THE
TOTAL
EMASCULATION
OF THE
WHITE
MAN

THE
TOTAL
EMASCULATION
OF THE
WHITE
MAN

DAVID VALENTINE BERNARD

STREBOR BOOKS

NEW YORK LONDON TORONTO SYDNEY

Strebor Books
P.O. Box 6505
Largo, MD 20792
http://www.streborbooks.com

© 2015 by David Valentine Bernard

ISBN 978-1-59309-580-2
ISBN 978-1-4767-6234-0 (ebook)
LCCN 2015934632

First Strebor Books trade paperback edition August 2015

Cover design: www.mariondesigns.com
Cover photograph: © Keith Saunders/Marion Designs

10 9 8 7 6 5 4 3 2 1

Manufactured in the United States of America

For information regarding special discounts for bulk purchases,
please contact Simon & Schuster Special Sales at 1-866-506-1949
or business@simonandschuster.com

The Simon & Schuster Speakers Bureau can bring authors to your live event.
For more information or to book an event, contact the Simon & Schuster Speakers
Bureau at 1-866-248-3049 or visit our website at www.simonspeakers.com.

For Misha Turner—whose passing has left a multitude of inside jokes that now only make sense to me.

"... *the meaning of all culture [is] to breed a tame and civilized animal, a household pet, out of the beast of prey 'man' .... We may be quite justified in retaining our fear of the blond beast at the centre of every noble race and remain on our guard: but who would not, a hundred times over, prefer to fear if he can admire at the same time...?*"

—FRIEDRICH NIETZSCHE, *On the Genealogy of Morality*
(Translated by Carol Diethe, Cambridge University Press, 2006, 24)

DAY ONE

After listening to his mother on the phone for twenty minutes, Edward Binkowski felt like going on a demonic rampage. In his mind's eye, little girls would scream at the sight of him; old people would be trampled by the terrified crowds; and everywhere, there would be violence and chaos until he finally managed to make his mother shut the *hell* up! …No more nagging about when he was going to get married and give her a grandchild! He could not care less about their neighbor, Mr. Shapiro, finding blood in his stool—or his mother's hairdresser getting a boob job! He was holding the cellular phone to his ear with his left hand; unconsciously, he found himself strangling the beer bottle he was holding in his right. His breath came quicker as the rage filled him; he gnashed his teeth—

But when he glanced up, the bartender was laughing at the depraved expression on his face; and when he looked at himself in the mirror behind the bar, he did look ridiculous, so he bowed his head and sighed.

Even though it was only about ten-thirty on a Saturday night, there were only three other men in the bar. Since college students were the bar's main clientele, the fact that most of them had gone home for summer break had something to do with the depressing atmosphere. The only customers left were hardcore drunks and fools like Binkowski—who had walked into the bar about forty minutes ago, after putting in a thirty-hour shift at the hospital. He thought he would relax here for a while before heading home to sleep; but as always, his mother's call had disrupted the simple pleasures of his life....

He was a medical student. Four years ago, in order to appease his mother's grand ambitions for a doctor son, he had moved to Athens, Georgia from New Jersey. Truth be told, the University of Georgia had been the only school that accepted him. He was a mediocre student at best; and the further along he got in his studies, the more he realized he had no real passion for it. He would do a good enough job when he finally became a doctor, but he was vaguely aware that if he did so, he would always hate his life—no matter how successful he became in terms of prestige and money.

His dream was to become a writer. In fact, his writing notebook was open before him. He had been leafing through some pages before his mother called; and to drown out her voice now, he leafed through some more pages. In his fantasies, when he saw himself as a successful author, he always saw a drunken Irishman: an otherwise brilliant poet who wallowed in filth and died a tragic, syphilitic death. His stories, likewise, tended to be tragically short mixtures of filth and brilliance.

His current scheme for literary fame was an anthology of short stories called *Treatise on the Penis*. His first piece was about a man— a paranoid schizophrenic, apparently—whose penis was literally his voice of reason. The penis talked to him—deep, philosophical conversations, actually—and guided him to love and happiness. At the end of the story, the man's penis dies—is *suffocated*—when the man finally has sex with the woman of his dreams. Binkowski had started writing it shortly after he broke up with his girlfriend about a month ago, so that probably explained the weirdness of it. The dying penis had seemed like a brilliant metaphor while his mind was still hazy and sentimental from the break-up; but since he had not yet determined whether he *liked* the story or not, he turned to the opening page and read through the first couple of lines. In the meanwhile, his mother updated him on a distant relative becoming a hooker on Hollywood Boulevard—or some such craziness he knew it was pointless to try to follow.

At moments like these, he felt like the words he scribbled on the page were the only things keeping him sane. He dreamed about literary success the way virginal teenage boys dreamed about sex. He was a prolific writer—but in the same way that virginal teenage boys were prolific masturbators. He had never actually *finished* one of his stories. Words and scenarios poured out of him like diarrhea—but they never seemed connected to any kind of plot; and in truth, after reading a few lines of the talking penis story, an objective voice told him it was pure crap, so that he grimaced and sat there glumly.

When he allowed his mind to refocus on the phone call, he realized his mother had gone back to nagging him about not having a mate yet—and the usual stuff women in their late sixties complained about when they had too much time on their hands. Since his father died a year ago, she had been calling him more—and, to be honest, a side of him did feel it was his duty as a son to receive her weekly naggings. However, when the whiny tone of her voice reached a new threshold, desperation overpowered his sense of duty, and he blurted out the first lie that popped into his head:

"—Ma, another call's coming through! ...It's from the hospital! They must have an emergency or something. I've gotta run! I'll call you tomorrow. I love you. *Bye!*" After his high-pitched, frenetic delivery, he pressed the button to end the call and sat there panting.

Ending the call before she could speak was always the key—otherwise she would ask questions and go on tangents until he was there for another hour. When he glanced up, the bartender had a knowing grin on his face. Binkowski nodded at the man awkwardly, gulped down the last of his beer, and left.

He was suddenly restless. He knew his mom meant well, but he felt as though he was still trying to escape her womb—as if he was still connected to it through some invisible strings, and that if he relaxed his resistance for the slightest instant, the strings would be yanked and he would find himself back in her belly. He sighed—both because he knew the thought was ridiculous and because he did not want to be thinking anything at this point. He needed sleep—or some state beyond sleep, where none of the annoyances of his life would be able to reach him.

…There was a woman loitering in the upcoming intersection. For a moment, a sense of terror came over him—especially after she waved at him like she knew him—because his first thought was that she was his mother! She had the same height, weight and over-processed hairdo as his mom. She waved again, and stepped into his path, smiling. As she moved out of the shadows, he stared down at her with trembling eyes; but once he saw she was a stranger—and that his mother had not somehow managed to teleport down to Georgia—he allowed himself to breathe. His heart rate slowed; relieved and exhausted, he smiled. But—

"Good!" the woman began excitedly, "—you're finally here."

His smile faded: "Huh?"

"I've been waiting here over half an hour," she said with the same urgency

He frowned. "For *me?*"

"Of course. We have important business ahead of us, Edward."

He paused, scrutinizing her face. "You *know* me?" he said, frowning. Plus, only his mother called him Edward. To everyone else, he was Ed or Eddie—

"Of course I know you, Edward," the woman began, smiling strangely.

Binkowski's frown deepened. "Someone *sent* you?" he asked.

She shook her head: "*You* sent for me, Edward."

There was something cultish in her eyes—a gleam seen only in people who had absolute faith in something *crazy*. All Binkowski could do was stare. Eventually, he took a deep breath and stood straighter, trying to refocus his mind.

"Who *are* you?" he said.

"I'm your conscience," she replied simply.

"What...?" he said, blinking drowsily.

"I'm the embodiment of your innermost being," she announced as if she had been practicing the line in front of a mirror for the last month.

After staring at her blankly for a few seconds, Binkowski found himself chuckling.

However, the woman's expression remained grave. "This isn't a joke, Edward. I'm here because you *called* to me: because you're *hurting*—"

Once again, Binkowski laughed at her corny lines—

"You can't *run* from this anymore, Edward," she warned him.

"Run from *what?*" he said with a weary chuckle.

"Run from your *conscience*. I am always there. I *see* everything... *hear* everything. I *am* you."

"I'm a middle-aged woman?" he asked sarcastically.

"In your mind you are."

Binkowski laughed heartily. "...You're definitely crazy enough to be my conscience," he countered. A side of him had hoped the insult would force her to break character and bring this farce to an end, but her pleasant visage remained. His smile faded. The only logical thing to do at this point was to get away. He tried to walk around her—to leave, before his budding annoyance turned to rage. However, that was when she hugged him. Her gesture *shocked* him in fact, and he stood there frozen. Her body was warm and good. It was like a mother's warmth, but better. He felt his rage melting away—

"That's it," she encouraged him as she tapped him on the back, "Let it all go…all the senselessness…all the *hurting*—"

But that corny word again made him grimace. He let go of her and took a step back—as if the smell of her were intoxicating and he had to distance himself in order to think clearly. "What the hell do you *want* from me?" he asked with a strange combination of bewilderment and exhaustion.

"It's not what *I* want from you, Edward. It's what *you* want from me."

He shook his head, as if still fighting off the intoxication. "Okay, what do I want?" he asked half-mockingly.

"You want what every man wants: to live fully and freely—to be *one* with his conscience."

That seemed reasonable enough; and despite himself, Binkowski nodded. Or, maybe the exhaustion was finally dragging him into the abyss. He stared down at her bleary-eyed. "And how do I do that?" he asked before he had thought better of it. He expected a long, philosophical answer that would keep him there longer—or another maddening riddle that would push him closer to madness—but the next thing he knew, the woman pulled up her blouse and exposed her breasts!

Binkowski jumped back. As the panic set in, he instinctively searched the empty street for any onlookers—

"No one else can see me, Edward," she said in the same pleasant, matter-of-fact way. "I'm your *conscience*, remember."

He was staring at her wide-eyed…and her breasts actually weren't half bad—especially for a woman her age. They were definitely suppler than his last girlfriend's—but he shuddered when he realized he was actually getting aroused. He shook his head again, trying to force himself to come to his senses. When he felt he had regained enough of his faculties, he took a deep breath and looked at her objectively. He glanced at her chest one last time, then made an effort to look her in the eyes: "Why are you showing me your...your *breasts*," he said, fighting to get out the word.

"These aren't really breasts," she said, looking down at herself with the same pleasant expression. "As I said, I'm your *conscience*. I'm not actually here. These aren't really breasts—"

"Well they *look* like breasts!" he said in frustration.

"But they're not," she corrected him gently. "These," she said, massaging them, "represent everything you want."

"All I want in life is *breasts?*"

"Metaphorically, yes. These breasts represent everything you've ever wanted," she purred as she continued fondling them. Despite himself, Binkowski was being hypnotized by the gentle movements of her hands.

"You *want* these breasts," she declared, the way one might declare that the sky was blue. "You *like* them don't you?" she said, her fingers kneading the tender flesh with more urgency. He found himself nodding. In fact, he head felt light, as if he were floating away—

"Embrace your freedom!" she encouraged him now. "Take hold of everything you've ever wanted, Edward, and become one with me!" As she said these last words, she reached up and grasped the back of his head. In the next motion, she brought his head down to her nipple. Instinctively, he sucked. ...*God* help him, he sucked—at first with bewilderment and shock, then with some deeply hidden hope that the magic would actually take hold and he would become his true self...just as the woman had said—

But that was when the woman laughed and pushed him away. Her laugh was horrible and cackling. As he looked at her confusedly, the sliding doors of the van parked on the curb opened, and the camera crew revealed themselves. All of them were laughing at a joke that Binkowski could not bring himself to grasp. He looked at their faces, but they were all a blur at that point.

By the time the woman darted into the van and yelled, "Antoinette sends her love!" Binkowski's sleep-deprived mind was teetering over the edge. Within seconds, the van was hurtling down the street; but even then, all Binkowski could do was stare at it with a dazed expression.

"…What the hell?" he whispered at last.

Binkowski stood there at least thirty seconds after the van had disappeared, staring blankly into space. Had that woman really mentioned Antoinette? Antoinette was his ex-girlfriend: an unassuming woman his mother had chosen for him—apparently because she had "good, child-bearing hips" or something like that. She had been nice, but after dating her for two years, he realized her only redeeming quality was her virtuosity at oral sex. As he had found himself thinking upon occasion, Antoinette could suck the juice out of a stone and make it beg for mercy…but every time she opened her mouth to actually *speak*, her nasally voice reminded him of his mother and set off some deep psychological urge to flee. On top of everything, it had been a long distance relationship— since she continued to work as a dental hygienist in New Jersey. When he ended their relationship a month ago, it had been more like a mercy killing. If Antoinette had really been behind all this, then he only felt sorry for her—because she still had not realized they were useless together. In fact, when it occurred to him there was no hatred in him—no resentment that needed further revenge— his spirts began to brighten. He was over all that, ready to embrace the next chapter of his life. The only thing he felt for her now was sorrow—and perhaps a little guilt as well, since he had allowed their brain dead relationship to linger on so long before pulling the plug.

...So, all of that had been a prank. As he nodded his head, a bittersweet smile came over his face. Now that he thought about it, this bore all the hallmarks of that Revenge Prank website everyone was talking about. The premise of the site was that people who wanted revenge could upload their victims' weaknesses and psychological vulnerabilities. The site then got local actors to carry out scenarios designed to humiliate the victim. The actors were usually unpaid students who were hungry for exposure on a site that attracted millions of viewers a day; as such, the site was wildly profitable. Binkowski, himself had visited it and laughed as unwitting fools were pranked by ex-lovers, former students—and a never-ending stream of petty, vengeful people. It had all seemed like "good, honest fun" to him before, but now it was only more evidence that society was screwed up. ...And maybe he was screwed up as well. What psychological vulnerability had Antoinette showed the world about him? His mind returned to the actress fondling her breast and making him suck. He grimaced as he considered all the sick possibilities. Maybe he had always had problems with women—on some deep level he had never considered before. There was a queasy feeling in his gut as he considered all the horrible relationships he had had with women. He seemed on the verge of a genuine breakthrough, but as the vague outlines of the epiphany began to form, his exhausted mind finally ground to a halt.

Damn, he was tired...

Remembering his bed, he began walking languidly. In ten minutes, he reached the building and walked up the three flights of stairs to his apartment. After he closed the door behind him, he turned on the kitchen light and looked around absentmindedly. Ten seconds passed before he caught himself and groaned. Frustrated and exhausted, he turned off the light and shuffled down the hall, toward his bedroom. When he glanced into his roommate's bedroom, he saw the bed was empty and remembered his roommate was attending a function at a professor's house. He nodded his head as if proud of himself for remembering, then he continued walking to his bedroom.

He seemed to fall asleep the moment his head touched the pillow; but by one in the morning, his beer-filled bladder felt like it was going to pop. It was only through an extreme act of will that he managed to return to the lewd dream he was having—about a nurse at the university hospital. Unfortunately, about fifteen minutes later, he awoke to a sensation like someone hammering spikes into his bladder. He groaned, got out of bed gingerly—since he felt like his bladder was going to *explode*—then he opened his bedroom door and began waddling toward the bathroom.

In the haze of his mind, Antoinette's revenge prank was like a half-forgotten piece of a dream. His full bladder was the only thing that mattered now; and as the pain intensified, he quickened his pace as much as he could without setting off the bomb in his abdomen.

There was a street lamp outside the bathroom window, so he did not bother turning on the light as he stepped in. The bathroom was cramped, even for an apartment that catered to broke college students. Instead of a bath tub, there was a nook in the wall—perpendicular to the toilet—which functioned as a shower. There used to be a door on the shower, but it had come off in an unfortunate accident involving his roommate and vigorous sex with a *huge* Mongolian woman who claimed she was on the shot put team. Instead of a door, there was now a plastic curtain, which was open.

Binkowski had fallen asleep in his jeans. As his bladder cried out in agony, he pulled down the zipper, pushed up the toilet seat with his foot, and moaned as the torrent began filling the commode. Three seconds passed with him standing there with his eyes closed and a simpering smile on his face. In fact, since stumbling to the toilet in the middle of the night had become a regular activity, he had literally learned to do it with his eyes closed. For this reason, he had not noticed the two legs sticking out of the shower. It was only when the man snoozing in the shower shifted his weight slightly that Binkowski looked down and noticed the legs. His eyes grew wide as he stared into the darkness and saw the outlines of a large man's body! When he screamed, the man in the shower screamed as well. Terrified, Binkowski turned toward the man, inadvertently peeing on him. ...Actually, it was only inadvertent for the first few moments. As the man screamed louder, Binkowski began to see the steam of piss as a weapon. He was actively aiming it now—as if his attacker would melt under the deluge.

It was only when the presumptive attacker started cursing—and *spitting*, since some of the fluid had gone into his mouth—that Binkowski recognized his roommate's voice. Mercifully, by then, Binkowski's bladder was also empty, so the incident ended with him shaking the last few droplets onto the floor, returning his penis to his jeans, then retreating two steps to flick the light switch on the wall.

His roommate, Cletus Jones, was a large black man—a doctoral student, actually—who was big enough to be mistaken for a football player, but too ungainly to be a match for anyone with real talent. Jones was still spitting. In fact, on his face, there was a look of stunned horror. Binkowski felt he should apologize or do something else to make amends, but there was no real way to make things right after *peeing* on a brother.

Nevertheless, "I'm sorry, man," he began feebly. He grabbed a towel from the rack and proffered it to his roommate; Jones grabbed it and began rubbing his face. He tried to get up, but then groaned and grasped his head. Binkowski frowned. "You okay?" When Jones looked up threateningly, Binkowski smiled uneasily and added, "...Besides being peed on?" Then, as the entire scene replayed itself in his mind, "What were you doing in there anyway...in the *dark?*"

At the question, Jones frowned; after a few seconds, his eyes grew wide as he remembered something—but then he frowned again when it occurred to him his memories were insane. He was in a tan linen suit—which he realized, with *new* horror, was soaked with piss. He cursed again and began stripping. Within seconds, his jacket was off. Still sitting in the shower, he started taking off his pants—but as the horror of warm piss took hold of him again, belt buckles and shoelaces were suddenly too complicated and time-consuming. Desperate, he fumbled to his feet and removed his shoes by stepping on the heels and kicking them off. In his madness to be clean, he removed his socks in a similar manner, stepping on the toes and pulling them off. He again made an attempt to remove his belt—but succumbing to the madness, he turned on the shower with half his clothes still on. Apparently, the water was freezing, because Jones cried out again. He was dancing under the shower now, cringing as every freezing droplet hit his skin—but the prospect of being clean and piss-free gave him the fortitude to withstand it. He tried taking off his dress shirt, but the buttons again confounded him, so he merely stood there, shivering.

As the plastic curtain was still open, the cascade fell onto the floor. Binkowski looked down at the pooling water anxiously, thinking of the downstairs neighbor filing another complaint with the landlord, but he figured he had to mop up the urine on the floor anyway. About thirty seconds passed with Binkowski staring at the scene, captivated by the weirdness of it all. It was only when Jones turned off the water and looked over at him menacingly that he jumped and came to his senses.

"Sorry!" he apologized. Thinking quickly, he darted out of the bathroom, grabbed some towels from the hall closet, and returned within six seconds. He handed one of the towels to his friend, retained two to put on the rack, and tossed the rest onto the floor. It was actually the perfect time to retreat from the bathroom and leave them both with some modicum of dignity, but he still stood there, staring, waiting for his roommate's explanation.

"…You got drunk?" Binkowski coaxed him. Jones had been rubbing his head with the towel vigorously, as if trying to wipe off a stain that only he could see and feel. However, at Binkowski's question, he stopped, frowning.

"Yeah, I guess…."

Binkowski laughed—both because drinking was always an adequate explanation for craziness between men, and because Jones *never* got drunk. Jones was the steady, responsible one in their relationship, who never lost control and always had the money to pay their bills. Binkowski may have grown up in the suburbs, but he had grown up listening to the *hardest* rap music; as a consequence, he was culturally blacker than Jones—who hailed from an upper middle class Georgia community where all the houses had plantation-style columns like in slavery days. It was Binkowski who drank too much and "acted a fool" and fed off Jones' drunken scraps when they went to the club to pick up women. In fact, once Binkowski had a few beers in him, he could lie to the devil and make off with his lunch money. Jones would look on in awe as Binkowski weaved elaborate tales that rarely failed to loosen the party girls' flimsy restraints on their panties. Usually, it was something about Jones being a star football player and Binkowski being his agent. He would tell them about pending million-dollar professional contracts and other foolishness until Jones would almost begin believing it himself. All was fair in love and war—especially in the off-campus clubs where the gold diggers did their prospecting. However, to Jones' credit, he would always set the scheming miners straight when they asked about his contracts. That kind of moral uprightness was precisely why Binkowski laughed at his friend's reactions now—since Jones was exhibiting the telltale signs of *hard* drinking.

"What the *hell* were you drinking?" Binkowski teased him now.

By then, Jones had managed to undo his belt. He put the towel around his waist and let his pants and underwear slip to the floor. At Binkowski's question, Jones paused to think. Once he remembered, he winced and looked over at his friend helplessly: "Hillbilly Champagne."

"*What?*" Binkowski said, laughing louder.

"That's what he called it," Jones mumbled, frowning at his recollections.

Binkowski laughed again, but when Jones' face remained grave, Binkowski frowned as well. "Wait, you're *serious?* You *really* drank something called 'Hillbilly Champagne'?"

"I guess so," he said as if shocked by his own memories.

Even though the shower was off now, there were still puddles on the floor, so Binkowski pushed around some of the towels with his foot—to sop up the water. Jones still seemed disturbed. His movements were languid now. In fact, since he still had on the wet shirt, his trembling had gotten worse. Jones was staring off into the distance with a distraught expression on his face, and Binkowski could see his friend was not right.

Coming to his senses, Binkowski held out his hand, to coax his roommate out of the cramped shower. Next, acting quickly, he closed the lid of the commode, flushed the toilet, and made his friend sit down. He began unbuttoning Jones' shirt—since the man's trembling hands were useless. Medical training told him to engage his patient in conversation:

"So, you drank this 'Hillbilly Champagne' at the professor's party?"

"No," Jones replied in the same distracted way, "…on the way there."

"Doesn't your professor live out in the woods or something?"

"Yeah."

Binkowski frowned: "So, you stopped at a bar before you left town?"

"No, there was a stand by the side of the road."

"…Wait, you stopped by the side of the road, at *night*, to buy booze?"

"Yeah, the hillbilly stepped out into the road while I was driving."

"…Hillbilly?"

"Yeah, he had a long, white beard and a banjo and *overalls*."

Binkowski chuckled, eying his friend skeptically. "…Okay."

But Jones was frowning again. "He was selling the Champagne out of these jugs…and there was a magazine rack to the side, with like a *million* porno mags."

Binkowski laughed. "*What?*"

"…Was like he had every porno magazine ever made. Magazines you never even heard of…all kinds of fetish ones with *weird* covers—with midgets riding donkeys and other craziness."

When Binkowski surrendered himself to the laughter, Jones found himself chuckling as well—even though he still had a dazed expression on his face.

By now, Jones' shirt was off, showing his chiseled chest. "C'mon,"

Binkowski began, sobering up, "let's get you into something warm." He coaxed Jones to stand by gripping his upper arm, then he began leading him out of the bathroom. Binkowski had put one of the towels over his friend's shoulders, like a shawl; as they walked, Binkowski still gripped him by the upper arm, as if his roommate were an old lady. Yet, his friend was still staring ahead in a daze as all the bizarre recollections flashed before his eyes.

Jones' bedroom was annoyingly clean and well organized. There were dozens of books and technical manuals on five shelves against the wall. There were old physics textbooks and manuals on nano-technology: the kind of hard science that only a handful of people probably really understood. Jones was one of those people.

Binkowski made him sit on the edge of the bed before pulling the heavy bed spread—a quilt—over his shoulders.

"You feeling better?"

"Yeah, I guess," Jones mumbled. He glanced at his digital alarm clock on the nightstand. It was one thirty-seven. He stared helplessly, so that Binkowski laughed at him.

"You're still thinking about that hillbilly, aren't you?"

"Yeah," he said in the same distracted way.

Binkowski looked at him with a certain amount of exasperation. "You *do* realize that hillbilly thing had to be a dream, right?"

Jones wished he could agree, but he shook his head. "I don't know, man."

Binkowski tried to move him away from the hillbilly: "So, what happened after you left the stand?"

"…The hillbilly told me to take a swig—to test the Champagne before I bought it."

Despite himself, Binkowski chuckled. Jones went on quickly:

"I took a sip, but then the next thing I remember, I was at my professor's house. It's like I blacked out or something.… Anyway, the professor's mom was there, visiting from Atlanta. She met me at the door and said the professor was busy—and that she would keep me entertained."

"Entertained *how?*"

Jones looked away uneasily. "Well, I gave her a drink from the jug—"

Binkowski laughed. "You took the Hillbilly Champagne to the dinner?"

"Yeah," Jones went on quickly, "…she took a swig, and then we started…" He faltered, his eyes growing wide.

"You made out with your professor's *mom?*" Binkowski practically screamed. As he said the words, the breast-fondling woman from the street popped into his mind. It still seemed like a hazy dream, but he frowned momentarily, asking himself if it really could have happened. However, Jones was still in shock; and at the moment, his issues seemed more pressing than half-forgotten dreams. That was when something new occurred to Binkowski:

"How *old* was she?"

"I don't know…seventy-five, maybe *eighty.*"

"Damn!" Yet, his mind still could not conceptualize it. "You had *sex* with her?" he asked, his face contorted with a combination of awe and disapproval.

Jones again looked up at him helplessly: "She said she wanted gravy on her giblets."

Binkowski stared at him blankly for a few seconds. "What the *hell* does that even mean?" he asked at last.

"She took me to a bedroom…I guess it was the professor's son's room. There were these pictures—teenage crap: rock band posters with blond skanks, car posters…the usual stuff—"

"And you had sex with her *there?*" Binkowski asked breathlessly.

"…We were still drinking the Hillbilly Champagne, and she was talking about giblets and other craziness…and then she grabs my dick and screams, '*Fuck* me, nigger! Fuck me like I was your slave master!'"

"*Shit!*" Binkowski whispered, too stunned to laugh. His face merely twitched as he stared. "…What *you* do?"

Jones scratched his head and stared ahead with the same helpless expression. "I said, 'You want this nigger dick, you *dried* up cracker bitch?'"

Binkowski doubled over with laughter!

Jones chuckled uneasily and shook his head as if to say that was the tip of the iceberg. "She kept screaming about giblets and gravy. At first, I was worried the professor would hear; but after a while, the Hillbilly Champagne must've kicked in, 'cause I just didn't give a shit."

"Damn!" Binkowski said mutely, but then the voice of reason rebelled in him again, and he shook his head. "You can't really believe *any* of that happened," he said flatly.

"Why not?" Jones said defensively.

"Hillbilly Champagne…? Puttin' gravy on granny giblets…? Just *think* about it for a second. You're a black dude in Georgia—does *any* of that sound like something you'd do?"

"I know how it sounds, but…"

"But *what?*" he said, losing patience.

Jones sighed. "…Well, there's more."

Binkowski stared at him, sighed heavily, then nodded for him to continue.

Jones took a deep breath as well. "…So, while I was going at it with the professor's mom, her grandson opened the door."

"*Damn!*"

"He starts going crazy: screaming…throwing stuff…clawing at his head as if a bomb had gone off in his skull or something…. I look down at his grandmother, thinking she'd be horrified, ashamed…

whatever, but she had this annoyed expression on her face. And then she screams, 'Get out, you little shit! Can't you see I'm fucking!'"

When Binkowski chuckled, Jones inadvertently laughed as well, accepting the absurdity of it. However, he sobered quickly when he remembered the rest of the scene.

"…After that, the kid *lost* it…grabbed a baseball bat. He must have knocked us out or something, because the next thing I knew, we were in this dark place…and there was this light—this *beautiful* light—and the professor was sitting there naked, licking his tit—"

"*What?*" Binkowski said, lost again.

Jones shrugged, as if to say, "That's what I remember."

"How the *hell* could he be licking his tit?" Binkowski scoffed.

"He had man boobs—*flaps*—and he grabbed one and was licking it."

Binkowski wished he hadn't asked. His face wore a disgusted grimace now. At the same time, he had come that far, so there was no point holding back now: "*Why* was he licking it?"

"How the hell should I know?" Jones returned; and in retrospect, even Binkowski acknowledged it was a fairly stupid question.

Binkowski went on quickly, hoping to redeem himself: "What about the granny and the kid?"

Jones paused for a moment, frowning. "…The old lady was standing above the professor as he licked his tit, patting him on his head lovingly, as if to say, 'Good job.'"

"…Okaaay," Binkowski said, drawing out the last syllable, since he could think of nothing else to say. His face was blank for a few moments, until something occurred to him: "What about the kid?"

"…He was gone. …I felt…*jealous* of him, because he had gone into the light. *Yeah*," Jones said, remembering. "The rest of us were staring at the light, and it was so beautiful—as if we were staring at…*God*…and then the next thing I knew, I was here, in the shower…getting peed on."

Binkowski was about to apologize once more, but his mind again rebelled against the entire story. *"None* of that could have happened, man!" he protested. "What's more likely: that you drank some hillbilly's moonshine and had drunken sex with your professor's mom, or that you dreamed it all when you passed out in the shower? And what's with that 'beautiful light' stuff? You sound crazy as hell, bro," he said with a laugh. "Maybe you died and this is the after-life," he mocked him. In fact, at the thought, Binkowski laughed louder. "Maybe that crazy kid killed you after witnessing that *fucked* up scene with his grandmother." However, when he saw the deflated expression on Jones' face, he sighed and tried a more supportive approach. "Does *anything* you told me sound realistic, man?" While Jones was considering it, Binkowski took a step to-ward him and started checking his head. When Jones pulled his head away in annoyance, Binkowski said, "There're no head wounds, bro. *Nobody* knocked you out with a baseball bat."

Jones checked his head before he nodded uneasily.

"Occam's razor, man: the simplest explanation is usually the correct one. Isn't that what you always say when I tell you my crazy con-spiracy theories?" Despite himself, Jones smiled as he remembered some of Binkowski's theories about those free porn sites being used in government mind control experiments to breed the perfect soldier. While Jones was still smiling, Binkowski pressed home his point: "That's right. So, let's get some sleep before morning. Once the sun's out, you'll call your professor and clear up everything. I bet you'll both laugh about it. ...Leave out the part about screwing his mother, though," he said with a chuckle. Jones wanted to be-lieve, so he smiled faintly and nodded his head when his friend gestured to the bed. Unfortunately, he lay in bed for the rest of the night, staring up at the ceiling as if seeing the bizarre events of the professor's home.

DAY TWO

The new gods looked at what they had created, and it was good. After ten minutes of strenuous effort, they had finally managed to get their creation into the skintight leather outfit. They styled her long, flowing hair perfectly; and in order to accentuate her full lips, they applied a shade of lipstick that was ironically named "Demon Red." Truth be told, the new gods were horny bastards, so a few of them contemplated taking off the clothes again in order to caress her creamy skin and follow through on their depraved fantasies. The naughtier ones had let their hands linger on her breasts and crotch—and propped up her legs to get an unobstructed view—but the Zeus of the Athens, Georgia gods had slapped their hands away and reminded them of their grand vision.

"We're *gods* now!" he had scolded them. "We can get pussy any time we want!" At that, the other gods had bowed their heads in shame and submitted to his will….

After giving their creation precise instructions, the gods opened the door and watched as she stumbled out into the world. Outside, it was a little after ten at night. Her legs were unsteady at first— partly from the fact that she was still dazed, but mostly because she was wearing stiletto heels and the parking lot was composed of gravel. Even then, after a few tentative steps, her stride became confident, and she held her head high—like a woman who *knew* she looked good. Within thirty seconds, she walked the entire length of the parking lot, past all the pick-up trucks and motor-cycles, and strolled into the shady-looking bar on the far side of the parking lot. The bar's main feature was the gigantic confederate flag over its front window; otherwise, it was essentially a large wooden shack on the edge of the woods.

Seeing that their weapon had been deployed, the new gods sat back and waited for their will to be carried out. Five minutes later, their creation exited the shack and began walking back the way she had come; a short while after that, the first of the pot-bellied farmers and truckers and biker gang members began shuffling out, all of them nude with zombie-like expressions on their faces.

The new gods grinned.

DAY THREE

Whenthe man opened his eyes that first time, the world was a blur. He stared at the confusing mess for minutes or hours—until his head hurt from the effort to make sense of it. He was about to clamp his eyes shut from the pain when something finally clicked in his head—some new neural connection was made—and his vision became clear. He was in a car, sitting in the driver's seat. His eyes focused on the car's dashboard; beyond the windscreen—and the lonely dirt road—there were thick, dark woods. When he turned his head to the left, he realized he was on a mountain—since there was a lush valley below him. The sun was setting over the valley, bathing every-thing in a soothing amber light. He stared at the sun dreamily—until his eyes burned from the glare and his head throbbed from the pain. Grimacing, he clamped his eyes shut....

Where was he...? With the pain, his dizziness ebbed and flowed. When a wave of nausea washed over him, he rested his head against the seat until he regained his equilibrium. As he did, it occurred to him the car was not moving: it was merely parked there, in the middle of nowhere. He tried looking around again; but with his sun blindness, the world only registered as improbable geometric shapes. Desperate, he scoured his mind, trying to retrace his steps; but the more he asked himself how he had come to be in this place, the more he came to realize he could not remember anything—including his own name.

Maybe he had had some kind of car accident...? Instinctively, he touched his head, thinking he must have hit it in the crash...but there were no wounds; the car, from what he recalled, had not *seemed* wrecked. However, he did feel *unreal*—as if he had been drugged. A voice within him was screaming for him to wake up—to come to his senses, before it was too late. He had a sudden suspicion that he was being watched—that someone was laughing at him from the shadows. Someone or something must have stolen his memories and dumped him in this place. As paranoid as it seemed, he was *certain* of it. He sat up straighter, balling his hands into fists in case he had to protect himself—

And by now, his sun blindness had dissipated to the point where the world began to take shape again. He looked down at the steering wheel; his eyes moved lower, to where the seatbelt was secured around his torso...but he had a sudden need to be free, so he unbuckled the strap—

The glove compartment! Maybe something in there would give him a clue of what was going on. He opened it in hopes of finding his license and registration—*anything*—but it was only jammed with junk: balled up wrappers and tissues from fast food restaurants, loose change, half a bottle of soda...He pulled it all out eagerly, depositing it on the dusty floor mat, but none of it was *useful*. Desperate, he pulled down the car's visors, thinking his documents might be there, but there was nothing.

Glancing down again, he noticed he was dressed in a shirt and tie. He loosened the tie and unfastened the first two buttons of his shirt, as if they had been strangling him. Still looking down, it occurred to him there might be some clue in his pants pockets. After he dug his hands into them, he saw one of the pockets was empty, while the other had thirty dollars and some coins. He stared at the money blankly for a few seconds before he jammed it back into his pocket in frustration.

...And he could not get over the feeling he was overlooking something obvious. He scoured his mind again, going over a checklist of what he had done and what he *should* be doing...until he realized he had not checked the back seat! He swung around, terrified, half-expecting a monster to be behind him, baring its fangs—like in the movies! ...But there was nothing behind him— or at least, so it seemed on first glance.

That was not enough for him, so he got out of the car and looked into the back window; after that, he opened the back door and checked again. When that was not enough to reassure him, he walked around the entire vehicle, checking all windows, opening all doors...Then, at last, in order to cover all contingencies, he got on his hands and knees, and looked under the vehicle. There was still nothing there, and yet he sensed a residual presence—as if Satan, himself had just been there—

Up in the sky, a hawk cried out; the man jumped to his feet, ready to fight for his life. He was trembling now—and still fighting to breathe, as if all the air had been sucked out of the world. ...*Where was he?* He looked around again—at the verdant valley, at the dirt road beneath his feet—but he recognized none of it. When his eyes returned to the setting sun, the prospect of being alone in the darkness filled him with a sense of dread. He felt that if he did not escape this place before night came, he would be trapped here forever. He was about to turn back to the car when he noticed a structure in the valley. He frowned.

Down in the valley, about four hundred meters from the road, there was a house. He took a few hopeful steps in that direction— but beyond the dirt road, there was a precipice. As he looked down, the dizziness took hold of him again, causing the world to swirl before his eyes. When he began to lose his balance, he made sure he stumbled backward, away from the edge. He groaned, grasping his head; but luckily for him, the dizziness passed quickly. When it did, his eyes returned to the house in the valley. ....He could not explain it, but he felt that all the mysteries of his life would be revealed if he went to it. In his mind, the building suddenly seemed like a Temple of God. It made no sense, and yet he was again certain of it. Mesmerized, he found himself stumbling toward it like a drunkard—until he remembered the precipice, and stopped abruptly.

As he looked down, the dizziness seemed on the verge of returning; for an instant, the valley floor went out of focus...but in time he saw there was a ledge on the side of the mountain; and when he looked closer, he saw there was a path on the ledge, which led down to the valley floor. Indeed, he realized it would be simple to step onto the ledge and follow the path; and when he navigated the path with his eyes, he saw it led straight to the structure. More than that, the path seemed to stand out against the valley floor, like magic. None of it made sense; and yet, with each passing second, he felt the house was his only hope.

Driven by that hope—or *madness*—he climbed over the edge of the precipice and lowered himself onto the narrow ledge. His patent leather shoes were slippery against the damp sod. He lost his balance—but managed to grab onto a shrub growing out of a rock. He wavered again, seeing how crazy this was—but the ledge widened up ahead, and he again saw the path led straight to the structure. To push himself along, he allowed his mind to be blank; then, as soon as the ledge was wide enough, he quickened his pace once more.

When he reached the valley floor, there was a stream. He jumped over it, desperate to reach the Temple of God. While he was jogging down the path, he saw a snake's tail disappearing into the brush. He hesitated a moment, giving the snake a chance to disappear, then he ran on at full speed, blocking out everything until he reached the Temple.

Yet, when he was finally standing before the structure, he was startled to see it was only a wooden shack. The glass in the window panes had long been shattered; the door hung precariously on dislodged hinges. From the road, it had had the appearance of something majestic; but now that he was there, it was clear no one had lived in the shack in decades. There was no furniture inside—only dusty crates and some rusting cans. Where the wooden floor used to be, grass now grew through the rotten boards.

Frustrated with the world, he turned and looked back the way he had come. His car seemed disconcertingly small and distant. As he looked back at the shack, he wondered about the madness that had made the structure seem like something out of Paradise. In fact, he was about to sigh and return to the car when he glanced through one of the shattered windows and noticed something odd.

There was a crate in the middle of the shack; and lying on top of it, there was a bright—almost *shining*—envelope. In fact, everything had dust on it except for the envelope. It looked as if someone had placed it there only moments ago. He stared into the window; and in the same way the shack had called to him from the road, the envelope called to him now. He walked over to the door; in attempting to open it, it came off its hinges with a loud bang that startled some birds in a nearby bush. He swung around at the sound of flapping wings. He was panting again, but when he saw there was no immediate danger, he took a deep breath and placed the door on the ground. Still uneasy, he stared into the darkening shack. The envelope was lying right there—but it suddenly seemed like a trap. He remembered the feeling he had had when he woke up in the car: the sense that someone or something had done this to him.

He stood there tentatively, trying to think through his options. His mind was so dazed that he would probably have stayed there forever. However, his strange fear of the night pushed him forward. Now, he was in the shack, walking on the rotten boards. There were crunching sounds with every step he took—as if he were walking on a gigantic egg, and would crack through the shell at any moment. He tried not to think about it....

When he was about to grab the letter, something caught his attention to the left; and when he looked, he saw a man's form! He cried out and jumped back, ready to run—or to fight for his life if it came to that. ...But when he looked again, he saw he was only seeing his reflection. There was a full-length mirror against the wall. When his heart rate began to slow, he walked up to it, staring at himself.

Incredibly, even then, he did not recognize the man in the mirror. He seemed to be in his mid-fifties. Except for a paunch, he was not exactly fat...but his body was soft—undefined beneath his wrinkled clothes. There was some kind of emblem on his chest, over his heart. He tried to read it via the mirror, but it was backwards—and too small. Forgoing the mirror, he grabbed his shirt, twisted the emblem and looked down at it. It read, "Security." He was a security guard! He had not realized it before, but he was wearing a uniform: white shirt, grey pants and a red tie. The pants had stripes down the side, but they were so short that his white socks showed at the bottom. He looked like a bad stereotype of a security guard: middle aged, gut hanging out of his shirt, high water pants...and he was not even the type of security guard who had a real badge: his was *painted* on.

He raised his arm and sniffed the pit, grimacing at the stench. Besides being wrinkled, his clothes were *filthy*. He looked at his face, bewildered. His eyes were red—as if he had not slept in *days*; his hair was disheveled—a graying thatch of receding hair. His lips were quivering. He stared, disappointed with himself and his life—even though the only thing he had to judge was a stranger's darkening image.

He would probably have stayed there forever, lost in his thoughts, but the impending darkness again pushed him to act. He turned from the mirror and went to the crate. As he had thought before, the letter had been placed there recently. The envelope was so white that it seemed to glow. He picked it up and saw it was heavy. When he twirled it in his hand, he realized there was no writing on the envelope whatsoever...but on the back, there was a wax seal. The wax had a peculiar odor that he could not place—but which made him slightly sick to his stomach. He was about to frown—

But outside the shack, there was an indistinguishable rustling sound. In the man's mind, it sounded like a beast's footsteps. Before he knew it, he was running. He jammed the letter into his pants pocket and *ran*. He saw no monster outside the shack, but he still sensed something menacing, so he ran for his life. Soon, he was ascending the path and navigating the ledge; once again, he slipped on the damp sod—but all he could think was that he had to get back to the car and lock himself in before darkness came....

At last, he clambered over the top of the precipice and returned to the dirt road. The sun had set. He was panting and exhausted, but the urge to flee this place was stronger than ever. He looked at the car: it was a grayish sedan—one of those huge, ugly American cars that only police departments, cab companies and old men used. It was missing its hubcaps—and there were signs of rust beneath all the dirt and grime.

It was the type of car the loser he saw in the mirror would drive. At the same time, if it had brought him here, then it was his only hope—the only thing that could save him. All he had to do was make his way back to the main road...wherever that was.

He rose to his feet and took a step toward the car, but his legs faltered as the same creepy sense—of a residual presence—came over him. He stood there for about five seconds, rocked by the same urge to open all the doors and check every crevice of the vehicle for evidence of a hidden monster. ...Mercifully, the spreading darkness again overrode his other fears. He was moving quickly now. Within seconds, he was inside the vehicle. He hesitated before putting on his seatbelt, still wary of being *trapped*, but he snapped it in place. The car key was in the ignition: he turned it with a desperate motion...but the engine only whined!

He stared ahead in a daze, his mind going over his options frantically. He could either spend the night in the car or try to walk back to civilization in the darkness. He shook his head, overcome by the sense that he was either going to drive out of here now or he was *never* going to make it. He grasped the key again, offered up a silent prayer to the universe, and turned it.

He was so numb inside that it took him a few seconds to realize the engine had started. When he did, he grinned like a simpleton. Desperate to leave, he gripped the steering wheel and put the car in gear. He was about to stamp on the accelerator...but which way should he go? He looked down the road: should he keep going straight or turn around? Staring ahead, the only thing he could see was darkening woods. He turned in his seat and looked back, through the rear window. There was no sign of civilization there either, but the woods did not seem as dark in that direction, so he decided to go that way.

The road was not really wide enough to turn a car safely; it was a miracle he did not roll the car off the precipice, but his fears—of the darkness and hidden monsters—filled him with urgency.

Once the vehicle was turned around, he stamped on the accelerator. The darkness had fallen quickly, so he turned on the headlights. As he glanced at the fuel gauge, he saw he had about half a tank of gas left…but he had no idea how deep he had come into the woods. He stamped on the accelerator again, and braced himself for a long, terrifying haul through the darkness—

But after about two or three minutes, he turned a bend in the road and slammed on the brakes. There was a woman standing in the middle of the road! The braking vehicle slid and went askew—and almost flipped into a ditch; but thankfully, it came to a screeching halt before it reached the woman.

The man sat there panting; the woman did not even flinch. In fact, he stared at her in disbelief. She had long, raven hair and bright red lipstick—against which her creamy skin seemed deathly white. She had on a skintight outfit, which in time he saw was composed entirely of leather. She posed unnaturally—the way a model posed, with her left arm resting on her hip and her head raised high. There was a cigar in her right hand. She put it to her lips and took a long drag before she removed it and sashayed over to the driver side window. As she walked, she blew smoke from her mouth, like a machine releasing exhaust. The man could only stare.

When she reached the car, she bent over dramatically and leaned into the window. Then, as the man looked on incredulously, she sighed and asked, "Have you been a good boy, or have you been naughty?" The residual cigar smoke stung his eyes and burned the back of his throat. He realized her accent was British. She had a stern expression on her face; and as her chin was still lifted, there was something haughty and off-putting about her—

"What?" he said as she stood there waiting for his response. When he eventually came to his senses, he blurted out, "Where is this place? How do I get back to the highwa—"

She put her index finger over his lips, so that the acrid odor of the cigar flared in his nostrils. "Something tells me you've been naughty," she mused.

When she removed her finger, he opened his mouth to say something, but no words came. Considering how she was dressed, and her stilted behavior, her words sounded like something out of a bad porno. At the same time, even bad pornos had their uses. The woman was still bent over. His eyes moved from her stern eyes and gravitated lower—to where her ample cleavage spilled over her leather bodice. She wore a crystal pendant, which was nestled smugly between her breasts. His eyes lingered on the creamy flesh—past the point where it was merely rude—

"Move over," she commanded, opening the door so abruptly that the man almost fell out. Her quickness startled him. He tried to protest, but her voice was louder—more *authoritative*. "Move over," she said again. "…I know where you need to be," she added, disarming him. "I know *everything* about you," she purred, so that the man's eyes grew wide and the last voices of resistance were stifled within him. He found himself complying: unsnapping the seatbelt and maneuvering over the gear shift, into the passenger seat.

She climbed into the vehicle. He stared at her long, slender legs, noticing, for the first time, that she was wearing stiletto heels. Her movements were decisive. Within a matter of seconds, she put the car in gear and began speeding down the dirt road. She took the corners like a rally car driver. The man only stared, his eyes gravitating back to her pendant—and, of course, the breasts that surrounded it. He stared longingly—until she took a corner so sharply that his head banged into the window. He cursed, grabbing his head.

"I suggest you put on your safety belt," she advised him in an offhand way—even though she, herself was not wearing one. The cigar dangled from the corner of her lips; but as the smoke wafted up into her eyes, she did not even blink. The man stared, frowning—

The car went into a pothole and jolted to the left.

He winced. "Maybe you should slow down?" he suggested.

Her voice remained steady: "If I slow down, you aren't going to get where you need to be."

His frown deepened as he wondered if this conversation—if *any* of this—could really be happening. Did women like her really exist— or was she only a figment of his imagination? Now that he thought about it objectively, this had all the hallmarks of a sex dream. Soon, she would contrive to be naked, and he would possess her...and then wake up in the real world, wishing he were still dreaming.

It all made sense intellectually; and yet, even if this were a dream, the woman still seemed to know what was going on. While he was hopelessly lost, she was decisive; while he was a slovenly mess, she was young and mesmerizingly beautiful. Seeing no reason to keep fighting it, he sighed and looked out of the window. The woman seemed to be driving impossibly fast—and the dark blur outside the window was like a computer-enhanced scene in a bad movie. Nodding his head, he was again reassured that none of this was possible.

A strange smile was on his lips now. He exhaled loudly and looked over at her casually. "Where you taking me?"

She looked at him quizzically before she stamped on the brakes and brought the vehicle to another screeching halt. She looked peeved: "You mean you haven't opened it yet?" she screamed.

"Opened *what?*"

She shook her head disapprovingly. "I see you've been a naughty boy," she scolded him, "—*very* naughty." Then, reaching over the gear shift, she grabbed the letter from his pants pocket and thrust it toward him. She was glaring at him. When he took the letter timidly, she resumed driving—albeit at a slower pace. "Read," she commanded.

He stared at her anxiously for a few seconds, but he knew it was pointless to resist any of this. If this were a dream, he had no choice but to follow it to whatever demented conclusion his mind was concocting. He nodded his head and looked down at the envelope. He had been right after all: the envelope had been waiting in that shack for him. It had been placed there for him to retrieve, and it was pointless to resist. The strange woman and the letter had to be plot devices in this crazy dream. It was the only thing that made sense as he turned the envelope over in his hands.

The peculiar odor of the wax did not sicken him as much this time—but he again found it odd that nothing was written on the envelope. He broke the wax seal by pulling open the flap. There was a sheet of fine stationery within. He turned on the ceiling light so he could see. At first, he stared at the sheet with a frown, because there was nothing written on it. ...But then, as he looked on with gaping eyes, words began to form. They appeared out of nowhere, glowing against the stationery. His jaw dropped and he leaned forward, frowning as he read the elegant penmanship. The words read:

Your name is Felix Higginbottom, and you are on a mission from God.

The man stared. ...And his name really *was* Felix Higginbottom. It was suddenly clear to him. Yet, before he could make sense of it, the words on the stationery began to fade away. He panicked, as if he were losing the key to his salvation. Mercifully, before the words disappeared entirely, new words began to form. They read:

Look up and see where you are.

When Higginbottom looked up from the letter and stared out

of the window, his eyes grew wide once more. Down in the valley, he saw the highway—or rather, the lights of cars going to and from the city in the distance. He recognized the city below: it was Atlanta, Georgia…and he remembered he lived in Athens, Georgia—a city a couple hours' drive away. He was a security guard at the University of Georgia. He was fifty-seven years old and he was married…no: he had gotten divorced five years ago, when his wife left him for a young woman. However, before his wife's turn to lesbianism, she he had given him two sons, both of whom were adults now. Like their father, the sons were also finding unimaginative ways to destroy their lives. Indeed, all his old memories filled his mind now, and he sat there helplessly, absorbing them. It was clear now that he had not been happy in years. He remembered the sense of disappointment he had felt when he looked at his reflection in the shack, and he nodded his head uneasily—

The British woman took a hearty puff of the cigar; at the sound, and the sudden infusion of smoke, he looked over at her sharply.

"Who *are* you?" he asked breathlessly.

She did not even bother to look at him. Instead, she addressed him in the same exasperated way: "What does the letter say about me?"

He was about to tell her the letter had not mentioned her; but when he glanced down, he saw new words forming. In fact, he had to read them twice before they seemed to sink in. They read:

Her name is Cassiopeia, and she is an angel, sent by God.

He looked over at her, stunned—both at the reality of the words and the realization that words were really appearing on a blank sheet of paper. However, when he looked back down at the fine stationery, he saw the page was again blank. He waited expectantly for the magic to return, but the page remained blank, and the magic seemed gone forever. Had he imagined it all? He thought back to the words on the page: *A mission from God?* Was he even a religious man? He searched his mind, but then shook his head: the choice between going to church and watching Sunday football had always been decided in favor of football...so no, he was not a religious man—or even a *spiritual* man. ....*Mission from God?* No, everything in this dream was impossible. At the same time, given the state of his life in the real world, maybe an impossible dream would do him some good. Even if Cassiopeia was only the product of his depraved imagination, he was suddenly eager for the dream to continue. The real world, with his ex-wife and dead-end job, was a nightmare, so he could see no harm in letting this dream continue for a little while longer.

He sat up straighter now, open to all the possibilities of this place. Cassiopeia had said she was taking him to where he needed to be, and he was suddenly hopeful. When he looked over at her again, his eyes paused at her cleavage, and he stared longingly. After an uncertain period of time, he looked up at her face and realized she was smiling.

"Are you ready to do God's will?" she asked, "—or are you going to be naughty?"

Put in those terms, he felt he had no choice.

Edward Binkowski's head was totally screwed up, and he *knew* it. Most straight men had probably had some version of the gynecologist fantasy. To spend one's working days between random women's legs was the ultimate form of "playing doctor." Accordingly, that morning, when Binkowski began his stint in the hospital's gynecology clinic, it had been with a secret thrill. Of course, he had intended to conduct himself professionally—and refrain from salivating as the women spread their legs for him. He had even taken the precaution of wearing an unusually tight pair of underwear that morning—in order to hide any potential erections. However, after what he had seen and smelt today, he feared he might never be able to have an erection again!

Now, he viewed every woman with suspicion, wondering what rancid stink bomb she might be hiding between her legs. His fertile imagination conjured images of women as terrorists, ready to decimate civilization with their dirty bombs. Intellectually, he knew women making emergency visits to the gynecologist were more likely to be victims of some unfortunate infection or another. Nevertheless, once one had witnessed a terrorist bombing first-hand, one began to see terrorists everywhere. Anyone who looked like the terrorist sparked wild panic and bigotry—and triggered recollections of carnage and death.

…And it occurred to him that human sexuality was largely about illusions. He had to forget everything he had seen and smelt today. To revive his sexuality, he felt he needed counseling—or an intensive regimen of brainwashing. Like a meat eater after his first visit to the slaughterhouse, he had to forget how the meat was made. Indeed, after the day's events, he was terrified his stomach might never be strong enough again—and that he would either starve or go mad.

In truth, much of this had to do with sleep deprivation. With only five hours of sleep in the last three days, his mind was unfortunately susceptible to a wide range of stupid thoughts.

Once Arlo Rasmussen sensed the baby was asleep, he lowered the five-month-old to the bassinet—cautiously, as if his son were a sensitive bomb. After an hour of trying to coax his son to sleep, Rasmussen did not want this moment ruined by a careless jolt or a sudden noise. In fact, he held his breath as he lowered the baby. Then, once he was sure his son was resting snugly, Rasmussen pulled his hands away with carefully honed agility, stood up straight and allowed himself to breathe.

Thank God that little cocksucker's asleep! he thought, grinning. He was too tired to feel guilty—or to actually grasp the thoughts fluttering through his mind. It seemed as though it had been days since he had slept. The slightest noise provoked the baby to shriek for hours; and lately, even when Rasmussen managed to sleep, he would dream about the baby crying and keeping him awake....

He sighed softly and backed away from the bassinet—gently, lest one of the floor boards creaked. After five or six steps, he turned and looked around the room absentmindedly. He was in the spacious living room. It was late afternoon, and the chamber had a strangely menacing quality he had never considered before. It was somehow too big—too *opulent*. The ultramodern furniture was more like art than something meant for human comfort. Every time he sat on the strange, angular couch, he half expected an angry museum curator to chase him away. His wife had picked out all the furniture; and even though he usually loved what his wife loved, he suddenly realized he hated it all—

He shook his head, sensing his thoughts going in an unsavory direction. He needed some fresh air, so he left the living room and walked down a side corridor, to exit the house. When he got outside, the sun was a few minutes from setting. He stared dreamily as the long shadows crept across what he called the "side yard." Most houses could boast a front yard and a back yard, but Rasmussen's lawn surrounded the entire house. In fact, it was a more like a park than a lawn. There was enough space for dozens of children to run freely; there were huge oak trees, colorful flower beds, and a wide range of artistic nuances that made the Mexican gardeners earn their pay. A tall, expertly manicured hedge bordered the front and side portions of his lawn, blocking his view of the outside world. However, beyond the hedge, there were other million dollar homes, and woods…and a meandering road that led to the highway. A year and a half ago, when Rasmussen and his wife moved to Atlanta from New York City, the realtor had boasted that you knew you were in a wealthy neighborhood when you could go for weeks and months at a time without seeing or hearing your neighbors. That thought had appealed to him at the time; but as he looked around now, he only felt trapped and isolated—as if his wealth and good fortune had damned him.

Most of his wealth had come from a series of books he had written for lazy college students: *Calculus for Numbskulls, Trigonometry for Numbskulls,* and so on. The ironic thing about most mathematics and science professors was that the more they knew, the less they seemed able to teach the basics to their students. Rasmussen was the exception, which was why he and his books had achieved a kind of cult status on college campuses.

Besides material wealth, Rasmussen was a tall, good-looking man with sandy hair and large, blue eyes. At thirty-five years old, he had relative youth in addition to wealth; and as he had been married to the woman of his dreams for about two years now, his life seemed perfect by all outward appearances.

Yet, everything had happened so quickly that he felt *lost.* Only a year and a half ago, he had been a star professor at Columbia University in New York. Eight months before that, he had met his wife through one of those dating services that catered to busy professionals. He could not remember the details of their first date, but they had gone out for drinks—and then they had ended up at his place, making love. He remembered it all as a vague series of thrusts and moans. In the morning, she had been gone and he had had the feeling that even though he had possessed her totally, she had not really been his. The next few times they made love, she had always been gone in the morning—or in the middle of the night, when there was an emergency at her office. The more he had her, the more desperate he had been for *more* of her, until he had felt himself possessed by an escalating mania.

…And their conversations had been like their sex: he would talk to her for hours yet come away thinking he knew nothing about her. Even now, he was not sure if he had proposed to her or if she had proposed to him. One night, after making love, the conversation had moved to children:

"Promise me we'll raise our kids ourselves," she had said suddenly, "—that we'll never hire nannies and babysitters…that we'll never *pay* someone to love our kids for us…."

Her voice had trailed off, but he had been so startled by the strange tone that he had been unable to speak. After an awkward silence, she had begun a rambling story about her youth. She had told him about being raised by a nanny and moving to a boarding school as a twelve-year-old. As she talked, there had been a lifetime of pain and resentment in her voice. It had been a jarring insight into her soul; and he had thought then that everyone was scarred from a childhood trauma—limping around from the unhealed wound. Most forgot when exactly the wound had taken place, or they had been wounded so many times that all their scars had been mysteries to them.

Rasmussen's wife, to her credit, had never lost sight of her wound; she had never fallen prey to the belief that growing up meant forgetting; and that night, as Rasmussen held her in the darkness, there had been something amazingly powerful and compelling about her awareness. He had made her a promise right then—that he would always be there for her and for their children when they came; and in the morning, there had been a tacit understanding that they were going to marry.

The engagement lasted only weeks. The wedding was a semi-formal affair, held on a private beach in the Hamptons of New York. His wife planned the entire thing with the same attention to detail that made her a rising star in her firm. She even got her parents to emerge from their mansion in Connecticut. Rasmussen was happy to meet them at last—since they were a part of his wife and he was always hungry to know more about her. Yet, when he eventually met her parents, the only concrete thought he had about them was "well-groomed and well-mannered"…as if they were a breed of dog.

Compared to his wife's family, his relatives had seemed rowdy. His father was a retired firefighter, his mother was a school teacher, and his brother was a famous drag queen at a Greenwich Village revue, who would have provided the musical entertainment if Rasmussen had not bribed him with a case of cognac. His relatives made loud, embarrassing toasts at the wedding reception, got drunk, and danced too lewdly and animatedly for the music. However, they were uncomplicated in a way that was strangely comforting.

On the wedding night, Rasmussen made love to his wife for *hours*—provoked not so much by lust or love as the need to reassure himself she was his. However, even after all his energy was spent, and he was lying there in the silence, listening to her breathing, she was still like ether in his arms….

A month later, her job offered her a promotion if she agreed to lead the Atlanta office. By then, Rasmussen would have done anything for her, so he agreed to leave the university and move to Atlanta with her. He figured he could teach and write his books anywhere; and in the beginning, everything went as planned. He got a job at a local college and his wife ascended the corporate ladder. They moved into this million-dollar home—which his wife assured him would double in value in five years—and he put the finishing touches on a book his excited publishers insisted would be another bestseller.

He may not have been able to say for sure he was happy; but for a few months, his life had had a kind of mathematical predictability. He had known what was expected of him and what his wife needed, and he had appreciated that.

Unfortunately, that all came to an end with his wife's unexpected pregnancy. In fact, five months passed before they realized she was pregnant. She had no morning sickness—none of the usual symptoms of pregnancy. Moreover, since she was one of the twenty-five percent of women who experienced some form of vaginal bleeding during pregnancy, she had mistakenly thought she was still having (irregular) periods. Even when the growing baby began moving around in her womb, she had assumed the stress of her job had given her indigestion. Up to her fourth month of pregnancy, she had been relatively slender. In her ignorance, she had attributed her growing belly to a lack of exercise and the afore-mentioned stress.

Also, with his wife's busy schedule, weeks would sometimes pass between their lovemaking sessions; and when they did make love, it would often be rushed—not because either of them did not want it to last longer, but because her cellular phone always seemed to be ringing. In time, Rasmussen felt like a thief, trying to pilfer pleasure from his wife's body. Her true lover was on the other end of the phone call: a commanding voice that could get her to leap out of bed on the slightest whim. Indeed, as the months passed, and her ringing phone ate away at their intimacy, he found he enjoyed making love to her less and less. He did not press her for sex—and caught only glimpses of her nakedness—so if she put on "a few extra pounds" he neither noticed nor cared.

However, all doubts were put to rest in her fifth month. She was at work, getting ready for a meeting, when a particularly savage kick from the baby made her rush to the emergency room. There, the overworked doctor glanced at her belly and asked her for her due date. Her first reaction was to curse him, since he seemed to be saying she looked fat; even when he explained himself, she had protested, saying she had been taking birth control pills since she got married…but there was no getting around the image on the sonogram—or the sound of her son's beating heart.

That day, when Rasmussen came home from teaching, he found his pale-faced wife sitting at the kitchen table, waiting for him. Like many of their conversations, the details eluded him afterwards. His first reaction was actually joy, but something about his wife's tone and deportment had made that reaction seem inappropriate. …His wife had always been a planner. She had made an elaborate diagram of her future, which ended with her being the chief financial officer of her firm and pregnant within four years. The unexpected pregnancy had upset that timetable; and as the leader of a busy business enterprise, her only options had been to quit her job or take an extended leave that would doom her career. When she reminded Rasmussen of the promise he had made the night they got engaged—that they would raise their children themselves—he had made the sacrifice again, and agreed to give up teaching at the end of the term, in order to take care of the baby.

Logically, he understood why his wife could not quit her job—*and he did not want her to*—but he needed help! Most days, his wife was either off on a business trip or working late at the office, which meant Rasmussen sometimes went days or weeks without a break. Worse, when he suggested hiring some help two months ago, his wife had screamed and shed tears and accused him of going back on his word; so that in the end, he had found himself pleading with her to forgive him—and swearing he would never mention it again…and so, that had been that.

He had always deferred to his wife's dreams—since she was more ambitious than he was—but after five months of caring for the baby, he was afraid. The act of proving one's love—and deferring one's dreams for the sake of love—was neither natural nor sustainable. The more one made a *conscious* decision to act out of love, the more that love died…until all that was left was bitterness. Even though he resisted it, Rasmussen was beginning to feel bitter and used. After all, he had already quit a prestigious job at Columbia University in order to come to Atlanta and support his wife. Out of love for her, he had gone from the Ivy League to a backwater college; and in order to keep his word, he had given up working all together, so that he could stay home and be a kind of *househusband*.

…And there was something else: he could not help thinking she had planned all this. As the obstetrician had said, if she really had been taking birth control pills for five months into her pregnancy, it was unlikely the baby would have been healthy. In truth, his soul had been poisoned by so many doubts and resentments that he found himself questioning everything now—including his own sanity….

The sun was setting on Athens, Georgia. Athens was a classic university town: since it was the middle of summer, the neighborhoods around the campus were dead to the point of being depressing. There were still thousands of people about; but as most of the students had returned to their homes, the life and energy of the town was gone.

The man's eyes were wild, and the huge bags beneath them combined with his droopy skin to give him the appearance of a depraved bloodhound. Fifteen minutes ago, he had stolen a car on campus and driven to the "interesting" part of town, where university students found cheap housing—along with the questionable food and entertainment that fit their budgets.

There was an envelope in his pocket. Before starting his rampage fifteen minutes ago, he had ripped open the flap eagerly, breaking the wax seal. He had followed the letter's instructions meticulously; and now, he had reached his destination. The greasy-looking fast food joint did brisk business when school was in session; but at this time of year, the parking lot was mostly empty. The man found a spot near the entrance, looked around to make sure no police cars were about, then he turned off the engine.

Getting his bearings, he looked up at the restaurant's gaudy neon sign. It read, "Roadkill Chicken and Bar-b-cue," and had some cartoon critters—a chicken, a pig, a squirrel, a raccoon and something that was either an opossum or a giant rat—lying flat on a road with their faces in agony and their eyes bulging out of their sockets. In order to establish that they were, indeed, road kill, there were black tire marks over their flattened torsos. It was clever in a juvenile sort of way that catered to "edgy" college students with cast iron stomachs—but the thought of such a bar-b-cue turned the man's stomach (since he was middle-aged with ulcers and acid reflux).

Feeling he had lost his way, the man retrieved the envelope from his pocket and extracted the neatly folded letter. Instantaneously, words began to appear. He sat up straighter and leaned forward, his bloodshot eyes growing larger as he read the message.

The letter was explicit, and since the man prided himself on his attention to detail, he reached into the glove compartment and took out the black marker the letter told him would be there. Next, turning on the overhead light and looking at himself via the rearview mirror, he drew one of those old time cartoon villain mustaches with dramatic curlicues. A triangular goatee on his chin—along with dark circles beneath his eyes—completed the effect. Indeed, as he considered his handiwork in the rearview mirror, a lunatic stared back at him, so he smiled with satisfaction, knowing he had done a good job.

To carry out the letter's final instruction, the man turned to the back seat, where there was a costume. As he stared at it, it finally occurred to him the stolen car must have belonged to one of Roadkill's delivery guys, because the costume was designed to look like a mangy critter; the aforementioned tire tracks were on the stomach, and the bizarre head covering had two veiny eyes bouncing about on springs like antennae.

He hesitated a moment before putting it on—but mostly because it was hotter than the devil's ass crack outside. On top of that, the outfit had the stomach-churning odor of stale sweat, bar-b-cue sauce and vomit—or maybe that was only the car. Either way, the inside of the costume was damp and musty; once he put it on, he felt as though bugs were crawling over his skin. He began to itch; worse, sweat soon began pouring down his temples—especially after he put on the hat. At the same time, he had followed the letter precisely, so he felt the same sense of satisfaction as before.

Once he got out of the car, it was as if his body went on automatic pilot. He stormed into Roadkill's, where a pimply teenage boy was tending the cash register. There was a large television against the wall, and the teenager was looking up at the main story on the local news. Apparently, dozens of bikers and truckers had been arrested for riding through town in the nude; and no one, including the dazed men, could explain why....

Anyway, the teenager had on the same bizarre head piece with the antennae eyes. The kid was about to give his usual greeting to customers when he finally turned from the television and looked at the man. Seeing the man's costume, the teenager's first thought was that the delivery guy had returned—but of course, the cartoon mustache and the other bizarre enhancements made the man look like a maniac. The teenager instinctively jumped back and stood there frozen as the maniac leaped over the counter and grabbed one of the bar-b-cue chicken legs from the serving tray. At first, the teenager only stared confusedly. It was not until the man yelled, "Eat my chicken!" and came at him with the greasy bar-b-cue, that the youth began to scream.

By now, Rasmussen was sitting on a bench at the side of his house. He was tired, but he knew he could not sleep. He was about to consider his next move when an unusually loud car zoomed past his house. He looked in the direction of the car, but the high hedge impeded his view; and soon, even the whining noise of the engine was gone, leaving Rasmussen to question if a car had really passed. He sighed.

He sensed himself unraveling in this place. He was profoundly lonely here. As his realtor had promised, he had never really seen one of his neighbors; he knew none of their names. At most, he caught glimpses of delivery trucks and luxury cars as they sped past his house. Sometimes, when he was feeling particularly lonely, he went to the mall and lounged about the hordes of bored grannies and giggling teenage girls. Unfortunately, in time, the grannies always started giving him annoying baby tips from when they had their children fifty years ago; and after a few minutes, the teenage giggling would grate against his nerves as well, until he found himself fleeing the mall and speeding back home to have some peace.

When the sun finally disappeared over the trees in the distance, Rasmussen took a deep breath and sat straighter. Another day was gone; more days like this one lay on the horizon.

In time, he remembered the mail. He was not expecting anything, but checking the mail had become a cherished daily activity—since there was always the chance of something new and unexpected showing up in the mailbox.

He stood up, groaned from his aching back muscles, then began to walk around the house, to get to the front. His minivan was parked in the driveway. It was lime green; and like everything else in the house, his wife had picked it. In the garage, his Porsche went unused—a relic of his past life and his past manhood....

He was dressed in a t-shirt, running shorts and a pair of sneakers. There was a towering security gate in front of their house, but Rasmussen usually left it open—since the iron gate had begun to seem more like prison bars than a security feature....

The mailbox was beyond the security gate. He paused after he had crossed the threshold of his property, then he looked up and down the lonely road. In the distance, he could see the upper stories of some million-dollar homes. As twilight descended on the world, the buildings all looked like things out of horror movies: the kind of dark, imposing structures that drove people to madness.

He missed New York. He missed crowds and sidewalks; he missed walking to the corner deli, riding the subway—and all the other loud, messy conveniences that made New York City seem real and *alive*—

He shook his head, annoyed with himself for wanting impossible things. Pushing himself on, he opened the mailbox and pulled out the mail. He flipped through the envelopes in quick succession, but his wife's name was on all of them. All the bills were in her name, and that was suddenly yet another insult to his manhood. A side of him wanted to rant and rave, but he knew his thoughts were stupid....

He was about to sigh when a car horn suddenly blared behind him! Rasmussen jumped and cried out as the car sped past in a gust of wind. Even after the vehicle was safely past him, the shock left him panting on the side of the road. It was actually a mini-van—the same model as his, but another hideous color. In truth, the minivan had not been going that fast, but as the road was empty, there was no reason it should have been that close to him.

Amazingly, even after the near miss, the minivan did not stop—it merely continued on as if nothing had happened. Rasmussen stared in disbelief—until the outrage of it triggered the hostile New Yorker lurking inside of him. He was about to unleash a torrent of cuss words...but when he looked at the minivan's roof, he saw someone had forgotten a baby seat on top; and when he leaned in to get a better look, he saw the baby was still in the seat, squirming around!

At first, he could not believe what he was seeing. Two or three seconds passed before he allowed himself to believe it. When that happened, he dropped the mail and ran. Now, he was screaming for the driver to stop as he sprinted after the vehicle. In his mind, the minivan driver was an overworked father like himself. Rasmussen ran as if he were trying to save his own soul and his own life. He screamed like a madman, practically *begging* the driver to stop. Luckily, as the minivan was still going relatively slow, Rasmussen was soon at the rear bumper. He yelled louder, so that the veins on his neck bulged, but the minivan continued on at the same leisurely pace, as if the driver were deaf.

The windows were tinted, so he could not see inside. However, he noticed the driver's window was open. He screamed again; but by now, he was out of breath and his legs were beginning to burn. As his strength began to fail him, he thought about flinging himself at the vehicle and latching onto the door...or anything else that would get the driver's attention. By now, he was at the side of the vehicle—and as his legs burned, he knew that was as far as he was going to get. As he lifted his hand to bang on the window, he instinctively looked up at the baby seat. It was only then that he realized the squirming baby was actually a hairy, frog-looking doll!

From watching children's TV with his son, Rasmussen knew the doll was the latest craze: when you squeezed it, it jumped around and began giggling like some kind of demented drug fiend. Someone had tied the safety belt around the doll's pressure sensor!

Rasmussen stopped in his tracks, bewildered and exhausted. The minivan stopped a short while afterwards; then, as Rasmussen looked on in disbelief, a grinning teenager with neon orange hair poked his head out of the driver's side window. The rear door opened next, revealing more laughing teens with strange hair and disturbing facial piercings. One was holding up a video camera and giving Rasmussen "the finger." Another one was grabbing his crotch and making other crude gestures. The three teens were congratulating themselves now: bored suburban kids, entertaining themselves with mischief.

From Rasmussen's idle moments of wandering the Internet, he had come upon that Revenge Prank site. Now that he thought about it, these kids had probably been inspired by it. He was staring at them in disbelief when the kid with the camera leaned forward, as if getting a close-up. It was that slight motion that sent Rasmussen over the edge.

He did not know where he found the strength or the speed; but in the blink of an eye, he was at the open rear door. The laughing kids were not laughing anymore. They screamed for the driver to take off, but Rasmussen was already there. He grabbed the camera and flung it out of the vehicle, smashing it on the road...and then he was flinging blows.

The frog-faced doll's maniacal giggles could be heard clearly now, providing the perfect soundtrack for the carnage. The camera-man was the first to catch a blow to the nose; Rasmussen backslapped some other kid, then he reached over the back seat, to grab the driver by the hair...!

The teenagers were all screaming now—mostly yelling for the driver, or some other brave soul, to *do* something. ...But by that time, Rasmussen was like a vengeful demon. Even though he was a thirty-something college professor, he was twice as big as any of the teenagers. He was practically frothing at the mouth as he dis-pensed his justice—

The driver stepped on the accelerator, as if that would some-how shake off Rasmussen. It was pointless of course; and as the driver kept looking back to see which of his friends was being pummeled, it was only a matter of time before the van flew off the road and into someone's hedge. The jolt threw Rasmussen off balance, so that one of the bloody-faced teens managed to shove him out of the back with a lucky kick to the stomach. Rasmussen landed on a neighbor's plush lawn. After that, the minivan made a U-turn, grinding up the lawn and nearly capsizing in the process. Another hedge was knocked down; then, once the vehicle had fi-nally returned to the road, it accelerated again and disappeared into the twilight.

When Rasmussen stood up and looked around, he saw the doll on the ground, still going into fits. He stared at it for a few seconds before he burst out laughing. ...*Damn, he felt good!* The rage had been building within him for weeks or *months* now. He had needed to release it—and beating the *crap* out of those brats had been just what the doctor ordered!

As he was about to laugh again, he suddenly remembered he had left his son alone! Coming to his senses, he took off running again—back the way he had come. All he really had left was the cultivated illusion of being a good father. To the outside world, he was the dutiful father, giving up everything for his son. It was perhaps all a lie, but it was the only thing he had. Worse, if something happened to his son, none of the sacrifices he had made would have meant anything…and his wife would hate him forever.

He ran faster, past the point of exhaustion and probably past the point of madness. In front of his house, he saw his wife's letters strewn on the ground. He ran past them and up the driveway. The front door was locked—

Damnit!

He sprinted around the house, to get in the side door. His mind was numb by then; his limbs pulsed with pain. When he darted into the living room, the baby sprang up from sleep, startled. At first, they stared at one another, both of them wide-eyed. However, when the baby began to shriek, Rasmussen smiled and walked up to his son.

After the frantic way Cassiopeia had driven to Atlanta, Higginbottom was confused when she swung the car into one of those shady-looking strip mall motels. It was right off the highway, on the outskirts of town; as Higginbottom looked through the windscreen, he saw about five or six prostitutes parading on the curb, in front of the management office. He could tell they were prostitutes because they had on their "hooker uniforms": towering platform heels; huge, hideous wigs; shorts that dug into their crotches and ass cracks, and so on. As Higginbottom was about to ask Cassiopeia why they were there, she got out of the vehicle, barked, "Come!" and slammed the door behind her.

Higginbottom fumbled out of the car and ran to catch up to her. She walked toward the management office in her usual authoritative, no-nonsense way. Higginbottom followed nervously in her wake, instinctively frightened by the rough-looking prostitutes. Most of them were black, layered in excessive makeup and cheap, overpowering perfume that could not mask the odor of stale, musty sex. He held his breath and stared at the ground to avoid making eye contact with the women; but at the sight of Cassiopeia (and her skintight leather outfit) the prostitutes started snarling and yelling threats—apparently thinking Cassiopeia was another prostitute trying to infringe on their turf. She walked past them as if they were not even there—which only infuriated them further. One of them grabbed Higginbottom's arm, as if she were taking back what was rightfully hers. When Higginbottom looked, she was missing a few teeth. She moved in closer, as if to kiss him, and he *squealed*—like an old lady who had just laid eyes on a *humongous* rat! Terrified, he darted to Cassiopeia's side, where he hoped to receive the protection of Heaven....

In the management office, a heavyset white man with a stained, too-tight T-shirt looked up confusedly when Cassiopeia walked through the door. Higginbottom stumbled over the shag rug and bumped into her back. She turned and gave him a disapproving look. He took a step back and bowed his head.

"Y'all want a room?" the attendant drawled. He was in the process of eating some kind of sauce-filled sandwich—which explained the stains on his shirt.

"Yes, sir," Cassiopeia replied. "We'll take the finest suite in your establishment." From her statement, it was as if she had walked into a five-star hotel in London. The attendant stared at her confusedly. His first thought was that she was being sarcastic, but her face had its usual stern expression. Her accent had also thrown him off balance. He stared at her, chewing the contents of his mouth mechanically, like a cow chewing its cud. He took in Cassiopeia's leather outfit and saw, in Higginbottom's body language, the shy, embarrassed deportment of most johns. Adding it all up in his head, he reached for his beer and guzzled the last of it to wash down his sandwich. Next, he nodded his head and began his usual sales pitch: "We charge fifty dollars an hour—"

"How much for a week?" Cassiopeia interrupted him.

"A *week?*" he said in surprise. In fact, his tone seemed to say, "Why the *hell* would you want to stay here for a week?" In that sense, he and Higginbottom were in total agreement. Higginbottom was about to step up (to ask her what they were even doing in this place) when she reached into her pants, dug something out of her crotch, and pulled it out. It was a wad of one hundred dollar bills. She counted out five bills and slammed them on the counter.

"I assume this will be adequate recompense for now?"

The attendant stared at the bills, stunned; after that, he nodded and reached for the bills eagerly. He raised them before his eyes and stared in amazement. Higginbottom looked at the attendant with a vague sense of shame and empathy, because he knew the man was going to sniff those bills once he and Cassiopeia were gone.

Cassiopeia shoved the remaining wad back into her crotch. When the attendant and Higginbottom looked, they saw the wad gave her the illusion of a manly bulge. At the realization, they looked away uneasily. Suddenly flustered, the attendant got the keys; once he handed them over, Cassiopeia stormed out of the office in the same way she had stormed in. Higginbottom followed her, again stumbling over the ill-placed rug.

Outside, they walked past the same horde of prostitutes. The "finest suite in the establishment" was of course a roach-infested dump. The walls were painted in a greenish-pink color—as if the painter had run low on supplies and decided to mix all the paint he had into a vat. A hideous shag carpet from the nineteen seventies covered the floor. It was a kind of neon purple, with various blotches, bald patches and stains from decades of abuse. There were two beds. The sheets were grayish—either by design or from years of accumulated filth. Higginbottom shuddered at the thought of what must have happened on those beds.

Yet, he did not gawk at the room for too long, because the moment the door was closed behind him, Cassiopeia began to strip. Within thirty seconds she had thrown off all her clothes. Her body was flawless; her uncovered breasts were everything Higginbottom had imagined. His mouth salivated at the sight of them. Her scant pubic hair had been shaved into a triangle. His penis became fully erect for the first time in what seemed like years; his breath became short—

However, as he was getting ready to fling himself at her, she turned her back on him and walked over to the adjoining bathroom. He stared at her uncertainly, wondering if he had been given an invitation…and she was such an odd woman that he could not assume her nakedness was itself an invitation to sex. She had left her clothes in a pile on the floor; when he looked down, he saw the wad of bills was still in her lacy underwear.

While she showered, he stood there in a state of anxious horniness, wondering if he should join her (with or without an overt invitation). Unfortunately, her shower was a quick one. As he was beginning to believe he had lost his chance, she began toweling off. There was something graceful and unreal about her movements. She was like something out of a dream, and his penis sprung to life again.

By the time she put the towel back on the rack and headed out of the bathroom, he felt like his heart was going to bust out of his chest; he prepared himself, again ready to fling himself at her and work off five years of sexual frustration—but once she was out of the bathroom, she turned sharply to the right, lay on one of the beds, and pulled the covers over her nakedness.

Higginbottom stared, again wondering if he had been given an invitation. However, the situation became clear when she raised her head from the pillow and yelled, "Go wash up and get some sleep! God is going to call on us in the morning." Then, looking disapprovingly at Higginbottom's filthy clothes: "After you shower, wash your clothes in the sink, so you can have something clean to wear in the morning!" At that, her head returned to the pillow. Higginbottom stared for a few seconds, unsure of what had just happened; but when he realized his penis had gone limp, he bowed his head and slunk off to the bathroom.

At Roadkill's, the teenage cashier passed out after a few seconds of having a greasy chicken leg shoved down his throat. Luckily for him, he landed in such a way that the bar-b-cue was expelled. The restaurant's only two customers were a scruffy couple—a man and woman in their early twenties—with matching nose rings and tattoos. As was the way of their generation, the two of them soon had their smartphones out and trained on the maniac in the mangy suit. In fact, they were so excited by the prospect of their videos receiving a million hits on the Internet that it did not once occur to them to call the police.

As he looked down at the unconscious cashier, the maniac grinned triumphantly, seeing that his work was done. To celebrate, he returned to the tray with the bar-b-cue, grabbed a piece and took a hearty bite. "Eat my chic-*ken!*" he screamed again, so that the half-chewed meat tumbled from his mouth—and the scruffy couple stepped in closer to get a better view.

It was then that the manager/cook came running from his office to investigate the commotion. The bizarre scene stopped him dead in his tracks, and he frowned. The manager was a short, fat, middle-aged man whose stubby limbs and unusually large bald head gave him the appearance of beach ball with arms and legs. The manager and the maniac stared at one another for two or three seconds—as if each were witnessing the most ridiculous thing he had ever seen.

However, the maniac was the first to regain his senses, because he grabbed a plastic bag from behind the counter and began shoveling the bar-b-cue into it. After about five handfuls, he giggled maniacally, screamed, "Eat my chicken!" one last time, and fled.

Beyond the window, the maniac could be seen shuffling toward a car in the parking lot. Within the restaurant, the scruffy couple ran past the manager with their phones aloft, hoping to capture the maniac's retreat on their cameras. When the manager looked, their faces wore wide, excited grins—which were all the more ghoulish because their faces were still smeared with bar-b-cue sauce. Either way, by the time the couple reached the door, the manic was already in the car, speeding out of the parking lot.

A few tense seconds passed, with everyone staring out at the darkening parking lot and trying to figure out what had happened. That was when the teenage cashier groaned from the ground. In his first futile attempt to get to his feet, he toppled a stack of serving trays, which rained down on his head. At the commotion, the scruffy couple once again held their phones aloft and ran to get a better vantage point; and to his credit, the manager finally came to his senses and rushed over to rescue his employee.

After what Binkowski had seen and smelt today, he definitely needed some stiff drinks. It was a little past ten now, and the bar was dead—especially as it was a Monday. His writing pad was before him; and as usual, he was staring down at the sheets, trying to figure out if he had written nonsense or not. He sighed, drained the last of his beer, then signaled the bartender for a refill. Half an hour later—after about three more beers—his brain belched and vomited up yet another one of his profanity-laced train wrecks. Excited by the new idea, he leaned over his pad and began scribbling furiously:

Protagonist:
Freddy Fischbach; late 40s; slightly overweight.
Opening Scene:
He's in bed having sex with his plump wife. He's really into it: sweat's pouring; the bed's shaking…but when he looks down, he sees she's fast asleep. In fact, when he stops his thrusting (and the bed stops squeaking) he realizes she's snoring—loud. To be honest, he hadn't been feeling anything either. He looks down, to where his penis entered her vagina, and it seemed like a toothpick in a donut hole. His wife had started shaving her pubic hair about a month ago—since it started going gray. Before, the mass of hair had hidden the brutal reality of it from him, but now it was undeniable: he had a tiny cock. He had of course known this all his life, but looking down at his little twig, he felt like the victim of a cosmic joke. His wife did not even pretend she was feeling anything anymore. Half the time, when he was finished, he merely looked up at him like a patient mom whose retarded son had managed to tie his shoelaces.

As his erection died a horrible death, Fischbach crawled from between her legs—as if worried she would awaken and see him. He wanted to hide in fact, but when he got out of bed, he stood there watching his wife. Her panty was around her left ankle. When he followed her leg up to the gaping maw of her vagina, a sudden terror came over him, as if the thing would grow fangs and devour him. The thought was weird, even for him, and he found himself fleeing the room.

His two daughters had left for college, so there was nobody else in the house to see his nakedness. He went down to the living room and turned on the television. It was past midnight, and one of those infomercials was on. As Fischbach was about to turn away and fetch a snack from the kitchen, the TV announcer said, "Do you have a little cock?"

Fischbach's head jerked around! On the screen, there was a midget in a lab coat.

"I used to have a little cock," the midget confessed. After he said it, a nude picture appeared on the screen: one of those bathroom mirror selfies taken with a cellular phone. In the picture, the midget was standing on top of the sink, his toddler-sized pecker barely visible in the mass of pubic hair. Fischbach shuddered at the sight.

However, after about two seconds, the picture disappeared from the screen, and the midget again looked into the camera self-assuredly. "I used to have a little cock," he said, tossing down his coat and ripping off his pants like a stripper, "but look at me now!"

Fischbach stumbled forward, his jaw hanging lose, his eyes bulging…! The midget's cock seemed bigger than he was! When the man took it in his pudgy little hand, it looked like he was holding a bazooka!

"Look at me!" the midget demanded. "My cock's so big I have to rest it on this shelf to keep it from dragging," he said, grinning. Appropriately enough, a shelf had been set up so that he could demonstrate his technique.

Fischbach stared, mesmerized. Was this some kind of midget porno? Had the cable company started up a risqué fetish channel? He saw the remote control on the coffee table, reached for it and pressed the MENU button. To his amazement, he saw he was watching a regular network channel! He frowned, but—

"Look at my cock!" the midget demanded again. "You want a cock like this, don't you! Look at it!"

Despite himself, Fischbach leaned in further—

"What the hell you waiting on?" the midget screeched. "You see the goddamn number on the screen, don't you? Call it, you dumb bastard!"

Suddenly flustered, Fischbach reached for the cordless phone on the coffee table and dialed the number frantically. The phone rang once before someone answered:

"About time!" the person said. "What took you so long?"

It took Fischbach about three seconds to realize the person on the phone was the midget. When he did, he instinctively looked up at the television. That was when his eyes grew wide, because the midget was holding a telephone to his ear.

"Yeah, it's me, you dumb bastard," the midget cursed him. By then, Fischbach's mind was moving so sluggishly that a few more seconds passed before he accepted the fact that the midget was talking to him live. He looked down at the phone—

"What the hell are you looking at the phone for?" the midget said impatiently. "Do you want a big cock or not?"

"Yeah," he said breathlessly, surrendering to the madness.

"What? Speak up!" the midget demanded.

"Yeah!" Fischbach practically screamed, so that he cringed afterward, wondering if his wife had heard. Then, in a more even tone, "I want… a big cock," he said shyly.

"Of course you do, numb nuts! I see that noodle you're packing."

It was probably only then that it occurred to him the midget was actually seeing him through the television, but he was too stunned to cover his nakedness.

"How are you doing this?" he said in the same breathless way.

"How?" the midget said in annoyance—as if it should have been obvious. "I'm your fairy godfather, you dumb bastard!"

Fischbach could only stare ahead; and then, the next thing he knew, there was a flash of light and the midget was actually there, in the room with him! Both of them were naked and the midget's massive cock was dragging on the floor like a hose. Fischbach trembled as he looked down—

"There's no time to waste!" the midget said now. "I have a schedule to keep, you know."

Surrendering totally to everything going on around him, Fischbach nodded and peeped, "What do I have to do?"

Once again, the midget looked at him in annoyance. "Grab my sack, of course! Don't you know anything?"

"What sack?" Fischbach said, confused—since the man's hands were empty.

"My nut *sack, you dumb fuck!" the midget exploded. Then, with more exasperation, "Everyone* knows fairies keep their magic in their sacks!"

Fischbach had of course never heard of such a thing, but he was willing to accept his ignorance on the issue—the same way he was willing to accept his ignorance of the latest teenage heartthrob—

"Hurry up and grab it!" the midget demanded.

Flustered once again, Fischbach reached between the man's legs and grabbed his sweaty balls—

"Goddamn it, Binkowski!" the bartender screamed. "Why the *hell* are you still here?"

Binkowski looked at him confusedly, emerging slowly from his writing trance. Startled, he looked around at the empty bar. Somehow, he and the bartender were the only ones there. The television had been turned off; the chairs had all been turned over, onto the tables—

"Get the *fuck* out!" the bartender screamed, so that Binkowski jumped from the bar stool, grabbed his pen and pad, and fled.

Once he was outside, his pace slowed, and he again looked around confusedly. His buzz from the beer had long worn off; the comfort of the writing trance had gone as well, leaving him disillusioned and *empty*—like a junkie coming down from his high. He felt beat up and worn out. Much of that had to do with the shift he had put in at the hospital, but he felt a strange spiritual component as well, as if part of his soul had been taken from him. The tendrils of the Fischbach story retreated from his mind; the excitement he had felt while writing was gone as well; and in his dazed state, he could now barely remember where he had meant to go with the plot. It was all unraveling, and he felt the usual feeling of frustration at being unable to finish what he started. He sighed.

Wondering what time it was, he checked his cellular phone: it was twenty-six minutes past midnight. He stared at the phone's display in disbelief, but there was nothing to do now but go home.

It was about a quarter to one in the morning when Binkowski closed the apartment door behind him. Upon entering the apartment, he saw someone had shoved an envelope under the door. He turned on the light to reveal the cramped kitchen; after that, he bent down to pick up the envelope. As he turned it over, he saw there was no name written on it—but there was a wax seal. Shrugging, he ripped it open and pulled out the fine stationery. However, nothing was written on it either. After giving it some thought, he concluded someone in the building was probably having a party—and that the blank invitation was most likely a printing mishap. He made a mental note to check with likely party candidates in the building, but tossed the letter in the bin, turned off the light, and headed down the hall, to his room.

He assumed nobody was home—or that his roommate was sleeping—since all the lights were off and the place was quiet.

However, while he was passing his roommate's open door, he looked in and saw Jones lying on the bed. His roommate had a habit of listening to music when he was trying to figure out a complicated problem, and his headphones were on now.

Indeed, Jones had been moping about the apartment for the last few days, still convinced the story he had told the night of the infamous pissing incident was true. When Binkowski lingered by the door, Jones looked up, noticed him, and turned on the lamp on the nightstand. His face wore its usual forlorn expression as he took off the headphones.

"Still no word from your professor?" Binkowski ventured.

"Nah."

"Did you contact your department?"

Jones nodded his head. "They said he went on sabbatical," he replied, sounding skeptical.

"You don't think so?" Binkowski pressed him.

"They said he sent them a *text* message, but who does that?" he began, his voice already rising with emotion. "We were supposed to start work on a major project this week. He *just* got funding. When I went over to his place the other night, it was to celebrate. He was going to tell me the details. ...So, why would he take off *now?*"

"So, you still think he's licking his tit in the dark somewhere?" Binkowski said mockingly, unable to help himself. Yet, once he saw the aggrieved expression on Jones' face, he put up his hand apologetically. "Either way," he went on quickly, trying to be constructive, "you can't mope around here for the rest of the summer. I've got some late shifts for the next two nights, but why don't we do something Friday? We can hit he clubs, find some new pussy...unless you're still craving that eighty-year-old?"

At Binkowski's jibe, Jones laughed, despite himself. Eventually, he nodded, seeing Binkowski was right. Staying locked up in his room was definitely not doing him any good.

Seeing his friend emerging from his malaise, Binkowski smiled. "Good," he said, heading off to his room. "Get some sleep then."

"Alright," Jones said, turning off the light.

The prostitute in the room next to Higginbottom's seemed to be doing good business, because her squeaking bed (and her fake screams of ecstasy) started up every fifteen minutes, like clockwork. On top of that, Higginbottom quickly became convinced there were lice or some other bugs in the bed, because something kept biting him. By then, Cassiopeia's calm, steady breathing told him she was sound asleep. He did not want to turn on the light or do anything that would disturb her—and risk incurring her wrath. Thus, he lay there for hours, listening to fake screams and being eaten alive. Worse, in the parking lot, there seemed to be constant flare-ups, with a sting of johns and disagreeable prostitutes being put in place by a pimp whose name was apparently "Big Slug." At least, that was the name Higginbottom kept hearing—as in, "Beat his ass, Big Slug!" (from prostitutes) or "Please, stop, Big Slug!" (from johns and prostitutes getting their asses beaten).

Slug had a thunderous baritone, which shook the walls and left Higginbottom trembling inside. Every time he heard it, his mind conjured images of a monstrous black man who had done *hard* time in prison for "Regulating fools"—as Big Slug, himself, had put it all night.

With all that, it was not until three or four in the morning that Higginbottom finally drifted off to sleep; but even then, he had horrible dreams—about Big Slug, his whores and the wretched johns who endured his regulations.

DAY FOUR

When the baby began to cry, Rasmussen jumped up from bed and looked in the corner of the bedroom, where there was a crib. The baby was grabbing the bars, like a convict trying to escape. They stared at one another. Rasmussen felt too drained to move, so he let his head return to the pillow.

What time was it? By the height of the sun outside the window, he knew it was at least after ten in the morning. He looked absent-mindedly to the empty space beside him on the bed, trying to remember if his wife had come home last night or not. He was not sure. Either way, she would be long gone by now. He sighed, got out of bed, and went to tend to his screaming son.

He felt like he was sleepwalking. Soon, the hours were passing him by. He changed his son and cooked and did laundry. The next time he looked up at the clock, it was about three-fifteen in the afternoon. He did not even try to make sense of it anymore….

He was in the living room now, watching a shameful TV show while the baby played with some blocks on the floor. On the talk show, a man and a woman—ex-lovers—were yelling horrible things at one another. The recurring premise of the show was that there was some doubt about the paternity of the couple's baby. Typically, the tearful woman came on first, saying she had no idea why the father was denying paternity; the father then appeared, usually on video, calling the woman a slut and claiming there were at least four or five other men who could have been the father. In a perverse way, it all became a proxy war for the battle of the sexes. The worst stereotypes about men and women were on display. The men (usually black) were thugs who refused to accept their responsibilities. The women, on the other hand, were either portrayed as scheming jezebels trying to trap unsuspecting men in their webs of deception or reckless party girls juggling an endless procession of lovers. The all-mighty arbiter was the paternity test, revealed after all the recriminations, taunts and threats had been made. The moment of revelation, when the host told the unusually silent man if he was Baby Leroy's father, was the moment when the skirmish in the battle of the sexes was settled. Either the man jumped up triumphantly, having narrowly missed out on becoming a whore's baby daddy, or the woman reigned supreme, having kept another irresponsible man from shirking his duty to his offspring. Rasmussen felt his brain cells melting as he watched, and yet he was honest enough to acknowledge a feeling of vindication every time the host told the man that little Shinqueedah was not his. It made no sense, yet he knew he had been thoroughly pulled into the stupidity of it all. At such times, he would find himself thinking that if he were still teaching, he would be too busy for this foolishness— and that idleness really was the devil's entryway into the soul....

Presently, the baby let out one of his petulant cries to warn Rasmussen he had better pay more attention to him. Since Rasmussen had been well trained by now, he rose, picked up the baby, and took him to the kitchen to fetch some food.

Rasmussen placed the baby in the high chair and went to the refrigerator to get some juice. He was washing his son's favorite bottle when he looked out of the window and saw a blue-haired creature grinning at him! He jumped back, so that the plastic bottle slipped from his hand and bounced against the floor. He stood there gasping for air—until it occurred to him the blue-haired creature was only an old woman. She was still grinning. He stared at her for two or three more seconds, as if waiting for her fangs to appear or the telltale tentacles to emerge from beneath her flowery church dress. Nothing appeared, but he was still not convinced.

After a few seconds, the woman held up a serving dish—as a kind of peace offering, perhaps—and gestured with her head for him to open the kitchen door. When he nodded reflexively, she disappeared from the window. Yet, he was still uneasy. Something about her grin was unnerving. He glanced at the baby, who was looking at him anxiously, then he took a deep breath and walked over to the door.

"Good morning, Mr. Rasmussen!" the woman yelled as soon as he opened the door. "I'm your neighbor, Mrs. Stanko—but everyone calls me Granny Stanko," she said, putting so much emphasis on the "stank" that her name came out sounding like "Stank Hoe." Rasmussen instinctively flinched, but, "I made a casserole," she announced suddenly, holding up the serving dish for him to see.

Rasmussen listened without really hearing. Somehow, the woman was inside his house now. She placed the casserole on the table and gestured with her head for Rasmussen to sit. He had been holding the door, staring at her as if she were a stray thought that had escaped his head.

"I've been living in the house next door for thirty years," she began after Rasmussen sat down, "but I've been sidetracked these last few months. Today, I woke up and *swore* I'd come see you, in order to get us back on the right track as neighbors." She made more small talk—about the neighborhood and its history—but

Rasmussen only stared at her anxiously, as if waiting for demonic horns to sprout from her head. She was dressed like a television granny from the 1950s—a stock character of an old southern lady with a flowery church dress and a lace shall. Yet, she seemed like a really bad actress. Looking down, he noticed she was wearing the kind of platform pumps that only strippers and porn stars wore. Hers were bright red, with dazzling rhinestones.

Rasmussen was frowning at the shoes when the old lady noticed the baby. She gasped and practically ran over to the little boy, her face beaming. "What a *beautiful* baby!" she exclaimed. When she began spouting some gobbledygook and making bizarre faces, the little boy eyed at her as if to ask what the *hell* was wrong with her. Now, she was rambling on about her first baby, and the horrible diaper rash he used to get. As she did so, she walked over to the cabinet. There, she fetched a plate as if this were *her* house; on her way back, he retrieved a knife and fork from the drainer by the sink. Rasmussen only stared in disbelief, but she was soon hovering over him again, arranging the plate and utensils before him, cutting out a piece of the casserole and putting it on the plate. In the mystery dish, he saw chicken and potatoes—and bacon. Since Rasmussen only stared at the dish in the same dazed way, she cut off a piece with the fork and fed him.

Despite his initial protestations, it tasted...*heavenly*. Rasmussen moaned and his eyes went back in their sockets. At the sight, Stanko's grin widened and she handed him the fork. Soon, he was shoveling the casserole into his mouth. He could not help himself. It was as if Stanko's dish filled a hole in his soul. When he glanced at the baby, there was a disapproving look there, but he did not care. He got a second helping of the casserole while Stanko went to the refrigerator to get him something to drink. Rasmussen felt like he was eating the way the gods ate.

Unfortunately, things began to unravel when the woman turned her attentions to the baby once more. Too young to appreciate bacony treats and Southern hospitality, the little boy promptly began to bawl when she pinched his cheeks and came at him with her pruney lips. Infuriated by her strange affections—and her inability to take a hint—the baby unleashed a tirade of epic proportions. His little face turned purple; his pudgy fists sung at her bluish hair, until Rasmussen leapt up from the table and pulled her away, fearing for her safety. She seemed so sorrowful that Rasmussen felt guilty and ashamed. This was all more proof that he was a horrible father. In fact, he saw his son's life in a flash: in kindergarten, the little boy would beat up the other kids and be banned; by first grade, he would begin torturing animals in the woods; by ten, neighborhood kids would begin disappearing; and sooner or later, Rasmussen would be revealed as the father of the Antichrist—

The baby screamed louder, banging his little fists against the high chair's table. Rasmussen apologized to the woman as he ushered her toward the door. She told him he could hold onto the casserole container until he was finished; but at her suggestion, the baby seemed to scream louder, so Rasmussen grabbed the dish and handed it to her as he issued more apologies. She stood at the door, staring at him sorrowfully—so that he practically felt like crying. However, when the baby's tirade passed a new threshold, Rasmussen instinctively slammed the door on her and turned away guiltily.

As the prostitute in the next room was beginning her chorus of fake screams, Higginbottom sprung up from the bed with a terrified expression on his face. He was panting for the first five or six seconds—and his eyes were wild as he recalled all the implausible events from the day before. There was daylight outside the window now, but the digital alarm clock said it was after three-thirty. Either it was wrong or he had somehow slept deep into the afternoon. He stared at the clock in disbelief—

"*Get this pussy!*" the prostitute screamed. Higginbottom stared at the wall uneasily, imaging the perverse scenes on the other side of it. Glancing down, he realized he was nude—and remembered washing all his clothes the previous day. However, the john in the next room seemed to be thrusting away with wild abandon now—so that Higginbottom began to fear the thin walls would come crashing down. Instinctively, he moved lower down on the bed, to get away from the wall. He got on his knees and inched away; he looked down at his penis again—as if it would somehow help him make sense of all this—but it only hung there limply, mocking him.

Remembering Cassiopeia, he looked toward her bed, seeing it was empty. In fact, it had been *made*. Suddenly frantic, he looked first at the open bathroom door, then went to check the empty room. How long had he been sleeping? What if Cassiopeia had *left* him? His heart was thumping in his chest now. He felt like an abandoned child, ready to cry for his mother—

Outside the room, in the parking lot, there was a bloodcurdling scream. Higginbottom looked toward the window, but the blinds were closed. A man was screaming as if someone had lopped off his arm; Higginbottom went over to the window to take a look. When he got there, he pulled down one of the horizontal blinds, glanced out surreptitiously, and saw a towering blob of a white man—with long, hazel hair, tattooed arms and gold teeth. The blob was beating up a middle-aged white man who was dressed in nothing but a pair of shorts. As for the blob, he was wearing one of those "wife beater" undershirts—but his gut was so huge that the undershirt had risen up and taken on the appearance of a bikini top. Even the man's belly had a tattoo—a grinning skull with fangs.

Higginbottom stared, fascinated as his gut jiggled—and gave the fangs the illusion of movement.

Now, the blob was brandishing his fist in the john's face: "Don't lie to Big Slug!" he warned the john, grabbing him around the neck with one of his huge paws. Higginbottom's eyes grew wide: he would never have guessed Big Slug was white. Big Slug must have hit the john in the face before Higginbottom got there, because the man's nose was bloody. At Big Slug's new threat, the john began to cry—

Higginbottom closed the blind, turned from the window, and leaned against the wall. He felt sick again—the same combination of nausea, dizziness and *panic*. This place was getting to him. Twenty-four hours a day, it was the same thing: a steady stream of prostitutes and johns—all of them trapped in a cycle of sex and violence. The prostitutes were mostly black; the johns were mostly white and—like Higginbottom—past their prime. They had faces like his; whatever pleasure they received in the motel rooms was short-lived, since most of them did not stay longer than fifteen minutes. When they did, Big Slug always went to check, followed shortly thereafter by scenes like the one he had just witnessed.

Where the hell was Cassiopeia? Higginbottom went to the window again—to check for the car—but it wasn't where they had parked it last night. Panic was about to set it again; but with his last iota of dignity, he rebelled against the feeling of childish helplessness. He was a *man*: he had to hold it together. He nodded his head absentmindedly. Besides, it was possible Cassiopeia had only left for the store. Maybe she would return with food shortly. He wanted to believe that, so he nodded his head once more.

At the same time, without Cassiopeia's actual presence, thoughts of missions from God seemed even more ridiculous than they had last night. Without her, *everything* from yesterday seemed impossible, so that he stumbled back into the bed, lay down heavily, and sighed. If all of this were a dream, then he wanted to be unconscious again—a dreamer within the dream—until the time came when he had to wake up. Bewildered, he took a deep breath and closed his eyes.

It was not until ten minutes after Stanko was gone that the baby calmed down. Rasmussen returned to the living room—and the sordid television show. A new couple was on the screen, accusing one another of the usual things. Rasmussen stared at the television, but did not really see. His mind kept returning to Stanko—and her platform heels. Something about her had been *off*, so that his mind vacillated between two totally disturbing explanations of her sudden appearance. Either she was a figment of his imagination or some kind of spy, sent for a nefarious purpose he could not yet grasp. It was the kind of idle thought that only paranoid idiots had, and Rasmussen bowed his head in shame, thinking of this as a new low.

By then, the baby was drowsy, so Rasmussen lowered him to the bassinet and turned the channel. He was flipping channels when he came upon one of those news channels. The announcer was giggling as she read the report:

"...So, you've probably heard about a story out of Athens, Georgia—where the Roadkill Maniac became a sensation after an Internet video of his rampage went viral." Now on the screen, the videos captured by the scruffy couple's smartphones were being shown. The lunatic—*the Roadkill Maniac*—paraded on the screen in a mangy costume, brandishing the bar-b-cue and screaming, "Eat my chicken!"

The announcer was still giggling. Rasmussen stared at the screen, trying to get the joke; but in the end, a newfound feeling of frustration—of disillusionment with the world around him and his *life*—overcame him, and he pressed the remote control once more, to turn off the television.

He lay down on the couch, with his head back and his eyes closed. However, almost immediately, the doorbell rang. His first thought—indeed, his *fear*—was that Stanko had returned! He looked back at the baby uneasily. However, when the bell rang again—in a lingering way that implied impatience—Rasmussen sprung up and went to the attached foyer.

After answering the door, he was initially relieved to see someone besides Stanko. However, two huge black men were standing there. Both men were wearing designer suits and shades—and had completely shaved heads. Their faces were hard and grim, and Rasmussen looked up at them uneasily. One had a tattoo on his neck—a frenetic design that looked like barbed wire—

"Do you have a Chevy minivan?"

Rasmussen stared at the questioner for two seconds before the words made sense to him. "Oh, *yes*," he said, remembering.

"Did you wreck Don Cole's lawn yesterday?"

Rasmussen again had to think about it for a few seconds before the surreal images reentered his mind. "Oh, *no*," he said, shaking his head; he was about to laugh, remembering the squirming doll and beating the *crap* out of those kids—

"Is this you?" one of the men said, producing a grainy picture from the security camera. It was Rasmussen standing on the dug-up lawn, laughing.

A faint smile came over his face as he remembered. "That's me," he began, "but—"

"Is that your minivan?" the same man said accusingly, producing another grainy picture."

"No, it's not," Rasmussen answered—this time without needing to think.

"Didn't you say you owned a Chevy minivan?"

"I do, but it's not my car. These kids—"

"Don Cole don't tolerate no disrespect to his property, Mr. Rasmussen," the huge man said ominously.

Rasmussen looked up at him anxiously: everyone seemed to know his name today! "…This is all a misunderstanding," he began cautiously. "It will sound crazy if I try to *explain* it," he said with an awkward laugh," but there's an explanation."

"Then come on then," one of the men said.

"What?"

"Don Cole's waiting."

The other man rested his heavy hand on Rasmussen's shoulder, as if taking him into custody—"

"But I *can't* now," Rasmussen protested as the man began pulling him out of the door. "I'm watching my baby," he said, gesturing over his shoulder, "—and nobody else is here."

The man paused, pursing his lips, "Then bring it then."

"What?" Rasmussen hedged, looking for a way out of this; but besides kneeing the man in the crotch and locking himself in the house, he saw no manly options.

"Go get it," the other one commanded; and seeing he was trapped, Rasmussen nodded his head and went to fetch his son.

After a few minutes, Higginbottom opened his eyes, realizing he could not return to sleep. He rose from the bed and went to the window. In the parking lot, the melodrama with Big Slug and the wayward john had reached its dénouement. Now that dominance had been reestablished, Big Slug was patting the john on the shoulder as he walked him to his car. Maybe he was offering the john a discount on his next screw or something, because the man seemed genuinely grateful. Higginbottom closed the blinds and looked about the room aimlessly.

He felt *lost*. He wished Cassiopeia had left him a note—or some tangible proof that she actually existed. Instead, he found himself wondering if she was something he had *dreamed*. He shook his head, frustrated with his thoughts. When he glanced down, his limp penis again mocked him, so he went to the bathroom and began to dress himself in the clothes he had washed yesterday. They were still damp and wrinkled, but at least the musty stench was gone.

He reflexively checked his pants pockets again, and saw the thirty dollars were still there. He was hungry: he literally had no idea when he had last eaten. He was in a strange town with nothing to eat, and the money was the only thing keeping him from total helplessness. Deep down, he still held out hope that Cassiopeia would return and take him away from this place—to carry out their grand mission from God—but if all of that was madness, at least he had *something*.

When Rasmussen exited the house with the baby, the huge black men were standing by a Mercedes Benz sedan, staring at him with their arms crossed ominously—like actors on an action movie poster. He hesitated for a moment, considering his options; but when he saw none, he continued on. The baby was still in the bassinet, sleeping. He knew he should have transferred the little boy to the protective car seat, but he was wary of waking his son. Besides, they were literally only driving a few hundred meters.

As Rasmussen neared the sedan, one of the men opened the back door for him, while the other walked around to the driver's side door. Rasmussen entered the spacious vehicle with a vague sense that he had been apprehended. He put the bassinet in his lap and gripped it for dear life. After the man who had opened the back door for him got in the passenger seat, they took off.

The front gate was wide open, as it usually was, and Rasmussen made a mental note to begin closing it from now on. He looked down at his son, relieved for the simple blessing that the baby was still sleeping—but his stomach became queasy when he contemplated what the next few minutes had in store for him. Had the men really called their boss "Don Cole"—as in *mafia* don? Rasmussen tried thinking back, but his mind seemed shredded.

From the road, he could see the top story of Stanko's house. In a year and a half, he had never even heard a peep from that house; other than the automatic porch lights and occasional visits from the gardeners, he had never seen any signs of life. Now, Stanko had appeared like a ghost from a 1950s TV show: the doting granny, always eager to fill everyone's belly with "home cookin'." His mind kept flashing back to her platform heels, as if they were the clue that would unlock the entire mystery. He tried thinking about it for a moment, but he knew there was no sense to it. Exhausted, he sat back in the luxuriant leather seat and closed his eyes.

Within twenty seconds, the car was there. Rasmussen opened his eyes when the vehicle began to slow; however, the scene at the front gate left him staring. There was a woman there, dressed in a skintight leather outfit. Her hair was dark and long; her skin seemed impossibly white as she stood there staring at them. She was like a supermodel—or, with that leather suit, like some patron saint of sadomasochism. Rasmussen sat up in the seat, staring at her. What made the scene especially jarring to the senses was the fact that she was leaning against an ugly *monstrosity* of a car.

Don Cole's henchmen glanced at one another—to make sure

they were really seeing what they thought they were seeing. The driver stopped at the monstrosity's rear bumper. Actually, since the ugly car was blocking the gate, they could not progress anyway. After they stopped, the woman pursed her lips and sashayed over to the driver's side window. The two black men again looked at one another confusedly before the driver lowered the window. The moment he did, she bent over—supposedly to talk to them—but since she did not say anything, Rasmussen surmised her purpose was to give them a better view of her large, succulent breasts. The two black men leaned in closer, mesmerized. In fact, they ogled her without any reservations or discretion; and to be clear, the woman seemed to have no problem with them looking. If anything, she pushed out her chest further, so they could get a better view. At least ten seconds passed with them staring at her in the awkward silence; Rasmussen looked down at the baby to preoccupy himself; he wondered what he was going to eat for dinner—

"Open the gate and let me in," the woman commanded them.

"Okay," they droned in unison, so that Rasmussen looked up and frowned at the weirdness of it all.

After the henchman in the passenger seat pressed a remote control, the gate opened. Within seconds, the woman returned to her car and drove through the gate, leaving them. When Rasmussen looked at the black men, they both had slack-jawed expressions on their faces. Five or six seconds passed. Rasmussen looked ahead, seeing that the ugly car was actually driving on the lawn! To be fair, there were several cars and trucks parked in the driveway, so driving on the lawn was the only way to get to the house. However, even then, Rasmussen was expecting Don Cole's henchmen to be going into fits at the sight of the monstrosity grinding up even more of the lawn; but when he looked, the men were staring ahead blankly, as if in a trance. His frown deepened.

The woman had reached the house by now. Rasmussen watched her get out nonchalantly and sashay up to the front door. In fact, given all he had seen, he came to the conclusion the woman had to live there—or was a frequent visitor—because she opened the front door and walked in.

Five more seconds passed. As Rasmussen's gaze returned to the henchmen, he saw they were still staring ahead like zombies. "Excuse me," he called, "—are you guys alright?" When the men said nothing, Rasmussen leaned in closer, but did not raise his voice—since he did not want to awaken the baby. "*Excuse* me?" he said, resting his hand on the shoulder of the man in the passenger seat.

After about two seconds, the man finally stirred. Rasmussen removed his hand; the man first looked back at him confusedly, then over at the driver—who was still staring ahead. As the man tapped his colleague on the shoulder, the driver jumped. They once again stared at one another confusedly, then they looked back at Rasmussen for a few seconds—as if they suspected he were the cause of their confusion. After Rasmussen put up his hand to plead his innocence, the men looked at one another once more. Eventually, they shrugged their shoulders; and with nothing else to do, the driver put the car in gear and passed through the gate.

Looking out the window, Rasmussen noticed the gap in the hedge—where the minivan had gone through. As a temporary measure, someone had dragged the butchered plant back into the hole, but it was clear the plant was drying. In fact, the entire thing was an eyesore, and Rasmussen's guts clenched when he remembered he was being blamed for it.

Since all the cars and trucks were blocking the way, the driver parked about ten meters beyond the gate. The henchmen were getting out of the car now. Apparently they were all business once more, because their movements were curt and decisive. Rasmussen's door was opened for him. Still not wanting to waken the baby, he exited the vehicle as gently as he could. The henchmen walked before him, leading the way; he followed, his mind numb....

There was loud rap music playing—the southern variety with computerized drum tracks and simplistic melodies that sounded like a tone-deaf five-year-old had made it on his cell phone. By now, Rasmussen was thinking Don Cole was probably a young rapper—instead of a mafia kingpin. Looking at the henchmen again, it occurred to him there probably weren't too many blacks in the mafia....

They walked around to the back of the house. The music got louder, so that Rasmussen could feel the bass in his chest. When he looked down, the baby was beginning to stir in the bassinet. Rasmussen grimaced and braced himself....

The henchmen led him around some high shrubs; once he cleared them, he saw a chaotic scene, with flashing lights and gyrating bodies. The henchmen had stopped on the periphery; Rasmussen reflexively stopped beside them and stood there taking in the scene. There were at least a hundred people—bikini-clad women, mostly—dancing around the huge, in-ground pool. There were three or four camera crews dispersed around the back yard; and on the other side of the pool, an impromptu stage had been set up for the stars of the show. Two rappers were jumping about like they were having seizures. One was black, with flowing dreadlocks that whipped in the air threateningly; the other was white—perhaps as young as thirteen—with blond hair that had been done in corn rows. While the rappers continued their convulsions, some bikini-clad women cavorted around them and occasionally bent over to receive mock thrusts from the dreadlocked rapper. There was a massive banner behind the stage, on which the name "Don Cole" was set against images of money and jewels. Rasmussen nodded his head uneasily, concluding the dreadlocked rapper had to be Don Cole—

At that moment, to his left, one of the women's bikini strings popped, so that her huge breasts flopped out. However, even then, her gyrations continued, as if she were under some kind of pagan spell. Rasmussen looked away and took a deep breath—as if trying to resist coming under that same spell. Yet, the song continued blasting; the dancing became more frantic, with hips thrusting and breasts bouncing. As Rasmussen listened to the rapper's lyrics, it occurred to him the song consisted of a single line, repeated over and over again:

When you horny, you tend not to give a fuck!

Don Cole said the words; the white sidekick merely added flourishes like "Yeah!" and "Huh!" in time with the beat. Completing the scene, there was a middle-aged white man behind them, sitting on a golden throne. Something about him reminded Rasmussen of the guy on the Kentucky Fried Chicken container. The man had the same white suit, girth and goatee. Apparently, his contribution to the performance was to hold up his golden chalice periodically and nod his head approvingly. Every once in a while, he even took a sip and gave another satisfied nod.

Rasmussen could only stare. When he glanced down, he saw the baby was glaring at him as if to say, "You'll pay for this, you bastard!" However, the gyrations of one of the bikini-clad black women soon left the baby mesmerized. She was about three meters away, and moved her body as if she had a detachable spine. One of the camera crews came over to capture her. Her hips and torso seemed to move at impossible angles. Her luscious breasts pulsed with her motions; her long, lean legs flexed with athletic perfection. Rasmussen found himself staring as well. Initially, he was probably more amazed than aroused. However, in time he realized he was definitely aroused as well! Damn, he knew what he'd be fantasizing about if he and his wife ever had sex again. For a moment, he tried to recall the last time they made love. Was it weeks? Maybe even a month had passed. *Damn....* He was still staring at the black woman—indeed, the *goddess*—his mouth inadvertently watering. When he looked up, he saw the goddess was smiling at him—perhaps laughing at the depraved lustiness in his eyes. He looked away, ashamed—and confused as well, since he was definitely still horny! Yes, indeed:

When you horny, you tend not to give a fuck...!

Rasmussen nodded his head as the ghetto wisdom finally seemed to register—

The music stopped. "Cut!" someone—the *director*—screamed into a megaphone. "That's a wrap!"

Women stopped their gyrations and began clapping; soon, they were dispersing and talking amongst themselves. When Rasmussen looked back at the goddess, she winked at him and laughed again as she turned toward the house. He had to force himself to look away from her perfect, round behind. He shook his head, like a fighter in the ring trying to remain conscious.

When Rasmussen finally looked to his side, he noticed the two henchmen were gone. He had no idea when they had left, but it must have been while he was salivating over the goddess. Instinctively, he searched for her again, but when he realized she was gone, he felt deflated. He grimaced when he caught himself, and yet the strange emptiness was still there. Looking down, he saw the baby had an annoyed expression on his face again—as if to ask why they were still there, and why there were no snacks. Rasmussen sighed.

Scanning the area again, Rasmussen noticed the two henchmen on the stage, talking to the Kentucky Fried Chicken guy. Now, the henchmen were pointing out Rasmussen to the guy; the man stared at Rasmussen blankly. Rasmussen had the impulse to wave, but he was still holding the bassinet, so he merely nodded. The Kentucky guy either did not notice or did not care, because he turned away dismissively, said something over his shoulder to the henchmen, then walked away. He walked with a cane; but from his easy stride, Rasmussen guessed the cane was a stylistic accessory, rather than a medical one.

Presently, the henchmen were gesturing for Rasmussen to come. He nodded and began walking around the pool. As soon as he reached the men, they motioned for him to follow. Now, they were leading him into the house—through a side door. Inside the house, the video shoot seemed to be transitioning into an after party, because many of the bikini-clad women were lounging in the living room and sipping drinks. Rasmussen felt old and out of place—and *white*—especially after an R&B song started playing and the women instinctively began to dance. He noticed Don Cole groping a few women in the corner of the room like some kind of depraved octopus. Rasmussen looked away uneasily, perhaps a little jealous. As he walked, a few of the dancing women noticed the baby and got that excited expression women often got when they saw a beautiful baby. Rasmussen smiled awkwardly as a few of them gathered around, but he apologized and moved on to keep up with the henchmen.

Soon, he was being led down some side corridors. The music faded into the background and there was nothing but the grim solemnity of this march to whatever fate awaited him. At last, the henchmen opened the door to a spacious office and motioned for Rasmussen to enter. On the far side of the room, the Kentucky guy from the stage was sitting behind a mahogany desk with his feet up. To his right, perpendicular to the desk, there was a long leather couch, on which the white rapper was lounging. Up close, the rapper seemed scrawnier; after a few moments, Rasmussen realized the kid was giving him "the stare down"—that menacing gaze inmates gave one another in the prison yard to establish dominance. It seemed ridiculous, but the two black henchmen were lurking behind Rasmussen now—and seemed ready and able to back up the kid's intentions.

Rasmussen looked away from the boy and concentrated on the man behind the desk—who he assumed was some kind of business manager. There was something strangely affable about him. He had taken off his jacket, and there was a snifter of brandy in his hand. Rasmussen knew it was brandy because the bottle was on the desk. The man took a sip before leaning back to assess him.

"Hi," Rasmussen began inanely, still gripping the bassinet. There were two chairs in front of the desk, but he got the sense he was to remain standing. The henchmen continued to hover behind him—as if prepared to club him in the head and carry out his corpse as soon as the man behind the desk gave the word. In fact, at that moment, the man took another sip of the brandy, took his feet off the desk, leaned forward in the seat, and sat there sizing Rasmussen up.

The man stared with pursed lips—as if looking deep into Rasmussen's soul—then he said, "What kind of man are you, Mr. Rasmussen?"

Rasmussen opened his mouth, ready to fumble around for an answer, but he soon realized the question was a rhetorical one, because the man continued, "What kind of man destroys another man's property—his *lawn*—and stands there laughing about it? What kind of man then runs off like a *coward?*"

When the man paused, it occurred to Rasmussen he was being prompted for a response. "This is all a misunderstanding," he said quickly. On the couch, the kid grunted to show his disapproval; behind Rasmussen, the henchmen shifted their weight menacingly, as if preparing to tackle him; and behind the desk, Colonel Sanders raised one of his bushy eyebrows.

"Then explain it to me?" the man said, as if baiting Rasmussen to incriminate himself.

"Okay," he started again, searching for the right words. "...After I went out to get my mail yesterday, a minivan drove past: the same minivan you saw on your security video. When I looked at the top of the van, I saw what I thought was a baby. I ran after it, thinking someone had forgotten the baby seat on top of the car. I'm a father, as you can see," he said, lowering the bassinet slightly so the man could see the baby, "—so I panicked, as if that was my baby. I took off running, trying to reach the van before they reached the highway; but when I got close enough, I saw the thing in the baby seat was only one of those dolls—the ones that move and talk," he clarified. "...When I stopped, the minivan stopped too. The back door opened and I saw these kids. They were filming it all and *laughing*. It was all a prank," he said as if he still didn't believe it. "As they sat there laughing, this sense of...rage took over me. I saw *red*. The next thing I knew, I was in the vehicle, beating the *crap* out of them. The driver started up the minivan again, but I was already in there.

"They drove for a while, but with all the chaos, they crashed into your hedge and tore up your lawn. While they were doing all that, I lost my balance and one of them managed to kick me out of the rear door. That's how I ended up on your lawn. After that, they took off again. It's obviously not as though *I* was driving," he said for emphasis. "They kicked me out and left. ...When you saw me laughing on the video, that's because…"—he paused, looking down shyly—"because it felt good, as a *man*, to take revenge. It felt good, and I laughed," he said simply. "Afterwards, when I ran off, it was because I remembered I had left the baby home by himself. As good as I had felt on your lawn, I felt that panic a father feels… that if something happened to my son…" He looked down at the baby now—who was mercifully sleeping again. When Rasmussen looked up, the man behind the desk had a pensive expression; but from his body language, Rasmussen could tell he was being convinced. To press home his point, Rasmussen continued, "So, you see, this is all a misunderstanding; but as a show of good faith, I'll be willing to pay for any repairs."

At the mention of money, the Colonel lost his calm veneer. "This was *never* about the money," he said testily. "Don Cole can't have people disrespecting his property."

"I would never disrespect his property," Rasmussen assured him. "You can tell him that."

The man behind the desk frowned. "*I'm* Don Cole," he said.

"Oh," Rasmussen replied, confused. "I thought the rapper with the dreadlocks—"

"Nigga Nutt?" Cole asked.

Rasmussen stared at him confusedly: "Huh?"

"Nigga Nutt: that's his name—the rapper from the stage."

"Oh," Rasmussen said again, unable to think of anything else to say.

"And this is Nigga Fross," he said, gesturing to the white boy with the cornrows, "—my son."

"I see," Rasmussen said, visibly uneasy.

Don Cole laughed. "That word—*nigga*—bothers you, don't it?"

Rasmussen thought about it for a few seconds: "Yes it does," he said frankly.

The man smiled. "You look at me and you see a middle-aged white man exploiting these poor blacks—these *niggas*," he said, jutting out his chin at the henchmen. Rasmussen looked back at the men apologetically, but their faces wore the same inscrutable expressions.

"Sheeet," Don Cole continued, "we's all niggas here," he drawled. "We all got some nigga in us. You know what my real name is? Winthrop Colchester III. My son, Nigga Fross, is Winthrop Colchester IV. I was a *banker* before all this—a high society Georgia cracker. In those days, if I saw a nigga, I looked down on him. But you know what happened? I started researching my family tree. My great, great, great granddaddy was a nigga—but was able to pass for white. Sheeet, half of us passing today and don't even know it. This country was founded on the backs of the nigga. Nigga values are *American* values—"

"That's *real* right there," Colchester IV interjected, pronouncing his "there" as "thar" in the Southern fashion.

Looking on in a daze, Rasmussen found himself wondering if all this was part of an elaborate joke. Maybe the kids from the minivan were pulling another prank on him. He told himself to pay attention—so that he could outwit them. At the same time, he was *trapped* in this place, unable to do anything but nod to all the craziness he was hearing—

"What's nigga values?" Don Cole continued thoughtfully, "—shiftlessness, thieving...? Nah," he said, shaking his head, "—*hustlin'*—"

Colchester IV and the henchmen grunted to show their approval; Rasmussen nodded timidly once more. Don Cole was scrutinizing him again, nodding his head: "I looked into you, Rasmussen, and I see you did alright by yourself, selling them books and whatnot. You's a hustler too, nigga."

"Okay," Rasmussen said feebly.

"So, embrace your nigga-ness, son—"

"True, true," Colchester IV interjected.

"Strive to be a *real* nigga—to reach your full potential of a *hustler!*"

"Yup, *yup!*" Colchester IV chimed in again, so that Rasmussen looked over at him and nodded awkwardly.

Now that Don Cole's sermon was over, Rasmussen opened his mouth again—to perhaps give another one of his inane responses—but that was when the door suddenly opened. Looking over his shoulder, Rasmussen recognized the leather-clad dominatrix woman from earlier. She walked up to them with the aggressive sexuality of a model on the catwalk.

Don Cole barely managed to say, "What the *fuck* you want, bitch?" before she zipped down her top and exposed her breasts like Superman ripping off his shirt to reveal the "S" on his chest. Instantly, a slack-jawed expression came over Don Cole's face. In fact, as Rasmussen looked around, he realized everyone in the room had the same expression.

To be clear, even Rasmussen had to admit she had nice breasts, but the entire thing seemed more bizarre than sexy. More to the point, when the woman bellowed, "Get on your knees, you *useless* scumbags!" Rasmussen knew it was time to get the *hell* out of there—especially after the others crumpled to their knees and looked up at her like repentant dogs groveling before their master.

The rest of the house—and the after party—passed him in a blur; and even when he was on the road, walking home, he kept asking himself if he had really seen what he thought he had seen.

Higginbottom was lying in bed, staring at the ceiling. Since his room faced the east, the room became darker as the afternoon sun moved lower in the western sky. As he blinked drowsily, Cassiopeia suddenly flashed in his mind. Turning his head, he looked over at the digital alarm clock on the nightstand and saw it was five-fifteen in the afternoon. He had waited here for hours, hoping for an insane fantasy. All at once, he saw this moment as an opportunity to test his courage and put an end to this farce. There was an entire world out there, waiting for him, yet he was hiding in here like a scared child. Besides, he was hungry. He remembered seeing a strip mall on the ride to this place. The thirty dollars in his pocket were suddenly a ticket to freedom—and *life*. He began moving toward the door, where his shoes were resting on the mat. He put them on, his mind blank.

There did not seem to be a room key. He scanned the room but saw nothing; at the same time, he was not leaving anything behind: the clothes on his back, the shoes on his feet and the thirty dollars in his pocket were literally the only things he had.

He closed the door behind him, but left it unlocked. The prostitutes must have been changing shifts or something, because the parking lot was clear. He moved on quickly, his mind still blank—even as he felt a vague sense of hope.

He was not entirely sure where he was going, but maybe this was how he had been all his life. Maybe this was the first time in his adult life he had acknowledged the fact that he was lost....

About two hundred meters beyond the motel, there was a warehouse of some kind. It had long closed, since the truck loading bay only had rusting shipping crates in it. It was getting darker outside, and Higginbottom realized it was not safe to be walking here. Something crunched underneath his shoes; when he looked down, he saw drug vials of some kind. He remembered the thirty dollars in his pocket. For an instant, he considered turning back—since Big Slug's domain at the motel was probably safer than anything in the surrounding area.

At the same time, it felt good to walk...and he was beginning to think that if he really was on a mission from God, then there was nothing to fear. If his mission was more than madness, then he had to live up to the task that God had put before him. Maybe God was testing him with all this as well—just as He had tested Job and the other wretched men in the Bible. If he really was a soldier of God, then he should be able to walk through hell, itself, knowing that God had his back. ...And if this was only madness, then maybe it would be best for it to end like this—with him alone in the darkness, facing off against shadowy attackers and his personal demons. Given everything he had experienced, it occurred to him he would rather be dead than go back to pretending to be alive....

Beyond the warehouse, there was a gravel road. He followed it for about five minutes, until it came upon some train tracks. The world was getting dark and gloomy, and whatever sense of adventure he had had was dying quickly. He wished he could have gotten in the car and driven to the center of the city, where there was life—instead of walking around the rusting remains of the warehouse district. He wanted to look upon something good—something that would revive his decaying soul and let him know it was good to be alive. He was tired of seeing the worst in people—and the worst in himself. He yearned to hear real laughter ringing in the air, and genuine joy, but the world around him seemed to have nothing to offer but darkness.

That was when he looked beyond the train tracks and saw the strip mall in the distance. All at once, it was like a beacon from God—a reward for his faithfulness. He nodded his head hopefully and quickened his pace....

He had to jump over a ditch to get to the other side of the tracks; after pushing through some bushes and climbing over a shoulder-high concrete wall, he was in the strip mall's parking lot. Beyond the parking lot, there was a two-lane road, but traffic was not that heavy. On the other side of the road, there were woods and some dreary little houses that instinctively made Higginbottom shudder—as if they were nothing but traps for the human soul. There was something depressing about the entire scene. Yet, he had come this far, so the only thing to do was keep moving ahead.

Higginbottom looked from the road to the four wretched-looking stores that comprised the strip mall. Business did not seem to be very good, since there were only five cars in the parking lot. The first establishment was one of those twenty-four-hour convenience stores that looked like it was always getting robbed. The second establishment was a bar, with half a dozen neon signs in the window, advertising various beer brands. Higginbottom took a hopeful step in that direction, but as he looked past the third establishment— some kind of tattoo parlor/gun store—his eyes came to rest on the fourth business. On first glance, he could not tell what it was or what it sold, but its sign got his attention. It read, "God Bless America." As he looked, the word "God" seemed to glow in the dwindling daylight. Higginbottom stepped forward, mesmerized....

Soon, he was in the store. Behind the counter, a man about Higginbottom's age and weight was snoozing with his head resting on the back of his chair. A portable radio on the counter was turned to one of those confrontational talk radio shows. The host was in the middle of a tirade, warning his listeners about demonic creatures called "libruls"—

The door slammed behind Higginbottom; a doorframe bell was triggered—presumably to let the owner know he had a customer— but the thing was so loud that the poor man was startled out of his sleep. In his terror, he almost fell out of the chair. He looked up at Higginbottom with wild terror in his eyes. However, after

Higginbottom put up his hands to show he was harmless, the man behind the counter nodded—either to acknowledge that harmlessness or to extend a greeting to the store; and of course, with this being Georgia, the shotgun behind the counter reassured the man as well.

Higginbottom nodded his head, turned to the right and headed down one of the aisles to browse. As far as he could tell, this was some kind of thrift store. Everything seemed to have the American flag on it: coffee mugs with the American flag; T-shirts with the American flag; snow globes that recreated presumably patriotic scenes...all of which of course featured the American flag. The goods all seemed as though they had been there for years. The flags were all faded; many of the shelves seemed as though they had not been dusted in months; the floor was unswept, and muddy shoeprints littered the linoleum tiles. Given the slovenly appearance, and the lack of customers, Higginbottom wondered how the store managed to stay in business. However, when he glanced back at the counter, he noticed a lottery machine on the far end; and as he looked, the scrolling text on the machine announced there was a ten million dollar jackpot for Saturday. ...Ah, the state lottery: the last refuge of wretched people and wretched stores....

The radio host was still on his rant; the owner continued to eye Higginbottom suspiciously, as if he were going to run off with one of the faded T-shirts. In truth, by then, Higginbottom was convinced there was nothing in the store for him; but with small, depressing stores like this one, once one had made the mistake of stepping in the door, one was trapped—obligated to at least pretend to browse. Thus, feeling he had no choice, Higginbottom walked deeper into the store.

Against the back wall, there was a bin full of books. By the dog-eared appearance of the books, Higginbottom suspected these were the owner's private stock: more junk he had pulled out of his attic. Feeling he had browsed for the mandatory time, Higginbottom was about to turn around and leave the store. However, it was then that one of the books caught his attention. Its title read, *The Total Emasculation of the White Man: A Treatise on the Demise of Western Civilization.* The title was so bombastic that he could not tell if it was ridiculous or utterly brilliant. Curious, he picked it up. It was thick and heavy—and felt strangely good in his hands. There were no pictures or graphics on the cover: only the title against a black background. He turned to the first page and began reading:

The White Man will survive. No matter what happens, he will live on. Just as rats have learned to survive in a sewer, subsisting on what people have thrown into gutters, the White Man will learn to survive. However, survival is not living; and here, one must remember that the rat lives in the sewer because he is afraid to dwell in the world of men. He is afraid of the light and open spaces…and so the sewer becomes his domain, and the offal of the human world becomes his sustenance.

It was cowardice that drove the White Man to the sewers—fear of other races and fear of his woman! It was the total emasculation of the White Man that has brought civilization to this precarious place. The White Man, on whose broad shoulders Western Civilization was built—

The floor creaked behind Higginbottom; he jumped when he glanced back, because the owner was standing right at his shoulder, grinning. The man looked at the book Higginbottom was reading, then he grinned wider, so that his purplish gums and yellowish teeth stood out prominently. "That's a good book, right thar," the man drawled.

Unsettled, Higginbottom glanced down at the thing in his hands, as if the owner had caught him holding porn. He opened his mouth, perhaps hoping to explain—

"I've met the author," the owner boasted now. "He lives in this area."

Higginbottom stared down at the book again. The author was someone named Stewart Goodson; Higginbottom turned the book over, to look at the back cover, and saw a picture of an avuncular man with a grey beard, horn-rimmed glasses and a pipe in his mouth. The picture seemed to be from about thirty years ago; and as Higginbottom looked down at it, he realized Goodson had a perturbed expression on his face, as if he had sniffed a disgusting fart.

"...Oh," Higginbottom said, in response to the owner's statement on knowing the author.

That was when the owner nodded and announced, "That will be twelve dollars and fifty cents."

As Higginbottom looked on confusedly, the owner turned and began to walk back to the counter. "Oh," Higginbottom said again. Then, assuming he had somehow agreed to purchase the book, he followed the man back to the counter and retrieved the money from his pocket.

Once Higginbottom was outside the store, he felt a peculiar combination of relief and disillusionment. The relief was a consequence of having escaped the store; the disillusionment was because he had felt compelled to buy the book, a lottery ticket, and a large bag of corn chips that looked like it had been there for *months*. He only had twelve bucks left; and since he doubted such purchases could possibly be part of God's plan, he bowed his head in shame.

By now, night had fallen. The first time he saw this place, he had merely found it depressing; now that dusk had given way to night, he sensed something sinister lurking in the darkness. He remembered how terrified he had been of the night when he woke up in his car a day ago. The same panicked feeling was filling him now. Something was in the breeze—a scent perhaps, or an electric charge—making his skin crawl. A prickly sensation went down his spine, as though a cold finger had caressed the nape of his neck—

He was running! He ran without thought, but the motel room instinctively rose up as a safe harbor. It was the only place he knew he could turn on the light and lock the door. He scrambled over the wall, pushed through the bushes and jumped over the ditch; once he was on the other side of the tracks, he began running again. His mind and body went numb, so that running became his entire existence.

As the deserted warehouse again came into view, he ran faster. He tried not to look at all the shadows and hidden recesses—or think about what might be hiding in them. The book was dangling from a plastic bag in his right hand, and it occurred to him it was heavy enough to use as a weapon. If he swung the bag, he was sure the force would be enough to knock out an attacker. Yet, even these thoughts only registered as tiny blips in his mind. His fear of the night overrode everything; as he ran, he saw nothing and felt nothing…and then, miraculously, he was standing in front of his motel room's door. It was as if he had blacked out—or as if the trip from the strip mall to the motel had taken only *seconds*.

When Cassiopeia popped into his mind, he turned from the door and scanned the parking lot frantically. However, the car was still not there. In fact, at that moment, a new john arrived in a pick-up truck, and half a dozen prostitutes exited their station at the management office and went over to his door to parade their wares.

Higginbottom looked at the scene for a second—before he turned back around, opened the door, and entered the motel room.

The lights were of course off, and something about the darkness again unnerved him. If he really was on a mission from God, then maybe there was a devil out there as well. Maybe demons were being sent against him, hiding in the darkness, waiting for their moment to strike—

He switched on the light and stared at the room with wide, trembling eyes...but there was nothing there. Given Cassiopeia's continued absence, he did not know if the empty room left him relieved or terrified. ...What if he had been abandoned in this place? He stumbled over to the bed and plopped down on the mattress like a corpse. The plastic bag with the book was dangling from his hand; in his dazed state, he landed on top of the book—so that the hardcover edge dug into his stomach. The bag of corn chips popped as well, and a few of the chips were expelled onto the bed. He grunted, cursed out and took out the book. He stared at the title again; then, compelled by the same curiosity he had had in the thrift store, he opened the book and read a paragraph, then another, then another, until he had read entire chapters. Hours passed. Yet, even after devouring the first hundred pages, he could not figure out if Stewart Goodson was a sage or an old bigot whose time had passed. The author had a way of making unabashedly racist and sexist comments in a way that made them seem perfectly rational. For instance, from page seventy-six:

The White Man fails for the same reason other men fail: laziness, a lack of imagination and a dearth of talent. However, it has only been recently that the White Man has become comfortable with his failure. For two thousand years, failure was unacceptable to him. He saw failure, rightly, as an act of capitulation. God demanded excellence from the White Man! God made him exceptional so that he could prepare God's Kingdom here on earth. But the White Man lost his way—precisely because he allowed himself to believe the jealous lies of others. They called his victories historical atrocities. They said his advancements were based only on barbarism—and he believed them, and gave up his claim to being exceptional...and look at him now: cowed, subdued by the whining of other races! What some call equality, should rightly be seen as a crime against God. With such twisted, demonic logic, the White Man has begun to see his failure as a compromise for social advancement. He is told the strong should not conquer the weak; and so, in an age where the weak are tolerated by the strong, the strong invariably become weak and pitiful. Look at yourself, White Man!

From page one hundred and twenty-seven:

One day, while walking in the woods, I came upon a pair of box turtles. The first one was walking steadily up a rise; but at the bottom of the hill, I saw the second one. He was overturned, lying helplessly on his back; and by the way he was wedged against a rock, I knew there was no way he would right himself. Sooner or later, a predator would come for him, or dehydration would get the better of him—so, in an act of what I thought to be kindness, I reached down and turned the turtle over. More than that, I carried the turtle up the hill, to where the first turtle was walking, assuming them to be companions.

In this sense, I acted as an unjust god. I did not ask how that turtle had ended up overturned. In other words, I did not ask if it was his own folly. Maybe that overturned turtle was only the doomed chaff of the turtle race. Maybe that turtle had a genetic predisposition to capsize: a fatal genetic flaw which, if allowed to spread to the general population, would doom the turtle race. In my supposed act of kindness, maybe I had outwitted nature's safeguards; in saving one, I may have killed them all. By unnaturally putting the overturned turtle on equal footing with his comrade, maybe I had committed an unspeakably evil and catastrophic act.

This is how our society has been run since the so-called Civil Rights Era of the 1960s. In attempting "a simple kindness" to downtrodden races, we may have doomed all races!

Was that genius, idiocy or bald-faced racism? The distinctions were too nuanced for Higginbottom. The only thing he knew for sure was that Goodson's rants made his skin tingle. ...And he remembered it suddenly: the first time his skin had tingled this way. It had been when he was about eleven or twelve. Everyone had congregated at his uncle's house for Thanksgiving that year: dozens of relatives from all over the country. After the meal, while everyone was lazing about, he had wandered off by himself and entered the basement. To his childish eyes, the old junk had seemed like a treasure trove. ...And for some reason, one box had stood out. It had been the highest one, reaching almost to the ceiling, yet he had gone for it immediately, ignoring more accessible ones. As soon as he opened the box, the "gentleman's magazine" had been right there. It had either been a *Playboy* magazine or one of its equivalents. He could not remember exactly—but his skin had tingled with the awareness that he had come upon something that would change his life forever. The naked women in the magazine had cast a spell over him. He had put the magazine under his shirt and snuck back upstairs, lest anyone missed him. Yet, twice, he had gone to the bathroom to look at the sacred goddesses within the magazine. After he got home, it had taken him about a month before he learned how to masturbate; but once he had, he graduated to a new level of obsession with the magazine. He had been like a crusader, uncovering some kind of Holy Grail of perverts. …Unfortunately for him, about three weeks into his crusade, his mother had found the magazine under his bed, burned it, and grounded him.

In a strange way, Goodson's book filled the empty place his mother's vandalism had left; and as he lay there reading, he realized he did not want anyone to take this book away—or to hinder any of the discoveries that might emerge from it. In fact, by then, he viewed Goodson's book as a revelation from God.

For this reason, when Higginbottom finally put the book aside in the wee hours of the morning, he was thoroughly convinced he knew God's plan for him—and the *world*….

DAY FIVE

Rasmussen awoke in the master bedroom. It was either early morning or late at night, because it was dark outside the window. The plasma television on the far wall was on, but the volume had been muted. A news program was playing, and another announcer was laughing at the Roadkill Maniac's antics. Rasmussen stared at the screen with heavy eyes; in the attached bathroom, he heard movement. It occurred to him his wife was saying something. At first, he thought she was talking to him. He opened his mouth to ask her what she had said; but as she went on—about some task that was to be completed—he realized she was talking on her cellular phone. Seeing she was occupied, he closed his mouth, shut his eyes, and allowed the sleep to retake him....

Higginbottom had no idea if he had slept or if he had merely lain there for hours, thinking. However, when he opened his eyes, it was dawn. He glanced at the clock, seeing it was six twenty-five. Instinctively, he turned his head and looked at Cassiopeia's bed. It was empty; but strangely enough, he was relieved. He could not explain it, but he felt revived and hopeful—and he did not want to be weighed down by anyone else's will right now.

Goodson's book was still lying next to him on the bed, like a lover. He stretched out his hand and caressed it—either to make sure it was real or to reconnect with its wisdom. Now that he had read it, he felt sanctified—as though God had saved his soul and set him on the right path after a lifetime of aimless wandering. He did not know if Goodson's words were *the* truth, but there had definitely been some unmistakable truth there. He felt he only had to open his soul to it and everything would become clear. More to the point, he was tired of hiding in this place—and being afraid of the world around him. Imbued with the power of God, he felt a kind of intoxicating strength flowing through him. He sat up in bed now, and looked about the room. There was still nothing there for him—and no logical reason for him to *stay*—so, as simply as that, he rose, put on his shoes and walked to the door. As he was about to turn the knob, he looked back at the room and saw Goodson's book was still lying on the bed, next to the empty bag of corn chips. He returned, picked up the book, and placed it in the plastic bag. After checking his pocket to make sure his meager funds were still there, he walked to the door and stepped into the new day.

Even at this time of the morning, there were still three prostitutes lurking about the management office. Higginbottom did not know if they were the morning shift or if they had been there all night. It was probably his imagination, but he was convinced he could smell them from across the parking lot. He unconsciously held his breath and began walking—back toward the strip mall. He figured he should get some breakfast before deciding his next move. Either way, he was through with this place....

One of the prostitutes—a huge black woman with a blond wig—noticed him and said something to her coworker. The coworker had on a greenish wig that made her look like one of those troll dolls. The woman glared and him and then yelled "Roscoe!" over her shoulder.

Higginbottom looked over to see the attendant/manager from the first night emerge from the office. Either he was wearing the same stained shirt or he had stained another one in the exact same spot. When the prostitutes pointed out Higginbottom, the man glared at him in the same way as his hookers.

Higginbottom eyed them, but had no time for their foolishness, so he walked on—

"Where the *fuck* you going?" the manager demanded.

Higginbottom looked over at him curiously—the way one instinctively turned toward a backfiring car or another loud, inarticulate noise. At first, Higginbottom figured the manager was talking to someone else, but the man was still glaring at him.

Higginbottom stopped and turned to him: "What?"

"You ain't settle your bill yet!" the man screamed. "Cash is due, motherfucker!"

Behind him, the prostitutes nodded their heads, as if they were getting a cut of the money.

"What bill?" Higginbottom began, growing annoyed.

"Fucker!" the manager cursed him, "I said fifty dollars an *hour*. You already been here *two* days! You owe me *thousands*, you dumb fuck!"

Higginbottom found himself laughing. What the manager was proposing was preposterous—as if he really did believe this was a luxury hotel. Still chuckling, Higginbottom continued walking away.

"Where *you* going?" the manager screeched.

Higginbottom ignored him, still smiling—

"Big Slug!" the manager screamed now, "—Slug, come out here and handle this business right quick! *Slug!*" he yelled louder when the man didn't instantly appear, "where you at?"

A few seconds later, a door behind Higginbottom opened and Big Slug waddled out. Higginbottom looked over his shoulder, wondering if he should run. Big Slug was shirtless and his extra, extra, extra large jeans were unzipped. He was holding up his pants with his left hand while he scratched his tattooed gut with his right—

"Grab him, Slug!" the manager screamed. "He ain't paying what's due!"

Higginbottom again went through the permutations of running, but a newfound sense of calm made him stop and turn to face the man. He had no real intention of fighting—yet he knew running was pointless and beneath the dignity of the man he was trying to be.

"You guys got paid already," Higginbottom tried reasoning with him, "—and I've got no money for you." At that, he turned to leave, but the dismissive gesture stirred Big Slug from his early morning sluggishness (so to speak).

"Where *you* going?" the man began. "We ain't *dismiss* you, mother-fucker!" he cursed. "You leave when *we* say leave."

Higginbottom knew that tone from two nights of listening to johns getting their asses kicked. When he turned, the man was waddling toward him. By now, Big Slug had buttoned his pants and his pendulous gut jiggled with every monstrous stride.

Higginbottom told himself he would not run. He had no idea what he would *do*—especially as a physical confrontation seemed imminent—but he knew he would not run, and this reassured him. He braced himself for whatever was to come. He took a deep breath and was amazed by how calm he was: how assured he was that no harm would befall him. It seemed like madness, and yet there was something like a smile on his face now—

"You ain't answer me," Big Slug said threateningly, while the glee-ful prostitutes and the manager came over to watch the impending carnage. "Where you going, when you *know* we got funds due?"

"I'm leaving this place," Higginbottom said simply. He took an-other deep breath—

Big Slug let loose a right cross! Higginbottom moved—almost

effortlessly—and Slug swung at empty space. Slug swung again! Higginbottom was surprised how slow and clumsy the man seemed. If one of those blows connected, Higginbottom knew he would be messed up. However, Big Slug was like one of those huge, immobile predators whose only hope was getting his prey to come within reach. Higginbottom evaded his first two blows with minimal effort, while Slug was already breathing hard. Adding insult to injury, Higginbottom was still holding the plastic bag with the book—as if Big Slug posed no threat whatsoever.

The disappointed prostitutes were screaming for Big Slug to handle his business; the manager was hurling threats—either at Slug or Higginbottom. When Big Slug made his third attempt to connect a blow, instinct took over: Higginbottom stepped toward the man, pivoted—so that the man again swung at empty space—then he brought the full force of his knee into the man's gut. Instantaneously, Big Slug squealed like a skewered pig and stumbled back. In fact, the behemoth was so clumsy that he tripped over his feet and landed on his butt like a big baby who was still learning how to walk. The sight was pathetic, and Higginbottom stared down at him almost apologetically. How the hell could so many johns succumb to this guy? Or was it something else? Higginbottom still felt calm and revived. His breathing was still even, and his eyes grew wide as he considered the possibility that he really had been imbued with the power of God....

Big Slug was now rising to his feet, his breathing labored and his face beet red from the blow he had taken to the gut.

"Let it go," Higginbottom pleaded with him, but Big Slug reached into his back pocket then, and fished out a switchblade. In his huge, pudgy hands, the knife seemed like a small twig, so that Higginbottom still felt he was in no real danger. "Let it go, man," he tried reasoning again, while the prostitutes and the manager yelled more threats and epithets. In fact, when Higginbottom looked up, he realized the crowd had tripled. Prostitutes had come from their rooms to watch, waving their arms wildly as they cried for blood. Higginbottom watched them uneasily for a few moments—before his gaze returned to Big Slug. By then, the man was lumbering toward him with his gold teeth bared and his flab jiggling like a bowl of Jell-O. The man's arm was raised high; Higginbottom focused on the knife. He took a deep breath—

The man swung! Higginbottom moved in the same effortless way—but the clumsy oaf had put so much force into the swing that he could not stop his own arm in time. Higginbottom looked on incredulously as Big Slug's huge arm swung in an arc, imbedding the knife blade in the man's own thigh!

As Big Slug squealed out and crumpled to the ground, Higginbottom could only stare. Even the prostitutes looked on with stunned expressions, unable to believe their eyes—

"Goddamn it, Slug!" the manager cursed him now. "You been sniffing glue or something?"

Some of the prostitutes began cursing him as well.

The extremes of human nature were always an ugly sight, and Higginbottom shook his head. "Why don't one of you call an ambulance?" he suggested.

"Shut the *fuck* up!" the manager cursed him. "Ain't nobody ask you."

"Can't you see he's bleeding?" Higginbottom pleaded with them while Big Slug whimpered on the ground.

"You must be a goddamn retard!" one of the prostitutes addressed Higginbottom now, "—ain't no ambulance gonna pick up *nobody* around here."

"Then why don't you drive him to the hospital," he said with the annoyance creeping into his voice again. When he looked, blood seemed to spurt from Big Slug's wound—

"Why don't *you* drive him if you care so much?" another of the prostitutes yelled now. "We got a living to make."

Incredibly, they were walking off now. Even the manager had turned his back and was returning to the office. They were like an audience exiting a bad movie—dissatisfied with the ending and grumbling about their wasted time.

"Damn," Higginbottom whispered as he watched their backs, "—you got some messed up friends, brother."

"Help me!" Big Slug begged, tears practically flowing now.

Higginbottom sighed. "You got a car?"

"That truck!" Big Slug yelled, gesturing with his head. "The keys in it."

Higginbottom nodded faintly and began walking over to the truck. After Big Slug squealed out again, Higginbottom began to jog.

Curt Streusel was Athens, Georgia's leading roving reporter. Every morning show had one: someone who specialized in "feel-good" stories in odd locations. Streusel was a heavyset man in his early sixties, whose goofy antics had garnered him the nickname "The Strudel." Today, Streusel was at a local park, doing tai-chi with some elderly Chinese people. The lone cameraman captured Streusel as he did the exercises and made playful complaints about how stiff he was. It was all typical morning show filler before a man burst from some bushes behind Streusel. Within seconds, the man was at the Reporter's shoulder; startled, Streusel turned as the man—indeed, *the Roadkill Maniac!*—snatched off his toupee. Streusel stared at the grinning man, stunned…then his trembling eyes focused on the thing the Maniac held in his right hand.

When it occurred to him the man was holding his toupee, Streusel grabbed his bald head, shrieked like a little girl, and ran off. The

old Chinese people, unsure of what was going on, fled as well. However, the camera remained on the Roadkill Maniac, who dug his
hand into the pocket of the mangy suit and pulled out some greasy
bar-b-cue:

"Eat my chic-*ken!*" he screamed with a demented grin on his sauce-
smeared lips. After three or four monstrous bites, the chicken leg
was reduced to bones. The lunatic swallowed without even chewing,
then he sprinted off and disappeared through some bushes in the
background. By then the director had already cut the feed and
returned to the studio anchors, who could do nothing but stare
blankly into the camera.

When Rasmussen opened his eyes once more, the television
was off and the baby was screaming. As he turned his head, he saw
there was sunlight outside the window. His wife, he knew, was
long gone, and yet his eyes still gravitated toward the dark doorway of the bathroom. He sighed.

Today, beyond the usual exhaustion, he felt a sense of dread that
he could not place. It was like a sore spot on his body, so he was
trying to retrace his steps over the last few days, in order to discover
when the blow had been struck. He lay down flat on the bed once
more and stared up at the ceiling, trying to make sense of it; but
eventually, when his mind remained blank, he rose from the bed
and began his day.

Higginbottom went to the truck and drove over to where Big
Slug was lying on the ground. He parked with the passenger side
of the vehicle facing the man, then he got out and walked around
the truck to reach him. Big Slug held out his hand for Higginbot-

tom to help him up. Higginbottom looked at him doubtfully; and as he suspected, when he pulled on Big Slug's large, sweaty hand, the man did not even budge. If anything, Higginbottom felt like lying down after the effort.

"You're going to have to get up on your own, brother," Higginbottom explained.

Big Slug tried to get up, but he yelped as he tried to move his leg—since the knife blade moved in his flesh. The man's face was streaming with sweat now. Higginbottom grimaced and bent down to look at the wounded leg. Given the man was at least sixty percent fat, Higginbottom doubted the blade had reached any major veins:

"It might be easier if I just pulled out the knife," he ventured.

As soon as Big Slug nodded, Higginbottom grabbed the knife and pulled it out. Slug cried out again; but since the worst seemed over, he lay down flat on the ground to rest for a while.

Given that Big Slug's pants already had a hole in them, Higginbottom used the knife to rip them further—and get a better look at the wound. He was about to apply some pressure to the wound, to staunch the flow of blood, when he looked at his hands and frowned. They were *glowing*—irradiating the most beautiful light he had ever seen. As he held up his hands to stare at them, he was so mesmerized that the knife inadvertently fell from his hand.

Big Slug was still panting on the ground; Higginbottom looked over at him and held up his hands for the man to see:

"Do you see…the light?" he said breathlessly.

"What?" Big Slug said, looking up.

"My *hands*," Higginbottom said excitedly, stretching them out further, "—don't you see the light?"

At first, Big Slug stared at his hands confusedly, but then his eyes grew wide as he, too saw the light.

Acting on instinct, Higginbottom rested his hands on Big Slug's wound. As soon as he touched the man's skin, he felt the energy intensify; the light grew brighter, so that he practically had to squint now. After about five seconds, Higginbottom pulled his hand away; and when he did, both he and Big Slug leaned in closer to look. Indeed, the men were silent and still for a long period afterwards. The wound was gone.

Even after he was awake, Cletus Jones stayed in bed, listening to the ambient sounds of the morning—birds and traffic and the upstairs neighbors having a quickie before work. Even though the day had only begun, Jones already felt exhausted and frustrated. Despite what Binkowski had said, he *knew* something was wrong. Something had happened at his professor's house, and the more people tried to convince him otherwise, the more certain he felt. Intellectually, he could appreciate why everything he remembered from that night was insane, but *something* had happened, and he had to find out what. In fact, that was the only thought guiding him now.

He waited patiently, listening as his roommate showered and ate breakfast. As soon as Binkowski left the house, Jones rose from the bed and got dressed. It was a little after ten in the morning. Within fifteen minutes, he was on the road out of town, headed toward his professor's house. He passed through a rural community before heading down a quiet road. Everything was going fine until he turned a bend in the road and saw something that made him lean forward in the seat. He slowed down the car, unable to believe his eyes....

The same hillbilly was at the stand, dressed in overalls and playing a banjo! After the man waved at him, Jones waved back and stopped the car. The man was really there, at the side of the road. At the man's feet, there were the same ceramic jugs, each with three exes on it. To the side, there was an impossibly large rack of porno magazines.

Totally convinced he was hallucinating, Jones looked away and scanned the road—to see if any traffic was coming: if anyone else could actually see the man. Unfortunately, the road was deserted in both directions—

"Howdy!" the hillbilly yelled cordially. "I see you's back for more!" he said, grinning widely. He was missing at least five teeth, but he was such a perfect stereotype of a hillbilly—down to his long, white beard and straw hat—that Jones was now convinced he had to be a hallucination. The man seemed like a stupid black person's idea of a rural white man, just as a thug nigger was perhaps a stupid white person's idea of an urban black man.

The man was still grinning at him.

Jones took a deep breath. "You remember me?" he began tentatively.

"Of course!" the hillbilly said gleefully, "not too many colored folk stop for the Champagne; but once folks get a dose of Uncle Enus' special brew, they can't help but come back for more!"

Enus' face beamed after his boast. He stuck out his chest and grabbed the straps of his overalls. Jones stared at the man helplessly, overcome by the suspicion that if he tried to touch the man, there would be nothing there. Eager to test his hypothesis, he exited the car and stood before the man; in his mind, he would attempt to grab hold of him—

"How many jugs should I put you down for?" Enus enquired.

Jones heard himself saying, "I'll take two jugs." He produced ten dollars, remembering the jugs were five dollars each. When Enus handed over two of the jugs, Jones put one under his left arm and took the other in his left hand; next, deciding to test his hypothesis, he put out his right hand for Enus to shake. He braced himself—but when the man shook it vigorously and tapped him on the shoulder, the only thing Jones could do was stand there numbly. Bewildered, he turned away. He was about to retreat to his car, but Enus interrupted him.

"Don't you want to taste her first?" the man asked coyly. From the last time, Jones remembered Enus liked to refer to his concoction as a woman. Still bewildered, Jones gestured to his car with his head, as if to say he did not want to drink and drive; but before he could actually voice any protests, Enus filled a dented pewter mug with his brew and proffered it with a wide, excited grin. Seeing no way out of it, Jones sighed, rested the jugs on the ground and took the mug uneasily. He looked down at the clear liquid, wary, but when Enus began giggling, he took a swig—if only so that he would be able to get the hell out of there.

Once he swallowed, and his eyes started watering, Enus put back his head and laughed heartily—so that Jones got a full, disturbing view of the man's rotten teeth and bare gums. Even before the concoction reached Jones' stomach, he staggered back, his vision growing blurry. By then, the hillbilly's laughter was thundering in the air like something out of a nightmare—

"Goddamn...!" Jones managed to whisper before everything went black.

Big Slug was driving and Higginbottom was in the passenger seat. Higginbottom kept looking over at the rip in the man's pants; Big Slug, himself, looked down at it periodically as he drove. They had not spoken since the incident—the *miracle* or whatever it had been. They were like two virgins after their first sex session, trying to figure out what the act had meant. They were in a new, unexplored world of possibilities now. Behind them, they had left their childish ignorance. New pleasures awaited them, but perhaps new horrors as well....

Fifteen minutes later, they entered a lower middle class suburb where white flight and gentrification had canceled one another out over the decades. Whites who could flee had long done so, leaving behind those who could not afford to move, those who *refused* to move (since they stubbornly considered this place their home) and those who still held out hope that gentrification would win out in the end and free them of all the shiftless niggers in their midst. To be fair, many of the blacks also clung to this hope as well....

"...I always wanted to know," Big Slug began abruptly.

"What?" Higginbottom said, looking over.

"...that there was something else out there...besides all this bullshit."

Higginbottom nodded and turned his head to stare out of the windscreen once more.

"I ain't never had faith like Mama wanted," Big Slug explained. "I needed to see and touch and *feel*, you know...but I've *seen* now," he said with new resolve. "I'm *ready* now. I'm gonna be a soldier from now on—for *Jesus*."

Higginbottom had been listening passively, preoccupied with his own thoughts, but when he realized what the man was saying, he shook his head: "Keep cool for now," he began, "we don't know what's happening yet."

"What do you mean we don't know?" Big Slug said heatedly. "Can't you see my leg? I'm *healed*. Sheeet, I was a bullshit thug a few minutes ago, but God healed me...*through you*," he said almost shyly. "I always thought there was goodness in me," he began with rising passion, "but I needed to *see* it, you know? I needed to see

God's plan before I could take that step. I'm not a man of faith, but of *action*…and now that I've seen, I know what we need to do."

Higginbottom was looking over at him uneasily. "What do we need to do?" he asked cautiously.

Big Slug laughed and eyed him coyly: "I see you testing me now, brother, and a hardheaded fucker like me needs to be tested. But I'm gonna pass the test," he said confidently, "'cause I've *seen*. I'm ready, brother: ready for *war*."

"*War?*" Higginbottom said hoarsely, alarmed.

"Why else would God choose me?" Big Slug reasoned. "I ain't a thinker. I ain't a planner: I'm a man of *action*. I'm the one you call when you need fools regulated," he said self-assuredly. "I'm a *soldier*, and I'm ready to do battle. Sheeet, everything I did before this—putting them hoes and dumb fuckers in they place—that was just training, brother. God was *preparing* me. Everything happens for a reason—I see that now," he said with a strange staccato laugh. "…Yeah, I see that now," he repeated in a lower, more thoughtful tone. The man was looking over at Higginbottom with unblinking eyes now, his face eradiating a kind of grim certainty. "I feel I can do *anything* now," he explained, "…now that God has let me *see*."

Higginbottom stared back, but he was no match for the overpowering certainty in the man's eyes—so he nodded, turned away and looked through the windscreen, at the ugly suburb.

The kitchen counter had become Rasmussen's favorite place to change a diaper. It was tall enough, yet had enough space to spread everything out. He was sure there was a sanitary concern somewhere; but like the weird, smiling housewives who appeared on daytime TV commercials with mops and miracle cleaning solutions, Rasmussen had become a firm believer in the power of disinfectant. …And it was amazing what the human nose and stomach could tolerate with practice. The first time Rasmussen opened a diaper, he had rushed to the bathroom to throw up. Now, he could change a diaper while still eating his breakfast. The peculiar combination of feces, disinfectant and baby powder was no longer nauseating to him— and that was a good thing, since the house seemed to reek of it.

When he was finished changing his son, he stood up straight and looked at his handiwork. His son, by all accounts, would be a heart-breaker when he grew up, and Rasmussen felt a sense of fatherly pride. Indeed, looking at everything objectively, he was succeeding. Despite his doubts and uncertainties, he was holding it together. Even though he was thoroughly exhausted—and felt his life had gone off the rails somewhere—being a father was the one thing about his life he would never change. In fact, if all the recent crazi-ness in his life was the cost of being a father, then he felt it was a price he was willing to pay. He smiled at that moment; and when the baby smiled back at him, Rasmussen felt the same sense of wonderment he had experienced the first time he held his son.

Still smiling, he picked up the baby and headed for the living room. He had an errand to run at the mall, so he was looking for his car keys now. After a few seconds, he saw them on the coffee table and walked over to pick them up. He was heading toward the foyer with his son when he glanced out of a side window and saw a head pop up!

He jumped, startling the baby—who began to cry. After the initial shock, Rasmussen saw it was only Granny Stanko. He had to remind himself she was a real person—instead of a character in an insane daydream. She was still at the window, grinning widely and gesturing with her hand for Rasmussen to let her in the front door. After Rasmussen nodded, she left the window and headed to the front door. He grimaced.

Why the hell didn't she just ring the doorbell in the first place!

His son had stopped crying, but Rasmussen was in a foul mood now. While Stanko waited at the door, he considered his options and came to the conclusion he was not in the mood for her craziness today. His escape plan formed haphazardly in his head, but he committed to it totally. First, he walked over to the door, took a deep breath and made sure he had the keys; then, opening the door, he smiled and blurted out, "Sorry, Granny Stanko—you caught me on my way out!" She opened her mouth to say something, but Rasmussen stepped past her, deftly pulling the door shut with his foot. "I'll catch up with you later," he said now as he fled toward the garage. "—We'll have coffee cake," he added, knowing how old ladies were suckers for coffee cake. He did all this without allowing her time to respond; indeed, within a matter of seconds, he had dashed to the garage, loaded his son into the rear child seat and gotten behind the steering wheel.

When he was heading down the driveway, he looked back at his home and saw Stanko was still standing on the front step. She looked lonely and forlorn, and a wave of guilt made him hesitate. He considered going back and being sociable; but when he glanced down, he saw she was wearing a new pair of bright yellow stiletto heels—which seemed totally bizarre against her grey church dress. Had she walked all the way here in those things? …Or maybe she really was a figment of his imagination—some depraved projection from his collapsing mind. As he looked at her, he found himself wondering what kind of underwear she was wearing under that church dress. Maybe she had a thong—or maybe she was even *naked* under all that—

He shuddered when the actual thoughts registered in his mind— and looked away uneasily. Disturbed, he waved to Stanko hastily and stamped on the accelerator, so that the minivan lurched forward.

Luckily, the baby had drifted off to sleep again. Rasmussen watched his son via the rearview mirror, then he allowed himself to sigh. Moving to the next item on his agenda, his mind went to the errand he was supposed to run for his wife. Today, her dry cleaning had to be picked up; a few days ago, she had had a craving for corn chips from a specialty health food store. All these tedious tasks were beginning to get to him, but he realized as well that love was all about tedium. Love was boring, manifesting itself in all the mundane daily routines that allowed couples to live comfortably. Love was keeping the house clean and the bills paid—whereas passion and romance were like gaudy decorations on Valentine's Day: hollow representations of a much grander idea....

Less than a minute into his drive up the meandering road, he turned a bend and saw a heavyset man running ahead of him. At first, he thought the man was dressed in a skintight, skin-tone jogging suit. However, when the man emerged from the shade of a gigantic elm tree, Rasmussen saw the man was totally nude— except for a pair of white socks!

There was something hypnotic about the way the man's droopy ass jiggled with every stride. Unconsciously, Rasmussen slowed down. It was like driving by a car crash: you knew it was unseemly to watch, but you couldn't help yourself.

At the same time, one could only watch droopy ass for so long. As the reality of it began to set in, Rasmussen shuddered and came to his senses. From the man's deteriorated muscle tone, Rasmussen gauged him to be in his sixties or seventies. By now, Rasmussen was close enough to see the man was limping; and when he looked down, he saw the soles of the man's socks were bloody. Adding it all up in his mind, Rasmussen concluded the man must have forgotten his medication, run away from his nurse and stepped on a sharp stone along the way. If Rasmussen were still in New York, he would have left the man to roam, secure in the knowledge that the police would pick him up eventually. However, he lived in the suburbs of Atlanta now, and a sudden sense of neighborly duty urged him to corral the man until an ambulance could be called.

He pressed on the accelerator, intending to overtake the man and cut him off. ...And at first, when he drove up to the runner's side, he did not recognize his neighbor. The man's hair was disheveled, his eyes were blank and zombie-like, and he looked like he had neither shaved nor slept in days. Unconsciously, Rasmussen's eyes drifted down, past the man's gut, to his crotch. The man had an erection—and his huge, purplish testicles were slapping against his thighs—along with his erection. The sight instantly made Rasmussen queasy. When he looked back at the man's dazed expression, his eyes grew wide as he recognized Colchester's profile.

Even though the vehicle was at Colchester's side now, the man was still staring ahead blankly, as if he were in his own little world. The man's eyes barely blinked; his jaw hung open, so that the drool literally pooled on his chin. However, the most discordant thing was the sound of balls slapping against thighs. Rasmussen was taking pains not to look past the man's chest, but the sound was still turning his stomach. He was trying to figure out how to corral the man when Colchester tripped over a rock and fell headfirst into the ditch. Acting instinctively, Rasmussen slammed on the brakes and ran out of the vehicle to help. Colchester was lying there as if dead.

"Hey...you okay?" Rasmussen said. He knew it was an inane thing to ask, given the man was lying naked at the side of the road, but what was one to say in such circumstances? He looked around anxiously now—partly for help, but mostly because he still had no idea what he was supposed to *do*. Colchester's face was still blank; his body was limp and corpse-like. Rasmussen leaned in closer, frowning. When he saw Colchester's chest rise and fall, he was relieved. "…Colchester?" he called tentatively. The man seemed to rouse somewhat, so Rasmussen called his name louder, and bent down to touch his shoulder.

It was then that Colchester blinked several times in quick succession, as if coming out of a trance. After the man's eyes focused on him, Rasmussen smiled reassuringly and asked, "Are you okay?" At first, Colchester only stared, but then his eyes narrowed with recognition.

"Rasmussen?" he drawled. He looked around confusedly for a few seconds, until he glanced down and noticed he was naked! "—*Goddamn!*" he yelled, suddenly seeming animated and alert. He was trying to get up now. Rasmussen grabbed his right hand and pulled him out of the ditch. When Colchester tried to stand, he winced from his injured feet. He swayed, so Rasmussen held his arm to support him. That was when Rasmussen noticed the man was clutching a sheet of paper in his left hand—an envelope, actually. It was odd; but given Colchester's predicament, Rasmussen's only thought was to help him to the passenger side of the minivan. Once the man was sitting in the vehicle, Rasmussen walked around to the driver's side.

Yet, as he looked into the window and saw Colchester still had an erection, he cringed and looked away. He thought about it for a moment; then, remembering the baby blankets he kept in the back of the minivan, he went to the rear door, grabbed a blanket and closed the door as silently as possible (since his son was still sleeping). As soon as he entered the vehicle, he handed the blanket over to Colchester, who took it eagerly.

Even after the man had the thing over his lap, Rasmussen tried not to look at him. They sat there in silence for about five seconds, both of them in shock.

"Should I take you home?" Rasmussen ventured at last. And then: "How are your feet? You want me to take you to the hospital?"

Colchester looked down at his socks, wincing when he saw the blood. However, he was beginning to think clearly now—to digest how surreal this situation actually was. He searched his mind for an explanation, but there was nothing. Desperate, he looked over at Rasmussen. "What the *fuck* happened to me?" he asked.

Rasmussen looked at him uneasily, but since he had no real explanation, he merely he shrugged. "You were running down the road...like that," he began, gesturing vaguely with his hand to refer to Colchester's nakedness. "...You don't remember anything?"

The man shook his head, disturbed.

Rasmussen remembered that dominatrix woman storming into the room yesterday, and telling them to get on their knees. Yet, even as he recalled the scene, it seemed too crazy to be *real*. "...What's the last thing you remember?" he asked Colchester now.

Colchester stared ahead, his frown deepening. Ten seconds passed. He scratched his beard stubble. "...What day is it?"

"Wednesday."

"Wednesday?" he said confusedly.

"Yeah." And then, trying to focus Colchester's mind, "What's the last thing you remember?"

"I don't know. ...It's all jumbled up."

"Maybe I should take you to the hospital?"

"No!" he said forcefully, as if the shame of being seen by Rasmussen were all he could stand for one day. "Just take me home... please." He looked at his body, fidgeting when his eyes passed over the bulge in the blanket. "...You think anyone else saw me?"

"I doubt it," Rasmussen tried to reassure him. "You know how dead the neighborhood is at this time of the day."

Colchester nodded his head hopefully. Then, after a pause of six seconds or so, "Hey, I'd appreciate it if—"

"No need to mention it," Rasmussen cut him off. "We'll keep it between us."

Colchester nodded appreciatively, but in truth he was still in shock, trying to piece together something that seemed *impossible*.

It took about a minute for them to reach their destination. When Rasmussen pulled up to the gate, Colchester nodded awkwardly to give thanks. After that, he practically fled from the vehicle. The gate worked with a remote control; but of course, Colchester did not have it on him. Rasmussen assumed the man did not want to risk being seen by his house staff, because he squeezed himself into a gap in the hedge and disappeared. Rasmussen heard him howling from a thorn or sharp twig, but he was gone, and Rasmussen felt somewhat relieved that that was behind him. He sat there for a few seconds, staring at the place in the hedge where the man had disappeared; but after that, he allowed himself to laugh. He took pains to keep his voice low, lest Colchester was still within earshot; but now that he thought about it, that was the craziest thing he had ever seen! Colchester must have done some good drugs last night, Rasmussen mused. To each his own...

When Rasmussen was getting ready to leave, he glanced toward the passenger seat and saw Colchester's letter was lying there. In the man's haste to leave, he had forgotten it. Rasmussen picked it up and looked at it. Strangely, there was no name or address written on it. However, the paper was heavy and exquisitely made: fine stationery. Rasmussen turned it over: it actually had a wax seal—like official letters from olden times. The seal did not have a recognizable emblem, but the wax gave off a sickly sweet odor, like over-ripe fruit. His face soured. He was sure the letter was important, but he wondered if he should return it to Colchester right away. After all, the man had just snuck into his home by shredding his skin in the hedge: the most discreet thing to do was to return later—after the man had had a chance to rest and get his bearings.

Rasmussen opened the glove compartment and tossed in the letter. He remembered the errands he was supposed to run, so he made a U-turn and prepared to leave. However, when he glanced back at the Colchester estate, a chill went through him. He was suddenly unsettled—*terrified*, even. It was as if his soul had been poisoned—as if he were *dead* inside. It made no sense, but as the strange terror took hold of him, he felt a desperate need to be somewhere safe. He began to drive—but without urgency and purpose. He felt *lost*.... He glanced in the rearview mirror and saw his son was still sleeping. When he looked out of the window—at the quiet, unmoving suburb—he felt suddenly doomed: trapped in something he had no hope of understanding....

As he came upon Granny Stanko's home, a strange thought occurred to him: he needed to see and talk to her. Maybe it was only desperation, fed by his terror of the Colchester estate. However, he knew he couldn't be alone right now, so he turned into her open driveway and honked the minivan's horn to let her know he was there.

Big Slug's house was not exactly a pigsty, but there was dust and clutter everywhere. The furniture was old: stuff from thirty or forty years ago that Slug had probably inherited from his parents. The only new item seemed to be a flat screen television in the living room.

Big Slug took Higginbottom to the kitchen, where the man immediately started cooking. The kitchen smelled of burnt and rotten food—partly because the garbage needed to be thrown out and partly because there was a layer of charred muck on the greasy stove. Luckily for Higginbottom, his mind was too preoccupied to register the full extent of it; and soon, the smell of sausages and French fries overpowered everything else. Big Slug seemed to buy both items in bulk quantities. Once his first batch was complete, he flung it on a plate and deposited it in front of Higginbottom as if he were feeding slop to a pig. The plate was heaped with enough food for three or four people—so at first, Higginbottom thought they were to share the food. However, when Big Slug returned to the stove and pushed some more sausages into the greasy pot, Higginbottom nodded and took a deep breath. There was a bottle of ketchup on the table—next to the glass of orange juice Big Slug had poured earlier. Higginbottom reached for the ketchup—

"Cassiopeia told me this would happen," Big Slug began abruptly, startling Higginbottom, "but I didn't believe. I hadn't *seen* yet, so my mind was closed, you know." He looked over his shoulder at Higginbottom, grinned, then returned to the pot as a grease fire flared up.

Higginbottom sat there with the bottle of ketchup held in mid-air while Big Slug slammed the lid on the pot to stifle the flames. Higginbottom frowned, asking himself if Big Slug had really mentioned Cassiopeia by name or if he had merely imagined it. He put down the bottle of ketchup and picked up the orange juice. He took a long swallow—to clear his throat and his mind. "…What did you say?"

By now, Big Slug had opened the pot once more and was assessing the damage. Nothing seemed amiss, so he turned to Higginbottom almost immediately: "Cassiopeia—the angel you came in with. She told me she'd need me in the war, but I thought she was crazy."

Higginbottom blinked drowsily. "*When* did she say this?"

Big Slug pursed his lips as he tried to remember. "The morning after you guys came. She told me when she was leaving." At that,

Big Slug returned to the pot, flipping the sausage links over in a clumsy way that almost started another grease fire.

Higginbottom sat up straighter. "She told you she would use you in a *war?*"

"She said you and me was soldiers," he replied over his shoulder. "...Soldiers for *God*...and that a great battle was coming."

Higginbottom did not know what to believe anymore. He had foolishly allowed himself to believe he'd escaped Cassiopeia and her madness; but from what Big Slug was saying, all of this seemed to be her will. Even when she was not physically there, her will—indeed, *God's* will—was inescapable. He felt himself sinking into it like quicksand. He shuddered at the possibility of losing himself inside some mysterious abyss—and yet he was also coming to grips with the possibility that he had lost himself a long time ago. From what he could tell, everything that had happened since he woke up in that car three days ago had been carefully orchestrated. He had no idea where it could all be going—and what role he was to play—but his skin tingled with the reality that he was at the center of something, and that it was *vast.*

Higginbottom ate about a quarter of the food before he felt stuffed and unwell. Big Slug was in the chair across from him, gnashing his food as if he were angry with it—or as if he were eating a live creature and had to make sure it was dead before he swallowed it. The man ate with his mouth open. Food toppled from his mouth to the floor; grease covered the man's face. Higginbottom looked at him for a few moments, but the sight only turned his stomach further, so he looked away to keep the nausea at bay.

While he was allowing his stomach to settle, he looked down and remembered he had carried Goodson's book into the kitchen with him. It was lying on the table, still in the plastic bag. He wiped his greasy hands on his pants and took out the book. He looked down at the title, then up at Big Slug, wondering what Goodson would make of a man like that. He was still convinced the book would guide them somehow, but he did not know *how*. Feeling he needed some kind of corroboration, he turned the book around, so that Big Slug could read the title. When Big Slug continued stuffing his face, Higginbottom pushed the book toward him to get his attention:

"Have you heard of this book?"

"Huh?" Big Slug mouthed through the half-chewed food.

"…This book: I think it's important."

Big Slug stopped chewing and looked down at it confusedly.

"I think you should read it," Higginbottom said at last.

Big Slug was still looking down at the book in the same uncomfortable way. "I don't see too good," he said, looking away.

Higginbottom understood instantly. "Then let me read some of it to you," he said. When Big Slug nodded, Higginbottom turned to the first page and began reading.

Initially, Jones had no idea where he was. As he opened his eyes, he saw he was inside a building; and from the ambient light, it seemed to be late in the afternoon. About ten seconds passed before he recognized the bathroom of his apartment—and a few more seconds had to pass before he realized he was lying in the shower again!

As if fearful Binkowski would pee on him once more, he practically jumped to his feet, willing the spinning world to be still and his throbbing head to be calm. His cellular phone was in his pocket. He leaned against the wall and retrieved it. When he checked the time, he saw it was five-fifteen in the afternoon. He frowned.

The last thing he remembered was Enus' laugh. How had he gotten back here? He tried retracing his steps, but he knew it was pointless. Distraught, he fumbled over to the commode and sat down heavily with his head in his hands. Even though he had started the day with the determination to find out what had happened to him, it had all been a waste of time. Given everything that had happened, he sensed the workings of something *godlike*. Whatever it was, he felt powerless against it, and there was a sick feeling in his soul....

R asmussen opened his eyes and looked around confusedly, seeing that a new day had begun. He was in the nursery, sitting in a rocking chair by the window. He was not sure if he had slept or not, but his head hurt when he tried to move it. He groaned before he yawned. The last thing he remembered was being up at five in the morning as he tried to rock the baby to sleep. He looked at his wrist watch: it was a little after eight in the morning. The baby was up, looking irritable. Neither of them had had a full night's sleep in days, and they really did not like one another at the moment.

Rasmussen wondered if his wife had left for work yet. He stared at the watch again: his mind was so sluggish that he had to concentrate to remember his wife usually left at seven in the morning. Actually, if he remembered correctly—and he probably didn't—she was supposed to have left for a business trip at the crack of dawn. Either way, the rest of the house was silent and empty now, and Rasmussen sighed.

He and his wife had had one of their "anti-arguments" again. Anti-arguments were like regular arguments, but instead of getting angrier, the Rasmussens became more polite and cooperative. … Last night, when they had sex, his wife had faked her orgasm. Granted, both of them had been tired and overworked, but when she let out that fake-sounding scream, he had stopped and stared down at her in disbelief. What had hurt him the most was that she had actually thought he would not notice. The only thing he had been able to do was stare at her; she, in turn, had stared back at him—at first, with confusion; and then, when she realized he had seen through her, with alarm.

Mercifully, the baby had begun to cry, and Rasmussen had gotten out of bed to tend to his son. Even after he came back to bed, they had only talked about an errand his wife needed him to run—so that the only thing between them had been politeness.

Presently, as Rasmussen turned his head to look out of the window, a sharp pain went through his neck. He cursed under his breath, so that the baby glared at him.

It looked like it was going to be a bright, sunny day. The nursery was on the second floor, and had a view of the back yard. Glancing down, he saw the towering fence that separated his yard from Granny Stanko's. When he allowed his vision to focus, he realized Stanko was actually bent over one of her flower beds, doing some gardening. For whatever reason, he smiled. Since that strange moment of terror at the Colchester estate—when a yearning for safety and companionship had driven him to Stanko's doorstep— he had felt closer to her. That entire sequence of events did not exactly seem *sane* to him, and yet it was so.

The only thing that had marred their meeting was her outburst when he mentioned Colchester. At the sound of the name, she had started ranting about how horrible the family was, and how their immoral music was eroding the fabric of society. The rant had gone on for *minutes*, as if the word "Colchester" had triggered some kind of demonic possession. When he asked her if he could have another piece of pie, she had switched back to the sweet grandmother, and rushed to the kitchen. Indeed, she had stayed sweet for the remainder of his visit, but the entire thing had set off alarm bells in him, even as he began relaxing again.

Either way, he had talked to her more in one afternoon than he had talked to his wife in the last six months. He was not sure what any of that meant—and what role Stanko was playing in his life—but he was grateful she had been there in his moment of need. There was definitely something *wrong* about her—and her strange hatred of the Colchesters was only the latest evidence of it—but at the end of the day, he was happy she was there.

While he was sitting there, staring down at Stanko dreamily, she stood up to stretch her back, and noticed him. When she waved, he waved back. Now, she was stepping closer to the fence. "I have a present for you," she announced. "I'm coming over."

Rasmussen tried to nod, but his neck was still too stiff, so he waved his hand to give his assent. Stanko returned his wave before disappearing from view. In truth, his mind was still too lethargic to react one way or another. As he turned from the window, he made eye contact with the baby again. The five-month-old glared at him, still irritable. The child probably needed to have his diaper changed or something. Rasmussen picked him up and headed downstairs. He would make breakfast, change the baby, see what Stanko wanted…and perhaps, if there was time, and the baby allowed it, he would get some rest.

When he reached the kitchen, he saw his wife had left him an updated list of errands. He felt like one of her employees. …But he did not want to think about that now. He allowed his thoughts to shift to coffee. The coffeemaker was constantly brewing, since caffeine was probably the only thing keeping him relatively alert. He filled a cup with one hand, while still holding the baby to his hip with the other. He was taking his first sip when Stanko rang the doorbell. He had no idea how she moved so quickly—and he was not sure he wanted to know. Maybe there was a hole in the fence or something. He shrugged.

He rested the cup on the counter before he exited the kitchen and entered the living room. When he opened the front door, Stanko was grinning like an escaped lunatic.

"Here!" she said abruptly, shoving a teddy bear at him.

Rasmussen instinctively stepped back, as if she had stuck a gun in his face. When he looked, the teddy bear's expression was *demonic*. It had a grin that went from ear to ear; its teeth, while not exactly jagged, were long and menacing. Its eyes were huge—like lemur's eyes—and seemed to glow preternaturally, even though it was broad daylight. Rasmussen wanted nothing to do with the thing; but while he was standing there, the baby grabbed the teddy bear and let out a squeal of delight. Rasmussen stared at his son, disappointed somehow—as if this were the first sign his son would grow up to be an imbecile.

Stanko was talking excitedly again: "My grandson wanted your son to have it. He dropped by unexpectedly last night. …Oh, and he gave me this bracelet, too!" she said, jangling it before his face in the same semi-aggressive way. The bracelet had crystals hanging from it, which caught the sunlight and blinded Rasmussen for a moment. However, the flash of color and sound pleased the baby, and he laughed out again, before returning to his new teddy bear.

By now, Stanko was unleashing her usual beatitudes about her loving family, and so on, and so on…Rasmussen allowed his mind to drift away. He stared ahead blankly, with a practiced half-smile on his lips. …*Damn, he needed some sleep.* His mind felt like sludge.

Yet, after about a minute of pointless chatter, Stanko surprised him by stopping. "I know you're busy," she announced abruptly, "so I won't keep you too long."

Rasmussen was ready to close the door, but even though she had said she was going, she lingered. When Rasmussen realized her intentions, he smiled at her lack of subtlety.

"Have you eaten breakfast yet, Granny Stanko?" he asked now.

She giggled, did a coquettish half-twirl with her gardening dress, and said she had not.

As Binkowski was leaving the apartment, he realized someone had again shoved an envelope beneath the front door. He bent down and saw it was the same kind of envelope as before. It had no writing on it and the same wax seal was there. After he ripped it open and pulled out the fine stationery, he saw it was again blank. He stood there confusedly for a moment, wondering what could be going on, but then he shrugged. Besides, he was running late for his shift at the hospital, so he shoved the letter into his pocket and continued on his way.

As he was about to reach for the doorknob, he noticed Jones' car keys hanging on a hook by the door. He had fifteen minutes to make it to the hospital, and he was definitely not going to make it if he walked. He craned his neck and called over his shoulder:

"Hey, Cletus!"

"Yeah," came the muffled reply a few seconds later.

"Can I borrow your car today?"

"Go ahead!" was the grumpy, sleep-deprived response.

"Thanks, man," Binkowski said, grabbing the keys and rushing out of the door....

Higginbottom woke up on Big Slug's couch. The couch smelled like the man—which was to say it had an unsavory odor that made Higginbottom feel slightly ill. He had to look around for a few seconds before he remembered where he was. As his mind began its usual catalogue of the last few days, he groaned wearily. Had he really healed Big Slug's wound? Had Cassiopeia really planned all this? Even now, he had to wonder if was he acting of his own volition or if some other entity—*God?*—was shaping his destiny. He nibbled his lower lip as he considered it; but eventually, as his mind faltered, he sighed.

He had read to Big Slug for *hours* yesterday. They had made it about a third of the way through Goodson's book—and *talked.* He felt he was helping the man—and helping himself to better understand Goodson's wisdom. Big Slug had seemed to appreciate it as well—since he sat at Higginbottom's feet like a little boy listening to a bedtime story.

Still smiling, Higginbottom sat up on his elbows and looked around Big Slug's living room as if he had lost something. It occurred to him he still had no idea what the man's real name was! Indeed, frowning, Higginbottom realized he had not given the man his name either.

Suddenly restless, he rose from the couch and went to the window to look out at the relatively quiet but bland—and somewhat depressing—neighborhood. He belched then, and tasted some of Big Slug's sausages from yesterday. The meal still felt like an indigestible lump in his intestines. He pinched the layer of fat on his stomach and grimaced. This morning, for once, his physical condition—his softness as a man—was unacceptable; and before he had given it much thought, he found himself outside. His shoes were not meant for running, but he was curious how far he could go. A block later, he was standing on the curb, wheezing, his hands on his knees. At the same time, it felt good to sweat. He felt like he was purging his body of weakness; and whether it was part of God's plan or not, he needed to be healthy again, so he ran another few blocks once he caught his breath. After that, he headed back to Big Slug's place with a new sense of hope and urgency.

It was nearing five in the afternoon. Jones had locked himself in his bedroom since yesterday, trying to make sense of something that made no sense. Now, as he emerged from one of his pointless forays into his memories, he looked at his blank walls and knew he would go insane if he did not leave the room soon. He decided to go for a walk. He put on some nylon sweat pants, running shoes and a T-shirt—since he figured he might go to the university track and run some laps.

He left the dreary apartment behind him and headed to the campus. He put on his headphones and listened to some "high energy" music on his smartphone. The music kept his thoughts from wandering too far into the abyss of the last few days, and that was the main thing he needed now. It felt good to be moving. He kept his pace brisk, taking the opportunity to run through a few intersections. He began to sweat, but he felt good—even in the Georgia heat.

Shortly before he arrived on campus, he looked up and saw a black woman walking through the upcoming intersection. She crossed the street and headed away from him. In fact, she was more than a woman. When he looked, she was bathed in the most beautiful light he had ever seen. It was as though the sunset cloaked her: that's how he thought of it. More than that, he felt as though he had never seen colors before he laid his eyes on her—as if he had been *blind* before all this.

He had stopped walking when he saw her, too stunned to move. However, as the woman continued down the street and disappeared behind a building, he found himself running—darting across the street before the light changed. He had panicked when she disappeared from view, but he was relieved when he saw her again— and that beautiful light. He was like a moth attracted to a flame now—acting more on some hardwired impulse than any purpose.

He stumbled forward, dazed—almost blinded by the light now. If he had been trying to resist it before, he surrendered himself to it totally now. He felt giddy and *high*. He laughed out as the sensation of utter bliss enveloped him. Dazed, he stumbled forward, picking up his pace.

It was only after he had *grabbed* the woman that some of his reason returned. She was looking up at him wide-eyed and *shocked*. He stared down at her in the same way, holding his breath. However, her light was still beautiful. He felt he had to concentrate to resist disintegrating into it. She was still looking up at him; and now that she was in his arms, he felt he wanted to *kiss* her. In fact, it was the only thing he wanted in the world—the only thing he had *ever* wanted. Before he could reason any of it out—or ponder the consequences of his act—he reached down and kissed her. He kissed her fully and deeply. He sunk into the depths of her and was happy to lose himself—

"Damn, Cletus!" she said breathlessly, pushing him off.

He stared at her, at first still dazed, but then he frowned when he realized she had said his name. "You *know* me?"

She looked up at him confusedly, but then laughed sardonically. "Very funny," she deadpanned. "You don't call me in a week—especially after the day we had," she said with bitterness creeping into her voice, "—and you think you can just push up on me as if I'm some *hoochie*."

His frown deepened. He looked her over, but her light was still too overwhelming. He felt he had to concentrate to see her. He shook his head, closing his eyes, as if trying to shield himself from the glare.

When he looked down at her again, he considered his options. He had absolutely *no* idea who she was—and yet he felt in his soul that he knew her...maybe even that he *loved* her. He opened his mouth, but then realized anything he said would seem insane—especially if it was the truth. Taking note of the bitterness that had crept into her voice, he knew he had to tread lightly. Adding it all up in his mind, he came to the conclusion his only real option was to buy some time:

"Can we go somewhere," he began, "and talk—"

"Oh, *hell* no!" she said, taking a step back, as if preparing to defend herself. "The last time we 'went somewhere to talk,' we ended up at your place—then you ran off as soon as we were done, Mr. Romantic."

He blinked drowsily, trying to keep up with what she was saying. "I ran off?" he asked, still attempting to buy time.

"You had that dinner thing, remember—with that professor and his crazy family." After she said the words, she suddenly began to laugh.

"…I told you about the dinner last Sunday?" he said breathlessly.

She looked at him oddly, but then laughed, assuming he was being sarcastic.

"What's so funny?" he asked cautiously.

"I'm remembering that crazy story you told me," she said, laughing louder.

He was vaguely aware that meeting her like this was too good to be true—and yet he was so desperate for answers that he threw caution (and reason) to the wind. The same impulse—to *grab* her—came over him again, and it was only through an extreme act of will that he managed to restrain himself.

Yet, by now, she had stopped laughing and was looking up at him quizzically. Even though he had resisted the impulse to grab her, the effort had *taxed* him. In the intuitive way of women, she sensed something was wrong—and he felt the longer she stared at him, the quicker she would see through him. So, again acting on instinct, he embraced her and pulled her to him. He held her in the same full, deep way he had kissed her, and they stayed like that for a few moments.

"Let's go for something to drink," he whispered into her ear. "I'm not trying to get you home again," he reassured her, "but I don't want to let go of you." In fact, all at once, he was overcome by the fear that if he let go of her now, she would disappear forever, and he would lose his last chance to know himself. That was the remarkable thing about her: he had absolutely no idea who she was, and yet he had the sense she knew him better than he knew himself. All of it was insane, yet he held her tighter and closed his eyes, thoroughly at peace for the fleeting moments she was in his arms.

For the most part, Binkowski's day went as it usual did. He reported to the hospital and made the rounds with the other residents. For his late afternoon break, he went to the cafeteria, ate a tuna fish sandwich and tried talking to a nurse who made it clear she had absolutely *no* sexual interest in him whatsoever.

Now, he was walking back to his station glumly, his mind in a far-off, lonely place as he shuffled down the busy corridor. As he was walking past one of the private rooms, he glanced through the window and suppressed a yawn. After taking about two more steps, he stopped and frowned. Something about the patient in the room had been odd, but he could not quite place it. He walked back to the room and looked through the window. A middle-aged man was there, his face in agony. The man's midsection seemed bandaged, so Binkowski originally thought he was having some kind of abdominal distress. However, when he looked closer, he realized the thing that was bandaged was the man's huge cock! The tip of it reached the man's *chest*.

As if mesmerized, Binkowski opened the door and stumbled into the room. After he picked up the man's chart, his eyes grew wide, because he saw the patient's name was Freddy Fischbach—

"Doc, I'm *dying!*" the man pleaded as he tossed and turned.

Binkowski looked up at him, still in shock. As he did so, he realized the man was handcuffed to the bed.

Fischbach noticed where he was looking: "I killed my wife," he said, matter-of-factly. "...But it was an accident," he said, gasping for air. "She just couldn't handle all this good pipe," he said, gingerly tapping the thing on his chest with his free hand.

Binkowski was still staring, too stunned to move or *think*—

"Oww!" Fischbach screamed, his face contorted in agony.

Seeing the man's distress, Binkowski came to his senses and went over to the side of the man's bed.

"What's wrong?"

"It's my cock, doc! It's *still* growing!"

"Huh?" Binkowski said, but as he looked down, he saw the man's penis was visibly larger now. The bandages were beginning to rip—

"Awwww! I'm *dying!*" Fischbach screamed.

Binkowski couldn't move! When he looked down again, the bandage ripped completely, revealing a cock of *gargantuan* proportions. In fact, the sight of the thing made Binkowski stumble back in terror. It was *still* growing! By now, it was at least two-thirds the length of the man's body. It moved past his face, muffling his cries as it grew—

And then, the next thing Binkowski knew—*boom!*

It was as if there had been a stick of dynamite in the man's thing, because blood and tissue were hurtling everywhere. Binkowski had instinctively ducked down and shut his eyes; but when he finally looked around, the room looked like someone had flung spaghetti and meatballs at the walls.

Fischbach was definitely dead: Binkowski had a strong stomach, but he winced when the saw the bloody remains of the man's body. Then, with new horror, Binkowski realized there were clumps of bloody flesh in his own hair, dribbling down his face! He squealed out and began raking his fingers through his hair—as if a nest of spiders had just hatched.

As he took his first terrified step toward the door, he slipped on one of the bloody clumps. He only managed to maintain his balance by grasping the door knob. After that, he practically pulled the door of its hinges as he fled. In the busy corridor, he grabbed a passing doctor—an avuncular old man whose thick glasses made his eyes look like tiny peas.

"Help me!" he managed to squeak as he pulled the man over to the door. However, when they both looked into the room, there was nobody there. There was no blood either. Binkowski looked down at his own body, seeing his clothes were unsoiled.

When he looked up, the avuncular doctor was glaring at him—

"I'm sorry!" Binkowski tried to explain, but there was of course no explanation for what had happened. As he went back to staring into the empty room, the annoyed doctor stormed off. Yet, Binkowski stood there for a few minutes, still trying to make sense of something that made no sense.

Jones and the woman were sitting in one of those trendy cafés where everyone had a Mac laptop and the overpriced coffee came in humongous, handmade mugs that had supposedly been produced by Nicaraguan peasants or something. The café had literally been down the block from where he grabbed her on the street, so they had walked to it in silence.

After they got their coffee and found an empty table in the corner, they sat down awkwardly. The beautiful light still surrounded her. He stared at her helplessly—in an unrestrained way that probably left her a bit uneasy. Yet, she did not seem to be a shy, coquettish woman either, so she merely stared at him, trying to make sense of his strange behavior.

Probably about a minute had passed since they sat down. They had sipped the coffee in the silence, but the tension was clearly eating away at them. Jones was still overcome by the feeling this was his last chance—

"I know this must all seem…*strange*," he blurted out.

She eyed him sardonically: "That's one way of putting it."

He smiled uneasily and looked over at her in the same helpless way. "I'm going to say some things, and some of it is going to seem…crazy," he said at last, after searching for the right word.

"Okay," she said, putting down the coffee and giving him her undivided attention.

"…I've been having these…gaps…in my memory."

"What do you mean?" she asked, leaning forward.

He took a deep breath, mostly to buy more time to think. "Some strange things have been happening to me: *blackouts*, I guess you'd call them."

"Blackouts?" she said, frowning. "Have you seen a doctor?"

"No."

"Why not?"

He looked at her in frustration, sensing he would never be able to make her understand. "I don't think it's *medical*," he began, "I only know it's *strange*."

"How can you know for sure if you don't go to a doctor?"

Her statement was logical; in her own way, she was trying to be helpful—and he could appreciate that—but her suggestion only made him feel disconnected from the world. She lived in a world of sense and order that he no longer inhabited. Seeing this, he nodded his head, telling himself to forget the entire thing. Staring across at her beautiful light, all he could think was that he wanted to be around her for as long as possible—and that he would only scare her away if he told her his insane stories. She would react the same way Binkowski had reacted, and he would be alone again.

"You're absolutely right," he said flatly. He picked up the mug and took a sip of the coffee, staring down at the table glumly.

She smiled at him knowingly. "What aren't you telling me?"

"Huh?" he said, looking up.

"You want to ask me something, but you're afraid."

He stared at her; after a few seconds, he nodded his head, seeing he would lose her anyway if he said *nothing*. He took a deep breath and released it slowly. "I want you to tell me what happened the day I went to see the professor."

"Why?"

"Because…as I said…there are…gaps in my memories. I remember some things, but my roommate says there's no way…" His voice trailed off. "On the other hand," he continued, looking over at her steadily, "there are some other things that I can't remember at all."

"Things like what?"

"…Like your name."

She frowned. *"What?"*

"I don't remember anything about you—your name, how we met… *anything.*"

She was staring at him in the same expectant way, as if waiting for him to reveal the punchline of the joke. In fact, he could tell she did not believe him at all, because she smiled. "Then why'd you kiss me if you don't remember me?"

"I was *compelled* to do it," he said simply.

She laughed. *"Compelled?"*

"I look at you now," he went on quickly, "and…there's this *light* around you—as if you have your own little sunset surrounding you…and all I want to do is sit here and stare at it."

She was still looking at him suspiciously. After a while, she chuckled and took a sip of coffee. "This your way of trying to sweet talk me?"

"I'm being *honest* with you," he said simply. "…When I saw you on the street a few minutes ago, it was the first time—*in my mind*—that I've ever seen you. You're telling me now that we were together the day I went to see the professor. You say I told you about the dinner. I don't remember *any* of that. …Did I come see you afterwards?"

Her frown had deepened. He seemed too earnest for this to be a joke. "…No," she said distractedly, in response to his question, "you called me while you were there. You said the professor and his family were arguing at the dinner table, so you had come outside to get some fresh air." Then, as it all began to add up in her mind, "You *really* don't remember me?"

"*No*," he said, desperate for her to understand; then, on instinct, "…but I feel…I feel like I'm connected to you—that I *love* you." After the words flew out of him, they both seemed shocked. Yet, now that the words had been said, he felt there was no point holding back. "What I said about the light and sunset…I meant that *literally*. There is this beautiful light surrounding you—as if I can see your…soul. Maybe I *should* see a doctor," he conceded, "but until then, help me remember."

Her body language had stiffened with the realization that he was not joking. He could practically feel her slipping away from him, closing herself off. He reached across the table and held her hand—as if fearful she would withdraw it.

"I know how all this sounds," he started again, "—and how I must *seem*—but help me if you can. If you don't want to talk anymore…

if you need time to let all this digest, I can understand. I've been locked in my room for *days*, trying to figure it all out. Yesterday, I told myself I'd try retracing my steps. I tried to drive to my professor's house…but I blacked out and found myself back home." In the silence, he realized he had left out the part about the hillbilly—but he was relieved as well, since she was still struggling to accept the madness of what he had already told her. When she remained silent, he pressed her: "What was the professor's family arguing about?"

"Oh," she said, emerging slowly from her shock. She took a long drink of coffee. "…You said the professor's mom told her grandson that he dressed like a faggot, and then the grandson said she dressed like a slut and that she was probably thinking about screwing you and taking some hard black dick in her."

Jones blinked drowsily. "…*What?*"

Despite everything, she laughed at his expression. "We were laughing on the phone about it: high class, dysfunctional white folks…like something on Jerry Springer. …After a while, you said you didn't hear any more screaming, so you were heading inside to talk to the professor before you left. That was the last I heard from you."

Jones' mind went into overdrive. If what she was saying was true, then maybe his memories really were faulty. What she had told him sounded more plausible than Hillbilly Champagne and drunken sex with his professor's mom—but he had no idea how those memories could have gotten into his head. That was when he realized there was a simple way to corroborate all this. He had been holding her hand all this time. He let go of it now and reached into his pocket to retrieve his cellular phone. In a few clicks, he was scrolling through his call history. His eyes widened when he saw he had made a call six days ago, in the evening. The woman's picture was next to the call data. Her name was Artemis Clarke. He looked up at her, amazed.

While Jones was holding the phone, it rang. When he looked, he saw Binkowski was calling. After he pressed the icon to answer the call, he put the phone to his ear:

"What's up?" he asked.

"I...I...Something just happened," Binkowski said, sounding frazzled.

Jones paused, straightening his posture and leaning forward in anticipation. "What happened?"

"I don't know," Binkowski said in frustration. "...But I had to get out—of the hospital. I told them I wasn't...*well*. I had to leave."

Once again, Jones paused, trying to understand what his friend was saying. "Where are you?"

"I'm still outside the hospital. It was *crazy*," he said, remembering everything that had happened in the room. Then, "Whatever you had that day—you know, when you went to see your professor—I think I have it too."

Jones did not really catch what his friend was saying. He only knew the man was in trouble. "You want me to come get you?"

"I...I don't know, man," Binkowski said in the same frustrated way. It's all *crazy*," he said again.

"Stay there. I'll be right over." As he said it, he remembered Artemis. He looked over at her, freezing. He had been about to stand up—

"Okay," Binkowski said, before hanging up. Jones looked down at the phone, then up at the woman. He sighed.

"My friend's...something happened to him," he tried to explain even though he did not really understand either.

"You're leaving?" she said, mostly to corroborate what she had overheard.

He nodded. "I don't want to, but…"

"Don't worry about it," she said nonchalantly. "I had to leave anyway." She started getting ready—picking up her bag and making sure she had everything. He stared at her with a forlorn expression—like a wet puppy watching its master leave. She laughed when she saw his face—

"When can I see you again?" he asked pleadingly.

She turned her head to the side and scrutinized him with a smile on her face. "Call me tomorrow and we'll see," she teased him.

"I will call you," he declared, as if making a solemn oath involving the soul of his first-born son. His newfound earnestness made her chuckle. When she stood up, he was again overcome by the desire to grab her. He put his hands on the table and clasped them together, consciously telling himself not to move—and not to allow himself to be overcome by the beautiful light. Sitting there, he looked like a studious boy waiting for the teacher to pat him on the head. She again chuckled at his expression. Then, as if deciding he deserved a reward, she smiled at him:

"Since I still have to find out where you were going with that crazy story, I guess we'll have to meet soon."

His eyes shined with gratitude and joy, then he nodded his head with a broad smile on his face. "You definitely won't be disappointed…if you're into crazy stories."

She laughed again, and came around the table to hug him. He stood up to hold her. She felt good. He closed his eyes and pulled her to him. Time once again seemed to stand still—but then she laughed at him again, and pushed him off, before she began walking away.

"Let me know how it goes with your friend," she said over her shoulder. Within seconds, she was gone, taking her beautiful light with her. He stood there, alone and empty in the relative darkness. Deflated, he sat down heavily once more, until he glanced at the table, saw the phone, and remembered Binkowski. As he did, he bolted up, grabbed the phone, and rushed to the exit.

When Jones reached the hospital, Binkowski was sitting on the front stairs, grasping his head in his hands. Jones walked up to him and tapped him on the shoulder. Binkowski looked up sharply and stared for a moment, as if trying to place his friend's face.

"You alright?" Jones asked.

It was probably only then that Binkowski recognized his friend and remembered why he was there, because he said "Oh," and nodded his head.

Jones sat down next to him. "What happened?"

Once again, Binkowski stared blankly. However, like before, the only words he could find were, "It's *crazy.*"

Seeing him now, Jones instinctively recognized the madness of the last few days. As Jones nodded his head with patience and understanding, Binkowski was so grateful that he almost wanted to cry—

"I know it *couldn't* have happened," Binkowski continued now, "...and yet..." He went back to grasping his head, as if trying to protect it from an impure outside influence. Jones again waited patiently—with the kind of empathy that only came from shared madness. On Binkowski's face, he saw everything he had been experiencing these last few days: the frustration; the disbelief at seeing something you *knew* could not have happened, yet which felt no less real than anything else. Like him, Binkowski was now drifting through a vast ocean of doubt, rudderless and desperate. Seeing his friend now, Jones was suddenly clear about what they needed to do. Indeed, he was hopeful for once—since he was not alone in the madness anymore.

"Let's go," Jones said, getting up. Binkowski looked up at him uncertainly, but the same hopefulness entered his eyes when he saw Jones' newfound certainty. "We need to get to my professor's house," Jones said to the enquiry in Binkowski's eyes. "Whatever happened to me—whatever's happening to *us*—it started a week ago, at my professor's house."

Binkowski stared at him for a moment; eventually, he nodded—not so much in agreement, but as a way of acknowledging his friend's new confidence. He stood up as well, and they headed off.

Binkowski led them to where he had parked the car. Jones was driving now. They sat there in silence, both of them excited and terrified by what they would find at the end of their journey.

"I met a woman," Jones said when they were heading out of town, "…and I *love* her."

Binkowski looked over at him, struggling to make sense of the words in the context of everything that was happening to them. Eventually, he nodded. His mind fumbled about for what people usually said in such circumstances: "Where'd you meet her?"

"I don't remember," Jones said matter-of-factly, still staring out of the windscreen at the increasingly rural roads.

"Huh?" Binkowski said at last, frowning.

"I met her a week ago, I think—before all this. I ran into her to-day, on the street, and she told me…some things," he said vaguely.

"And you love her?" Binkowski said suspiciously.

"Yeah," he said excitedly. "She had this…*halo*—"

"What?" Binkowski said, lost again.

Jones looked over at him and sighed, frustrated that he could not make his friend instantly understand and see all the beautiful images in his head. "Her body was cloaked in this beautiful light," he explained again. When Binkowski took a deep breath and shifted his weight uneasily, Jones went on quickly. "I know how it sounds. It's crazy, like everything else…and yet, I love her."

"Okay," Binkowski said at last, taking his friend at his word and ultimately too mentally exhausted to ask the questions that needed to be asked.

They went back to staring out of the windscreen in silence, at the darkening world. The rural road was twisting and turning now, practically lulling them to sleep. Binkowski was about to yawn, but that was when Jones turned a bend in the road and slammed on the brakes!

When Binkowski looked over at him confusedly, Jones was staring ahead with trembling eyes. Binkowski followed his eyes and looked through the windscreen; but initially, he saw nothing.

Binkowski looked back at his friend, seeing the same horror on his face. "What's wrong?" he whispered.

"Don't you see…the hillbilly?" Jones said breathlessly.

Binkowski was about to say he did not see anyone, but when he turned his head, he saw the hillbilly emerge from the darkness. The man was grinning and holding up one of his jugs for their consideration. The hillbilly was exactly as Jones had described him; the stand was behind him; the banjo was leaning against the stand, and there was an impossibly large magazine rack with hundreds of porno magazines—

After the hillbilly hopped off the stand and onto the road, he began approaching the car. "How many jugs should I put you down for?" he called as he approached.

Jones could not move. His heart was thumping in his chest. He realized he was hyperventilating—

"Do you want to taste her first?" the hillbilly enquired, holding up one of the jugs and grinning—

Jones stomped on the accelerator, but the grinning hillbilly did not even flinch as the car raced toward him. For a moment, Jones told himself he would plow the man over; but at the last moment, he swerved the car and stamped on the accelerator again. He did not look back, but Binkowski did—

"Don't look back!" Jones screamed, so that his friend jumped. "We can't stop now! We can't look back or let anything distract us!" he declared. Then, in a calmer voice, "The drink makes you black out. We have to keep going—no matter what..." but even while he was saying the words, the road was becoming blurry. Feeling himself losing consciousness, he panicked and cried out. Binkowski screamed as well, because he saw his friend losing control of the vehicle. Yet, the world soon began to swirl before Binkowski's eyes as well. Everything became chaotic and blurred; and within seconds, the world was black and still—as if God, Himself had erased the universe around them.

Higginbottom paused after he finished reading the final page of Goodson's book, then he closed the cover. The way Big Slug was staring at him, he knew the man understood the significance of the words. For once, real thoughts seemed to be percolating in the man's head—instead of base, pointless violence. Higginbottom nodded his head, as if proud. Yet:

"What do we do now?" Big Slug asked excitedly.

Higginbottom stared at him, initially confounded by the simple question, but then he allowed himself to speak aloud something that had merely been an idle thought over the last few days: "We have to find Goodson. ...There's wisdom there—in his words...

in what he has to say about us...and what we've *become*. He's thought about the things that are affecting us—that are *killing* us."

"Things like what?" Big Slug interrupted him.

"...The things we do to ourselves. How we live—the *laziness* of it...the *self-destructiveness* of it. We have to change things in our lives. We have to do *better*."

Big Slug thought about it, pursing his lips, so that he seemed like a petulant baby. Eventually, he nodded his head; and as the man gave his assent, Higginbottom was relieved: he had told someone else his thoughts, and the other person had agreed with him—

"I'm gonna fix something to eat," Big Slug said, getting up. Seeing the remote on the coffee table, he grabbed it, turned on the television, then tossed the remote to Higginbottom.

The television was tuned to a gossip show. Higginbottom heard "Rap mogul Don Cole," and then found himself watching a grainy video with a heavyset white man tongue kissing a young, dreadlocked black man. Both men were groaning and moaning as they surrendered to their passion. The black man squeezed the white man's titty—

Higginbottom shuddered; and as the full horror of it hit him, he pressed the button on the remote, turned off the television and sat there panting. Big Slug had been waddling to the kitchen, but he stopped after Higginbottom turned off the television, and looked back confusedly.

"We're polluting our minds with that stuff," Higginbottom explained. Big Slug shrugged before he continued on to the kitchen. Yet, seeing the man's retreating bulk, and knowing Slug probably had another sausage banquet on the menu, it occurred to Higginbottom they had been polluting more than their minds.

"Hey," Higginbottom began, getting up and following the man into the kitchen, "I've been meaning to talk to you about the way you eat...."

It was getting late now. The baby continued to cry. Rasmussen was holding his son in his arms as he walked from one side of the nursery to the other. He hoped the movement would lull the baby to sleep, but it was pointless. The baby had already been changed and fed: as far as Rasmussen could tell, his son's only purpose was to cry and keep Rasmussen from sleeping. He glanced at his wristwatch. It was a few minutes past eleven. The baby had been crying nonstop since ten.

Still holding his son, Rasmussen left the nursery and walked down the hall to the master bedroom. When he got there, he stood in the doorway and looked around confusedly, wondering where his wife was. Three or four seconds passed before he remembered she had left on a business trip. He frowned, wondering how he could have forgotten, but he doubted he had gotten ten hours of sleep in the last five days. Time seemed to be slipping away: one day bled into another; whole days seemed to disappear into the nothingness. He felt like a hollowed-out husk of a man—

The baby's cries reached a new, teeth-shattering pitch; Rasmussen stirred from his stupor and looked at his son. As tears streamed down the baby's face and rivers of snot flowed from his little nose, Rasmussen was overcome by the irrational fear that a hidden observer was *judging* him. Someone was hiding in the shadows, writing all this down in a book of judgment—and his son's cries were proof that he was a horrible, callous father. After all these months, being a "good father" was all he had left—since his mind was gone. Earlier today, he had tried to add seven and five in his head, and had literally had to use his fingers to come up with the answer! *Him*: a man who had been doing differential equations in his head since he was thirteen.

With each passing day, he felt his intelligence slipping away. He had to concentrate in order to complete the simplest tasks; he was always tired and worn out; and as much as he had tried to convince himself he was a "modern man," a side of him had begun to wonder if the modern man was even a man at all. He loved his son dearly, but this strange, "stay-at-home-dad" existence was obviously not working for him. Was this really a gender-neutral world, where the roles of men and women were interchangeable, or was there something intangible about being a man and being a woman?

Indeed, he wondered if his wife was happy with her role. Had feminists fought for equal rights so that they could go to work while their husbands stayed home? He suspected they had all duped themselves into something stupid—something that none of them could possibly want, but which was the logical conclusion of their past stupidity—

His son's cries reached an even higher pitch. The rivers of snot and tears had pooled at his son's chin, so that the oozing snot hung like a goatee. Panicking, Rasmussen dried off his son's face with his shirtsleeve. When it occurred to him this was unsanitary, the same fear—of the hidden observer's judgment—made him panic even more.

He turned from the master bedroom now, but when he looked down the hall and saw the nursery, his soul rebelled. It occurred to him he had not left the house all day. These walls were becoming his prison, draining the life out of him.

Desperate to escape, he found himself moving toward the stairs. The baby cried louder, but Rasmussen felt like he was running for his life now. He allowed instinct to guide him. Soon, he was in the garage, fastening his son into the baby seat. Within minutes, he was driving. He had no destination in mind. At times, it seemed like the steering wheel turned itself. ...But there was something soothing about letting go.

His son continued to cry; in Rasmussen's dazed state, the sound merely became background noise—like the droning engine and the rush of air outside the window. ...And then, he was there, parked in front of an all-night diner in the middle of nowhere. He realized, all at once, that his son was not crying anymore. When he turned back to look, he saw the baby smiling at him and putting out his right hand to be held. In the baby's left hand, there was the creepy teddy bear Stanko had brought. Rasmussen frowned, because he was pretty sure his son's arms had been empty when he strapped him into the car seat. In fact, now that he thought about it, he was almost certain he had tossed the doll in the back of his son's closet—as a prelude to throwing it in the garbage.

When Rasmussen walked into the diner with his son, there was nobody else in there besides the waitress—and whoever was in the kitchen. The waitress was standing behind the counter, watching the TV on the far wall. On Rasmussen's entrance, she smiled reflexively. She was in her sixties or seventies, with reddish, blondish hair done in a kind of beehive. Her uniform was worn and too tight, but not tight in a way that flattered women's charms—since the only thing that bulged from her blouse was her gut. From her frumpy appearance, Rasmussen guessed she had been doing the same job for thirty or forty years.

"How y'all doing tonight?" she greeted him.

"Doing okay," Rasmussen returned. He smiled, happy to be talking to a real person for once.

"Baby couldn't sleep?"

"Something like that," Rasmussen replied, looking down at his son, who still seemed unusually jovial—especially considering he had been crying nonstop for the last few hours. "Can I have some coffee?" he said now. He noticed some pies in a display case on the counter. "Are those pies any good?"

"The best in Georgia!" the woman said with a grin. "How you think I got this fat?"

Rasmussen chuckled and moved toward one of the booths by the window. Amazingly, he was in a good mood. Only minutes ago, he had felt exhausted and rundown, but now he felt strangely refreshed. The change was almost supernatural; indeed, as the baby continued to giggle at nothing in particular, Rasmussen was slightly disturbed. …But no: feeling good was not something to be disturbed about, so he settled in the booth and tickled the baby's stomach so that the giggles would at least be connected to something tangible.

The TV was playing one of those annoying cable movies where all the cuss words and nudity had been edited out to produce bland, G-rated drivel, interspersed with a million commercials. It was doubly annoying since it was after midnight.

The waitress brought his food promptly. The pie was passable, but seemed a few days too stale. His son seemed eager to try some, so Rasmussen fed them both as he drank his coffee. His son continued to giggle through the entire thing, as if it were a secret game.

A few minutes into this, a car pulled up outside. Rasmussen looked out of the window and saw a figure emerge from the vehicle. He stared curiously, but the baby made a plaintive grunt, as if demanding more pie, so Rasmussen smiled and went back to his fatherly duties.

Rasmussen looked up as Cassiopeia entered the diner. She was still in the leather outfit, but Rasmussen had to stare at her to remember where he had seen her before. When he remembered the scenes at the Colchester estate, his eyes grew wide. In fact, as he looked at her now, her full, firm breasts seemed to glow—as if they were magical. He had a sudden thought that if he rubbed them a genie would emerge from her nipples or something, to grant him three wishes. He instinctively smiled at the thought, but his stomach clenched when he realized she was coming straight for him. Even when the waitress greeted her, she ignored her and walked toward Rasmussen.

Flustered, he tried to go back to playing with the baby, but the woman was soon at his booth. She sat down boldly, across the table from him. Rasmussen stared at her apprehensively. A side of him was terrified she would bark orders to him and he would lose his will like Colchester and his henchmen.

However, her tone was calm and formal when she spoke. "Allow me to introduce myself," she began. "My name is Cassiopeia."

"Hello," Rasmussen said inanely. He tried to think of something else to say; he opened his mouth to give his name, but she cut him off. "Have you accepted your destiny yet—or are you being a naughty boy?"

Her expression seemed so stern that he assumed she was playing the "straight man" in some kind of elaborate joke. At any rate, her British accent was somehow thrilling. What were the chances of running into a beautiful foreigner in rural Georgia? His spirits perked up—until he remembered the scenes at the Colchester estate and the minor complication that he was *married*. He looked down at his son guiltily, as if the baby would tell on him, but the baby was still jovial. When he looked back at the woman, his eyes instinctively went to her breasts. He tried not to stare, and yet he felt almost compelled to look.

Eventually, he shook his head, as if shaking off a spell; then, remembering her strange joke, he smiled and said, "My mama raised me right: I'm never naughty."

"I'm glad to hear it," she said in the same inscrutable way. While Rasmussen was looking on confusedly, she added, "What did your letter say?"

He frowned at her. *"What* letter?"

"Your letter from God."

Rasmussen sat up straighter and looked at her for a few seconds. Seeing the same (possibly sardonic) expression was on the woman's face, he allowed himself to laugh; but when her face remained stern, Rasmussen's laughter died abruptly, and they both sat there awkwardly, staring across the table at one another. Even the baby was staring.

That was when the waitress came over. "Y'all want anything?" she said, addressing Cassiopeia.

Cassiopeia answered her, but continued to stare at Rasmussen: "I'll have what he's having."

The waitress frowned: the odd couple set off some kind of heightened waitress sense, honed by decades of working the night shift in a backwoods diner. She lingered, looking at Rasmussen— as if to ask him if he needed her formidable skills. After he put up his hand to reassure her, she left.

As soon as the waitress was gone, Cassiopeia spoke up. "You were told to bring the letter," she scolded him.

Rasmussen frowned. "Told by *whom?*"

"You are being naughty, Mr. Rasmussen."

He paused before he spoke. "How'd you know my name?"

She spoke calmly: "I know because God has willed it. All of this is His doing."

Rasmussen stared, dumbfounded; but then, grasping at the only logical explanation he could see, he returned to the position that this *had* to be an elaborate joke. "Who put you up to this?" he said, smiling nervously; he noticed her breasts again, adding, "That's some outfit for a God-fearing woman."

She shook her head: "Adam and Eve were naked in the Garden of Eden, Mr. Rasmussen. It was only their sin that made them ashamed of that nakedness. I am free of sin, and so I am free of shame. Likewise, now that you have been cleansed by God, you have neither sin nor shame."

Still thinking this was some kind of "straight man" act, he chuckled. "Believe me, ma'am," he said, eying her cleavage, "my thoughts are pretty sinful."

She smiled for the first time, then leaned forward deliberately. "You like looking at my breasts?"

At her prompting, he looked. In truth, he had been looking all along, taking what he hoped were discreet glances—but he stared now, his eyes devouring her supple flesh. She smiled, straightening her posture and sticking out her chest—apparently so that he could get an unobstructed view. Rasmussen knew it was wrong, yet he could not tear himself away. Eventually, he clamped his eyes shut. When he opened them, he noticed the baby was looking at him sympathetically, as if to tell him he was no match against those breasts. Rasmussen took a deep breath, trying to clear his head, then he gulped down half the coffee.

Cassiopeia smiled. "Even though you've been naughty, I'll forgive you this one time." As she said those words, she twirled her fingers, so that an envelope miraculously appeared in her hands. Rasmussen's eyes widened…but his rational mind rebelled, telling him that it was only a cheap magic trick. She placed the letter on the table, in front of him. He was ready to dismiss the entire thing; but when it looked, he realized the envelope was exactly like the one Colchester had been carrying. For a moment, he thought it was the same letter, and that the strange woman had broken into his glove compartment. In fact, once he picked it up, he saw the envelope had the same seal and the same peculiar odor.

"Where'd you get this?" he started cautiously.

"It's a letter from God," she said simply.

"From *God?*" he returned, frowning.

The waitress approached the booth, carrying the pie and coffee on a tray. Rasmussen remained silent while the waitress hovered, but as soon as she was gone, he looked up at Cassiopeia:

"Who the hell are you?"

"I've already given my name," she said calmly.

Rasmussen's mind felt like sand being washed away by the waves. He felt he had to struggle to hold onto the little he understood. He shook his head in frustration. "What's this all about?" he said at last.

She seemed displeased; for a moment, she seemed on the verge of yelling at him, but then she sighed and took a sip of the coffee. After that, she took a bite of the pie and chewed it a few times before her face soured. "Horrid!" she cursed; she grabbed the coffee mug and gulped down a few mouthfuls to chase away the taste. When she saw Rasmussen staring at her confusedly, she addressed him in an offhand manner. "I've said all there is to say, Mr. Rasmussen. If you want to know anything else, you'd better consult the letter."

Rasmussen looked down at the envelope uneasily. He was still holding his son—

"Allow me," Cassiopeia said, taking the envelope from him and breaking the wax seal on the flap. She then handed him the page inside the envelope.

However, after Rasmussen took it, he frowned, because it was blank. He turned it over, then turned it back. He was about to tell her the page was blank, but then words suddenly began to appear. Rasmussen leaned in, unable to believe his eyes as he read:

Make yourself ready, Mr. Rasmussen, for God's will is to be done!

"What the hell?" Rasmussen managed to whisper.

"Not hell," Cassiopeia corrected him, "—in fact, just the opposite."

Rasmussen looked from her to the letter and back again.

"What kind of game is this?" he said with a deep sense of panic.

"This isn't a game," she corrected him in the same calm manner. "I am here because God *demands* it of me. Haven't you been feeling different lately?"

"...Different *how?*"

"As if you had the power of God within you."

Rasmussen laughed. "The only thing I've been feeling lately is *tired.*"

Once again, she seemed displeased. "You've been neglecting your gifts, Mr. Rasmussen—but we can clear this up quite quickly."

At that, she stood up and gestured for the waitress to come. In truth, the woman had been staring at them from the counter all that time, trying to overhear their conversation. As the waitress approached, Cassiopeia motioned for Rasmussen to move down, so the woman could sit next to him. Rasmussen complied in a zombie-like way—as if he suspected he would wake up at any moment to discover it had all been a dream.

Cassiopeia turned to him: "Have you ever met this woman before?" she said, referring to the waitress.

Rasmussen shook his head, still bewildered, but curious to see where all this was headed.

Cassiopeia turned to the waitress next: "Madam, have we met before?"

"Hardly," she said haughtily, as if Cassiopeia had asked her if she had ever been a hooker.

"Excellent," Cassiopeia said zestfully. "Mr. Rasmussen. Where did she go to high school?"

Rasmussen was about to ask her how he was supposed to know; but then, all at once, a name appeared in his mind. He saw it clearly, in huge, sparkling letters. "Jefferson Davis," he whispered.

The waitress jumped in his seat when he gave the correct name, but then she looked at him suspiciously. "You supposed to be a magic man or something?"—Rasmussen shook his head apologetically—"Well, I ain't falling for it. With the Internet, anybody can find out that kind of thing nowadays."

Cassiopeia smiled and turned to Rasmussen—who was still staring in shock. "See?" she began, "—the power of God is in you."

"Power of God?" the waitress repeated, her face creasing. Rasmussen gave her the same apologetic look. "What in the Sam Hill are you people going on about?" Then, turning to Rasmussen again, "If you're supposed to be a real magic man, then why don't you tell me something nobody knows?"

"Like what?" Cassiopeia encouraged her.

"...Like, who'd I lose my virginity to?"

Both women turned to Rasmussen. He went to shrug his shoulders, but the words seemed to fly out of his mouth. "Donnie Mathews," he blurted out, startling both the woman and himself.

"What the hell?" he whispered again.

"I told you already," Cassiopeia corrected him in her matter-of-fact way, "—all of this is *God's* doing. You have been endowed with His power, so as to be better able to carry out His will." Then, smiling in a way that implied their business was concluded, she said, "Now that you know your place, we'll be in touch."

At that, she stood up, dug her hand into her crotch, retrieved a wad of bills and slapped a fifty dollar bill on the table, in front of the waitress. "Thanks for you service, madam. Retain the surplus as a gratuity." She then shoved the wad of bills back into her crotch. Rasmussen stared, gape-mouthed; the poor waitress did not know if she was more stunned by the fifty dollars in front of her or the fact that Cassiopeia had pulled it out of her *crotch*.

Cassiopeia began to walk away now. In twenty seconds, the woman was outside. Rasmussen watched her get into the car—the same beat-up monstrosity from before—and drive off. When he turned from the window, he was startled to see the waitress was staring at him intently.

Amazingly, he realized he could see into her. Her thoughts were so clear that it was almost indecent—as if she were sitting there naked. She was trying to think of a question to stump him, and prove he was a fake.

"The birthmark is on your right breast," he blurted out, again startling them both. She rose from the table and backed away—as if he were a monster. When he looked down, the baby was grinning at him. Disturbed, Rasmussen decided this might be a good time to leave.

In Rasmussen's mind, the drive back home only seemed to take about five minutes. Much of that had to do with the fact that he drove like a madman. More than once, he had to make a conscious effort to ease his foot off the pedal. He had no idea where he was rushing to, but he had a desperate need to talk to someone—*anyone*. He thought about calling his wife, but he knew it was impossible—since there was no way to have that discussion without seeming *insane*. He had *been* at the diner, yet even he could hardly believe what had happened. …He had to test his so-called powers on someone else—some other random person—but it was the middle of the night. Maybe he could go to the mall tomorrow. His mind was working frantically, trying to provide options and context for everything that had happened to him—

and that *could* happen. ....And he remembered what Cassiopeia had asked—about if he had felt different lately. He was not entirely sure he had felt *different*, but strange things had definitely been happening. Now, every random event over the last month seemed connected. His head hurt as he thought about it. He winced....

He was wide awake now. ...And the way he felt at this moment, he doubted he would ever sleep again. It was as if a faucet of pure energy had been turned on inside of him. He felt the energy overflowing the confines of his body, flooding the world around him. Soon, everyone would be bathing in his energy—*drowning* in it....

He was almost home now. He was about to turn into his driveway when he looked ahead and saw a car was parked in front of the gate. He slammed on the brakes, narrowly averting a collision with the car's rear bumper. His heart was thumping in his chest; he gasped for air. Yet, for some reason, the baby was giggling—

A woman emerged from the car. As Rasmussen leaned forward, he saw it was Cassiopeia. He probably would have recognized the car sooner if his mind had not been in a daze. Either way, as she walked over to the driver's side window, all he could do was stare blankly. When she reached, she gestured with her hand for Rasmussen to lower his window. He complied, but felt disembodied—like he was merely an outside observer and someone else was carrying out the actions.

Cassiopeia leaned into the window once it was open: "Change of plans, Mr. Rasmussen," she began. "God is not ready for you to know your power yet."

Rasmussen opened his mouth—to ask her what she meant—but that's when she stretched out her index finger and tapped him on the temple. Instantly, everything went black.

DAY SEVEN

Winthrop Colchester IV—AKA Nigga Fross—yawned and got out of bed. He had been up for about an hour, fantasizing about the usual litany of freaks at his father's parties. He would have been content to stay in bed indefinitely, but his stomach had been growling for half an hour now, impinging on the pornographic imagery in his mind.

Presently, he exited his room and began shuffling down the stairs—toward the kitchen. When he was walking through the living room, the doorbell rang. It was such an odd occurrence that he stopped and looked over at the door. After giving it some thought, it occurred to him one of the guards had probably gotten locked out. Yawning again, he scratched his butt and began shuffling over to the door.

On the other side of the door, a woman in her mid-twenties was standing next to her middle-aged cameraman. After Colchester opened the door, they looked at him excitedly—as if he were a leprechaun holding a pot of gold. The woman spoke up quickly:

"Can you corroborate that it was your father *and* Nigga Nutt in that sex tape?" She was holding a microphone with the logo of one of those gossip shows on it. After she asked her question, she shoved the microphone in young Colchester's face.

He stared at her, having to concentrate in order to digest her question. In the haze of his mind, he conjured some of the freaky scenes from his father's parties—with three or four women for each of them. He figured one of the groupies had probably taped their orgy on her smartphone. Yet, even after he understood what the reporter was asking, his only tangible thought was to wonder how the woman and her cameraman had managed to reach the front door. When he instinctively looked toward the front gate, he remembered there were still holes in the hedge—from that minivan. He nodded when he remembered. However, as he looked back at the woman, he was suddenly taken aback by the crazed, expectant expression on her face.

To refocus him, she withdrew the microphone and asked, "So, can you corroborate it?" At that, she extended her arm, and the microphone, once more.

Colchester had a sudden impulse to kick her in the neck or something, but he instead took a deep breath. His tone was slightly sarcastic: "Pops loves pussy...so probably." He had hoped that would shut her up, but—

"Does he love ass too?" she said, sniggering.

Colchester blinked drowsily. "You mean *anal?*"

The woman nodded eagerly, a strange grin on her face. The cameraman did too. Once again, Colchester looked at them uneasily, but as his father had told him, the key to dealing with the media was acting calm and knowledgeable, even when you had no idea what they were talking about. He shrugged:

"He probably loves it," he said, "...knowing pops."

The women laughed out strangely—like a horse neighing. After that, she nodded to the cameraman in the same excited way. They were leaving now—fleeing as though they had robbed a bank and intended to be *long* gone before the cops arrived. In fact, she neighed again, and began galloping across the lawn, toward the front gate. Colchester watched them in the same uneasy way, but at least they were getting of the property, so he sighed, scratched his butt again, and closed the door.

Big Slug was driving; Higginbottom sat anxiously in the passenger seat of the man's truck, periodically glancing down at the sheet of paper he held in both hands. Fifteen minutes ago, Big Slug had done an Internet search for Goodson's address; a few seconds ago, they had left Big Slug's driveway, and now they were driving down the block. Higginbottom could not believe it was really happening—but then he looked down at the list of precise directions on the printout, and nodded his head. Anything seemed possible in the Internet age. Everything was *assessable*, and Higginbottom trembled inside, as if witnessing the wonders of God.

Indeed, after days of resistance, he had given himself totally to the idea that he was on a mission from God. He was also convinced Big Slug was pivotal to that mission. A few days ago, he had looked at the man and seen only a monster, but there was a sense of hope in Higginbottom now, as if they would all be transformed by what lay ahead. It occurred to him that maybe God had chosen Big Slug *precisely* because of his inadequacies and pathologies. The transformation, when it came, would not be miraculous unless there were extremes to be traversed. Jesus had gone from death to life; and while Higginbottom was aware of the heresy of the comparison, Big Slug would go from the utter depths of depravity and brutality to something else that Higginbottom had not yet worked out in his mind. That thing, whatever it was, would be glorious— and Higginbottom had complete faith in it. More than that, he worshiped the prospect of it, as if he were worshipping God, Himself.

In this sense, Higginbottom had finally surrendered to his fate.

Surrender was like falling: he was in midair, leaving his fate to gravity and whatever awaited him at the end of this journey. Instinctively, he closed his eyes and took a deep breath. He was about to smile, but—

"Now that I think about it," Big Slug began out of nowhere, "I let them touch my soul...just like Goodson said."

Higginbottom had opened his eyes at the sound of the man's voice, and was looking over at him confusedly. When Big Slug glanced over and saw the confused expression on his face, he flipped his hand dismissively:

"Them *niggers*," he clarified. "I let them guide me. *That's* how I thought a man should be: hard like one of them thug niggers. That's what I grew up seeing...in my neighborhood. *That's* the music I listened to. I let them *poison* me. ...I was just a white man pretending to be a nigger...just like Goodson said."

Higginbottom had been listening in the same confused way, but when his mind finally began to digest the terrible outlines of the man's words, he shook his head. "Is *that* what Goodson was saying?" he protested.

"Of course!" Big Slug fired back. "*You* read the book to me: wasn't you listening, too?" Then, with new confidence, "Goodson was right about *everything*. I mean, *look* at me. Look at what I've become because I was brainwashed by that nigger image of manhood: that nigger ideal. I was looking in the wrong place. I was looking to *niggers*, letting them *poison* me, when I should've been looking *within*, at our white greatness. It was white men—our *ancestors*—that built this nation...this *civilization*. We need to get back to that—to be our *true* selves again. That *true* manhood...what did Goodson call it again?" he asked, trying to recall, before smiling oddly when he remembered. "Ah, *yes*: '...the brutal, life-giving *strength* of the White Man. The strength that only the White Man has ever really demonstrated'...!"

Big Slug was like a college professor now: self-assured, calm, able to rattle off rhetorical flourishes with ease. Higginbottom felt his own will eroding—and his thoughts about Goodson's words being replaced with Big Slug's. It was again like falling and surrendering to fate, but he felt horrible inside—instead of the peace of a few moments ago. In the pit of his stomach, he suddenly felt as though they were racing headlong into some terrible disaster. His soul rebelled, but he had no idea how to stop what had already been put in motion. He was *falling*—and now, when he closed his eyes, it was in anticipation of the terrible *splat*—

"Look at them two niggers," Big Slug started again. When Higginbottom looked over, Big Slug jutted out his chin nonchalantly—in the direction of two little girls in the upcoming intersection. There was a strange grin on Big Slug's face now. "What would happen if I ran over them now?" he mused. At those words, he stomped on the accelerator, so that the vehicle lurched forward.

Higginbottom sat straighter in the seat—

"Heh?" Big Slug demanded. "What do you think would happen?"

The two girls had stopped in the middle of the crosswalk, terrified as the vehicle bore down on them. Higginbottom could not speak! When he looked over at Big Slug, he was startled to see the man was staring at him, his grin widening grotesquely. They were *seconds* from colliding with the frozen girls. Higginbottom opened his mouth—to plead or *scream*…but all he did in the end was shut his eyes and turn away. Big Slug had once again stomped on the accelerator. Higginbottom heard the girls screaming—but *damn* him, all he could do was look away and brace himself for the impact—

Big Slug was laughing. Higginbottom's heart was thumping so forcefully in his chest that he was unsure if they had hit the girls or not. He only knew that when he opened his eyes and looked through the windscreen, the truck was beyond the intersection, speeding down the street. He swung his head around, expecting a scene of utter carnage, but the two girls were still frozen in the middle of the crosswalk, staring at the retreating truck.

Big Slug was still laughing, his fat rippling as he surrendered to the joke that seemed to exist only in his mind. "…Relax," he said once he had regained some of his composure. "I wasn't going to hit them," he continued. Then, in the same dismissive way, "The last thing I need is niggers *suing* me…taking my hard-earned money." Higginbottom stared in amazement: Big Slug was so far gone that he didn't even realize his "hard-earned" money came from the prostitution of those so-called niggers. As Big Slug went back to chuckling at his joke, the only thing Higginbottom could do was stare; then, when he could stand it no more, he turned away and closed his eyes.

Rasmussen burst into the kitchen, inadvertently banging the door against the wall. At the noise, he stopped, winced and made a mental note that he had to fix the doorstop. There was already a dent in the wall, and he groaned as he stopped to look at it. After filing his mental note, his gaze moved on to the rest of the kitchen… but then he frowned, because he realized he had forgotten why he had run in here in the first place.

He tried to retrace his steps, but nothing came to his mind— except for the vague, anxious feeling he had had when he entered the room. He scanned the kitchen frantically, hoping that something would jog his memory—but nothing did, and the frustration began to build within him, like a kind of madness.

In truth, an anxious feeling had plagued him all day. A part of him was convinced something crucial had happened—or had *changed*—but he could not figure out what it was. He could almost see and smell and *touch* it, but it retreated into the shadows of his mind every time he came close. It was *maddening*—hence, the anxious, restless feeling he had had all day....

He was still scanning the kitchen, trying to remember why he was there. While he was on his third or fourth sweep, his attention went to the window. It looked out on the back yard; but from his current position, the only thing he could see was the towering fence that separated Stanko's property from his. Beyond that, he saw trees and the roof of her house.

He was about to continue searching the kitchen when a head suddenly popped over the fence! After the initial shock, he saw it was only Stanko. He knew he should have gotten used to it by now, but one never really got used to an old lady's head popping out of nowhere.

Plus, the fence was *towering*: how nosy did you have to be to get a ladder and peer into someone's back yard? A sense of rage joined with his previous frustration, and he set his jaw, as if preparing to do battle. After days of her snooping, today was the day he was finally going to tell her off! He took two or three menacing steps closer to the window—as if preparing to spring out of it and charge the old lady. However, now that he was closer to the window, he had a better view of Stanko's sweet, grandmotherly face. She was scanning the back yard with a kind of desperate loneliness. In fact, it was more than that. For the first time since he had met her, she looked tired—*haggard*—as if the life had been drained from her. Something was not right, and Rasmussen took a tentative step closer to the window, intending to call to her. However, as quickly as she had appeared, she was gone. Rasmussen stood staring at the top of the fence, feeling guilty and worried. ...And that was the annoying thing about Stanko: no matter how much her snooping provoked him, he always felt guilty about his anger afterwards.

He groaned. Maybe another five or six seconds passed before he remembered he had come into the kitchen to search for something—and that he had forgotten what it was. Frustrated, he looked about the kitchen absentmindedly again—until he heard the baby's distant cries—

The baby! That's right. He remembered now: he had been outside, in the minivan, getting ready to leave on an errand, when the baby began to cry from the back seat. After a few futile minutes of trying to calm his son, he had run into the house to get the baby's favorite toy. …How could he have forgotten that? He had only run into the house about a minute ago. He had checked the living room before coming in here. He shook his head at his forgetfulness—but a few sleepless nights would do that to you!

Scanning the kitchen again, he saw Stanko's demonic teddy bear looking back at him from the top of the refrigerator. Since yesterday, the baby had spent so much time chewing on its fur that it had taken on the diseased, mangy appearance of a stray dog. Rasmussen hoped his son would tire of it eventually, but the little boy almost seemed *addicted* to the thing.

As the baby continued to cry in the background, Rasmussen grabbed the toy (it was damp to the touch, and he grimaced as he grasped it) then he checked the kitchen one last time, to make sure he had not forgotten anything else—

His wife's to-do list! It was still lying on the kitchen table. He had been about to drive out to the mall to complete the errands on the list. How could he have forgotten the list? *Damn*. He shook his head at himself again; then, snatching up the list, he exited the kitchen and rushed back outside.

He had left the front door open when he ran inside to fetch the doll. It was a sunny August day in Atlanta, and he was still sweating from the few minutes he had spent outside. As a native New Yorker, he hated Atlanta in the summertime. He called it hell with a southern accent. The air never seemed to circulate in this town: it merely hovered over you, draining your strength and will to live. His son was still crying. Rasmussen moved faster—

But as he was exiting the front door, he glanced down and noticed a letter lying on the welcome mat. He froze, frowning. Either he had not noticed it before or someone had placed it there while he was in the house. He looked around but saw no one...so he must have overlooked it when he ran into the house. He nodded his head uneasily, seeing no other explanation.

He stood there for a moment, thinking about it; but as the baby's cries reached a higher pitch, he shuddered, reached down to grab the letter, and jogged over to the minivan. The moment he proffered the demonic doll to his son, the little boy grabbed it and seemed content.

Rasmussen sighed: one disaster averted...nine hundred and ninety-nine to go. But he was still holding the letter. He looked down at it, realizing there was no name or address written on the front. When he saw the red wax seal on the back, he suddenly remembered Colchester's letter. Only a few days had passed since that bizarre incident, and yet it seemed like something that had happened *months* ago. He had tossed the letter into the glove compartment and forgotten about it. He assumed this had to be the same letter— but his mind could not explain how it had gotten on his doormat. He stood there, mulling it over—until his son made a playful gurgling noise and roused him from his thoughts.

After making sure the child seat was secure, he closed the rear door and got behind the driver's seat. The first thing he did was open the glove compartment. He was expecting Colchester's letter to be gone, but it was still there. He took it out of the glove compartment and held it in his right hand; as he did that, he compared it to the new letter, which he still held in his left. They were identical, down to the emblems on the wax seal. What did it mean? ...He had a sudden flashback of Colchester's huge, purplish balls slapping against his thighs. He flinched. Maybe the letters were an omen of madness. Maybe it would only be a matter of time before he went over the edge, like Colchester had. The thought made him smile nervously—the way people smiled when they wanted to convince themselves a thought was too stupid to be true. After all, he was a mathematics professor: he did not believe in omens and other supernatural nonsense. There had to be a rational explanation for all this: something obvious he was overlooking....

He placed Colchester's letter on the passenger seat, so he could focus his attention on his own letter. The envelope was so exquisite that he could not bring himself to rip it open. He remembered there was a kitchen knife in the glove compartment, which he used to peel the baby's fruit. He reached for it and used it as a letter opener. ...When he pulled out the folded page, it was silky to the touch—but when he unfolded it, he saw it was blank. He turned it over a few times, and held it up to the light, searching for a hidden message, but there was nothing. He frowned; at the same time, he liked holding the letter. There was something soothing about the silky page...and he liked its creamy smell. He inhaled deeply, closing his eyes....

Maybe fifteen seconds passed like that. Eventually, he looked around as if lost. Colchester's letter was still lying on the passenger seat. Rasmussen thought about opening it—but a sense of decorum restrained him. Besides, remembering he had an errand to run, he sighed.

Suddenly determined to do something productive with his day, he put the blank page back in the envelope, picked up Colchester's envelope, and tossed them both into the glove compartment. As he did so, he told himself he would visit Colchester later and try to make some sense of all this.

He nodded his head, but when he inserted the key in the ignition, he saw his hands were trembling. In fact, he realized he was *terrified*. An image of his parents suddenly popped into his mind. For a moment, it was as if he were a child again, because he suddenly wanted to run to his parents' bedroom and wedge himself between them. As a grown man, the thought was shameful; and yet, he felt as though something had been reset in his mind. Common sense, reason, experience—everything that made him an adult—was suddenly gone. He felt the first tears beginning to form—

No!

He sat up straighter, sensing that if he surrendered at this moment, he would never be able to come back to his senses. He forced himself to move. He remembered his wife's errands, and nodded his head. Yes: he would concentrate on that and forget everything else. Performing a routine act would cure him of the madness, and he would come back home and rest. He nodded his head hopefully at the thought, but the malaise would not leave his soul....

Over a minute had passed since Rasmussen inserted the key into the ignition. He was still sitting there, struggling against his childhood terrors. He reminded himself to get moving; but as he was about to start the minivan, he remembered the baby. Through all this, his son had been unusually quiet in the back seat. Rasmussen craned his neck now, to look at the rearview mirror. His son returned his gaze, but there was something odd in the baby's eyes, so Rasmussen turned around and looked more closely. He and the baby stared at one another for a few seconds; then, all at once, the baby's emerging teeth took on the appearance of fangs;

his skin turned leathery and dark; his eyes became large and distorted and *black*—

Rasmussen clamped his eyes shut for three full seconds! When he opened them, he was relieved to see the baby's face was back to normal. Nevertheless, he was still shaking. His son had gone back to sucking on the teddy bear's ear; and despite how repulsive he personally found the doll, there was nothing out of the ordinary about the scene. Rasmussen was nodding his head now. He must have imagined it all: he was an absentminded wreck, and sleep-deprivation had caused him to hallucinate. Relieved, he turned back around in his seat, closed his eyes and leaned back.

Rasmussen sat quietly for about another ten seconds—until he remembered his wife's errands. He had put her to-do list in his shirt pocket. He retrieved it now and began reading her neat handwriting:

Pick up dry cleaning
Get the dress I ordered
Get the tampons I like (See if they still have the jumbo pack on sale)—

The baby cackled in the background, as if amused by what Rasmussen had been reduced to. Rasmussen felt himself flush with embarrassment. The baby's mocking laugher grated against his nerves—but he was so afraid of what he would see on his son's face that he resisted the impulse to turn around. He knew he was beyond the stage where he could laugh away his fears. Yet, as was the case with Granny Stanko, all his hidden frustrations began to surge to the surface. He was tired of being this pathetic husk of a man. He wanted to take revenge—and all at once, his wife was to blame for everything! Her neat handwriting suddenly seemed like a provocation. She had actually numbered the list! *See if they still have the jumbo pack on sale...?* He heard her condescending voice in his head; he saw her wagging her finger at him, standing there with her other hand propped on her hip. Instinctively, he growled like a beast...but as the baby laughed again, Rasmussen slumped in his seat, feeling ridiculous. He was definitely losing it....

There was nothing to do now but go to the mall and distract his mind with his wife's errands. He turned the key in the ignition, so that the minivan's engine came to life. Yet, as he was about to back out of the driveway, the passenger side door inexplicably burst open!

In the space of two seconds, someone had opened the door, jumped in and slammed the door shut! Rasmussen's cry got caught in his throat. His uninvited guest was ducking down in the seat now, practically stuffing himself into the foot space of the passenger side. When Rasmussen realized his passenger was Colchester's son, he allowed himself to breathe again. However, Colchester IV looked terrified. Rasmussen was about to ask him what was wrong, when—

"*Drive*, nigga!" the kid screamed.

The Colchesters' bizarre "nigga" philosophy popped into his head again, and he groaned. Colchester IV was dressed in baggy hip-hop attire, and wore his baseball cap tilted to the side. Rasmussen eyed his blond cornrows uneasily: "Winthrop," he began again—

"Don't talk to me, nigga," Colchester screamed, "—just *drive!*"

Rasmussen stared at the kid, still thrown off balance by the cognitive dissonance of being called a "nigga" by a rich white kid—

"*Drive*, nigga!" Colchester yelled again.

"Stop calling me that!" Rasmussen screamed, losing it. "Look, Winthrop—"

"*Winthrop?*" the kid screamed, outraged. "You *know* my name is Nigga Fross!"

Rasmussen stared at the kid for two or three seconds, lost and bewildered—

"Just drive, man—*please*. They coming for me, yo!"

Rasmussen went to ask the kid who he was running from; but given his experiences with the Colchesters, it occurred to him it was probably better not to know. ...And in truth, he did have errands to run—so there was no point in sitting around here arguing with this crazy kid.

He sighed, put the minivan in gear, and turned in his seat to back out of the driveway. The baby was staring at him intently, and there were the vestiges of a mocking smile on the five-month-old's lips. As Rasmussen looked on, the child clutched the teddy bear closer, as if trying to provoke him. Rasmussen forced himself to look away.

He began to drive; he looked about the upscale suburb, hoping something would distract his mind. At this time of day, the only people out and about were gardeners and delivery men. The lords and mistresses of the manors were all either at work or hidden behind their wealth.

When Rasmussen turned the next bend, he saw a heavyset white man prowling the road, dressed only in a robe. There was a baseball bat in his hand, and the expression on the man's face was *murderous*. It was Colchester III. Rasmussen chuckled and looked down at his passenger, who was still hiding in the foot space:

"What the hell did you do, kid?"

"They *persecuting* me, yo!"

Rasmussen smiled. "For what?"

"Hell if I know!" But this was perhaps the first moment of peace young Colchester had had since his father began terrorizing him fifteen minutes ago. When his father started brandishing the bat, the kid had fled the house and run for his life...but he frowned now, as something occurred to him. "Pops rushed into my room this morning and started asking me all these crazy questions… and then he said I had *ruined* him. That's when he started chasing me, saying he was going to *kill* me, yo!"

Rasmussen looked at him uneasily. "What did he ask you about?"

Young Colchester thought back. "Oooh," he said, finally remembering the reporter from earlier—and the fact that she had mentioned a sex tape. After talking to her, he had eaten breakfast and gone back to bed—until his father woke him up and started going crazy. In the frenzied confrontation that followed, young Colchester remembered hearing the gossip show's music in the background as he fled the house. He had no idea *what* he had done, but he sensed it was bad.

Young Colchester was staring down at the floor in a daze; after a few seconds, Rasmussen ventured, "Why'd your father say you ruined him?"

Colchester sighed. "I think he made a sex tape or something."

Despite himself, Rasmussen laughed.

"A sex tape ain't no joke!" the kid reprimanded him.

Rasmussen chuckled again, but then waved his hand dismissively. "Aren't half your songs about having sex?"

"Yeah?"

"So what harm can a sex tape possibly do to you guys?"

Young Colchester stared at him hopefully, not yet aware that his father had been with *Nigga Nutt* in the video.

Still trying to be supportive, Rasmussen added, "It's not like your father was running for governor or something."

"…True, true," young Colchester conceded.

"Good," Rasmussen said, chuckling one last time—and glad he could be useful.

They were about to head onto the highway now. Rasmussen craned his neck and glanced at the rearview mirror, to see what his son was doing. The baby glared at him with cold eyes; the smile Rasmussen had been wearing faded away abruptly, and he sat there looking wretched. Young Colchester caught his expression:

"What's wrong?"

The kid was still hiding in the foot space. Rasmussen addressed him in an offhand manner: "You can probably sit in the seat now— we're out of the neighborhood."

When the youngster was sitting in the seat, Rasmussen glanced in the rearview mirror again, saw the same expression on the baby's face, and looked away uneasily. Following Rasmussen's eyes, Colchester looked back at the baby; but when he saw nothing out of the ordinary (the five-month-old was chewing on the doll again) he looked over at Rasmussen quizzically.

"You seem kind of stressed, bruh," Colchester began.

Rasmussen smiled, as if to say that was an understatement.

"When's the last time you emptied your nuts?" the kid asked casually.

"Excuse me!" Rasmussen said, trying to scrounge up a sense of parental outrage, but:

"You got that pussy stress on your face, bruh," the kid explained.

"Pussy stress?"

"You know what I'm talking about: that stress that only pussy can relieve. Yo' woman ain't giving you none?"

Rasmussen laughed at the kid's phrasing.

Young Colchester sniggered knowingly: "How long's it been?"

Rasmussen was uneasy about going into this topic (especially with a kid!) but between Colchester's open manner and Rasmussen's exhaustion, he blurted out, "Not too long—*days*." However, as he remembered she had faked her orgasm, his face soured.

Adding it all up, Colchester nodded his head. "I always heard that having a baby *ruins* a pussy."

"What?" Rasmussen said before he again found himself laughing at the kid's bizarre phrasing.

"Don't laugh—you know I'm right. I saw a baby being born once, on one of them Science Channel documentaries. That was a horror show right thar: pussy ripping open, slime squirting out...sheeet, I couldn't even *look* at a pussy for a month after seeing that. I don't blame you for leaving that pussy alone, bruh!" He shuddered then, adding a disgusted "Sheeet!" for good measure.

Despite the crude statement, Rasmussen laughed again. It was strange, but he realized he missed talking to other men. Men needed other men to stay sane...and they needed women to balance them and keep them from pursuing the extremes of the male psyche. Unfortunately, Rasmussen had no close friends in Atlanta (male or otherwise). When Stanko wasn't snooping and acting crazy, she was a sweet old lady—but it was not as though he had anything in common with her. ...Not that he had anything in common with young Colchester either, but at least he had the comfort of knowing he could tell the kid to shut the hell up. There was no way to do that with Stanko; and of course, now that he and his wife were having their anti-argument, honest conversations with her were out of the question. His life was still back in New York City; and realizing this, he felt suddenly melancholy.

They drove in silence for a few seconds. Then, "You love your woman?" Colchester asked abruptly.

Rasmussen paused a second, thrown off balance. "...Of course."

"But you had to think about it," Colchester pointed out.

"I'm just tired, that's all," Rasmussen protested.

Young Colchester looked at him suspiciously. "Okay, let me ask you this: Does your woman love you?"

Rasmussen thought about it—

"Ah-ha! *See?* …There you go," he said as though a great secret had been revealed.

"See *what?*" Rasmussen said, annoyed.

"It's like Pops says: 'A woman can't love a man unless she feels in her heart that she *needs* him.' She's gotta need something from him: either his money, his dick or his power. That's what Pops says."

"So, you believe everything your father says?" Rasmussen replied, growing hot.

"Hell no, but Pops knows pussy! I respect a player when his game is *tight!* Pops knows his shit." Then, pressing home his point, Colchester continued, "What yo' woman need from you, nigga? She got you driving a minivan, taking care of *her* son. Sheeet, you *her* bitch, nigga!"

The baby began to laugh from the back seat; at the cackling laugh, Colchester started to laugh as well. "*See*," he began, "even the baby know what time it is!"

Rasmussen had a sudden impulse to open the door and kick Colchester out of the speeding vehicle, onto the highway. Besides, listening to the kid was like being drunk—and not in a "pleasant buzz" sort of way, but in a reckless, "what the *hell* did I do last night?" sort of way. The only thing he wanted now was silence— and *peace*. In truth, he was feeling more exhausted now—and he sensed a headache coming on. Luckily, the conversation petered out, and they drove in silence for a while, with both of them staring out of the windscreen, at the highway.

After a few minutes, something occurred to Colchester, and he looked over at Rasmussen, saying, "Where we headed, anyway?"

"…Oh…to the mall."

"Can you drop me somewhere?"

"Where?"

"With my crew. I can chill over there until Pops cools down."

Rasmussen's mind felt shredded. He sighed. "Let me run my errands first, then we'll see."

They returned to silence, but Rasmussen felt more wretched now. ...He remembered the baby. When he craned his neck and looked at the rearview mirror, the five-month-old glared at him. Rasmussen stared back, more disillusioned than alarmed. The baby was still holding the doll...but there was something odd about the teddy bear; and when Rasmussen looked closer, the doll suddenly lifted its head! The painted beads that had been its eyes came to life and focused their malevolence on him—

A terrified squeal escaped from Rasmussen's lips! He swung around in his seat to get a better look; but in his panicked state, he swung the steering wheel with him. The minivan swerved to the right. The driver in the right lane had to slam on her brakes. Horns were honked. Young Colchester was screaming. Rasmussen had to turn back around abruptly—to steer the vehicle away from disaster; he fought the minivan's momentum to stabilize it—

"*Damn*, nigga!" Colchester cursed. "Pull over, man! Pull over!"

"What?" Rasmussen mumbled.

"*Pull over!*"

Flustered, Rasmussen pulled over. The car he had almost forced off the road zoomed past him now, its driver honking her horn angrily—

"What the *hell*, man!" Colchester screamed after they had stopped in the emergency lane. Rasmussen looked over at him, but said nothing. He was still in shock. "You trying to *kill* us?" Colchester raged—to which Rasmussen only shook his head feebly.

The baby was laughing; Rasmussen's skin crawled, but he knew there was no way he was going to turn around and look. In fact, he was already telling himself he had imagined it all.

Young Colchester continued to rant; perhaps half a minute

passed with Colchester screaming and Rasmussen sitting there in a daze…and the baby laughing at the antics of the adult world. Eventually, even someone as dense as Colchester realized screaming was not going to accomplish anything—or maybe it was only that Rasmussen's blank expression disturbed him. He lowered his voice and frowned:

"What's going on with you?"

Even then, Rasmussen only sat there, staring straight ahead— out of the windscreen. Coming to the conclusion Rasmussen was in no condition to drive, Colchester decided to take charge. First, he told Rasmussen to switch seats with him; when Rasmussen continued to stare ahead blankly, the kid exited the vehicle, walked around to the driver's side, then goaded Rasmussen, the way one would an obstinate cow, until he moved over to the passenger side.

Rasmussen was lost in his own little world—paralyzed by fears and superstitions. The only thing he could think was *Don't look back!* The baby's laughter fluttered through his head like an invitation to madness; his mind kept replaying the scene: the doll looking up, fixing its beady eyes on him. *Don't look back…!*

Young Colchester began to drive. Rasmussen was staring to the right, out of the passenger side window; he wrapped his arms around himself, like someone shivering out in the cold. Colchester watched him with concern.

"Yo," he called, trying to get Rasmussen's attention. Rasmussen remained nonresponsive. "—*Yo!*"

Rasmussen jumped.

"Look at me, man," Colchester said in a lower voice. Rasmussen still looked wretched, but he seemed to be coming out of his stupor. "Talk to me," the kid coaxed him. "You all right?"

Rasmussen stared at him. He blinked deeply, as if trying to clear his vision—but then he instinctively glanced over at the baby—

Don't look back!

He forced his eyes away. He was shivering.

"Yo," young Colchester began again, "you want me to call your wife or something?"

Rasmussen went back to staring ahead blankly. He shook his head.

"Talk to me, man," Colchester coaxed him again. "What just happened? What's up with you and the baby?"

At his mention of the baby, Rasmussen looked up at him sharply.

Colchester pressed him: "You afraid of your son or something?" A nervous smile came over the youngster's face: the statement was supposed to be a joke, but it died in the silence. Rasmussen looked away and shook his head.

"Then what's going on?"

Rasmussen seemed to be going back to his nonresponsive state—

"*Yo!*" Young Colchester screamed, so that Rasmussen jumped again. "*Talk* to me! *Say* something!"—Rasmussen shook his head— "What you afraid—"

The baby's laughter reached a new pitch; rage suddenly filled Rasmussen, and he turned toward the baby—despite his fears. In that instant, he felt as though he could...

The baby looked back at him, amused—but the evil aura was gone; and when Rasmussen looked, the doll hung limply in the baby's arms. Rasmussen stared, looking for something that would confirm his fears about the baby and the doll, but there was nothing. Young Colchester looked over at him:

"You want me to take you to the hospital, bruh?"

Rasmussen looked up at Colchester, as if only then noticing he was there. He stared at him for about five seconds. "Winthrop?" he whispered; he looked through the windscreen, as if he had woken up in a strange land.

"You all right, man?" the kid asked.

Rasmussen stared at him again; then, as something occurred to him, he frowned. "You can drive?"

"You see me driving, don't you?" he said sarcastically.

"...But, how old are you?"

"Fifteen."

"I thought you had to be sixteen to drive?"

"You gotta be sixteen to drive *legally*," he said with a wry smile.

Rasmussen nodded, still fighting the effects of shock. He noticed he was not wearing a seatbelt; he put it on. ...What the hell was happening to him? He took some deep breaths, trying to clear his mind. He asked himself if he had really seen what he thought he had seen....

They drove in silence for a minute or two, but Colchester seemed reassured that Rasmussen was going to be okay, so he did not press him on why he had almost killed them. As for Rasmussen, it was clear to him now that he was not well—and that he had not been well for a while now. His mind suddenly flashed with that scene from a few days ago: Colchester III running naked down the meandering road. Was the same thing happening to him? ... And what was the story with those letters? Maybe they really were an omen of madness...?

He shook his head eventually: he was a mathematician. Once again, he reminded himself he did not believe in omens and superstition. At the same time, the felt the same dread feeling in his soul, and he shuddered.

His headache had gotten worse. It tightened its grip abruptly, so that he groaned. He rubbed his temples, hoping to soothe the pain, but it kept increasing. He felt a little sick to his stomach as well. Luckily, the mall was within sight now. He would run his errands, drop off Colchester, then go home and try to get some rest. Between his insane fears about his son, his crumbling marriage and this sudden headache, he felt like he was being squeezed to death by something *monstrous*.

Given the time of day, the mall parking lot was practically empty. Rasmussen took it as a good sign—since an empty mall meant he would be able to complete his errands quickly. As soon as young Colchester maneuvered the minivan into the parking spot, Rasmussen spoke up: "You can wait here if you want: I won't be too long."

The kid nodded and Rasmussen got out of the vehicle. The Atlanta heat ambushed him the moment he stepped out of the door. It rose from the asphalt in waves. He felt like he was being roasted alive; groaning, he forced himself to move quickly. Across the parking lot, the air conditioned mall rose up like an oasis in the desert.

For a moment, he considered leaving his son with Colchester, but he told himself he had to work through this. He had to act like everything was okay: as though he had not seen impossible things in the rearview mirror.

Within seconds, he opened the rear door and got out the designer stroller his wife had recently ordered. He hesitated when it was time to get his son out of the baby seat, but the baby seemed to be a baby again. The doll still hung limply in his son's arms. For an instant, he thought about grabbing the doll and throwing it as far as he could…but he knew it would be a sign he was giving in to his fears, so he left the doll with his son and fastened them both into the stroller.

Once that was complete, he looked around, as was his habit, asking himself if he had forgotten anything. He tapped his shirt pocket to make sure he still had his wife's to-do list; he felt his pants pocket, making sure he had his wallet. He was ready.

By now, Colchester had turned on the radio and tuned it to the local hip-hop station. The song's refrain was:

Girl, you better to jiggle it, 'cause I'm gonna grind on it!

Rasmussen slammed the door, waved to Colchester and began the trek to the mall entrance.

With his headache worsening, he did not want to think anymore, but his thoughts were returning to his wife. She would be coming back from her business trip tomorrow, and he did not know if he was happy she was returning, or fearful of what might happen when she did. Young Colchester had asked him if he still loved his wife, and the truth was he did not know anymore. He was in love with the woman he had married two years ago, but he was not sure if that woman still existed—or if she had *ever* really existed. In the back of his mind, he still suspected he had been conned. He yearned for their old life together—or at least those old illusions—before their move to Atlanta. In truth, he was in love with a memory; and during his moments of fantasy, when he thought about making love to his wife, he always saw the woman from two years ago; when he thought about himself, he always saw the man he used to be. He fully realized things were rarely as perfect as they seemed in memories; and yet, maybe he needed to fantasize now. Maybe he needed fantasies to chase away the doubts and nightmares....

Rasmussen was so preoccupied with these thoughts that he did not notice the black woman until he almost collided with her. In his dazed state, she seemed to appear out of nowhere. He almost plowed her over with the baby carriage, but when he looked at her, he saw she was stunningly beautiful: tall, slim and young, dressed in a halter top and miniskirt that would have made a devout monk lose his mind and say to hell with his vows. At the sight of her, Rasmussen froze, mesmerized…and then his eyes grew wide when he realized he had seen her before. She was the goddess from the video shoot at the Colchester estate—the one with the detachable spine. He instinctively found himself gawking at her in the same hungry way he had that day.

When he began to regain some of his sense, he opened his mouth to apologize to her; but at the sight of the baby, she laughed out and bent down to tickle the five-month-old's cheeks. In fact, as she bent over, her full, firm breasts seemed as if they would spring from the halter top. Rasmussen's eyes bulged. In the back of his mind, a politically correct voice told him it was improper to be staring like this, but the black woman had the kind of body that was *meant* to be stared at!

He was not depraved enough to pursue some kind of sexual interlude with her, but he certainly liked the thought of it! At that moment, the black woman looked up and said something to him; in his overwrought state, Rasmussen did not hear, but the woman's smile was infectious. There was something childlike about it: something free and invigorating. Rasmussen found himself laughing. In retrospect, he realized the black woman had asked him if she could hold the baby; but by then, the baby was already in her arms. She was doting on the child now, and his son responded by giggling. All at once, the baby was only a baby again—purged of dark intentions and malevolence. The Atlanta heat, which had moments ago seemed so oppressive, now did not bother him at all. And at that moment, the black woman squeezed the baby against her bosom, so that her breasts again seemed like they would pop out of her halter top. As Rasmussen looked closer, he realized he could see the outlines of her nipples against the fabric. Despite himself, he let out something like a whimper. He was suddenly aware of his erection. It pushed forcefully against his pants, and he swayed unconsciously, as if high from the sensation.

The black woman continued to squeeze the baby against her breasts; Rasmussen stared at the scene longingly, until he realized he was jealous of his son! The realization was jarring—but damn, his son was a lucky little bastard…!

Rasmussen was about to smile to himself; but when he made eye contact with the five-month-old, he saw the baby was sneering at him. The same mocking smile was on the child's face—as if he were deriving pleasure from Rasmussen's sexual frustration. The baby let out a squeal of delight at that moment; and then, still glaring at Rasmussen, the five-month-old's pudgy little hand went up and grasped the black woman's nipple—

She gasped; Rasmussen held his breath, caught between a kind of reverse-oedipal yearning and shock. …But when he looked at the woman, he saw her burst out laughing.

"I guess he gonna be a breast man!" she said.

Rasmussen tried to laugh along with her, but he felt a bit…*odd*. It was as if the combination of lust and jealousy had awakened something primal within him. He tried to get a hold of himself, but when his son grabbed the top of the woman's halter and pulled it down, exposing her perfect breasts, the primal onslaught became too much for him. His body convulsed and he cried out; but by then, he was beyond concepts like pleasure and pain. He felt something was taking over his body. He tried to withstand it, but it was pointless. Within moments, he felt like he was coming apart—as if an explosion had gone off within him, and his body parts were hurtling through the air. Everything was going black now. Rasmussen let out a weak cry; but in the background, somewhere in the infinite darkness, he heard the black woman laughing with his son. He listened to them for a while; yet in time, even they were gone, and Rasmussen lay still in the darkness, vaguely aware of his erection.

About an hour and a half had passed since Higginbottom and Big Slug set out for Goodson's. Forty minutes into the drive, Higginbottom realized he had left Goodson's book on the kitchen table. Yet, by then, Big Slug had revealed more of his philosophical insights: perverse interpretations of Goodson's book that Higginbottom was slowly beginning to accept as possible. He did not know what to think anymore; and in truth, he was merely trying to hold on until things began to make sense again.

They were deep into the mountains now, driving up a deserted gravel road. The final instruction on the sheet of paper in Higginbottom's hands was to follow the winding road for two miles. They passed no other houses; then, somehow, they were parked in front of a rustic wooden house.

There was a picket fence. An old dog appeared and began barking at them in a labored way—as if it were asthmatic. There was a rusting mailbox by the gate, and Higginbottom saw Goodson's name on it. It was probably only then that he realized they had arrived. Sighing, he folded the sheet of paper with the directions and placed it in his shirt pocket.

By then, Big Slug had exited the vehicle, leaving Higginbottom sitting there by himself. Still unsure about what he should be doing—and the logic of coming here in the first place—Higginbottom looked back at the house. It seemed solid and clean: the lawn was trimmed, and everything seemed in order; but like the rusting mailbox, the house seemed to be succumbing to some natural process of decay. There was a dreary quality about the entire place; and in light of the strange, quasi-religious expectations Higginbottom had had in coming here, he felt disappointed now. His soul felt deflated—which only made the place seem drearier.

Whatever the case, Big Slug was still a true believer. The acolyte was now the high priest of their religion, so the man walked up to Goodson's gate boldly. At first, the old dog barked louder at his approach, but then it retreated to a safe distance, where it wheezed for three or four seconds between barks. Higginbottom sat watching it all with a kind of grim fascination. Only when the front door opened, and an elderly man looked out, did Higginbottom take a deep breath and exit the vehicle.

Goodson was lean without seeming frail. Even though he had to be at least in his eighties, his frame was still strong and his back was unbent. At the sight of him, the dog seemed relieved. It stopped barking and went over to him, wagging its tail in a lethargic, gingerly way—as if its tail were ridden with arthritis.

Goodson stepped out of the door and came down the walkway. The dog followed silently. Higginbottom was at Big Slug's side by then, and he looked up at the man, seeing his excited grin. Remembering he had forgotten Goodson's book on the kitchen table, Higginbottom had a sudden fear that Big Slug would become enraged when he found out—and beat him to a pulp. The excited grin—indeed, the gleam of absolute adoration—was still on Big Slug's face as he watched the old man. On the other hand, while Goodson's expression was not exactly grim, there was a kind of wariness there:

"What y'all want?" Goodson demanded.

Higginbottom again found himself deferring to Big Slug, waiting for the man's response. After all, Big Slug was now the high priest of their religion. Slug nodded before he took another step forward:

"We're here for the struggle, brother," he declared with a wide grin that showed off his gold teeth. Higginbottom looked over at Goodson curiously, wondering how the man was interpreting the bizarre scene. The wariness was still there, along with a certain amount of exhaustion. However, there seemed to be an abundance of patience as well. Higginbottom suddenly found himself wondering how many men like them had showed up at Goodson's doorstep, looking for some bastardized version of God....

After reaching a resolution in his mind, Goodson sighed, nodded his head in the same wary but patient way, and gestured for them to follow him. At that, he turned and began walking back toward his house. Big Slug nodded excitedly and opened the gate; Higginbottom followed him wordlessly, his mind blank and his stomach queasy.

The inside of Goodson's house was clean but cluttered. Most of the clutter was from the thousands of old, faded books that lined the walls of the house. In fact, the place seemed more like a library than a house. Most of the books were on shelves, but sometimes they were merely stacked on the floor.

Beyond the entrance, the house opened into the living room. Goodson gestured for them to sit on the couch. As they did, he took the rocking chair that was across from them; then, in the way of old men, he groaned as he sat down.

"Tell me again why you think you're here," he said as soon as they were all sitting.

Higginbottom opened his mouth, but Big Slug again spoke for them:

"Your book showed us...what the world's been doing to the white man."

Goodson stared at the man—not exactly aghast, but with clear distaste. He nodded his head, then looked over at Higginbottom: "What about you?"

Higginbottom sighed. "I honestly don't know anymore. I thought there was something there—in your book. I *felt* something—"

"But now it doesn't feel right to you anymore?" Goodson pressed him.

Higginbottom nodded, feeling ashamed. He bowed his head. However—

"Good," Goodson said, taking a deep breath, as if relieved. Higginbottom looked up at him sharply; Big Slug leaned forward, a confused snarl on his face.

Goodson looked at them both, leaned back in his rocking chair, and continued, "Most of what's written in that book is pure nonsense."

"*Whut?*" Big Slug mumbled, his face twitching.

Goodson shook his head ruefully. "Every few months, some of you guys show up, driven by the same foolishness that provoked me to write the book in the first place. For one thing," he went on as Big Slug fidgeted on the couch, "it's the height of narcissism to believe the decline of your kind means that *civilization* is declining. Besides, what we call 'Western Civilization' was nothing more than fools gloating, 'Our music and art are the best! Our laws are the most just! Our values and standards for beauty are the closest to God's...!' If Western Civilization is dead, it wasn't done in by colored folk, or women—but the fact that we, white men, don't even believe our own bullshit anymore. Pure self-indulgence: that's all it was." Here, he paused, lowering his voice:

"I wrote that book because I thought, 'Life is supposed to be good for the white man—since Western Civilization is the greatest thing that was ever created. Thus, if my life sucks, it has to be because someone did something to Western Civilization! Those *undeserving* people—them blacks, women, Mexicans...*whatever*—they must have *broken* Western Civilization...but we can fix it by putting them folks back in their place...restoring the natural order!'...whatever that is," he said, his voice trailing off again.

"I used to believe Western Civilization was about *me*," he said with new energy, "—that it was something my *ancestors* built: something I should have *pride* in, as a *white* man...but so-called Western Civilization is a creation of kings, emperors, *bankers*—and all the other members of the parasitic classes. It was the parasitic classes that created so-called Western Civilization. They infused it with *their* values and norms, then they made true believers out of the rest of us—so that we'd become foot soldiers in their unholy wars. Men like you and me—*average* white men—were made to worship at their altar and make sacrifices out of ourselves. Every time we begin to see the system's screwing us—just as it's screwing the black and the woman—then some dumb fucker like me comes up with one of those 'Decline of Western Civilization' books. Of course, it doesn't matter if minorities are being screwed by it. That's fine: that makes white men—average ones like us—feel like we have to defend it. If other races hate it, and our ancestors supposedly built it, then we should rise to defend it from the infidels and non-believers...all those barbarians waiting at the gate.... But it's all a lie. It's the way the parasitic classes keep *using* us—keep convincing us to be foot soldiers in their unholy war—while they reap all the benefits. We live to *serve* them, yet Western Civilization convinces us that we're *gods*—that we're the thin line between chaos and order.

"Nah," he said, shaking his head with absolute clarity, "if we don't stand as tall as we used to stand, it's because the parasitic classes have sucked us all dry—sucked us to the *bones*—and left us fighting over the crumbs that fell from their table. Nah," he said again, "let Western Civilization *die*. Let all its lies be exposed. Make the parasitic classes fight their own goddamn battles—so that the rest of us can finally live free...."

Higginbottom's head was *spinning*—and yet, it all made sense. In the silence, he stared down at the floor, thinking of all the actions that had brought him to Goodson's door. Indeed, as the bewilderment threatened to stifle him, he grimaced and shook his head. "I really *believed* it," he said at last. "I really thought God had given me a purpose."

Goodson shook his head: "Unless you're a priest, you probably shouldn't rely on God for your life's purpose."

"What the *hell* is that supposed to mean?" Big Slug erupted at last. He had sat there in silence, struggling to digest Goodson's words, but mentioning God was the final insult.

Goodson looked over at the man in the same wary way, wishing he had kept quiet. However, Big Slug was staring at him so intently that he knew he could not simply change the topic. He took a breath to clear his thoughts. "...Many people read the Bible and hear God demanding, 'Praise me and your life will have purpose!' However, if your life doesn't have purpose *before* you praise God, it won't have purpose *afterward*. You don't praise God in order to *attain* happiness—you praise God in order to *celebrate* your happiness. Otherwise, that's where it becomes madness...."

When Goodson was finished speaking, Higginbottom glanced over at Big Slug, seeing the man's face was sweaty and red—as if he had swallowed some hot peppers....

The couch was low and deep, so it took extra effort for Big Slug to stand up. Both Higginbottom and Goodson looked on uneasily at the man's first few futile efforts to stand up. The man's face was still red and sweaty—and he seemed dazed as well. As he struggled to stand, he seemed like a drunk trying to leave a bar. There was the sense that something horrible would happen if they allowed him to leave in this condition. Higginbottom opened his mouth, about to ask him if he needed help. However, it was then that the colossus finally managed to rise to his feet.

Big Slug's face was still inscrutable as he took a single step toward Goodson. Then, with an agility and brutality nobody would have expected, he leaned back slightly and kicked Goodson in the chest! The old man was sent flying. At first, the rocking chair slid back on the rug, but then it capsized, leaving Goodson sprawled on the floor.

"Now I see why God sent me here," Big Slug began ominously as Goodson groaned and trembled from the shock—

"What you doing!" Higginbottom heard himself say. He had watched the entire scene as if he were a million miles away—as if he could not possibly be connected to any of this madness—

Big Slug kicked Goodson in the side then, so that the man grunted. "God sent me to punish those who have sinned against Him," Big Slug said now. He reared his foot back, to deliver another blow—

Higginbottom leapt up and threw his weight against Big Slug towering bulk, so that the behemoth stumbled over to the wall. "Shit, Slug!" Higginbottom pleaded with him, "—this is *crazy!*"

Big Slug eyed him, his face growing redder. "Whose side you choosing?" the man asked in the same ominous way.

"What the *hell* are you talking about!" Higginbottom screamed. Looking down, he noticed Goodson was trying to stand up. However, since the man was still in shock—and in pain—it was now his turn to flounder about as he tried to rise. Higginbottom bent down to assist the old man, his mind still frazzled. His back was turned to Big Slug now; as such, his only warning was the sound of the floor boards creaking as the behemoth descended on him. Higginbottom barely managed to turn his head halfway before he felt the blow to the back of his head. He saw colors and spots as he went flying through the air. He probably lost consciousness for a moment, because the next thing he knew, he was lying in the fireplace. His body had instinctively taken on the fetal position, as if bracing itself for more blows. However, Big Slug was not interested in him anymore. In time, Higginbottom realized the man was in the middle of another rant, screaming more gibberish about God's will and punishment.

By then, Higginbottom was either semi-conscious or hyperconscious. His body seemed to go on automatic pilot, acting of its own volition. Now, somehow, he was standing. He had retrieved a poker from a decorative metal pitcher by the fireplace. Next, with strength that could only have come from the devil, he squatted low to steady himself, held the rusty poker before him like a spear, and drove his body at Big Slug.

Big Slug had been about to kick Goodson once more, but then he realized the poker was in his chest. Both he and Higginbottom looked at the thing in amazement. After that, Big Slug stumbled back three steps and collapsed onto the glass coffee table. The noise was like an explosion, so that Higginbottom jumped back. He shielded his face—as if he expected debris and shrapnel to rip through his body. When Higginbottom looked, he saw a piece of glass had become lodged in Big Slug's neck. For about the first five seconds, the blood gushed from the wound; but eventually, it became a steady flow, and then a *trickle*, as the life literally left him. Higginbottom stared at the body from the same faraway place, preparing himself in the event that it rose again, like one of those movie monsters. It was only after about ten seconds of staring at the unmoving body that Higginbottom finally allowed himself to acknowledge Big Slug was dead—and that he had *killed* him. When he did, he stumbled back into the wall and slid down—into the soot of the fireplace.

Higginbottom seemed to sit on the floor for minutes afterward, staring at Big Slug's corpse as the blood dribbled across the floor. It was only when Goodson began to regain consciousness—and to groan from the pain—that Higginbottom came to his senses and rose to help the man. Some of Goodson's ribs were definitely cracked—but both men instinctively knew that calling an ambulance was out of the question. At any rate, there had been more pressing matters, which demanded their full attention. Higginbottom helped Goodson over to the couch—which was of course next to Big Slug's corpse. From there, the old man directed Higginbottom in the grim work that had to be done. In his dazed state, Higginbottom followed the instructions like an automaton. Besides, having something to do was a welcome distraction to his mind.

Following Goodson's instructions, he retrieved a tarp and a chainsaw from the shack in the back yard, along with a rubberized garbage container and a hand truck. He deposited everything in the living room, next to the corpse, and allowed his mind to be blank. Once he severed Big Slug's lower leg with the chainsaw, and tossed it into the garbage container, the rest followed naturally— which was to say, once he crossed that line, there was no going back. It took three cuts to detach Big Slug's entire leg. Since the garbage container was almost full, he placed it on the hand truck and wheeled it outside. Goodson had instructed him to burn the body first. There was to be a bonfire, so Higginbottom left the severed parts in a heap on the far side of the yard, and headed back to the house. As he was leaving, the dog came over and began licking one of the bloody stumps. Higginbottom turned away, willing his mind to be blank and his stomach to be strong.

Yet, he did feel different when he returned to the house. He could not quite place it, but he began to get a sense of it when he went to cut off Big Slug's other leg. With all the coagulated blood, the fabric of Big Slug's pants got caught in the chainsaw. Goodson directed him to retrieve some scissors from the kitchen to remove the pants. He did this, and was about to turn on the chainsaw once more, when he looked down at the leg and noticed a festering wound. Indeed, it was the same wound he had supposedly healed days ago. The entire sequence of events popped into his head again, and he frowned. The flesh around the wound was discolored and puss-laden. In his dazed state, he stared down at it, still not able to understand what the wound *meant*. Had the magic worn off, or had it been nothing more than a shared delusion? Everything seemed possible at that moment, and Higginbottom felt his mind closing down—*crashing* from all the contradictions and possibilities. It was only when Goodson asked him what was wrong that he reflexively started up the chainsaw again and completed his work.

Within half an hour, the dismembered corpse was outside. The dog seemed youthful again, and jumped about excitedly, as if sampling Big Slug's flesh had revived it. After taking out the last load—which consisted of the head and the left arm—Higginbottom returned to the house and helped Goodson outside. There was a pile of firewood by the shack in the back yard. Higginbottom used the hand truck to move the firewood over to the body parts. After pouring half a tank of gasoline over the mass of wood and flesh, Higginbottom retrieved a box of matches from the kitchen and handed it to Goodson. Once the old man lit the bonfire, the dog barked excitedly and jumped about in a fit of joy. On the other hand, the two men stood there silently, mesmerized by the flames and shaken by the reality of what they had done.

Binkowski had absolutely no idea where he was, but all of a sudden, a woman was there. Her body was amazing, and that was the only thing that mattered in this world. A skintight outfit displayed all her assets, so that Binkowski leaned forward hungrily. Now, they were in his bedroom. How did they get there? He had no idea. In fact, he did not care. She was dancing at the moment—gyrating her amazing body. Music was playing—a frenetic song that required her gyrations to increase to the point where he began to worry her ass would explode from too much friction. Now, he was in the bed—waiting and ready for her to come to him. How did he get there? He again did not care. She was at the foot of the bed, doing a sensual striptease that made his sex rock hard. He was practically salivating now, his eyes bulging as she began taking off her top. It was like some kind of string contraption that unraveled as soon as she pulled on it; but to tease him, she giggled and clutched the disconnected strings to her chest to prolong his agony. Presently, she hopped on the bed, onto her knees, and began moving toward him. He was *ready*—

But then, deciding to put him out of his misery, she tossed the remains of her top onto the floor. Her breasts, themselves, were perfect—everything he had dreamed them to be—but it took his mind a few seconds to actually register something that in truth made no sense. It was only when she began straddling him that his mind made the final calculations or connections, and he screamed at the horror of it—

"What's wrong, baby?" she purred.

He could not speak at first, so he raised his trembling finger toward the offense. "There's a...a little arm between your titties," he managed to squeak.

She looked down at the limb nonchalantly. "That's only Alice," she said at last, "—my twin sister."

The only logical response to such a statement was, *"Huh?"* When Binkowski looked again, he saw the little fingers on the hand were actually moving on their own! He shuddered.

Nevertheless, there was a pleasant expression on the woman's face as she looked down at the hand. "We never separated right during gestation," she said with a kind of clinical detachment. Then, still with a far-off smile, she reached down and started playing with the tiny hand. When the hand grasped her finger, she giggled, so that Binkowski jumped.

There was still an expression of horror etched into his face. She looked over at him objectively:

"Don't you like my body otherwise?" she purred now. As she said it, she pulled her finger away from Alice's hand and began fondling her breasts. She started gyrating on his thoroughly flaccid penis as well, hoping to turn him on, but the baby hand was flailing about randomly now, as if searching for the woman's finger. It was the only thing Binkowski could see. The fresh horror of it deepened his disgust, and he shook his head—

"You *really* don't like my body?" she asked again, almost pleading now.

"Yeah, I guess," he said in frustration, but he still could not pull his eyes away from the flailing baby hand. He was about to shake his head again, but—

"What if we did it doggie style?" the woman proposed now. Not giving him time to think, she turned around deftly on the bed, so that her perfect behind faced him. Despite his previous protestations, he was now wearing a slack-jawed expression. She began moving her hips seductively—*slowly*—giving him an unobstructed view of all the contours and recesses of her body. He found himself growing hard again. Damn, with an ass like that, he could definitely forget about baby arms growing out of titties and other craziness! He was *ready* again, and single-minded in his lust.

"Stay like that!" he instructed her as he moved to his knees and positioned himself behind her. He was ready to put in some hardcore sex work for sure—but when he pulled down her flimsy pants, his brain again locked up. He kept staring, trying to make sense of something that *again* made no sense. That was when the eyes on the woman's ass blinked, and the mouth above her ass crack opened, displaying jagged, *messed up* teeth.

"Hi," Alice said, smiling—

Binkowski screamed! Indeed, he screamed so forcefully that it seemed to tear through time and space. His bedroom—and the freakish woman—disappeared, replaced by a dark, blurry world. Yet, even then, the horror would not leave him. He was still screaming. ...And he soon realized someone else's arms and legs were wrapped around his! In his mind, the limbs belonged to Alice: a full complement of arms and legs to drag him into hell with her. Desperate to be free, he began throwing elbows and punches, trying to dislodge himself from Alice's death grip. However, the arms and legs—which had actually lain there passively at first—began to come to life. Elbows to the ribs elicited yelps of pain; and when the limbs started fighting back, Binkowski suddenly found himself on the wrong end of some numbing blows. Terrified, he tried to defend himself—by throwing *more* elbows—but when Jones started cursing, Binkowski suddenly realized he and his roommate were both lying in the shower. By then, Jones' large, powerful hands had begun choking the *crap* out of Binkowski's neck—

"It's me, Cletus!" Binkowski managed to whisper.

Hearing his name, Jones came to his senses and stopped squeezing. Yet, both of them were exhausted and sore as they lay there for a few moments, gasping for air and asking themselves what was going on.

Eventually, it occurred to Binkowski he was actually sitting on Jones' crotch—so he leaped up and rushed to turn on the light. He was panting again, trying to forget where he had been sitting.

Once the light was on, he and Jones stared at one another in the same wide-eyed way. They both seemed to recall the hillbilly at the same time. Bewildered, they instinctively looked around the cramped bathroom, as if searching for him—or as if a clue would be on the soap dish, or lying next to their toothbrushes. When they saw nothing, they looked at one another as if to ask how the *hell* they had gotten back here.

"…Shit," Binkowski said at last, to which Jones nodded, as if to say, "Welcome to the madness, my brother."

Binkowski was still in shock. "What *happened?*" he whispered, as if he feared being overheard by the devil.

Jones groaned, grasping his head. "This is how it happens: you see the hillbilly, then you end up here."

Binkowski was still searching for sense where there was none: "You think something *teleported* us?"

Jones paused and looked at him in the same uneasy way. Eventually, he sighed. "You're asking if something *supernatural* happened?"

"Yeah, I guess," he said, shrugging.

Jones shrugged as well, allowing his mind to return to the thoughts that had been confounding him for a week now. "That hillbilly is the key," he began. "I think he's some kind of…I don't know: a mental trigger, perhaps. Maybe, when we see him, we black out and drive back home—"

"And end up in the shower?" Binkowski said, frowning.

"Yeah," he said, putting up his hands to acknowledge how crazy it sounded. At the same time, it was the only reasonable explanation at this point. Everything else required him to believe things that were even more insane.

Binkowski was still not convinced. "But *why's* this happening?" he pressed his friend.

"I don't know," Jones said in frustration. "That's why I said we have to get to the professor's house. Whatever happened—whatever's causing all this—it happened at his house, and something is keeping us from getting back there."

Binkowski eyed him knowingly: "You're afraid of saying what that thing is."

Jones thought about it before he nodded. He *was* afraid. At the same time, since talking to Artemis, he felt stronger inside—as though she had revived something in his soul. In fact, at the thought of her, something occurred to him, and he looked up at Binkowski excitedly.

"We can get Artemis to drive us to the professor's," Jones announced, "—since she hasn't been...*infected*." (He did not know how to describe what was happening to them, but "infection" was the best his mind could offer.)

Binkowski pursed his lips, thinking about his roommate's suggestion. "...You want us to call your perfect mystery woman?"

"Yeah," Jones said quickly, not detecting the sarcasm in his roommate's tone.

Binkowski was still scrutinizing him. "Didn't it occur to you that she might be a part of this too: another figment of your imagination, or a mental trigger, or whatever you want to call it?"

Jones felt sick to his stomach once he acknowledged the possibility. Even now, he knew nothing about her—except that she was perfect in an unquantifiable way. Her shimmering halo was perhaps the strongest evidence that she had merely been a hallucination, hatched by whoever or whatever was causing all this. Seeing that possibility, he felt dead inside. At the same time, there was only one way to know for sure, so he reached into his pocket and retrieved his phone.

Looking down at the phone, Jones saw he had missed two calls from Artemis. More troublingly, when he looked at the time stamp on the last call—and compared it with the date on the phone—it occurred to him an entire day had passed!

"It's Friday!" he said hoarsely, staring down at the phone. When he looked up, his roommate was looking back at him in the same bewildered way. After Jones got out his phone, Binkowski had retrieved his as well, seeing his mother had called him *six* times. They stared at one another helplessly for a few moments, but this new information only heightened their urgency—and the sense that they *had* to reach the professor's house. Again seeing that Artemis was their best hope, Jones took a deep breath, pressed the button to return her call, and exhaled anxiously as the phone began to ring.

The phone rang three times before Artemis answered. Jones opened his mouth to say something—to apologize or beg her for help, but—

"So, you're still alive, I see," she began, sounding hurt.

Jones winced, knowing he was in the middle of a minefield. In the silence, he thought about what he would say to her. However, there was no way to be circumspect in this situation. At any rate, he knew his mind was not up to it, so he blurted out, "I need you, Artemis. I need your help—if you can come now. I need you to drive me somewhere," he continued cautiously, looking over at Binkowski for guidance and agreement. There was a long silence afterward. "...Artemis?" he said, wondering if the call has been disconnected.

"Yeah," she said, cautiously—since she was still digesting what he had asked and trying to figure out *why* he might have asked it.

"Can you drive us?" he pressed her.

"*Us?*"

"My roommate and I," he clarified.

"You want me to drive the two of you?"

"Yeah."

"Your car broke down?"

He shuffled his feet uneasily, knowing she would continue questioning him until he revealed the full extent of the madness. Yet, he also saw a way to escape for the time being, and he leapt at it frantically:

"I'll tell you all about it when you come over," he said abruptly. He literally held his breath during the long silence, wondering if she would allow herself to be bamboozled by such an obvious ploy.

However, her curiosity seemed to seal her fate. She had been waiting to hear from him all day, wondering where he was and what he was doing. On top of that, she yearned to solve the great mystery she sensed about him—and the only way to do that was to see him. "...Okay," she said at last. "I'll be there in half an hour."

Jones was about to give her directions when she hung up the phone. It was only while he was listening to the dial tone that he recalled she had supposedly been to his apartment before—and that they had made love. The realization left him staring blankly into space. His eyes wandered aimlessly for a moment—until he noticed Binkowski staring at him expectantly. That was when he nodded his head, put away the phone, and said, "She's coming over."

The two roommates went to get ready. Apparently, twenty-one hours had passed since they had last been conscious. What had they been doing all that time? Jones went to his bedroom and looked at himself in the mirror. He needed to shave—and to take a shower—but there was no time for any of that, so he only put on a fresh shirt, along with a fresh coat of deodorant.

Afterwards, the waiting became tortuous. He paced his bedroom a few times before he realized his restlessness would drive him crazy. When his belly growled, the prospect of food brightened his spirits—since eating would be something to *do*.

Upon entering the kitchen, he saw Binkowski was already there, making a sandwich. His roommate gestured to the meat and bread on the plate—as to ask Jones if he was interested—and Jones nodded. Soon, they were devouring the food. At the same time, they were still too restless to take a seat—and too lost in the complexities of their thoughts to speak.

After about ten minutes, they began making their way downstairs. Yet, even when they were outside, they only stood on the curb restlessly, lost in the same insane inner dialogues. Jones noticed his car was parked across the street. A side of him wanted to go over and check it out, but an increasingly irrational side of him worried he would be transported back to the shower if he even *touched* the car.

While he was shaking his head to drive away those thoughts, he noticed Artemis driving up the block. She stopped in front of the building and honked the horn. Since the men only stared at her blankly, she waved to get their attention. Jones nodded at last, but he continued to stare at her with the same combination of hope and fear—as if he suspected she might be a desert mirage. The shimmering halo still surrounded her. Remembering what Binkowski had said—about her being another delusion—he looked over at his friend in the same uneasy way.

"You see her?" he asked flatly. After Binkowski nodded, Jones grunted to acknowledge his friend's response. Then, taking a deep breath, he began making his way over to the car. Binkowski followed him; but by then, he was like a newborn animal in a wasteland, hotwired to follow any large moving object that might keep him safe.

Jones sat in the passenger seat; Binkowski sat in the back. Nobody said a word for at least five seconds after they had entered.

"…Well?" Artemis began, eyeing Jones in her usual suspicious way. "Where we going?"

"Oh," Jones said, coming to his senses, "…to my professor's house."

It was only when Binkowski began putting on his seatbelt that Jones realized he had not introduced his roommate. "This is Ed," he said, looking at Artemis while gesturing over his shoulder." Then, turning to his roommate, "This is Artemis: the mystery woman." He chuckled nervously after he said it, but his joke was flat. In the awkward silence, Binkowski and the woman exchanged greetings; then, perhaps to move past the awkwardness, she put the car in gear and began driving down the block.

"So," Artemis began when they reached the intersection, "where does your professor live?"

"Keep going straight," Jones replied, "—until we get out of town."

She nodded, but then glanced over at him in the same suspicious way. "*Why* am I driving you two again?"

Jones looked back at Binkowski uneasily before he responded. "Well," he began, "we tried to drive there earlier, but we…blacked out."

"Again?" she said, frowning. "You *both* blacked out?"

"Yeah."

"You didn't go to the hospital?"

"No," he said anxiously, wary of where this would lead.

"Why not?"

Jones opened his mouth, but his words faltered. Binkowski took over:

"…Because we don't think it's *medical*."

She was silent for a while. "What do you think it is then?"

Jones inhaled deeply. "We don't know. ….First, it was only me seeing stuff. Back then, Ed was telling me everything you've said—about it being crazy. He told me it was some kind of *delusion* or dream—but then he started seeing stuff too. So, it's *spreading*."

She was frowning again. "*What's* spreading?"

"Whatever I caught a week ago, when I went to the professor's house. We have to get back there—to figure out what it is…but every time I try, I black out…and then wake up in the shower."

"The *shower?*" she said, lost again.

"Yeah…I know it makes no sense," he preempted her protests. "I've woken up in the shower three times now. Ed and I *both* woke up there half an hour ago—after setting out for my professor's house *yesterday*. That's why I didn't answer your calls," he added, seeing an opportunity to make amends. "I don't know where I was…what I was doing…*anything*." When he saw Artemis' face had become contorted into a confused scowl, he added, "Yeah, I know it's crazy. …And the more I try to explain it to you, the crazier it will seem…but you're the only one who can help us now…if you haven't already started seeing stuff."

"Stuff like what?" she asked cautiously.

Here, Binkowski spoke up again: "Stuff like fictional characters coming to life and showing up at your job…exploding before your eyes…stuff like that."

Of course, that was totally meaningless to her, so Artemis only stared ahead blankly, wondering what she had gotten herself into.

Once they were out of town, Jones directed Artemis to the rural road that would take them to the professor's house.

Everyone was silent for a while, as they drove down the deserted road, then Jones looked over at Artemis uneasily. "Something might happen," he warned her. Here, he once again glanced back at his roommate.

"Something like what?" Artemis pressed him.

"Well, when we tried to drive there, we saw a hillbilly."

She instinctively smiled. "A *hillbilly?*"

"I know how it sounds," Jones preempted her again, "but we think"—he again glanced back at Binkowski—"…we think he may be some kind of mental block: a barrier we can't pass…since we've been infected. …And so, that's why we need you: to get us past that point."

Her face was again contorted into a scowl. "…So, *both* of you blacked out while you were driving?" she tried to clarify.

"Yes."

"How did you get back home?"

"I guess we drove back—since I saw my car parked outside."

"So, you're saying you're now *programmed* not to pass a certain point on the road?"

"Yeah."

"…And you're hoping I'm not 'programmed' too?"

Jones nodded.

"So, what if you two black out and try to stop me?"

Jones had not thought of that. He looked back at Binkowski helplessly, hoping his friend would have an answer, but his roommate wore the same deflated expression. Looking out of the window, Jones saw they were about five minutes away from the place where the hillbilly usually appeared—

"Pull over!" he cried as a new idea occurred to him.

The way he had screamed, it was as if they were about to drive over a precipice. Suddenly frantic, she swerved the car over to the side and stamped on the brake. When the car came to a jarring halt, she was panting and terrified. "What is it!" she demanded.

"You have to tie us up or something."

"*What?*" she asked, lost again.

"You have to tie us up—in case we try to stop you."

She was still staring at him confusedly. Then, once she digested what he was saying, an annoyed tinge entered her voice: "Do I look as though I carry rope around with me?"

"Do you have tape or something?" Jones ventured.

She was about to make another snide comment—and perhaps tell them both to go to hell with their craziness—but then she remembered she had some duct tape in the glove compartment. She signed before reaching over to open the compartment. However, once it was open, she did not take out the tape: she merely pointed, as if reluctant to play any part in their craziness.

"There it is," she said dismissively. Besides, a side of her was beginning to wonder if this might be some kind of childish prank. What other reason could there be for them bringing her out into the middle of nowhere? The only other reason that came to mind was that Jones and his friend were serial killers—who intended to take her out into the woods to carry out their mischief. At the thought, she considered calling one of her girlfriends, so that someone would at least know where she was and who she was with. Yet, looking over at Jones now, it occurred to her she could never be afraid of him. She was certain he was *hiding* something, but she was equally convinced he would never *harm* her—

"*You* have to tape us up," Jones said after he had retrieved the tape from the glove compartment. He held it out to her. "Tape our hands behind our backs…and our ankles together."

She looked at each man curiously, wondering where they could possibly be going with all this. Yet, their expressions were so grave that she finally began to consider the possibility that they might be *serious*. Jones was still proffering the tape. She took it and looked down at it anxiously.

"Let's stand outside," Jones was telling Binkowski now. "It'll be easier for her to tape us if we're standing up."

Now that the plan had been set, the men exited the vehicle excitedly. Artemis still sat there with the tape in her hand, but when she looked over and saw the men lining up outside, she sighed and exited the vehicle as well.

The two men stood with their chests pressed against the side of the car—like two apprehended criminals waiting to be frisked. Artemis still wondered where this might all be leading, but she had already come this far, so she sighed, gestured for Jones to get his hands behind his back, and pulled off a strip of tape. There was something mildly erotic about taping them up. She had to use her teeth to rip the tape—and get on her knees to do their ankles.

Once the two men were sitting in the back of the car, she had to lean over them to attach their seatbelts. Looking at them now, she liked the idea that she could have her way with them and they would be powerless to stop her. She smiled momentarily, but then shook her head to drive away the thought.

Since everything was complete, she shut the rear door and got behind the steering wheel. When she turned around to look at them, she found herself smiling once more. In fact, she was now almost certain this had to be some kind of elaborate joke. Why else would anyone go through with all this? Again wondering how far they would take it, she decided to play along for now.

"Where exactly is your professor's house?" she asked Jones.

"Stay on this road for another ten minutes or so. You can't miss the house: it's blue and yellow." Then, as a final warning, "Don't untie us until we reach—no matter what we say or do. ...And make sure we're *ourselves* before you free us."

She was about to ask who else they would be, but their grave expressions conjured an anxious feeling in her, so she nodded her head, turned around, and started up the car.

"Here we go," Jones said when the car started down the road once more. That was the last thing he remembered.

In the dream, or whatever it was, the professor's mom was a dominatrix dressed only in a black leather thong and some thigh-high leather boots that were so tall that they seemed more like stilts. In fact, he had to look up to see her. Her droopy titties dangled from the heavens like strange, misshapen fruit. He was staring up at them with a kind of morbid fascination when she suddenly reared her hand back and slapped the *shit* out of him! His vision became blurry; blotches appeared before his eyes, and a metallic taste filled his mouth—which in time he realized was blood.

His face stung for what seemed an interminably long time. Worse, as he was regaining his bearings, he saw the blurry image of her hand coming toward him again. He tried to duck, but since he was still dazed from the last blow, it was pointless. The hand stuck him so hard that he felt like the left side of his face was on fire—as if the skin were melting off the bones! He barely managed to gasp for air before he saw the hand coming at him again. By then, he *sensed* the hand more than he actually saw it. Knowing he could not duck it, he instinctively tried to put up his hand—to *block* it—but that was when he realized his hands were bound. In fact, his entire body was constrained, so that a feeling of helplessness killed off more of his strength and will. He was ready to surrender—to *cry*, even—as he sensed the hand coming again. He filled his lungs with air, like a drowning man about to go beneath the waves, and screamed, *"Stop!"*

...Somehow, the hand stopped. He waited two or three seconds, still holding his breath, but when he saw the blurry hand was frozen in the air, he finally allowed himself to breathe again—

"Cletus?" a voice called.

He looked toward the voice, his vision still blurry. However, when it occurred to him the voice was Artemis'—and not the professor's mom's—he squinted—

"Cletus, you back?" Artemis said again. Looking up, Jones' vision finally cleared to the point where he could see the concerned expression on her face. Even then, she was *beautiful*. For a moment, it was all he could think. The halo still surrounded her, and she was like an angel.

However, as his mind started working again, he remembered they had set out to reach the professor's house. The car door was open: she was standing outside and leaning into the vehicle. Once she saw he was regaining consciousness, she retreated from the doorway to give him room to breathe. "You all right?" she asked, scrutinizing him closely.

"Yeah," he whispered. He blinked drowsily as he stared up at her. As he regained more of his bearings, he saw he was still in the back seat of the car—and that his limbs were still bound with the duct tape—

But that was when something moved on the other side of him! When he turned his head, he saw Binkowski going into what seemed to be convulsions. In time, he realized the man was only trying to free himself, but his efforts was so ferocious that Jones reflexively tried to flee—

"You back?" Artemis asked Jones again, since he still seemed dazed.

He glanced at her before he looked over at Binkowski again—to perhaps check that the man had not gotten free. Yet, when he looked out of the car window, he saw they were parked in front of the professor's house. It was a modernist glass structure, totally out of character for the rural south. Jones found himself scanning the windows, looking for any sign of life, but the curtains were all drawn and he saw no light. Taking one last deep breath, he turned back to Artemis and nodded to reassure her he was okay.

"How long were we"—he searched for the right word—"*out?*"

She nodded as well—since his question confirmed that he was sane again. "About twenty minutes."

He grunted uneasily, nibbling his lip as he stared off into space. Yet, after a few seconds, Binkowski started stomping his feet against the floor, as if trying to knock a hole in it and escape that way. Once again, Jones stared at him in amazement.

"Was I like that?" he asked.

"Worse," she said with a wide-eyed expression. "I woke you first because I thought you were going to knock the door off or some-thing."

"Damn," he whispered. Then, after thinking about it for a while, he nodded his head gravely and looked back at the house: "Did you see anyone?"

"Nah. I rang the bell, but nobody's home."

"Or maybe nobody's *answering*."

She shrugged to acknowledge the possibility, but she saw a more pressing matter: "Do you want me to call the police or something?" After what she had seen, "or something" seemed to include exorcists and witch doctors. Something extraordinary was definitely happening; some kind of authority had to be consulted—either to administer human laws or to dispense God's justice.

Jones stared at her, sympathetic to the terror stirring in her soul, but he still held onto the belief that he would be able to make sense of all this somehow, now that he was finally here.

"Let's look around first," he proposed. Then, realizing he was still bound, "You can *free* me now."

After Artemis released the seat belt, Jones maneuvered his legs outside the car, so that she could free them. After that, he got out of the vehicle entirely, so she could untie his hands. Once he was free, she stepped back and stood watching him, still fighting to understand what was happening. Jones was flexing his wrists and ankles, trying to get the blood flowing to his limbs again. After a while, he found himself staring at her. Her halo was still there, tempting him to dissolve into its colors. He stared at her helplessly for a moment, before he shook his head to refocus his mind. He looked up at the house, again scanning the windows for any sign of movement, but there was nothing.

At that moment, Binkowski began kicking the front seat. Jones took a deep breath, looked over at Artemis apologetically, and began walking around the car, to get to his friend.

"Did you try to wake him?" he asked her as he walked. She followed him, as if afraid of being left alone again:

"No." Then, seeing a glimmer of humor in the situation, "I only just met him—I didn't feel it was right to smack the shit out of him yet."

Jones nodded, too lost in his own thoughts to even acknowledge the joke.

As soon as he opened the door, Binkowski tried to get out, like a rabid zombie from a movie. Jones stared at him, fascinated. Artemis came over to his side and held his arm. That gesture of trust brightened his spirits—and some deep-seated sense of maleness—so that he looked over at her and smiled.

She nodded, returning a faint smile, then looked back at Binkowski—whose antics had gotten even more frantic.

Jones sighed, nodded to Artemis, so that she would let go of his arm, then he bent down, leaned into the car, and unleashed a brutal pimp slap—a *backhand*—that immediately made Binkowski cease his foolishness.

The right side of Binkowski's face was now deep red. After a few seconds of pure shock, the man blinked drowsily, groaned—since his face was *stinging*—and looked up a Jones with a combination of raw terror and confusion.

"You back with me, Ed?" Jones asked.

Binkowski squinted at him—as if his eyes still could not focus. "Cletus?"

"Yeah."

Binkowski groaned again, still experiencing the ill effects of the pimp slap. Yet, seeing his friend was going to be okay, Jones unfastened the seat belt and pulled him out of the car. Once he was outside, Jones began pulling away the tape.

However, even then, Binkowski stared ahead blankly, still struggling to re-embed himself in this reality.

No real plan was made, but they followed Jones' lead—since he had been there before. He took them over to the front door. First, he rang the bell and knocked. When nobody came to the door, he tried the door knob. It was locked.

It was getting dark. Jones looked up at the sky—as if it would provide inspiration. Something occurred to him: "Let's try the back."

Once again, the other two followed him. Artemis instinctively held his arm again, and Binkowski shuffled behind them groggily.

There was a garage at the side of the house. Jones looked into the window and saw the outlines of a car, but it was too dark inside to see any details, so they moved on.

After they turned the corner of the house, there was a back door. Jones tried the knob, not even bothering to knock first, and it opened. The inside of the house was dark and imposing. A stomach-churning stench wafted out, so that they all turned their faces away in disgust. It did not exactly smell like death—only *filth*. As Jones was about to step across the threshold, Artemis pulled his arm back.

"Cletus," she pleaded with him, "let's call the *police*."

He stared at her, acknowledging the wisdom of what she was saying, but he felt they had come too far to wait on the police now. Besides, they had not exactly seen anything to *report*. He took a deep, thoughtful breath: "Let's check it out first." Then, seeing their reluctance, "You guys can wait outside if you want."

The accusation that he was afraid stirred Binkowski from his stupor, and he spoke up—as if to defend his manhood. "I'm coming too," he declared.

When Jones and Binkowski turned their gazes to Artemis, she knew she was trapped—since there was no way she was going to wait outside by herself! Seeing she had no choice, she sighed and nodded to say she would come as well.

Jones returned her gesture, turned back around, and entered

the house. As he entered, he flicked the light switch by the door. They were in the kitchen now, and it was *filthy*: cupboards were open; various containers were strewn on the table and floor—and several of the containers had rotting food in them. Flies were in the air, and there were chicken bones on the floor. Looking down, he saw maggots wriggling in one of the containers. He grimaced.

The filth explained the stench, but not what had happened. He looked around again, searching for clues. Through an archway on the far side of the kitchen, he could see the dark outlines of the dining room—and the stairs that led to the second floor. There did not seem to be any immediate threats in the other chamber, but something about the darkness made him shudder inside.

He took a deep breath to refocus his mind—and shake off whatever chills had a hold of him. In the kitchen, to his left, there was an open doorway. Directly across from the doorway—there was a closed door, which he knew opened to a small bathroom. He was not entirely sure *how* he knew this, but then he had a flashback of that night: of being in the darkness and looking at the beautiful light. That scene, he remembered suddenly, had taken place in the basement. Indeed, to the right of the bathroom, there was a staircase that led to the basement. His stomach clenched at the realization—

But at that moment, a huge rat scurried from one of the containers and ran toward one of the lower cupboards, where it disappeared into a crevice. They had all instinctively jumped back at the movement; Artemis yelped, but managed to keep her voice low by putting her hand over her mouth. In the aftermath of the terror, they all stared at the crevice, as if waiting for more creatures to pour out.

When more vermin did not appear, Binkowski and Artemis allowed themselves to relax. Yet, Jones grunted in frustration—since he could not figure out what had happened here—and what they should be *doing*. The only thing he knew for sure was that something was definitely *wrong*. The professor was fastidious to the point of almost being a germaphobe. There was no way he would be living like this. However, if the professor really had gone on sabbatical, then maybe a squatter had broken in. In fact, from the extent of the mess, an entire colony of squatters could be here. Jones had wanted to call to the professor—to see if the man would answer—but now he feared the squatters (or some other dark, hidden enemy) would hear. Indeed, looking around, Jones realized some of the food seemed *fresh*—as if the perpetrators had it flung to the floor a few minutes ago.

Suddenly alert to the danger, he realized the best course of action was to investigate the house *stealthily*—and see who was there before he played his hand. It occurred to him he needed some kind of weapon. Seeing a wooden rolling pin on the counter top, he picked it up. Binkowski followed Jones' lead and picked up a broom that had been leaning against the wall. Jones looked back at him as he tested the heft of it and assessed its usefulness as a weapon. This was rural Georgia, and practically every house had a gun, so chances were high that their stick weapons were going to be useless. However, when Binkowski nodded to say he was ready, Jones gestured for them to follow him into the dining room.

Dusk had fallen, but they did not want to alert anyone to their presence by turning on the lights. It was probably a silly precaution—since they had already ringed the doorbell and knocked on the front door. Either way, they crept through the darkening rooms like thieves. Jones remembered most of the layout from his visit, and the things he did not remember—like the placement of the living room—he attributed to the fact that it was dark.

The house was spacious and eerie—like something out of a horror movie. The rooms were unkempt, with cushions out of place and a few items left on the floor, but that was nothing compared to the squalor of the kitchen.

There was a bathroom beneath the staircase, but nothing was out of place when they opened the door. At the bottom of the staircase, there was a door that made Jones' stomach clench—since he remembered it was the son's room. When he opened the door, he expected to see rock band posters and the rest of the teenage paraphernalia, but the layout was completely different from what he remembered. By the dwindling light outside the window, Jones saw the bed had been made, so he doubted anyone had actually slept there in a while. He frowned, wondering about his memories, but the rest of the house still had to be checked, so he closed the door and motioned to the others to let them know they were heading upstairs.

There were two bedrooms upstairs, but they were both empty. In fact, the second story seemed cleaner—as though nobody had been up there all week. The beds had all been made, and the bathrooms seemed unused. More importantly, there was no evidence that someone else was in the house. They had heard no other noises—and none of the lights had been turned on. Whatever had happened, the kitchen had been the epicenter of it—and the person or persons who had done it did not seem to be there now.

In time, Jones signaled the others to follow him back downstairs—to the kitchen. Even though they had seen no signs that someone else was there, they still crept through the house, taking pains not to tread too heavily on the floor boards. The kitchen light was of course still on, and the back door was still open.

Artemis and Binkowski looked up at Jones once they were back in the kitchen, amongst the filth. Artemis was about to ask him what they were going to do next, but then her eyes came to rest on the open doorway that led to the basement. She gestured with her chin, and the two men looked in that direction. As he recalled the scenes from the basement, Jones had a sick feeling in the pit of his stomach. Unconsciously, he had avoided going down there—even though it should have been the first place he checked.

The only thing to do now was go down there and investigate. Jones made sure he was still holding the rolling pin—in fact, he looked down at his hand to check—then he nodded to the others and began walking toward the doorway.

Beyond the open doorway, there was a landing; beyond that, there was the door to the small bedroom; and to the right of the bathroom door, there was the flight of stairs that led down to the basement. Everything was cast in darkness. As Jones reached the open doorway, he remembered there was a chain hanging from the ceiling. He pulled it, so that a light bulb came on, brightening the stairs. However, at the very bottom of the staircase, where the light could not reach, there was impenetrable darkness once more. Indeed, the darkness down there seemed *thicker*, and a strange feeling of dread came over him—as if the darkness were a barrier to another world, and he would lose himself forever if he stepped into it.

He paused on the top of the staircase; but once again concluding his only option was to move forward—no matter what happened—he took a deep breath and began descending the stairs. He raised the rolling pin as he walked, as if he expected something to spring from the darkness at any moment. The floor boards cried out like a bag of cats being drowned, so that Jones grimaced for the first few steps. However, again figuring it was best to rush headlong into whatever was coming, he practically ran down the last few steps, as if he was hoping to catch any hidden monsters unawares.

There was a switch at the bottom. His mind was blank by then, operating more on instinct and fear than thought. He flicked the switch and stood there panting as he scanned the space. In his dazed state, his eyes merely roamed the chamber, not really digesting what was there. After a while, he made out some old furniture and some boxes…but there was no magical light—and nothing to suggest his recollections from a week ago had been anything more than madness.

When he looked back, the others were lingering at his shoulders, scanning the dimly lit chamber. While they were all relieved that no monsters seemed to be lurking down there, the empty house raised more questions than it answered. Deflated, Jones turned and began ascending the basement steps. The others watched his retreating form for a moment, then they followed him wordlessly.

Once they were back in the kitchen, they looked at one another as if hoping someone would have a breakthrough. Since Jones had become their de facto leader, the other two focused their attention on him.

"What do you want to do now?" Artemis asked. She had again kept her voice low—even though they had seen no one. He thought about it, but then put up his hands to say he had no idea. The other two nodded; and for a while, they all stood there with their heads bowed, deep in thought.

"…Well, I've got to use the bathroom," Binkowski said at last, breaking the silence. He looked toward the living room, and the bathroom they had seen under the stairs. However, there was a deep darkness about the house now, and a cowardly voice pointed out that he could urinate outside, behind one of the bushes.

Jones seemed to be reading his thoughts. "There's a bathroom right there," he said, pointing toward the doorway that led to the basement. They had left the light on in the stairway, so the illumination was encouraging—like a night light to a frightened child.

Binkowski nodded and began walking in that direction, but his second step was into some greenish, rotting goo. He stopped and grimaced as he looked down at the mess on the bottom of his shoe. However, noticing a hand towel lying on the ground, amongst the clutter, he wiped his shoe on it and continued on.

In the meantime, Jones had gone back to eying Artemis' shimmering halo. He stared at her in the same helpless way, wondering, as always, what it all meant—and how she might be connected to all this craziness. Artemis was about to ask about getting something to eat when Binkowski stepped onto the landing at the top of the stairwell, and opened the bathroom door.

The moment he did, he leaped back in terror—but as he was on the landing, he tripped over the step and collapsed onto the kitchen floor. Jones and Artemis turned at the commotion—and jumped back as well when they saw the thing sitting on the commode.

On first glance, the creature seemed like some kind of ape beast: what you'd get if an orangutan bred with a Neanderthal. Artemis instinctively grabbed Jones' arm again; but as they all looked closer, they saw the creature was slumped over as if dead. Its head was leaning against the wall of the cramped bathroom, and its body was limp.

From where he was sitting on the floor, Binkowski leaned forward out of curiosity—to see if the creature might really be dead—

But that was when the thing's head jerked up!

Everyone in the kitchen screamed! The thing's bloodshot eyes swept the room—as if trying to decide who might be the tastiest. Since Binkowski was the closest one to the creature, he realized he was in the most danger—especially when the thing fixed its eyes

on him and licked its chapped lips. Binkowski tried to scamper
back, but his hand slipped on the same mystery goo from before.
By then, the creature had leaped up from the commode, giving
them a full frontal view of its wrinkly pink penis—and the thick,
black forest of pubic hair that surrounded it. Binkowski and the
others cried out again—but that only seemed to enrage the creature
further, as if their screams had been a challenge to its dominance.
The thing went to charge—to reestablish dominance or whatever
its motive was—but since something was wrapped around its lower
legs, it tripped, banged its head against the door frame, and collapsed
onto the landing like a sack of rocks. For at least five seconds afterward, nobody said a word—or *moved*—and the only sound was
their terrified gasps for air.

The Colchester estate was like a graveyard now. After Colchester
III's meltdown with his son this morning, he had retreated to his
private chambers. In fact, no one had heard a peep out of him since
he returned from his (unsuccessful) mission to find and butcher
his son. The guards debated going to check on him—since suicide
was a very real possibility, now that his empire was crumbling
around him. The hip-hop community could forgive almost any
transgression—rape, murder, thievery...it even *celebrated* some of
those transgressions as badges of honor against "the man's" rules
and oppression—but consensual male-male homosexuality was
grounds for instant excommunication from The Church of Thug
Niggerism. Some of the staff were already considering where to
send their resumes. While the more empathetic ones were worried
their boss might harm himself during this moment of disgrace,
they also worried that he might *pounce* on them if they ventured
too close. In their eyes, Don Cole now had mystical powers of

seduction over black men. If a hardened gangsta like Nigga Nutt could succumb to Don Cole's charms, then ordinary brothers like them might be susceptible as well; and in hard times like these, brothers had to protect their asses at all costs....

The mansion's control room had a console with about a dozen security screens. In theory, at least two guards were always posted there, twenty-four hours a day; but in reality, they were usually goofing off or snoozing on the job. Given the unfortunate events of the day—with a camera crew able to get to the front door without any of the guards noticing—they were extra vigilant now. Rather, there had been a *renewed* sense of vigilance after Don Cole screamed at them and threatened to send them back to the projects. Now, with the day's excitement dying down, the two guards in the control room were watching one of those reality shows—about high maintenance women whose lives revolved around spending money and flaunting their fake breasts.

The two guards were the same ones who had picked up Rasmussen that day—and they were again dressed in the dark suits that had become a trademark of Don Cole's entourage. In order to fulfil their duty, they glanced up at the security monitors from time to time—but mostly they made suggestive jokes about the women on the TV, and made plans for what they would do after Don Cole's empire came to an end.

There was a coffeemaker in the corner of the control room— and a small bathroom through a side door—since, in theory, the guards were never supposed to leave their duties. Beginning to feel drowsy, one of the guards yawned and stretched before he got up and shuffled over to the coffeemaker.

That was when the buzzer at the front gate rang. The guards glanced at one another uneasily before their gazes went to the security monitor for the front gate. Some kind of delivery van was parked there...no, it was an armored truck. A middle-aged white man was standing at the gate, dressed in one of those ill-fitting security guard uniforms. There was an off-putting demeanor about him. For whatever reason, he was glaring into the camera as if he wanted to kill somebody. Reflexively, his hand went to his gun as he waited, and a kind of Clint Eastwood squint entered his eyes. Don Cole's guards again glanced at one another, then the one who was still sitting at the console pressed the button for the intercom.

"What you want?" he demanded.

Seeing everything was under control, the guard by the coffee-maker continued pouring, but he kept glancing back at the monitor.

"The money's here," Clint Eastwood said via the intercom. He gestured over his shoulder—toward the truck—as he squinted up at the camera.

The guard at the console again pressed the button on the intercom, and leaned forward to speak. *"What* money?"

"This *is* Don Cole's house, right?"

"Yeah," the guards answered in unison. The one who had been pouring coffee began walking back to the console—

"I have your delivery of five hundred thousand dollars."

Don Cole's guards again looked over at one another, their mouths gaping. The one who had been holding the intercom button leaned forward again, "Don Cole ordered it?"

"Yes, sir," Clint Eastwood said, but his tone meant, "Who the *fuck* else?"

There was another long silence.

"You still there?" Clint Eastwood asked, more annoyance creeping into his voice.

"Yeah," the guard holding the button said, still in shock.

"We'll inform Don Cole," the guard with the coffee added. At that, the other guard released the intercom button and they stared at one another again in the silence.

Since Binkowski was still the closest one to the creature—and the one who would be in immediate danger if the thing leapt up again—he was the first to come to his senses. He clambered to his feet and took a few precautionary steps back. He glanced over his shoulder—at Jones and Artemis—once he felt he was a safe enough distance away from the creature. In fact, they all stared at one another again, searching for some clue of what on earth was going on. There was of course no sense to be made of it, so they eventually refocused on the crumpled mass of hair on the landing. Jones and Artemis stepped to Binkowski's side—as if that were the established safe distance.

"You think it's dead?" Artemis whispered, looking up at Jones. However, Jones was frowning now. Something about the graying thatch of hair on the creature's head seemed vaguely familiar. He found himself moving over to the landing, his mind dazed as he struggled to accept what his eyes were seeing. There was a gash over the creature's right eye; but at this close distance, the outlines of a normal human body became discernable. In fact, when Jones finally allowed himself to acknowledge that the creature was his professor, his eyes grew wide, and he bent over to check. The man's hair was wild; his beard had grown out, and his body was covered with what Jones guessed was a week's worth of muck… but that was definitely his professor.

Since Jones now seemed more stunned than terrified, Binkowski and Artemis came up to his side. In time, they too recognized the outlines of a normal human body, and they frowned.

"You *know* him?" Binkowski asked Jones now.

Jones nodded his head faintly before he whispered, "Yeah…it's my professor."

Startled, the other two stared down at the nude, hairy thing on the landing. Artemis was the first one to pay attention to the mass of fur around the man's lower legs. Upon closer inspection, she realized it was a costume. The professor had zipped it down to use the bathroom, and when Artemis realized it was a mascot outfit, she gasped.

"Isn't he that *Roadkill* guy," she whispered as if she feared waking him up, "...that *maniac*."

Jones' frame stiffened once he realized what she was saying, and they all leaned in further, to get a better look.

One of Colchester's guards was waiting at the door when the armored truck stopped in front of the building. The other guard had stayed in the control room to oversee the security console.

Clint Eastwood and another armed guard emerged from the truck. The other man carried a shot gun, his hand on the pump in case his services were required. The man's head was totally bald— but with a mass of zits on it, as if someone had dropped a bee hive on it. Zit Head stayed by the truck, looking on grimly with his shotgun at the ready, while Clint Eastwood continued on. As he neared the entrance, Clint Eastwood looked up at Colchester's guard with a grimace that was probably his version of a greeting. The guard jutted out his chin in response, and they glared at one another—like a gang banger and a skinhead confronting one another in the prison yard.

Clint Eastwood was walking up the stairs now, carrying a briefcase in one hand and a clipboard in the other. Colchester's guard looked down at the briefcase, marveling that half a million dollars could be kept in such a small container. For a moment, his mind went through the permutations of robbing the man—like in the good old days—but, as if reading his mind, Zit Head shifted his weight slightly and raised the nozzle of the gun to get the guard's attention. Thrown off balance by that casual threat of violence,

Colchester's guard moved aside and let Clint Eastwood enter the building.

Clint Eastwood was all business, ready to get out of there as soon as possible—as if the place smelled of cabbage and toe jam. "I'll need Don Cole's signature," he announced after taking a few steps into the house. The guard was walking up to him when a voice came from the top of the staircase:

"I'll be right down, Puddin'."

Clint Eastwood and the guard looked up. The moment they did, they froze. Don Cole—or, more precisely, a freakish caricature of Don Cole—was now descending the staircase. The caricature was wearing a flowery robe, which was partially open in the front, revealing his pot belly and pink underwear that looked suspiciously like panties. In fact, Colchester's purplish balls poked through at the bottom, and when the men at the bottom of the staircase saw this, they groaned and stepped back. On top of everything, the caricature was wearing mascara and pink lip gloss. There was an unsettling daintiness to his movements as he descended, and the men at the bottom of the staircase found themselves staring down at the floor or off into space: anything to avoid making eye contact.

The caricature was like a bad actor trying to carry out a role he was totally unsuited for. Like most bad actors, he compensated by going overboard. His gestures were grand and ridiculous—and strangely terrifying to the men at the bottom of the staircase. At the same time, flamboyantly gay men, by definition, were probably always overdoing it, so the caricature's antics were probably appropriately inappropriate…depending on one's perspective.

The caricature was standing on the final step now; the men at the bottom were still avoiding eye contact—

"What you want me to sign, sweetie?" the caricature said.

Clint Eastwood roused himself from the shock and stepped forward. He looked at the caricature's chest as he spoke, neither wanting to look too high nor too low. He handed over the clipboard he was holding in his left hand:

"Sign on the dotted line," he said too loudly—as if he had to force words out of his throat.

In the meanwhile, Colchester's guard stood by the side, staring at his boss in bewilderment. Looking down, he saw the man was wearing high heels—but since they were made for a woman with much smaller feet, the caricature's gnarled toes poked out of them like half-chewed sausages. The guard looked away.

By then, the caricature had signed the form and handed it back. The guard took it and extended the briefcase. When the caricature took it and winked at the man, Clint Eastwood stared back with stunned horror. The caricature did not seem to notice—or to care— as he began walking back up the staircase. As the men looked on, they realized the caricature was swaying his hips in a manner that was supposed to be seductive; but of course, it was only grotesque.

Luckily for Clint Eastwood, that was when he remembered there was no longer a reason for him to be there. Coming to his senses, he looked over at Colchester's guard with a slightly sympathetic, mostly mocking smile—as if to say "Good luck, you dumb bastard." Then, as he turned and walked toward the door, he chuckled softly.

The guard glared at him for a moment, glanced at the retreating form of his boss, then he shuddered and went to close the front door.

…It was all too surreal. When Jones and the others did speak, it was minimal; most of time, they worked silently, deep in thought as they tried to figure out things that refused to make sense.

Jones asked Binkowski to administer first aid on the professor. They had spotted some bandages in the bathroom upstairs, so Jones went to fetch them. They felt free to turn on the house lights now, no longer afraid of squatters and other human threats. Rather, the thing they had to fear seemed supernatural—or at least beyond normal human comprehension.

After Jones returned with the bandages and some disinfectant, Artemis proposed calling an ambulance. Binkowski seemed willing, but did not think the professor was in any immediate danger. As for Jones, he still felt he needed to solve this puzzle on his own—in order to regain his sanity. He felt this was a crucial test for him; and after all he had been through, he definitely did not want the police or doctors taking away the single best clue of what was happening to them. When he looked up from his thoughts, the other two were staring at him expectantly.

He looked over at Binkowski and gestured to the professor: "Can you wake him?"

By then, Binkowski had finished applying the bandage. He shrugged before shaking the man's shoulder—but the professor remained unresponsive. "Maybe we should let him rest?" he said at last.

Jones nodded. "We should probably put him to bed then?"

"What do you mean, 'we'?" Binkowski said, sardonically. "I draw the line at carrying naked dudes."

Jones smiled and gestured for Binkowski to move from the stairwell. The professor definitely needed a bath! He smelled like stale bar-b-cue sauce and deep fried, *oily* funk: the stench you'd get if someone had tried to fry a dumpster with a homeless man in it. Jones held his breath—or, at least tried to breathe shallowly—as he carried the professor upstairs. He considered taking the man straight to the bath tub, but deposited him on the bed instead. Since the costume was still around the professor's ankles, he was still technically nude. To avoid having to make any decisions now,

Jones covered the man's nakedness with the bedspread: out of sight, out of mind....

Once that was done, they all stood about the bed, staring down at the professor. There was still no sense to be made of it, and Artemis looked at Jones uneasily again:

"What do you want to do *now?*" she asked once more.

Jones took a deep breath. "I guess let him sleep...then talk to him when he wakes up."

Artemis pursed her lips, thinking it through. "Maybe we should tie him up, too," she proposed, "—the way I did with you guys."

Jones nodded and looked over at her appreciatively—since her suggestions were always logical. When he remembered seeing some tape in the kitchen, he told them to wait there while he headed downstairs.

It was getting dark by the time Higginbottom was finished mopping the floor and clearing away all signs of the afternoon's activities. By then, the dying embers of the bonfire had produced an eerie glow in the back yard. The sickening odor of burnt human flesh was still in the house and his clothes and *pores*—but between pure exhaustion and shock, his mind registered only bits and pieces of what was going on around him.

After the work was done, he stripped off the bloody clothes in the back yard, tossed them onto the embers and poured on some more gasoline to make sure they burned. He used the hose in the yard to clean himself, then he put on some old clothes Goodson had laid out for him.

As for Goodson, the old man had been resilient for his age. After taking some painkillers, he had cooked their dinner. Higginbottom had wanted to leave right away—to return to Atlanta and make sure he left no evidence at Big Slug's place—but Goodson had insisted he eat first. Now, they were sitting silently at the dinner table, lost in their own horrors and revelations. Higginbottom ate but did not *taste* the food. On the few occasions when Goodson did talk, Higginbottom's mind glossed over the actual words. So, for the most part, they sat there wordlessly, until the plates were empty. In truth, Higginbottom felt as though there was a hollow place within him now: that he could sit there for hours, stuffing his mouth and stomach, yet would never be full….

When Higginbottom was getting into Big Slug's truck, Goodson handed him a sheet of paper with his phone number on it. Higginbottom nodded and put it in his shirt pocket, promising to call; but even as he did it, he knew he would never see the old man again. What had happened here tonight was not the kind of thing people had reunions to reminisce about. In fact, for their own safety, it was best if nobody ever figured out the connection between them. Nobody could ever know he and Big Slug had been there. As long as no one followed any bread crumbs to Goodson's doorstep, Higginbottom and Goodson would be safe. All they had to do was make sure Big Slug's existence faded into the ether. That would probably not be too hard, given the lifestyle the man had led. More importantly, if Higginbottom managed to remove all traces of his visit to Big Slug's house, then he would probably be safe—even if the police conducted an investigation. He went over a checklist of everything he needed to clean or get rid of. Big Slug's computer seemed to be the key—since the man had searched for Goodson's address on it. There was also the chance one of the neighbors had seen him and Big Slug together, but the only thing he could do at this point was hope nobody had gotten a *good* look at him—and that the police would not put in too much effort into the investigation…if it even came to that….

Soon, Higginbottom was driving down the dark, deserted road, dressed in another man's clothes, driving another man's car, and wondering where it was all going to end.

His mind gravitated to his ex-wife, conjuring images of their first date. It had been an unimaginative affair with dinner and a movie. She had been grumpy and demanding, and he had been clumsy and shy. In retrospect, they had both been fools who had lacked the courage to realize they had no business being together. At best, they had tolerated one another over the years, until she put an end to the farce. Strangely enough, he found himself smiling now as he stared out at the road; and to his astonishment, he realized all the bitterness was gone from him now. It was the first time in five years he had thought about her without resentment. Without the bitterness in his soul, he felt lighter—so that he sat up straighter in the seat.

Yet, in the same way that his loveless marriage had dragged on too long because he lacked the courage to end it, he saw the last few days as proof of a deep-seated personality flaw. Remembering the piece of paper Goodson had given him—with the man's phone number—Higginbottom took it out of his shirt pocket and tossed it out of the window, into the darkness. He also threw away the sheet of paper with the directions. Whatever happened from now on, he swore he would be *decisive*—and act without the sentimentality and self-deception that had plagued him for most of his life. Unconsciously, he nodded to himself, and pressed down on the accelerator, in order to reach his destination.

It was a few minutes to ten when Higginbottom reached Big Slug's neighborhood. He parked the car a few blocks away from the house, and walked the remainder of the way—since he did not want to drive up to the house and alert the neighbors. His plan was to sneak in, do what he had to do, then sneak out before morning. Given some of the dumb-looking bastards he had seen on his walks of Big Slug's neighborhood, he probably had nothing to worry about—since half of them looked like they couldn't even remember their own names. At the same time, it was better to be safe than sorry. On the evening news, it was always that skinny drug fiend you didn't notice sleeping on the porch who ended up being the key eyewitness. When a drug fiend was buzzed, he of course couldn't remember *shit*—but a drug fiend in *search* of a buzz was like Sherlock Holmes, able to remember cryptic clues and solve impenetrable mysteries....

Higginbottom kept looking about anxiously; after walking half a block, it occurred to him he was walking like someone who was "skulking" about the neighborhood. He told himself to relax—and to walk naturally. To settle his mind, he went over the plan in his head and told himself everything would be okay—but he still almost screamed like a little girl when a cat jumped from a hedge and ran across the street. He stood there hyperventilating, proud of himself for suppressing the scream, but well aware he needed to calm the hell down.

He took a deep breath and again went over the plan: he would walk around the house and enter through the back—since it would be foolish to linger beneath the porch lights, where the lurking drug fiend could see him and report him to the police later....

Everything was settled in his head now, but the moment he turned into the driveway, he froze! A car was parked there. ...Not *any* car: it was the one he had woken up in four days ago. Straining his eyes in the darkness, he saw a shadowy figure behind the steering wheel. His eyes widened at the realization, but he still could not *move*—

The car door opened. Cassiopeia's leather-clad form emerged—
yet all he could do was stand there, terrified out of his wits for a
reason he could not quite articulate. She walked up to him in the
same authoritative way. In time, it occurred to him she was talking.
She had stopped in front of him and said something. He squinted
at her, willing himself to hear, but all he deciphered was something about being naughty. She turned and began heading back
to the car. As she did so, she turned her head and spoke over her
shoulder:

"There's work to be done, Mr. Higginbottom, so make haste."

A side of him was relieved his ears and brain were actually work-
ing again. Yet, he was still overcome by the same unnamable terror.
He opened his mouth feebly, his heart thumping wildly in his chest.
Even now, he could feel his will eroding again—and he *panicked*.

That was when his soul rebelled against returning to whatever
madness Cassiopeia had in store for him. Once he'd regained enough
of his faculties to actually walk, he took a precautionary step back.

"No," he said at last. That first word was said meekly, but when
she stopped and looked back at him with genuine surprise, he filled
his lungs and said, "No, I'm not going." His voice was resolute
now—strangely calm, despite the thumping in his chest.

She stared at him as if he had been using a remote Tibetan dialect.
Needing to confirm she was talking to the right person, she stepped
up to him—almost cautiously—and stood staring at his face. Once
she seemed to confirm he had the right face, she looked at the
rest of him—his clothes and shoes—like she was searching for the
vital clue that would reveal him as an impostor.

"…What did you say?" she asked, frowning.

He took another deep breath: "I'm not going."

She took a step back, as if she needed to look at him from another perspective. "Why not?"

His mind flashed to Big Slug's dismembered corpse lying in Goodson's yard. His heart rate shot up again, but he shook his head to chase away the panic. Then, to answer her question, "There's something I have to take care of…in the house."

Once again, she seemed genuinely surprised.

Her posture straightened and she pursed her lips. "You're saying something in this house is more important than your duty to me?" Her voice was low and menacing.

"Cassiopeia…" but his voice trailed off. He kept his mouth open, but no other words came out—

"I understand fully," she said cryptically. "Come this way then," she said, grabbing his arm and pulling him toward the car. He tried to protest, but her grip was firm—and, in a strange way, he was curious about what she would do. His life depended on getting rid of the evidence in the house, so he knew there was no way he would leave with her now. This reassured him—even as she pulled him over to the car. He thought she was going to try to force him into the passenger seat, but she instead brought him to the rear of the vehicle. Now, it was his turn to be confused—especially when she left him and went to retrieve something from the driver's side of the car.

She was only gone for an instant; on the way back, she began, "God sees all, Mr. Higginbottom—and *knows* all." Her voice was calm and matter-of-fact. He stood there numbly, staring at her. Since she had brought him to the rear of the car, he thought she had gone to fetch the keys to open the trunk. Instead, as she neared him, she produced a box of matches. She took out one of the match sticks and held it up dramatically. "Those who trust in God will always be able to count on his protection," she reassured him. Here, she paused for an instant, perhaps waiting to see if he understood. He of course had no idea where she was going with all this;

but to push things along, he found himself nodding his head. That seemed to reassure her, because she nodded as well.

"God forgives *all* transgressions, Mr. Higginbottom," she continued, "—even momentary lapses of faith." As she said these last words, she struck the match and flung it to the ground. The ground must have been soaked with gasoline or something, because a fire immediately roared to life! Either that, or it was some kind of demonic miracle. He jumped back, shielding his eyes and face from the flames; but in seconds, the fire climbed the side of the house and was dancing on top of the roof. Higginbottom stood there in shock—until Cassiopeia tapped him gently on the arm and said, "I suggest you get in the car now, Mr. Higginbottom."

Coming to his senses—or succumbing to a new sense of awe and terror—he ran over to the passenger door and was waiting in the vehicle before Cassiopeia entered and turned the key in the ignition.

Now, they were driving down the street. He twisted his body in the seat, so that he could look at the house. The entire structure was ablaze—as if it had been marinating in gasoline for weeks. He asked himself if he had smelled gasoline while in the driveway, but he knew his mind was too frazzled to remember. He took a deep breath now, trying to see if he detected gasoline in the air— or on her clothes—but he did not even smell smoke....

When he turned back around in the seat, there was a distraught expression on his face—as if he realized his soul was damned, and that there was nothing he could do about it—

"Now then, Mr. Higginbottom," Cassiopeia began as they left the block—and the inferno—behind them, "it seems as though I have to reestablish some discipline in our relationship."

As he sat there staring at her uneasily, he realized his body and mind suddenly felt light. Before he even had time to panic at the thought of losing himself completely, he felt like he was hovering far above his body. The only thing he could see was a tiny speck that he could barely recognize as himself. He went to call out to himself; but the next moment, the speck was lost in the nothingness; and in those final moments of consciousness, everything was dark and still.

At the Colchester estate, the overnight shift of guards had come in about an hour ago. One, a self-declared "old school cat"—or simply, Old Cat to his friends, was in his early sixties with a huge Afro. The other one was nineteen, and went by the nickname "Niggatoni"—since he supposedly aspired to be a chef (or at least loved pasta) and Niggatoni sounded like rigatoni. Plus, his name was actually Tony, so the nickname was cleaver in a stupid way—if that was even possible....

Anyway, it was a little before midnight now, and the funeral atmosphere still pervaded the house. At the shift turnover, the guards had been in agreement that Don Cole was finished. Nigga Nutt, from all media reports, had gone into hiding. Nigga Fross—that is, Colchester IV—was still missing; and as he was a minor, some of the guards were concerned. At the same time, the consensus was that the entire melodrama was white folks' business, and that the only thing to be done was hold on here for as long as Don Cole's money lasted. Their best guess was that the money would be gone in a matter of weeks or days—especially after the guards from the day shift revealed what they had seen earlier. Now that Don Cole had come out of the closet and ripped the door off the hinges, there was no going back. It was over, and they all accepted it.

Truth be told, after the first two guards left, Niggatoni and Old Cat had a long discussion about what they could steal from the house—or what they could purchase on the expense account before the credit card company canceled it. The vultures would be circling soon, so the jackals had to gorge themselves while they could.

Presently, the two guards were in the control room, watching one of those sports highlight shows where the announcers screamed semi-clever catch phrases as athletes scored and racecar drivers crashed and boxers beat the crap out of one another. The guards stared at the screen silently, their minds on more pressing matters. In fact, they were both getting drowsy by then. Niggatoni was about to yawn when a voice behind them suddenly boomed, *"Toodle-doo!"*

Both guards almost fell out of their seats as they swung around! It was the caricature of Don Cole. The guards of course had not seen him yet—since they were the new shift. They stared. The caricature now had on neon green stretch pants. Old Cat recognized the pants from an incident about a month ago. Don Cole had picked up a young hoochie at a club and brought her home. Unfortunately, things had gone downhill quickly when she gulped down a bottle of Colchester's one hundred year scotch. He had gone to the bathroom to freshen up; when he came back, she had been lying naked on the bed, draining the last of the scotch as if it were Kool-Aid. That had been an outrage to a connoisseur like Colchester, and he had gone into a rage, almost flinging her off the balcony. The guards had had to come to her rescue, and carry her off before he strangled her. In all that chaos, the pants had been left behind.

The guards stared at the caricature, speechless and suddenly overcome by the same budding terror as the guards from the first shift—

"I need to be driven somewhere," the caricature began in a sing-song voice, resting his hand on his hip. He was carrying the briefcase from earlier; over his shoulder, there was a sequined purse that

Old Cat surmised Scotch Girl or some other unfortunate hoochie had left behind. Yet, the two guards were so stunned that they *still* only sat there staring—

"*Hello!*" the caricature said in exasperation.

"Yessir!" the guards said, coming to their senses and standing up. The caricature held out the briefcase daintily for one of them to take. Niggatoni took it while Old Cat rushed to the garage.

In truth, one of them should have stayed behind to man the control room—especially since it was highly likely one of the gossip shows would try to sneak someone else onto the property—but the caricature's impatience left them scurrying around like roaches on the floor.

After exiting the control room, Old Cat turned to the left and headed to the garage; Niggatoni was going to follow him, but after a few steps, the caricature released a petulant, "*Excuse* me?"

When the two guards looked back, the caricature was standing there with his hand on his hip and a perturbed expression on his face. "Don't you believe in opening the door for a lady?" he demanded.

The guards looked at one another askance. Seniority seemed to win out in this instance, because Old Cat gave his colleague a look that said, "You do it, son." Deferring to his superior, Niggatoni restrained the urge to shudder as he went to open the front door for his master/mistress. In the meantime, Old Cat continued on to the garage.

After Niggatoni opened the door and stood to the side, the caricature giggled and walked through. Once they were outside, they waited around in the awkward silence for about three seconds—until the guard blurted out that he would check on the car. He ran off before the caricature could say anything, but stopped as soon as he had turned the corner. Even though he had only run a short distance, he was panting and trembling.

The sight of the car coming down the driveway brightened his spirits—since he felt there was a kind of safety in numbers. Old Cat seemed sympathetic to his colleague's plight, since he had gotten the car quickly. That was the kind of thing that forged lifelong bonds between men, and the youngster was grateful. They nodded to one another when the car was close; then, remembering he would have to open the door for the caricature, Niggatoni rushed back around the house and arrived at the same time as the car.

Like a proper lady, the caricature held out his hand so that the youngster could assist him into the vehicle. Once that was over with, the young guard rushed around to the passenger door and entered the vehicle, his face dazed.

They were driving now. Old Cat looked back at the caricature via the rearview mirror: the man was applying some more lip gloss. The two guards looked at one another askance again....

At the front gate, Old Cat paused. "Where we headed, boss?"

"Oh, *pooh!*" the caricature protested, "Don't call me 'boss.' It makes me sound old."

Old Cat sighed. "What do you want me to call you then?"

"I'm thinking of going by 'Dame Cole' from now on. It sounds positively *regal*," he said with an excited giggle.

The guards again exchanged a glance. Old Cat shook his head and took a deep breath to force the strange mixture of rage and terror back into his gut. "Where we headed, Dame Cole?" he said in a slightly mocking tone. However, the caricature giggled again upon hearing the name, so that by now *both* guards had to repress the urge to devolve into rage and madness.

"Take me to the mall," the caricature said, still giggling sporadically. Old Cat stamped on the accelerator. However, after driving a short distance, a pair of headlights appeared in the rearview mirror: paparazzi, most likely. The guards grimaced, but that was when the caricature retrieved his cellular phone from the purse and called his ex-wife. He wanted to know the designer of some dress she had worn three years ago. The ex-wife could be heard screaming epithets through the phone. Old Cat stamped on the accelerator again—to see if the headlights would follow—and so that the roar of the engine would drown out the voices. In fact, in ten minutes they were there. The pair of headlights had maintained the same distance behind them, but the guards had not really cared by then. Despite the roar of the engine, the caricature had yelled into the phone as if talking to someone on the other side of a football field. Over the ten-minute conversation, the ex-wife had given him a thorough inventory of where to go, what bodily orifices he could suck, and so forth. However, when the caricature saw they had arrived, he ended the call by yelling a cheerful "toodle-doo!" into the phone and hanging up.

The mall parking lot was mostly deserted at this time of night. Old Cat glanced into the rearview mirror: the headlights were still behind them, maintaining the same distance.

"Take me to the rear parking lot," the caricature demanded, still cheery.

Old Cat complied. The rear parking lot was even more deserted. In fact, there were no other cars. Beyond the open space, there was a lonely road that led to another highway. Presently, Old Cat was driving through the empty lot slowly, waiting for directions—

"Let me out here and hand me the briefcase," the caricature instructed.

"Here?" Old Cat said confusedly. They were in the center of the lot, so that it would take a few minutes to walk to the actual mall.

"Yes. This is fine."

Shrugging, Old Cat stopped the car. Niggatoni exited, opened the door for his highness, Dame Cole, and handed him the briefcase. As soon as the young man handed it over, the caricature smiled coquettishly again and began walking even farther away from the mall. As the young guard looked over his shoulder, he saw the two headlights from before. They belonged to a van; looking closer, he saw a TV station's logo on the side of the vehicle. Yet, there was nothing he could do at this point, so he returned to the car and sat there glumly as the caricature wandered farther away from the mall.

After about thirty seconds, Niggatoni looked over at the other guard uneasily: "Shouldn't we follow him or something?"

Old Cat shook his head: "He wanted to be let out here. If he wanted us to come, he would have asked us."

The youngster was about to shrug his shoulders when a sports car suddenly sped out of the darkness—near to where the caricature was walking. For a moment, it seemed as though the car would run over the man; but at the last moment, it swerved and came to a screeching halt at his side. The driver's side window opened; something was said, then the caricature handed over the briefcase. This all happened in the space of three or four seconds; after that, the car sped off again.

The caricature stood there watching the car as it turned onto the road that led to the other highway. An interval of about ten seconds passed before the caricature turned around and seemed ready to head back toward the guards. However, that was when the man fell like a sack of bricks.

The guards sat there watching in disbelief. The youngster seemed to come to his senses first, because he looked over at Old Cat and yelled, "Yo!"

Old Cat stomped on the accelerator; behind them, they heard the news van speeding up as well. In a matter of seconds, the car was at the caricature's side. He was going into convulsions on the ground. Both guards ran out to him. Old Cat asked him what was wrong, but he merely kept convulsing. When the guards looked up, the camera crew was right there. A reporter demanded to know what was going on. Acting on instinct, the youngster picked up his boss and carried him to the car. Old Cat held the door open, so that their boss could be shoved in the back. Once that was done, the youngster jumped into the rear door as well, and tried to hold down his boss while Old Cat got behind the wheel. By the time Old Cat stomped on the accelerator once more, the caricature's convulsions had stopped for the most part. Indeed, in time, all that could be heard was the roar of the engine as they sped toward the hospital.

"Chicken! Eat my chicken!"

Jones had fallen asleep on the divan in the corner of the professor's bedroom. He leaped up, terrified as he looked around in the darkness and tried to remember where he was—

"Chicken!"

A few more seconds passed before Jones got his bearings and realized the thing squirming about on the bed was the professor. There was a floor lamp by the divan. After he turned it on, the squirming and screaming stopped—as if the light had stunned the professor into silence. Jones was still half asleep—and struggling to make sense of what he was seeing—but after staring at the professor for a moment, it all began to come back to him. Last night, after he taped the professor's hands together, he had put the hands inside the Roadkill suit and zipped up the suit to constrain him further. The man's ankles had also been taped up, giving him the appearance of a hairy worm.

The professor had been squinting to shield his eyes from the light. When he finally looked over and noticed Jones standing there, there was initially terror in his eyes. However, in time, there was dawning recognition—and confusion as well, since he still had no idea what was going on.

Seeing the stirrings of consciousness in the professor's eyes, Jones took an excited step toward him.

"Professor…? Professor Steinholtz?" he began. "Are you back?"

Steinholtz looked up at him and frowned. He tried to move—to perhaps sit up in the bed—but again saw he was confined. Frustrated, he opened his mouth (to ask what the *hell* was going on) but—

"*Eat my chicken!*"

Steinholtz lay there stunned after the words came out of him—as if someone else had said the words.

"Professor?" Jones asked, stepping closer to the bed—but cautiously now.

Refocusing his mind, Steinholtz again attempted to speak, but—"Chicken…?" His eyes widened with shock—and the realization that those were the only words he could actually say. Growing desperate, he filled his lungs again, as if intending to *force* other words out of his mouth, but—"*Chicken..! Eat…! Chicken…!*" A frustrated grunt escaped from his throat afterwards, and he lay there panting.

Jones looked on helplessly, wishing he knew what was going on—or what he should *do*. In any event, with all the yelling, Binkowski and Artemis came running, both of them bleary-eyed. Artemis had slept in the room down the hall. Binkowski had taken the bedroom downstairs; but unable to sleep, he had spent most of the night watching the television in the living room.

"He's awake?" Binkowski said breathlessly, entering the room first.

Looking toward the doorway, Jones noticed the clock on the wall. It was five-fifteen in the morning. He nodded to answer Binkowski's question.

In the meanwhile, the professor looked at the new arrivals as if to ask who they were and what they were doing in his house; but again, the only thing that came out when he opened his mouth was, "*Chicken!*"

Driven over the edge, he did perhaps the only thing he could do at that point—which was lift his head off the pillow and slam it back down again in frustration.

Artemis looked at him anxiously as he slammed his head a few more times. "What's wrong with him?" she asked.

Jones shrugged with the same helpless expression on his face. "I *think* he's back," he began, "but looks like he can only say that chicken craziness."

On the bed, the professor's eyes brightened, and he nodded his head gratefully.

Jones nodded as well, and looked over to the others, who seemed to be staying at a safe distance, at the foot of the bed. "See?" he said to his friends. "He *recognizes* me."

When the professor nodded again, Jones went over to free him. However, in his eagerness, he pulled the Roadkill suit's zipper down all the way, so that the professor's erect penis sprang out like the creature in the "Alien" movies—

"*Chicken!*" the professor screeched.

Jones reflexively pulled the zipper back up halfway, to restore the professor's dignity. Afterwards, Jones looked down at the man apologetically; but by then, the professor was so desperate to be free that he pushed his bound hands through the opening in the suit and held them up for Jones to free them.

Binkowski was still wary: "You sure you want to let him loose? You *sure* he's sane?"

In response, Jones looked at him fixedly and said the one thing that should have been clear to all of them by now: "Ain't *none* of us been sane for a long time now." After that, he turned back to the professor and began pulling away the tape. Now, he was giving the professor a frantic explanation of their presence: "Things been crazy for over a week now," he began. "All of us have *seen* stuff...

and you've been going around shoving chicken down people's throats—"

The professor's eyes widened after Jones said those last words. By then, Jones had freed his hands and was moving onto his feet. The professor was reflexively rubbing his wrists to get blood flowing back into them.

Jones continued, "Whatever happened to us, I think it began *here*—at your house...at that dinner a week ago." He was looking at the professor fixedly now: "We came here because we thought there'd be answers. ...Do *you* know what's happening?"

There was a drained, far-off, expression on the professor's face for a moment, then he sat up straighter as everything began adding up in his mind. Unfortunately, when he looked up at Jones excitedly, the only word that came out of his mouth was, "*Chicken!*"

The professor sat there dejectedly for a moment, but Jones soon got an idea:

"Do you have a pen and pad handy? Maybe you can *write*."

Steinholtz's face brightened. Since he was free now, he reached over to the nightstand and pulled open the drawer eagerly. There was a pad in there, on which mathematical formulas and half-completed thoughts had been scribbled: the kinds of things that came to scientists in the middle of the night. Steinholtz grabbed the pad—as well as the pencil that was lying beneath it. Next, he flipped the pad to a blank page and began scribbling furiously. Excited, Jones and the others came over to look, but after reading the first word, they all groaned: Steinholtz had written, "Chicken!"

The professor lay down on the bed heavily; Jones and the others went over to the divan and sat there with their heads bowed. Everyone was quiet and still for about ten seconds; then, all at once, Steinholtz leapt up and rushed out of the room!

The others looked at one another confusedly before they rushed after him. Since Steinholtz ran like a lunatic—almost toppling headlong down the stairs—the others wondered if he had gone mad again. At the same time, they were open to the possibility that he was leading them to the thing that would answer all their questions; thus, as they chased the man, they were buffeted between terror and hope.

Binkowski had left the TV on in the living room; and as the flickering light fell on Steinholtz, he seemed like a demonic spirit fleeing through the darkness. In less than fifteen seconds, the man made it all the way to the kitchen. Jones and the others had taken turns cleaning it the night before, looking for clues; but as Steinholtz rushed through, he inadvertently toppled a stack of pots. The clangor seemed to shake the foundations of the house; but even then, the man only rushed on wildly.

Now, he was descending the basement stairs. Jones was close behind him now, ready to subdue him in case he had a gun stored down there. However, when Steinholtz flipped the basement switch, he stopped dead in his tracks, and stared ahead in shock. After a while, he stepped farther into the basement—first, in a daze, then in a frenzied search as he pushed over random boxes and scanned the shadowy recesses of the chamber for the thing that was supposed to be there.

By now, Binkowski and Artemis had made it to the basement as well, and were looking on from the entrance as Steinholtz stumbled about with a horrified expression on his face. They were all taken aback by that expression, and felt a dread feeling in their souls from the sight of it....

Eventually, when Steinholtz saw there was no point being down there any longer, he stumbled past the others and began ascending the basement stairs. They watched his retreating back for a moment before they followed him.

In the living room, Steinholtz stopped by the couch and looked over at the television. It was tuned to a cable news channel, but Binkowski had turned the volume down. The same story had been playing for most of the night—the Don Cole melodrama—so Binkowski had heard all the relevant details *hours* ago. Now, there was only a reformatting and recycling of those details, to give viewers the impression that new information was actually being released. The grainy images from the mall parking lot were everywhere by now. On the cable news broadcasts, a never-ending tide of experts narrated over them—and demonstrated their ability to extrapolate nonsense from vague data. Steinholtz watched it all absentmindedly until Don Cole's actual picture appeared on the screen, triggering a thought about his mother that at first seemed totally unconnected. He reflexively looked at the phone on the desk as he remembered his mother; and as he did so, he saw the answering machine was flashing—to indicate that a message was waiting.

By then, the others were at his back, looking on curiously. When Steinholtz went over to the answering machine, they followed. It was common courtesy to let people listen to their messages in private, but Jones and the others lingered—and Steinholtz was so preoccupied by his own thoughts that he barely even acknowledged their presence.

Steinholtz pressed a button on the machine and a computerized voice announced there were eleven new messages. The first message was from an irate-sounding British woman, who began by chastising him for missing their appointment—and then, in a throaty voice, she began describing how she was going to tie him up and take out her whip—

In his haste to press the delete button, Steinholtz almost split the answering machine in two! He looked over his shoulder sheepishly after he had done so, and the others shuffled their feet uneasily and looked down at the floor. The next three or four messages were from the university—secretaries and colleagues calling to ask where he was. Next, some security official informed him his lab had been broken into; the same man was on two other messages, sounding panicked and demanding to know where Steinholtz was. The professor listened to each of the messages for a few seconds before pressing the button to delete it. There was an ad for a cruise ship vacation. Steinholtz deleted it as soon as he heard the treacly voice of the announcer.

After that, there was a message from Steinholtz's mom. Her voice had an airy quality, and he instinctively leaned in further when he heard it.

"Son, something strange is happening," she began. Three or four seconds passed before she spoke again. "I can't remember what I've been doing…and I keep waking up in these…*clothes.*"

Steinholtz unconsciously put a trembling hand over his mouth as he listened. The rest of the message was incoherent: half-completed sentences and references to things that apparently did not even make sense to her. Alarmed, Steinholtz picked up the phone receiver and dialed his mother's number. As the phone began ringing, he realized he would not be able to say anything meaningful to her (given his condition) but hearing her voice would at least reassure him she was okay.

Unfortunately, after four rings, her answering machine picked up. He hit the button to end the call and then he dialed again. When her answering machine picked up once more, he slammed down the phone. As much as he wanted to believe she was merely sleeping at this early hour, there was a queasy feeling in his gut now. It was when his eyes wandered back to the television that the queasy feeling became something more concrete and disturbing.

He took two frantic steps over to the television before he stopped, turned to the others, and pointed at the screen.

"*Chicken!*" he screeched, trying to make them understand—but when the others looked, they could make no sense of it. A studio anchor was on the screen now, giving the latest details of the Colchester case. At the bottom of the screen, story headlines scrolled. Seizing upon an idea, Steinholtz ran over to the screen and gestured for the others to follow. He waited at the screen for something to appear; and when it did, he jabbed at the screen so hard Jones thought it would crack. The word beneath his finger was "Atlanta."

Jones looked over at him: "You want us to go to Atlanta?"

"*Chicken!*" he screamed. ...After he grimaced, he nodded eagerly. The others looked back at the screen for a long while, still not quite following; but seeing they at least understood his intentions, Steinholtz left them and went upstairs to get ready.

Even though everything around him was pitch black, Rasmussen assumed he was still conscious. He stretched out his arms, but there was only empty space around him. As far as he could tell, he was merely floating through the nothingness. The only thing he could hear was his panicked breathing. When he inhaled deeply, his nervous sweat smelled pungent, like a wild animal's. ...But at the same time, there was something soothing about the nothingness. After months of running around like a madman, taking care of the baby and trying to hold his life together, he suddenly found this place soothing. The darkness did not judge him or confine him. Anything was possible in the darkness; and once he realized this, his breathing became more even, and his heart rate began to slow.

He remembered the almost orgasmic surge of power he had felt before everything went black: it was still there, on the periphery, feeding his soul. In fact, he no longer felt like a normal man. Whereas before, he had felt timid and unsure, he now had the sense he only had to wish for something and it would miraculously appear before him.

He could sense wonders happening all around him now—and *within* him. All at once, he became aware that birds were singing, and that the wind was blowing lightly through the leaves. The world had been pitch black before, but he now sensed light beyond the darkness; and after a moment of confusion, he realized the only reason the world was still dark was because his eyelids were closed. When he opened them, he looked about wildly for about ten seconds, soaking in the world and all its wonders…until he realized he was lying in his back yard.

He frowned. The mall and the black woman were the last things he remembered. His mind flashed with an image of her perfect breasts…but it was the beginning of a new day now; by the placement of the sun in the sky, it seemed to be about seven or eight in the morning.

Maybe the woman, the mall—and all the other craziness—had been nothing but a dream?

He pursed his lips, giving it thought. Besides, he still felt energized and *strong*. The plush lawn felt good beneath him. The sky was cloudless and perfect—and the morning breeze was cool and refreshing. At that moment, a sparrow flew from beyond his roof and disappeared over his fence. As he followed it with his eyes, his peripheral vision caught sight of his body. Startled, he raised his head and looked at himself: he was totally nude…and lying spread eagle.

In fact, he had a rock hard erection. When he sat up on his elbows to look at it, he remembered Colchester. Like Colchester, had he blacked out and done crazy things...? He searched his mind; but in the end, images of perfect breasts and Colchester's purplish balls seemed more like the products of a bizarre dream than clues to his present predicament. His eyes returned to his erection. It was lying against his stomach, pulsing with every beat of his heart. He had never seen it so hard before—so *full*. Despite everything, he felt potent and alive. He wanted to have sex—not the polite intercourse he used to have with his wife, but something animalistic and unencumbered. ...He remembered the black woman, and her amazing body—

But somewhere in the distance, a siren began to blare—or at least, Rasmussen became aware of it. The god-like euphoria had begun to course through his veins again, but something about the siren made him panic inside. He felt like he needed to hide; he began to tremble—like an escaped criminal finding himself cornered. ...And it was not only the police and the authority of men that he feared: he felt as though he had transgressed against *God*. His soul suddenly seemed lost; he felt hollowed out—*devastated*. He wanted to cry: to pray to God for mercy and understanding—

But when the siren stopped abruptly, and the strange panic faded away, he lay there gasping for air. Suddenly desperate, he tried to *will* his memories to return; but besides the black woman's perfect breasts, the only thing he remembered his son's doll coming to life in the rearview mirror. ...No, those "recollections" from the mall were too ridiculous. The only logical explanation was that it had all been a dream....

That was a start, but it did not explain what he was doing out here. He needed to talk to someone—to corroborate what was real and what was fantasy. His thoughts instinctively went to wife; but when they did, he suddenly remembered his son!

He sat up and looked about the yard frantically, searching…but his son was nowhere in sight. His heart began to race again. Typically, his wife would have left for work by now. Indeed, operating under the assumption that this was still Friday, he remembered she was away on a business trip. That meant the baby was alone in the house.

Rasmussen was getting up now. He was about to run into the building when he glanced to his left—toward the towering, wooden fence that bordered his back yard—and saw someone staring at him! He froze, a shocked cry gurgling from his throat. It was Granny Stanko!

When he could breathe again, he glanced down at his erection—then back at Stanko's startled face. His first impulse was to cover his nakedness—but on second thought, a side of him was glad someone was there to see him in his full glory! It was not as though his wife had been enjoying his manhood lately; and from the way Stanko's eyes were wide and unblinking, Rasmussen guessed it had probably been twenty years since she had seen a real dick. He stood there posing for her, showing her what a real man looked like. Seeing he had finally found a way to shut her up, Rasmussen grinned. …But something was wrong. After staring at her for about six seconds, he realized her eyes were glazed. He took a step closer to the fence, frowning. Eventually, he *gasped*. …She was dead! From the expression on her face, she had died of shock!

Remembering his salacious thoughts, he felt ashamed—but mostly, he felt shock…and a budding sense—or *hope*—that he was still dreaming. He walked over to the fence and looked up at her. Her claw-like, arthritic fingers were gripping the top of the fence. She had probably come out to do her morning gardening, peeped over the fence, and gotten the shock of her life….

On the one hand, it was her own fault for snooping—but death seemed like a *harsh* punishment. He noticed she was still wearing the bracelet her grandson had given her. All her proud stories—of her grandchildren and other relatives—suddenly popped into her mind. Had he really taken her from her loved ones? For a few moments, he tried to consider the implications of what he had done: the responsibilities that were now on his shoulders. ...But given the strangeness of the morning, he felt too disconnected from the world to do the things normal men were supposed to do. He knew how he was supposed to be *acting*; he knew he had to call the police and report her death; but on this strange day, it was like something vital had been severed in him. He had the sense he was floating above the world—like a drunken god, or a *demon*— testing his power. All the world's concerns and tragedies suddenly seemed irrelevant. ...And in the end, none of this actually seemed *real*. If he was to be a god in this dream, then there was no point in confining himself to manmade restrictions and social conventions. Instead of death, he exulted in the possibilities of life; instead of sorrow, he felt only the drunken joy of a god. Guilt and contrition were meaningless to him now. He was about to laugh out and surrender himself to the madness—

But that was when he again remembered his son. Even in a dream, his responsibilities to his son were absolute and inviolable. He was jogging now. In his mind, he saw the little boy crying for his morning feeding—terrified and alone in the huge house. As he moved toward the kitchen door, Rasmussen listened for his son's cries—but besides the suburban stillness, he heard nothing. He moved faster, his erection jutting out like a jousting lance—and slapping against his thighs like Colchester's. He grimaced—

But when he stretched out his hand to open the back door, he noticed how filthy his nails were. Had he been digging in the dirt? Instinctively, he turned and scanned the back yard. On the exact spot where he had been lying, the grass had been ripped away. It looked as if someone had dug a hole, buried something, then refilled the dirt. Rasmussen looked at his filthy nails. Had he dug the hole? The mystery sidetracked him from the impulse to check on his son. ...And a nightmare thought occurred to him as well: *What if he had buried his son in that hole?* The nursery's window faced the back yard. Glancing up, Rasmussen saw the window was open. If his son had been crying, he would have heard those cries clearly. ...What if Stanko had seen him burying his son? Maybe that was why he had a sudden fear of the police. Maybe he had blacked out and done something unspeakable...!

His stomach felt queasy as he stumbled back to the disturbed patch on the lawn. Stanko's unblinking eyes stared at him accusingly. He looked away; but as he did, he noticed something else out of place: a mound of ash deeper into the yard. He took note of it, but his mind was so frazzled that he did not have the mental resources to concentrate on more than one thing at a time. His wary gaze returned to the disturbed patch on the lawn. His mouth was dry by then; but after he swallowed, the sickly taste turned his stomach further, leaving him even more disillusioned....

As he reached the patch, he lowered himself to his knees and began to dig. The hole was only about twenty centimeters in diameter—yet, in his dazed state, it did not occur to him it was too small for his son's body. After pulling away three or four handfuls of dirt, he came upon a balled up sheet of paper. It was damp from the soil's moisture, so Rasmussen pulled it open cautiously, taking pains not to rip it.

Yet, even when the sheet was open, he still stared at it incredulously. There were symbols sprawled across it: ancient writing, by the looks of it. He had no idea what the symbols *meant*, but he recognized his handwriting.

He stood up now, still staring at the sheet of paper. Why would he have had written those symbols? In fact, he wondered about all of it: Why was he naked? How had he come to be out here? Was it still Friday or had an entire day passed him by...? Given everything he had seen, it occurred to him it could be Sunday, Monday, or any other day of the week. Maybe *weeks* had passed since he had last been conscious....

He took a deep breath, telling himself to calm down and *think*. He was nodding his head now: only objective facts would save him. Unfortunately, when his eyes returned to the sheet of paper in his hand, more questions and irrational terrors popped into his head.

Now that he thought about it, something about his nakedness and the symbols reminded him of a pagan ritual. He remembered the black woman from the mall: had she put some kind of spell on him. ...No, that was too stupid. At the same time, the only other reasonable explanation was that he was losing his mind. He took another deep breath and held it. Maybe the pressure had finally gotten to him. ...Or maybe he had only sleepwalked out here. Maybe the encounters with Colchester's son and the black woman were a convoluted dream, spawned by a lack of sleep and a lack of sex. Maybe he had sleepwalked out here while his mind was pursuing its depravities. He nodded his head feebly, desperate to believe—but there was no denying that that was really Granny Stanko over there, staring at him with those dead eyes. Either this was all a dream, or it was a *nightmare*....

Like before, Rasmussen's eyes wandered the back yard aimlessly, searching for something that would explain all this. When they eventually came to rest on the mound of ash, his stomach clenched and he ambled over to the spot on heavy legs. There had been a fire there. A large section of grass was dead from the heat. Amongst the ash, he saw pieces of fabric that had managed to survive the flames—as well as the warped, charred remains of some shoes. He frowned, wondering what it could all mean—until another nightmare thought entered his head: *What if his son's corpse was in there, amongst the ashes?*

As his mind reeled, he stepped onto the charred grass, scouring the ash for anything that looked like bone. When he saw nothing, he did not know whether he was relieved or bewildered that he had had the thought in the first place. Dazed, he stumbled away from the ash and charred grass. Then, once again remembering his son, he turned toward the house. As the sense of urgency filled him, he forced his limbs to move faster; but even then, there was a dread feeling within him: the near certainty that he had done something unspeakable—and that no matter what he did from this point, his soul was damned for all eternity.

Despite everything, the linoleum kitchen floor was cool and comforting against Rasmussen's bare feet. Something about it was like an electric shock, sending his senses into overdrive. Whether it was merely panic or the strange power he had sensed before, his body felt stronger and lighter. It was as if his soul had migrated into a god's body—or a *demon's* body. He darted through the living room in five athletic strides. Soon, he was climbing the stairs. Indeed, he ascended the stairs so effortlessly that it was like flying—but even then, he did not feel as though he *controlled* the power. There was something *reckless* about it—like a racecar hurtling out of control....

As he neared the nursery, he had to concentrate in order to slow down; and then, opening the door quietly, he looked inside. For a moment, he stood beyond the door, staring at his son's crib. The god-like euphoria left him, and he again became a man wondering if he had done something horrible.

The crib was by the window. Rasmussen looked for a sign of life—but the only thing he could see was the rumpled bedspread. He began the grim trek across the nursery. He held his breath, hoping to hear his son's breathing; but again, all there was, was the suburban stillness. His mind went blank. He was trembling—and his stomach felt *sick*—but when he finally reached the crib and saw his son sleeping peacefully, he sighed in relief.

The little boy had never seemed so beautiful before. Rasmussen would have whisked the baby into his arms had he not feared awakening him. That said, his son was still holding that demonic teddy bear. Rasmussen stared at the thing for a few seconds, part of him expecting it to come to life again; but when nothing happened, he allowed himself to relax.

In fact, a nervous smile was playing on his lips when he heard the siren again. The siren started off low, but grew louder and louder, until the sound was like a monster rampaging through his skull. He grasped his head, ready to cry out—but that was when the siren stopped as unexpectedly as it had started. In the relative silence, he realized he was panting again. He looked around confusedly, asking himself if there had really been a siren....

He sighed: he had to get himself together. His mind offered up the idea of a soothing cup of coffee. He nodded his head at the thought, but as he turned to leave the room, he froze!

The same ancient symbols from the sheet of paper were written on the wall. Rasmussen could only stare. Remembering that he was still holding the sheet of paper from the lawn, he stared down it, then back to the wall. He again saw the strange figures were written by his hand—even though he had no idea what they *meant*.

Looking down, he saw the floor was strewn with dozens of crayons. He must have ripped open the container and used the red crayon to write his message. He tried thinking back—to how he might have done it, and *why*—but his mind was still moving like sludge.

On top of that, he still had no idea what day it was. He wondered how long he had been unconscious—if that was even the word for it. Indeed, he had a sudden fear that the world had ended while he was away. Beyond this little pocket of suburbia, maybe nothing existed anymore. Maybe he and his son were the last two people on earth. His mind went off wildly for a moment, considering all the possibilities, but as the thoughts began to drag him into the abyss, he shook his head and chastised himself for thinking such stupid things.

Yes, only objective facts could save him now. Since confirming the day of the week would give him something to work with, he instinctively found himself scanning the room for a clue. When he recalled that cable news channels usually listed the date and time on the bottom of the screen, a new sense of hope and urgency filled him.

The closest TV was in the master bedroom, so he exited the nursery and practically ran down the hall. As he approached the bedroom, he looked through the open doorway and saw the bed was unmade—the way it used to look after a night of good love-making. He took one step beyond the doorway when he glanced at the bed again and saw a naked, smooth, *shapely* butt. The sheet was entangled around the woman's torso and right leg; the rest of her body was nude. Rasmussen froze, his first thought that his wife had returned—or that he had lost track of more days than he had thought. However, some budding sense of shock told him he was wrong.

Before it occurred to him the woman on the bed was black, he attributed the dark skin to the fact that the curtains were all drawn. ...And then there was that amazing butt—rounder and suppler than his wife's. ...And the hair color was wrong. When the shock made him backpedal, the floorboard creaked—and the woman stirred from sleep and looked up at him quizzically. A few seconds passed. Rasmussen realized she was the same woman from the mall—the *goddess*. An image of perfect breasts again flashed in his mind—but Rasmussen was still struggling to digest the fact that she was naked and lying on his bed.

She was still in that post-sleep haze. Her eyes seemed to focus first on his erect penis. She stared at it for about three seconds— as if trying to figure out what it was—then her eyes rose to his startled face. She stared at that for a few seconds as well, trying to place it. Then, as if her brain suddenly started working, her eyes grew wide and she looked down at his penis again. That seemed to be when she realized she was lying naked on a strange bed, because she screamed, turned over and retreated until her back was pressed against the headboard. After that, she pulled the sheet around her—to cover her nakedness—and screamed again.

During all that, Rasmussen got a glimpse of her succulent breasts and smooth thighs. He stood there in a petrified daze until she screamed once more. By then, her eyes had gone back to his penis. She tried to retreat further—but there was nowhere to go, since her back was pressed against the headboard.

He put up his hands to assure her he had no ill intentions—but of course, it was pointless. Even he did not know what his intentions were at that point; and regardless of how pure his thoughts may have been in theory, his pulsing penis told a different story—

"How'd I get here!" she demanded.

He was still holding up his hands to show her he meant no harm, but as her eyes kept going back to his penis, it occurred to him he probably had to cover up before they would be able to talk. He pulled his penis to his stomach with his left hand, and tried to shield it with his forearm. His other arm was still in the air to demonstrate his harmlessness.

"I don't know how you got here," he began, trying to keep his voice calm.

"What do you mean you *don't* know?" she said heatedly. "Did you *drug* me or something?" she accused him.

"Of course not," he blurted out.

"Then how'd I get here?"

"I just woke up—*outside*," he pleaded with her. "I was coming in here—to check the date on the television—when I saw you. I have *no* idea how you got back here. I don't even know how even *I* got back here," he said, panting after his lengthy delivery.

She frowned before taking a quick glance about the room. "Where are we?"

"It's my house."

She was about to launch into more accusations, but he preempted her: "Look, the last thing I remember is seeing you at the *mall*. I just woke up on my *lawn*." Then, in a lower voice, "I don't know what's going on either. It's all…*crazy*," he said at last, his body limp and vulnerable as he laid all the cards on the table.

Even though common sense kept her from fully believing his explanation, Rasmussen was hopeful—since she was at least *considering* it. Of course, she was still in shock, ready to scream and make more accusations if the evidence presented itself, but she seemed *persuadable*.

"What's the last thing you remember?" he asked to keep her talking—and *calm*. Also, consciously or not, he knew that if he kept her talking, it would shield his mind from the possibility that he had actually had *sex* with her. For now, she was merely a naked woman on his bed—instead of evidence of his descent into depravity.

However, as soon as the vague outlines of that horror began to come into focus, he felt sick to his stomach. The nausea engulfed him, and he found himself rushing to the attached bathroom. The vomit was already moving up his throat; his vision was already becoming blurry. In the bathroom, he flung himself at the toilet bowl and knelt before it. His body convulsed a few times, and his stomach muscles were sore afterwards; but when nothing came out, he collapsed onto the plush bathroom rug and lay there in a daze.

In time, the black woman came to the bathroom door and looked down at him curiously. She had wrapped the huge sheet around her body like a toga.

"You okay?" she asked. She was still skeptical about him, but she was probably more curious than anything else—since he did not exactly seem like a rapist.

He raised his head and looked at her. Even in a sheet, she was beautiful. At the same time, it occurred to him he would have to throw out that sheet and all other evidence before his wife returned. He would have to get her the hell out of the house as soon as possible and *burn* all evidence of her visit. In his mind, his wife would return at any moment. His heart began thumping in his chest. He groaned as the queasy feeling came over him again; and by now, he felt like sweat was *dripping* out of his pores. Distraught, he went to put his head back down—but that was when the woman chuckled.

As he looked up at her, he saw she was smiling. He frowned.

Her smile widened: "I never saw a man so freaked out at the thought of having sex with me."

He stared at her until the words made sense to him; but even after they did, he still felt sick. "I'm *married*," he whined.

She laughed again.

"Why are you laughing," he said with a hint of anger. "A few seconds ago, you thought I had *raped* you."

She made a dismissive gesture with her hand, "Well, now that I think about it, I doubt anything like that could have happened."

He frowned and sat up slowly.

"Why?"

"For one thing, if you had been having sex with me all night, there is no way you'd still be that hard." There was a smirk on her face, so that he began wondering if she was a madwoman—or if this might be part of a larger scam to blackmail him or drive him nuts...or maybe none of this was really happening. His mind went through the permutations for a few seconds before his reasoning abilities seemed to collapse entirely.

She giggled at the dazed expression on his face. Her reaction did not even seem *remotely* sane until she added, "Besides, I'm on my period. Unless you replaced my tampon, I don't think we did anything."

Rasmussen stared at her in the same confused way. "Oh," he mumbled.

"Where does your wife keep her tampons?" she asked nonchalantly.

When Rasmussen pointed to the cabinet beneath the sink, she stepped over him and went to it. He stared at her, still dazed. After she retrieved a tampon from the box, she looked down at him with a raised eyebrow:

"Are you finished with the bathroom or are you waiting for a show?"

"Oh," Rasmussen said again, getting up. On the way out of the bathroom, he remembered the robe hanging on the back of the door, and grabbed it—since he was still nude. However, he paused before he left, and looked back at her. "Thanks for...all this," he said shyly.

"No problem," she replied with another one of her disarming smiles. "I'm in the music industry: I'm used to crazy shit happening."

After Rasmussen closed the bathroom door, he turned and stared at it, wondering if any of that had really happened. He was tempted to open the door and check, but when he heard rustling within the bathroom, he backed away from the door. He looked around confusedly for a while—at the now sheet-less bed, then at the open doorway, through which he could see the edge of his son's crib. When his wandering eyes came to rest on the television, he remembered why he had come here in the first place.

The plasma TV was directly across from the bed. Rasmussen saw the remote control on the nightstand, next to his cellular phone, and grabbed it eagerly. When he turned on the TV, a commercial was playing; but the loud, cheerful voices of some kind of herpes treatment ad grated against his nerves. He pressed the mute button and turned the channel. Yet, after he found a news channel, and saw the date, he stood there staring in disbelief. Supposedly, it was seven-fifteen on *Saturday!* Logically, the black woman's presence, and the time of the morning, should have told him it couldn't still be Friday—but confirming it only opened him up to other unwholesome possibilities.

He walked closer to the screen and stood staring at the date—as if being closer would allow him to see he had made a mistake. When the date did not change, he retreated a few steps and collapsed onto the bed. He felt lightheaded, but the evidence was irrefutable: today was Saturday, and he had lost almost a full day of his life. He lay on the bed for about half a minute, staring up at the ceiling. However, when he heard the shower turning on, he shuddered. As he recalled his wife was supposed to return today, the same sense of panic came over him again. He had to get the black woman out of the house as soon as possible! Apparently, he had not raped her—or had sex with her—but he was fairly certain his marriage would be over if his wife walked up the staircase at this moment. At the thought, his head jerked up and he looked toward the doorway with trembling eyes. Even though no one was there, and he did not hear any footsteps, his soul felt *sick*....

He groaned: anytime he felt he had figured something out, two more crazy things appeared on the horizon to confuse him. On top of all that, he still could not get over the feeling that something terrible had happened while he was unconscious—something even worse than adultery. What had he been doing—and how he had appeared to the people around him? ...And he remembered how Colchester III had been confused about the date, too. There was no point denying the similarities anymore. They had both woken up naked; both of them had gotten those letters; and at the realization, Rasmussen bolted upright on the bed, seeing he had to talk to Colchester. In a world of madness, the man was his only solid lead. He was so eager to see the man that he sprang up from the bed—

But as he glanced at the television, Colchester picture was on the screen! Rasmussen stared at the picture with wide, disbelieving eyes—until he realized *hearing* the story would be helpful. He pressed the mute button again, so that the voices blared. By the time he managed to lower the volume, Colchester's picture had been joined by his son's. Rasmussen stared in shock. The story was about how the father had collapsed after giving away ransom money or something—and how the son was still missing. The FBI was now involved and a manhunt was underway.

The television show had taken the time to interview some of the neighborhood's startled residents. An old couple from down the road talked about how shocked they were that "something like this" could have happened in their exclusive community; but at the end, the husband mentioned Colchester III's association to rap music and "those people." Rasmussen's headache returned… and now the reporter was back on the screen, talking about how young Colchester was still missing. She was telling people where they could send information if they had seen him—and talked in a tone that implied he might be *dead*.

Rasmussen remembered driving the kid to the mall—and promising he would drop him off. However, those scenes were again joined by images of perfect breasts and his son's doll coming to life. It was all too much—too *crazy*—and it seemed impossible to accept any of it without welcoming madness.

He knew he needed to calm down—and to *think*—but his mind was chaotic. When a commercial break began on the show, something about the loud, cheerful voices on the Viagra ad drove him even further over the edge, so that he grabbed the remote control and switched off the TV. In the silence, his breathing seemed harsh and disconcerting. He looked about the bedroom anxiously, searching for something that would help him make sense of all this—but as always, there was nothing.

Outside the window, a car sped past. It did not merely *drive* past—it flew past so quickly that the tires screeched against the asphalt. The bedroom window looked out on the front of the house, but the blinds were drawn. All at once, it occurred to him the sirens he had heard earlier must have been from the police and FBI speeding to the Colchester estate. At that moment, he heard another car coming down the street; curious, he went to the window and pulled the blinds open to see. He reached in time to see a news van zoom past—but then he gasped as he looked down at his lawn!

His minivan was parked on the lawn.…Not merely parked: there were deep tire grooves on the lawn—as if the car had been going at a high speed before it slid to a stop. Rasmussen was trembling again. He remembered the news story about Colchester: was he an accessory to a crime? Could he have done those things? At any rate, he was probably the last person seen with young Colchester! What if a bystander or surveillance camera had captured Colchester at the mall? If Rasmussen and Colchester had been seen together yesterday, then it might only be a matter of time before someone traced this back to him. Even if that were not the case, certainly one of his neighbors—or one of the passing police officers—would notice the minivan parked on the lawn! With such a serious crime committed, the police would canvass the entire neighborhood, asking everyone if he or she had any information. At the realization, Rasmussen's skin crawled—as if a cold hand had grasped the nape of his neck.

He was running now. He had tossed the robe on the bed during all this. He grabbed it as he fled. Soon, he was descending the stairs—but in his haste, he almost tripped and broke his neck. His strange erection was still there—and it was not as though he was *aroused* by anything—it was just there, like a cumbersome appendage. He looked at it as he ran down the steps, trying to make sense of it—but of course, it was useless.

Within seconds, he was downstairs. In the foyer, he paused at the front door and tied the robe. Yet, his penis refused to be restrained. It was as if it had a mind of its own. Rasmussen cursed in frustration; and even when he covered his manhood with the robe, it jutted out so prominently that he may as well have been naked. In time, he realized that if he put his hand in the pocket, he could grasp his penis through the material and pull it against his stomach. He had to manually keep his penis at bay, as if the thing would attack the neighbors if let loose....

He was still unsure about stepping out of the door with only the robe; but after peeping through the spyglass in the front door and seeing there was nobody in sight, he decided to "make a run for it."

In the blink of an eye, he opened the door, sprinted across the lawn and was sitting in the minivan's driver's seat. The window had been left open and the door was ajar. The keys were still in the ignition. Rasmussen tried thinking back, to how this might have happened, but something caught his eye; and when he realized what it was, his eyes grew wide.

Young Colchester's baseball cap was lying in the foot space of passenger side! Rasmussen's stomach churned, but he resisted the impulse to reach down and grab the cap. First, he had to hide the minivan in the garage. He nodded his head. Unfortunately, the instant he took his hand out of his pocket to operate the vehicle, his penis sprung from beneath the robe like some kind of movie monster. He flinched, but there was no time for that now, so he turned the key in the ignition and drove across the lawn. When he reached the garage, he had to stop and search for the garage door opener. It was not in its usual place—in the tray by the gear shift. He searched the glove compartment. As the seconds passed and his heart began to race, he pulled out all the junk in the compartment and dumped it on the floor. The door opener was not there! The glanced in the back seat; then, thinking of a likely location, he began feeling underneath his seat. When he grasped something that felt like it, he pulled it out and held it before his eyes. He was about to ask how it had gotten there, but his heart was still racing.

In his mind, the FBI would knock on his door at any moment, so he pressed the button and sat impatiently as the door began to move. As soon as the opening was wide enough, he pressed on the accelerator, almost colliding with his old sports car. He barely managed to swerve at the last moment—and to slam on the brakes before he crashed into the wall. He was panting—and there was a *crazed* expression on his face. Remembering the FBI, he pressed the button on the garage door opener once more, to conceal the evidence.

As soon as he turned off the engine, he turned on the minivan's ceiling light and grabbed young Colchester's baseball cap. It was a white cap—but on the left side, there was a congealed red substance that he immediately knew was blood! He sat there staring at it. Maybe half a minute passed. ...As he had thought before, every time he convinced himself he had figured something out, two more horrors appeared on the horizon....

Rasmussen exited the minivan and took a few unsteady steps toward the door that led to the laundry room and kitchen. Yet, as his wandering eyes happened to fall on his sports car, he stopped and stared at it for a few seconds. He frowned. It was a Porsche Boxster. As far as he could recall, he had not driven it in months—except to the end of the driveway to wash and wax it...and caress it like a long forgotten lover. However, when he looked now, there were mud stains on the side. At the sight, a sense of outrage came over him—as if some other man had violated his woman. With everything that was going on, he definitely did not have time to be sidetracked by this; but seeing his car sullied like that, he rushed over to comfort it...dry its tears...assure it that he still loved it, despite the fact that another man had violated it...

He was almost on the verge of tears now. As he neared the car, he saw the rapist had left the window open. Then, as he drew even closer, he discerned a human form inside the vehicle!

Rasmussen froze, buffeted between pure terror and demonic rage. The rapist was still in there, lounging like the car was *his*. The seat was all the way back, and as Rasmussen stood frozen in the silence, he heard *snoring!*

That was the final straw. It was one thing to violate a man's car, but *sleeping* in it afterwards was beyond the pale! It was like a rapist expecting his victim to make him pancakes in the morning and snuggle with him afterwards. Rasmussen rushed at the car now, yanked the door open, and was already growling as he prepared to dispense his justice—

But now that the door was open, he saw the rapist was lying there *nude*. That, in itself, seemed to call for further punishment. The demon in him cried for *blood*, but the sight of the teenage cock left Rasmussen confused for a moment; and when he instinctively leaned into the car to see the offender's face, he finally made out young Colchester lying there, snoring with his mouth wide open and the drool pooling on the leather headrest. That sight roused Rasmussen from his momentary confusion, and he slapped Colchester across the chest to awaken him.

The kid screamed! Rasmussen stepped back from the vehicle, waiting for the offender to come out so that he could beat the *crap* out of him. Yet, as Colchester saw he was nude, he cried out again. He bolted upright, covering his penis with his hand. Then, he jumped once more when he saw Rasmussen lingering outside the car with evil intentions shining in his eyes—

"Where the *fuck* am I?" he cried at last.

Rasmussen eyed him with simmering rage. His voice was low and menacing: "Get the *hell* out of my car."

That was when Colchester glanced down and noticed the bulge in Rasmussen's robe. As soon as he did, he cried out in horror once more, and clutched his penis to his stomach. "What you do to me, you *homo* nigga!"

"Just get the *hell* out!" Rasmussen raged. ...But young Colchester's accusation of rape reminded him of the black woman upstairs, so that he frowned. What could have happened last night for all of them to end up naked and confused? When he looked over at Colchester, the kid had a teary expression on his face, as if preparing to experience his first prison rape.

Rasmussen sighed—and, for the second time that morning, put up his hand to show he meant no harm. After that, he again remembered the blankets he kept in the back of the minivan—and had a flashback of Colchester III running naked down the road. He winced at the thought, gestured for young Colchester to wait there, then he walked over to the minivan. He talked as he walked, taking pains to be as calm and clear as possible:

"It's Saturday morning," he began. "Something strange is happening—and I don't know what it is. You, me and that black woman from yesterday all woke up naked this morning...with memory loss."

Colchester put a cautious foot out of the car door and looked over at Rasmussen suspiciously, "You mean you didn't *butt* rape me?"

Rasmussen had opened the minivan's rear door and retrieved a blanket by the time young Colchester asked his question—

"*Damnit*, Winthrop!" he screamed when he deciphered the kid's words. "Would you shut the *hell* up with that nonsense!"

He was so enraged that he slammed the rear door and approached the Porsche with a murderous expression on his face. When he was close enough, he flung the blanket at the kid. "Cover up for now," he commanded. He was in a bad mood again, but his rage seemed to melt away when he saw the contrite expression on the kid's face. At the sight, he also remembered the story on the news, so that he grimaced again. He considered his options for a moment, but duty demanded that he tell the kid about his father.

"Winthrop," he began now, "I have something to tell you."

Young Colchester put the blanket over his crotch before standing up and wrapping the blanket around his waist like a towel. "About what?" he asked cautiously, taken aback by Rasmussen's tone and body language.

"About your father: …he's in the hospital."

"*What…?* Why?"

"Something happened last night"—but as he said those words, he recalled the video the news crew had filmed at the mall. He looked over at his Porsche, his mouth gaping: could he have been involved in the ransom pick-up…?

"What happened last night?" Colchester coaxed him, but Rasmussen was still lost. His stomach felt queasy again; and all at once, he felt *suffocated*—as if he would die if he did not get out of the garage and breathe some fresh air. Young Colchester was still looking at him expectantly, but Rasmussen's only thought was to flee.

"Wait here for a moment," he mumbled, waving his hand dismissively. At that, he headed for the doorway that led to the laundry room and kitchen.

"*Wait?*" Colchester said, confused. "What about Pops?"

Rasmussen opened his mouth, but his mind again faltered. Eventually, he shook his head in frustration: "Just wait here for a moment. I'll bring you some clothes…we'll figure it out…" Then, before the teenager could protest, Rasmussen turned and fled toward the door.

Get some fresh air and think. That was the only thing guiding Rasmussen now. As soon as he exited the garage, he took a deep breath—but it did nothing to help him. While he was fleeing through the laundry room, he stumbled and collided with the washing machine, banging his knee. He cursed, but did not stop— since he feared he would never be able to move again if he lingered anywhere too long. The only thing that could save him now was *motion*, so he gritted his teeth and moved on.…

Beyond the laundry room, he again found himself in the kitchen. His headache was worsening. He needed something to drink, so he went to the sink, opened the faucet and sucked water directly from the tap. Afterwards, he wet his head with the cool water. He wanted to sit down—so that he could relax and *think*—but there was no time.

His son… Somehow, he again needed confirmation that the little boy was okay. He was running again; but this time, he did not feel god-like as he ascended the stairs. He was panting for air—*desperate…*

Yet, he paused once he reached the top of the staircase. He was peering into the master bedroom now. From this position, he could see the door to the bathroom was still closed. He had perhaps been hoping the black woman was a figment of his imagination, but the sound of the shower running confirmed she was real. He groaned as well when he remembered Young Colchester was still downstairs, waiting on him, but—

One thing at a time, he reminded himself. Taking a deep breath, he turned and continued on to the nursery—where he again stood above the crib and the sleeping baby. After that, he looked around vaguely again, still searching for something that would help him make sense of all this. When his eyes focused on the wall with the symbols, he cringed and stood staring at it. He was about to sigh and turn away when something suddenly clicked in his mind, and he remembered a class project from his freshman year at university. His mouth gaped and he stepped forward. The symbols on the wall were a cryptogram! He pursed his lips, trying to remember the cypher. After it all came back to him, his eyes darted about the wall for a few seconds as he deciphered the message. It read:

You know who you are.

His frown deepened. Unable to make sense of it, he translated it in his head once more, to confirm. After that, he again asked himself what it meant, until his head began to hurt from the strain.

He groaned. There was a rocking chair near the crib and the window. Rasmussen had spent many a night sitting in it, trying to rock his son to sleep; but now, he felt like plopping down on the chair and rocking himself into oblivion. He was about to do so now, but when he glanced out of the window, he saw Granny Stanko's shocked face!

He grimaced, thinking about all the work that lay ahead. After he called the police about Stanko, they would want to talk to him, and he would have to think of something to tell them. He was sure they would attribute her death to natural causes—unless they found some connection to the Colchester case. ...And what if her death was connected to that case? With his memory loss, there was no knowing what he had done or where he had been. Even if he tried to lie, he had no idea what the *truth* was. ...No: there was no way he could go to the police now—since they would only put him at the top of their list of suspects. Given his memory loss, the prudent course of action was to assume he was guilty—and to hide all evidence....

He was nodding his head now: he would have to clean up the house...erase the symbols from the wall...find something to do with Stanko...then he had to get young Colchester and the black woman out of the house...clean the minivan and the Porsche...try his best to patch up the lawn (since he could not call the gardener!)... His body slumped as the list grew in his mind; his breath became more labored, but seeing there was no time to lose, he again forced his body to *move*.

After exiting the nursery, Rasmussen was about to head downstairs (to get some cleaning products) when he heard his cell phone let out that pathetic "Charge me, I'm dying!" noise. The noise was so pleading that Rasmussen was always overcome by the same guilty urgency he felt when the baby cried. He was sure there was something sinister behind it—and that corporate America was using mind control to enslave its customers—but he kept such paranoia to himself....

The noise had come from the master bedroom, so Rasmussen turned from the stairs and entered the room. The phone was in its final death throes, since it was now emitting its plea every thirty seconds. The black woman was still in the bathroom. Rasmussen eyed the closed door uneasily. At the same time, since the closed door *shielded* her, she seemed less real—and therefore less *threatening*.

He saw the phone lying on the nightstand and went over to soothe its cries. The cable to charge it was already plugged into a power strip on the floor, so he attached it to the phone. When the phone made that cheerful, "I'm charging!" sound, Rasmussen had the same reassured feeling he had when the baby stopped crying and began suckling from his bottle....

While he was placing the phone back on the nightstand, he glanced at the screen and noticed he had missed three phone calls and received four text messages. Opening the folders on the phone, he saw the messages were all from his wife. She was one of those people who never used voicemail. In fact, the voicemail message on her phone said, "Send me a text message."

The messages were all in his wife's curt, efficient style. From Friday afternoon: "Finished last meeting. I'll call you later." ... From three hours later: "I called, but didn't get you. Are you okay?" ...From midnight: "Still can't reach you." ...From three hours ago: "I'm leaving for the airport...where are you???"

He thought about calling her now—to let her know he was okay, but he knew he did not have the mental capacity to talk to anyone now. Besides, he was still in "hide the evidence" mode. He first had to find out where all the corpses were buried before he talked to anyone and inadvertently incriminated himself.

He put down the phone and left it to charge. After that, he looked about the bedroom absentmindedly. The shower had stopped running. He stared at the closed door, having to reacquaint his mind with the fact that there was a naked black woman in there. At the thought—both of her nakedness and his wife's imminent return—he cringed. However, he realized he could solve the black woman's nakedness easily enough by getting some of his wife's clothes. In a few seconds, he went to his wife's walk-in closet and got out some sweatpants and a T-shirt. He wondered if the black woman needed shoes as well, but then remembered the warped shoes from the ashes in the back yard. Maybe it was only then that Rasmussen realized what had happened to their clothes. It still did not make *sense* but at least it was a start.

He took a pair of his wife's sandals from a nook in the closet before he returned to the bedroom to deposit everything on the bed. Remembering young Colchester would need clothes as well, he went to his closet and retrieved some likely items.

Rasmussen returned to the kitchen, but he only stood about once more, looking around absentmindedly. He was still holding the clothes for Colchester, but he felt he needed to fortify himself before he dealt with the youth—

...*Coffee:* maybe some coffee would help him. Besides, somewhere in the back of his mind, he still believed this was all a bad dream—or an escalating delusion. Maybe, if he revived himself with coffee, he would literally wake up from all this. Given everything that had happened, anything seemed possible....

He rested the clothes on the counter and went to the coffee-maker. After he filled his favorite mug, he gulped down the bitter drink as if it were a shot of whiskey. His senses must have been delayed, because it was only five or so seconds later that his mouth and throat registered the scalding hot liquid. He yelped, rushed over to the sink and gulped down some cold water again; once he had his fill, he slunk over to the kitchen table and plopped down heavily on a chair. He had hoped the coffee would revive him, but he felt even worse now.

He was about to sigh when he heard a loud thumping sound. Terrified, he swung around in his seat, a cry already forming on his lips. As the adrenaline flowed through him, he fully expected a monster to be behind him, baring its fangs...but there was nothing. After a few seconds of staring about the empty room, he allowed himself to breathe—and told himself he must have imagined it. Exhausted, he was about to turn back around—and chastise himself for being so jumpy—when the thumping sounded once more! Again holding his breath, he stared in the general direction of the noise, his eyes trembling. Eventually, when he felt strong enough, he rose from the chair and went to investigate....

He walked as if in a dream. The sound was coming from the foyer—where there was a power room and a coat closet. He crept into the foyer, scanning the area for anything out of place. He saw nothing—and was about to tell himself he had imagined it all—when something banged against the closet door. He jumped back, his heart again racing.

The closet was right by the front door. Rasmussen stared at the closet door, imaging the horrors that might be on the other side of it. However, when he heard the noise again, he frowned and leaned in closer. The sound was like confused shuffling—as if an animal had gotten trapped in the closet. ...A rat, perhaps, he thought. There was a basket by the front door, which held half a dozen umbrellas. Rasmussen grabbed a sturdy-looking one before he returned to the closet door. After that, he raised the umbrella in the air, grabbed the doorknob, braced himself, and pulled the door open.

Rasmussen had prepared himself for a scampering rat—or an opossum or some other southern critter—but instead he saw the pale, droopy torso of a middle-aged man. Rasmussen jumped back! Since the intruder had been leaning against the door, he tumbled out and seemed even more shocked and terrified than Rasmussen.

It was probably a reflection of Rasmussen's strange morning that he regained his composure as soon as he saw the man was totally nude. However, the man was growing more frantic now. His first few attempts to stand up were futile. Something in the closet seemed to be wrapped around his legs, and he was flopping around like some kind of stranded merman. Rasmussen leaned the umbrella against the wall and went over to help.

"Keep calm," he advised the man. "Take a deep breath. ...Give me your hand," he said when the man looked up at him confusedly. He nodded to reassure the man it was okay, and the man stretched out an unsteady hand.

After Rasmussen grasped it and hauled the man up, he saw one of his wife's shawls had fallen on him and gotten tangled around his legs. However once the man was standing—and the shawl fell away completely—he panicked again as he realized he was totally nude. He tried futilely to cover himself with his hand.

Since Rasmussen was getting used to the routine by now, he calmly said, "Wait here," and went to retrieve the clothes he had brought down for Colchester. He returned within ten seconds. The man was crouching awkwardly, trying to hide his penis and reserve his dignity. It was of course pointless—and he was too traumatized by the strange way he had woken up to realize he could have used the shawl to cover himself.

Rasmussen handed over the clothes and averted his eyes. The man took the clothes eagerly—the way a starving man would take food. Unfortunately, in his haste to put on the pants, he lost his balance and tumbled to the floor. Yet, even then, he was so desperate to cover himself that he rolled onto his back, raised his legs in the air and pulled the pants on. He was actually quite agile for a man his age, because he was on his feet again within seconds. Now, the man was putting on the T-shirt in the same frantic way; within seconds, he was standing there panting—and staring at Rasmussen in a wild, unbalanced way.

Rasmussen had been looking on with a certain amount of awe; but once he came to his senses, he cleared his throat and began reciting the relevant facts: "My name is Arlo Rasmussen. This is my house. Something strange is happening. So far, four of us have woken up like this," he said, gesturing to the man's body to indicate nakedness. "None of us can remember how we got here or what happened last night." Here, he paused to see if he had forgotten any relevant facts. When something occurred to him, he looked over at the man again. "What's your name?"

The man blinked a few times in quick succession, as if struggling to remember. Then, after the momentary confusion, he willed himself to stand straighter—and to *think*. "It's Felix," he said breathlessly. "Felix Higginbottom."

Rasmussen was about to ask him the last thing he remembered, but then the doorbell rang. The front entrance was right next to them, so they shuddered as they turned toward it. Given everything that had happened to them, both men were instinctively terrified as they glanced at one another. Then, after a voice boomed, "Open up—it's the police!" the men jumped again and staggered back.

When Jones and the others were heading out of Athens, they gave the professor an update of everything that had happened: his time as the Roadkill Maniac; Hillbilly Champagne and repeatedly waking up in the shower; Fischbach's penis exploding at Binkowski's hospital, and all the bizarre but seemingly connected events that had been pushing them toward madness. Unfortunately, the fact that the professor could say nothing but, "Eat my chicken!" made conversation awkward—if not impossible. Eventually, when all conversation petered out, Jones turned on the radio and found a random AM station. Thus, the long on the sort of it was that their minds had been numbed by country music for about an hour now—and no one had really *talked* during that time.

Since Steinholtz was the only one who knew where they were going—and his condition made it impossible for him to relay instructions—he was driving. The professor had showered and changed into some clean clothes, but since his hair was wild and he had not shaved—and his bulging eyes were red from a week of being a mindless maniac—he still looked like a lunatic. More troublingly, he drove like a lunatic as well, speeding at twice the limit and changing lanes like there was nobody else on the road.

In the passenger seat, Jones had been numb to most of it, lost in his own thoughts; in the back seat, Artemis and Binkowski had initially exchanged terrified glances as the professor carried out some of his more questionable driving maneuvers. However, after a while, they all seemed resigned to their fates. Sleep deprivation probably had something to do with it, but after everything they had been through, they all seemed to conclude it was pointless to hold back now. Jones and Binkowski had been living on the edge for a week now; and after a period of skepticism, even Artemis had become a true believer....

As Steinholtz cut off yet another driver and swerved into the off ramp at a speed that would have caused most drivers to capsize, the passengers did not even flinch. Lunatic or not, Steinholtz drove like a seasoned racecar driver, his eyes squarely on the road and all his faculties focused on reaching his destination.

Presently, they were in a posh residential area with mansions. Steinholtz reflexively slowed to accommodate the narrower, more sinuous roads. It was a good thing too, because as they turned the next bend, there were about five police cars parked in front of one of the estates. News vans were there as well. Jones and the others swung around in their seats to gawk, but Steinholtz was still staring ahead blankly.

Soon, he was turning into a driveway. The house appeared. Steinholtz slammed on the brakes, but the vehicle was still rolling forward slowly when the man opened the door and ran out.

Thinking quickly, Jones pulled back on the hand brake. After that, they all sat there confusedly as Steinholtz ran up to the front door and disappeared into the house. A few more seconds passed before they came to their senses and followed him into the building.

Steinholtz was yelling "Chicken!" as he searched the house. By the time they entered the front door, he had already searched the first floor. When he headed up the staircase, Jones and the others followed—but they stayed out of his way, like hunters allowing their frenzied dog off its leash. Plus, to be honest, even though they had gotten used to his antics by now, he still seemed thoroughly nuts.

Presently, Steinholtz pushed open the door of the master bedroom and looked about wildly—but the room was empty. His shoulders slumped with disappointment; but when he realized the bed had been slept in recently, he yelled, "Chicken!" and rushed to check the attached bathroom. Unfortunately, there was no one there either. He emerged from the bathroom with frantic eyes, trying to think of where his mother might be. He began scanning the room, searching for a clue. In the meanwhile, the others stood by the doorway—out of his way.

It was only when the professor neared the window, and looked down into the back yard, that he saw his mother standing by the fence. *"Chicken!"* he screamed again. In his haste to open the window, he almost broke it. "Chicken!" he yelled again, but the woman did not even flinch—as if she were deaf, or totally captivated by the scene on the other side of the fence....

Three or four seconds passed before Rasmussen was able to move or *breathe.* After the policeman banged the door again, Rasmussen shuddered and came to his senses. Higginbottom was looking over at him with gaping eyes. Thinking quickly, Rasmussen gestured for him to get back in the closet. The man nodded anxiously and complied, pulling the shawl—and some of the other articles on the floor—into the closet with his foot.

Rasmussen waited until the man closed the door behind him, then he drew a deep breath—to compose himself before he opened the door—

"Police!" the voice boomed again.

"I'm coming!" Rasmussen said at last. He took a step toward the door before he remembered he was still only in a robe. There was no time to dress now—no time to do anything but put on a façade and try to get through this. He made sure the front of the robe was tied securely; then, once again reaching through the pocket and grabbing his penis, he pulled it to his stomach. He knew he would look suspicious with one hand in his pocket, but there was nothing else he could do on such short notice.

As he reached for the door with his free hand, he tried to con-jure any possible lies he could tell, but his mind deserted him. He thought about trying to smile, but he knew it was pointless, so he braced himself and turned the knob.

From the policeman's booming voice, Rasmussen had expected a hulk of a man to be on the other side of the door; but when he opened it, he found himself looking down at a puny codger in a rumpled suit. It was a plain-clothes detective in his mid-fifties at least. He flashed a badge and said his name, but Rasmussen did not really catch either. He was still trying to reconcile the man's size with the booming voice. The detective had bulging eyes; and with his stature, he reminded Rasmussen of a Chihuahua.

"We have some questions to ask," the man boomed again. He was scrutinizing Rasmussen now; his eyes lingered on the mid-section of Rasmussen's robe, where he was grasping his penis. Rasmussen fidgeted; mercifully, the detective's eyes moved on. He was looking past Rasmussen now, into the house. "Do you have time to answer our questions?" the man asked. He had said "our," even though he was the only one standing there. Rasmussen stared at him for a few uncomfortable seconds, searching for a way to tell him to go away. There was of course no way to do that, so he stepped aside and allowed the detective to enter.

"Would you like some coffee?" Rasmussen ventured when they were both inside.

The detective thought about it before shaking his head. Apparently, this one was all business.

"You're aware of what's going on down the street?" he asked tersely.

"Yeah," Rasmussen began without any real thought, "I heard all the cars and sirens going past...then I watched the news." He grimaced after he was done, reminding himself he had to consider every word before he said it.

The detective assessed his story and body language, and came to the obvious conclusion he was hiding something. "Did you hear or see anything—before all the 'cars and sirens'?"

"No," he said too abruptly.

"Really?" the detective said skeptically. Slowly, he looked at Rasmussen from head to toe. His eyes again lingered at Rasmussen's pocketed hand. Rasmussen shifted his weight nervously, from one leg to another. "—I talked to some of your neighbors," the detective continued.

When the statement lingered, Rasmussen blurted out, "And?"

"Last night, some of them mentioned seeing bright lights and hearing some kind of..."—he consulted his notepad to get the right word—"...some kind of *screams* coming from this house."

Rasmussen stared down at the man incredulously. "*This* house?"

"Yes. They said it came from the second story," he said, instinctively looking up.

"A neighbor said he saw something on my second story?" Rasmussen said—both because he was skeptical and because he was trying to buy time to *think*.

"Yes, they were driving by in a car and reported seeing a light. Possibly a fire...but I guess your house didn't burn down," the detective observed.

Rasmussen shrugged, as if to say he had no idea what the man was talking about—which was of course the truth—but his mind was racing! He remembered the charred patch in the back yard. ...But how could anyone see the back yard from the road? The road faced the *front* of the house. The only person in a position to make such a report would be Stanko—

Stanko: he suddenly remembered Stanko's corpse was still out there! On the spot, Rasmussen decided that if the detective discovered her body, he would pretend to be shocked. He nodded his head unconsciously, trying to determine how he would act, if he would cry...how frantic he would be when he pretended to see his neighbor's corpse for the first time—

"Do you mind if I take a look upstairs?" the detective proposed.

In his dazed state, Rasmussen blurted out, "Go ahead." However, as they were ascending the stairs, Rasmussen remembered the symbols on the wall. On the surface, there wasn't anything incriminating about the symbols, but Rasmussen feared the symbols would seal his fate if anyone else saw them. ...And the black woman was still up there too! Rasmussen's stomach convulsed when he remembered—even though having a black woman in the house was not exactly a crime. ...But if the detective found young Colchester, Rasmussen would definitely be in trouble. He would have to explain why he had not called the police to have the search called off; his story would unravel; the police would search the house and match the Porsche against the car on the video...! Rasmussen felt *sick*...!

When they reached the second floor, Rasmussen's trembling eyes went to the master bedroom—and the closed bathroom door. However, the detective was walking straight for the nursery now. Rasmussen had left the door open—so that he could hear his son's cries. Now, as he and the detective walked down the hall, they could see the crib and the window. Rasmussen tried to brace himself, because he knew the moment the man looked out of the window, he would see Stanko.

By then, Rasmussen felt like he was going to pass out. As he walked two steps behind the detective, it occurred to him he could easily subdue the puny man. He could club him in the head and hide the corpse in the attic. Nobody probably knew the man was in here anyway. ...But Rasmussen shook his head, unsettled by his thoughts. Besides, it was too late now. The detective entered the nursery and began looking around deliberately. Rasmussen remained outside, waiting for the inevitable question about what the symbols on the wall meant, but the question never came. In fact, when the detective looked toward the wall, his eyes did not even linger. He continued searching. Confused, Rasmussen entered the room; while the detective looked over at the crib, Rasmussen turned his head and looked at the wall.

His eyes widened and he stood there shivering: somehow, the wall was clear! There were no symbols—and no sign that the symbols had ever been there. He looked toward his son's dresser, searching for the sheet of paper, but it was gone. There were no crayons on the floor either. Rasmussen's trembling eyes returned to the wall. He *stared*—

"What are you looking at?" the detective asked.

Rasmussen jumped. "—What?" he said, as the man stepped up.

"Were you looking at something?"

Rasmussen glanced at the blank wall again, then he returned to the detective. "No."

The detective looked at the wall for three or four seconds; after that he shrugged. "Can I check some of the other rooms?" the man asked now.

"Sure," Rasmussen said, his mind still reeling. ...And it occurred to him that staring at the wall like a paranoid lunatic had probably saved him. The distracted detective had concentrated on Rasmussen, instead of looking out of the window and seeing Stanko's corpse. Rasmussen took a deep breath, relieved for now—but his heart was still racing, and his body felt numb.

The detective was walking toward the door now. Rasmussen was about to walk out with him, but when he glanced back, he noticed the baby was up. His son was standing in the crib, with his pudgy little hands grasping the bars. The little boy was smiling at him. Rasmussen's instinctive reaction was to smile back; but as he stood there staring at his son, he realized there was something unsavory about the baby's smile. It was self-assured—almost mocking. Indeed, something about it frightened him—so he fled from the room and caught up to the detective.

The detective was headed to the master bedroom. Rasmussen winced when he realized what that would mean. He had to buy some time—to *think*, or pray for the woman to miraculously disappear like the symbols on the wall.

"What exactly are you looking for?" he heard himself asking the detective. The man turned and faced him:

"A car was parked on the road in front of your house."

Rasmussen paused, trying to figure out if that might incriminate him in something—but as far as he knew, all his cars were in the garage. He looked at the detective with a frown: "...And?"

The detective reached into his pocket and retrieved a cellular phone. He pressed some buttons and brought up a picture. "Is this your car?"

In Rasmussen's dazed state, he was terrified the man was going to produce a picture of his Porsche; but instead, it was an ugly American car. "...No, it's not," he said, relieved—but then it occurred to him he had seen that car before. He had a flashback of the dominatrix woman waiting at Colchester's front gate—and then ripping off her top like Clark Kent. He frowned—

"Something wrong?" the detective asked him.

Rasmussen came to his senses and tried to smile, but it was a fake smile, and they both knew it was fake. He shook his head to say nothing was wrong, but the detective stared at him nonetheless. Worse, since Rasmussen tried to *maintain* the fake smile, he only raised more suspicions in the detective.

Luckily for him, that was when the black woman opened the bathroom door. The detective turned toward the master bedroom, his hand instinctively going to his gun. When he looked, the black woman was standing there, naked. For once, the detective seemed discomfited…and who could blame him: the black woman was a goddess. Rasmussen found himself staring; after the initial shock, the detective averted his eyes—

"Sorry!" he said, turning back to Rasmussen. "I thought you… were alone. His eyes reflexively went back to where Rasmussen was holding his penis to his stomach, and things finally began to add up in his mind. He figured he had come while they were in the middle of a session—and if there was one thing every man knew, it was to leave a brother alone when he was in the middle of a session. The detective figured the black woman was Rasmussen's mistress—and that she had snuck in while his wife was gone. Since that seemed to explain Rasmussen's suspicious behavior, the detective mumbled something else and began moving toward the stairs. When Rasmussen glanced back at the black woman, she had a confused expression on her face. However, he figured he would fill her in later. For now, all he felt was relief as the detective began descending the staircase. Rasmussen began to follow; but as if shell shocked by the black woman's body, the detective did not even turn around. Once the man was downstairs, he went straight to the front door, opened it, and walked out without saying goodbye or even closing the door behind him.

Rasmussen rushed up to close the door, then he slumped against it, breathing heavily. He was actually about to smile, but as he took his hand out of his pocket, his penis again sprang out, startling him. He groaned.

He stood there for a while, letting the adrenaline ebb from his system. Remembering the baby was awake, his first impulse was to go and fetch him—to get him breakfast—but thoughts of his son's peculiar smile left him uneasy, so he forced his mind elsewhere. That was when his wandering eyes came to rest on the coat closet. In his dazed state, he had to stare at the door for a few seconds before he remembered Higginbottom was still in there. Nodding to himself, he tightened his robe, walked over to the closet, and opened the door. Higginbottom was looking at him like a panicked dog, ready to flee for its life—or *bite*.

"The police are gone," Rasmussen said to reassure him. When the man seemed to relax somewhat, Rasmussen gestured with his hand, so that Higginbottom would follow him to the kitchen. Once they were in the kitchen, Rasmussen pointed to the refrigerator and said, "Get something to eat." Yet, given everything that had happened, Higginbottom only sat down heavily at the kitchen table and grasped his head.

Rasmussen left him like that and went to the garage. There, he found young Colchester pacing restlessly with the blanket around his waist. After Rasmussen gestured for the kid to come, Colchester moved toward him eagerly. In the kitchen, Higginbottom and Colchester looked at one another confusedly. After that, they looked at Rasmussen for some explanation.

"Just sit down for now," Rasmussen said, "—or get something to eat," he continued, pointing to the refrigerator.

Colchester must have been starving, because he rushed to get something to eat. By then, Higginbottom looked like someone who was trying to rouse himself after being clubbed in the head. Yet, seeing that things were settled in the kitchen, Rasmussen left to retrieve the black woman. He entered the living room and took a few steps before he looked up and saw her coming down the staircase. She was dressed in the clothes he had left out. He had seen his wife in those clothes countless times, but the black woman added something to the outfit that had him thinking evil thoughts. He looked away guiltily, praying for strength—or at least, *composure*—

"Did he leave?" the black woman whispered.

"Yeah," he said, coming to his senses. Then, "Come meet the others," he said as she reached the bottom of the staircase. He turned and headed back to the kitchen now.

"The others?" she asked, her eyebrows rising.

"Yeah," he said, but did not explain any further. As he opened the kitchen door for her, he merely announced, "…The others."

The three of them stared at one another confusedly—then back at Rasmussen, since he was the only one acting as though there was some kind of logic to all this.

He sighed, realizing he was to be the host of their weird house party. He recited the lines he had given before: "My name is Arlo Rasmussen, as I said. This is my house. I know Colchester and…"—it occurred to him he did not know the black woman's name—

"Stephanie," she revealed.

He nodded. "Yes, I know Colchester and"—

"That's Nigga Fross!" Colchester corrected him.

Rasmussen gave him a murderous look again, until the kid looked down sheepishly. *"Anyway,"* Rasmussen continued, turning to Higginbottom, "I know these two, but how do you think you got here?"

Higginbottom's mind flashed with images of Big Slug's house going up in flames and Cassiopeia sitting next to him in the car as they drove away. He opened his mouth—and was about to tell them he had *no* idea how he had gotten there—when someone tried to open the door that led to the back yard. When the person found it locked, he banged on it, and screamed, "Hey!"

Everyone in the kitchen jumped. There was a window in the door, but a curtain covered it. As the others again looked to Rasmussen for guidance, he gestured in the direction of the garage and motioned for Colchester to show them the way.

The person outside the door banged again, but Rasmussen waited for the others to disappear before he went to it. Indeed, he was surprised by how calm he felt. It was almost as though all of this were becoming routine. It was definitely still nuts, but he was getting used to it....

Once again, he took a deep breath before he went to the door and opened it. As the door was swinging open, Rasmussen remembered the bulge in his robe; but by then, it was too late to cover up. Besides, as soon as the door was open, one of the scruffy-looking teenagers held up a hand-sized device, which emitted a light that momentarily blinded him. Rasmussen flinched and clamped his eyes shut. After that, he blinked rapidly, trying to clear his vision. "What the *fuck!*" he cursed when he looked back at them.

The two teenagers looked at one another anxiously, then their gazes returned to Rasmussen. They frowned. The first one had a nose ring and about ten piercings in his ears. The other one had dyed his hair black and had thick eyeliner in the "Goth" tradition. The one with the piercings decided to take charge: "Bring us the money," he demanded.

Rasmussen frowned: "*What* money?"

The Goth one looked at his friend uneasily: "Dude, I don't think it's working on him anymore."

Rasmussen was beginning to lose his patience. "What the *hell* are you two doing on my property?" he said threateningly—but that was when he suddenly remembered running after that minivan a week ago—and beating the *crap* out of those teenage brats. He remembered these two from the carnage! Indeed, when he frowned and looked closer, he saw the Goth one still had the remains of a black eye. "*You* guys!" Rasmussen yelled, his mouth gaping—

"What's keeping you two ass wads?" someone whined, turning the corner of the house. "How long does it take to pick up a freaking briefcase?" It was the same orange-haired kid who had been driving the minivan that day. The kid strolled up nonchalantly, but began to suspect something was wrong when he looked up and saw the ashen expressions on his cronies' faces.

"Dude," the Goth one started, "I don't think it's working on him anymore." He looked back at Rasmussen anxiously; still struggling to understand what was going on, Rasmussen stared at him with a confused scowl on his face—

"What do you mean it's not working?" the orange-haired one complained. "Did you do it right?"

"Yeah," the one with the piercings said defensively. "We flashed him and everything," he continued, holding up the device. "But, *look*," he said, pointing his thumb at Rasmussen, "he's not doing it."

They all turned to Rasmussen to observe him. They leaned in closer and frowned, as if he were a fascinating bug they had found crawling under a rock in their back yard.

When Rasmussen's frown deepened and he said, "Who the *hell* are you people," they all stepped back.

It was at precisely that moment that Professor Steinholtz reached the fence and screamed "Chicken!" when he saw his mother was dead. Everyone in Rasmussen's yard turned toward the fence. Steinholtz was about to be overcome with grief, but as he and the orange-haired kid made eye contact, the demonic rage consumed him. At the sight of his son, Steinholtz screamed, "Chicken!" again—and vaulted over the fence. The people in the yard seemed too shocked by the superhuman agility to move at first. Steinholtz went straight for his son; and by the time the youth realized he should run, his father was already there, swinging wild blows.

The youth was no match. After two blows, he was on the ground, squealing like a little girl while the rage demon in Steinholtz rained down more blows. Everyone looked on wordlessly, not quite able to grasp what was going on—and too enthralled by the spectacle to look away. Presently, as Rasmussen glanced at the fence again, he saw more people had gathered. Two men and a woman were standing by Stanko now, craning their necks over the fence to witness Steinholtz's death match; and with all the screaming and commotion, Higginbottom, Stephanie and young Colchester were soon at Rasmussen's shoulder as well, looking on in stunned disbelief.

The orange-haired kid was weeping now—so pathetically that even Steinholtz's demon began to lose its appetite for further carnage. Driven by a new motive, Steinholtz began searching his son's pockets; when he found nothing, his head jerked up—like a creature sensing the scent of its prey—and his eyes focused on his son's cronies. The two teenagers cried out in horror, and thought about running—but Steinholtz pointed at them threateningly, and glared at them, as to warn them of grievous bodily injury if they attempted to move.

Now, Steinholtz was walking over. As the two teenagers cried out again, Rasmussen was beginning to feel he should put an end to all this—since they were on his property. However, it was then that Steinholtz pointed at the device the kid with the piercings was still holding.

The youths glanced at one another, considering their options; but, *"Chicken!"* Steinholtz warned them again. The threat worked, because their bodies slumped and they bowed their heads, resigned to their fates.

The kid with the device held it up tentatively—like a fool holding out a piece of raw meat to a wild lion. The professor snatched the device out of his hands as soon as he was close enough, then fiddled with some buttons on the console. After that, there was a flash of light that seemed to consume the entire world. There was no point turning from it; and after a while, their souls grew hungry for it. Indeed, as the light filled them, all their lost memories began to return as well, and they shuddered.

At first, the returning memories were more confusing than insightful. Apparently, a few nights ago, the teenagers had showed up at Rasmussen's back door as well, and flashed him with the device, telling him to drive out to the diner and meet Cassiopeia. While he stood there like an automaton, they had cursed him for beating the crap out of them. One of them had slapped him across the face—but the orange-haired one had told them to focus on their plan.

First, they had filled his head with useless knowledge about the waitress at the diner: her birthday, high school, first lover and other pointless trivia that would later seem like miracles. Rasmussen saw himself complying with all the teenagers' instructions: going to the diner as if the entire thing had been his idea; reciting lines like an actor in a demented play...

He saw Cassiopeia making him forget by tapping his temple—and half a dozen other things that filled in some of the blanks of the last week. However, none of it made *sense*....

Eventually, he saw himself with Stephanie and young Colchester at the mall. He also realized the person laughing in those scenes was not really *him*. After what the teenagers and Cassiopeia attempted to do to his mind, something in him had rebelled. Indeed, there had probably always been a voice of resistance in him—a natural immunity to the mind control, or whatever it was—which was why he had been able to walk away when Cassiopeia barged into his meeting with Colchester and told them all to get on their knees. He had been partially immune; and after a while, his mind had rebelled against *all* outside control—so that by the time he blacked out at the mall, no one had really been controlling him. At first, he had been driven by a spirt self-preservation and freedom; but as his soul went from freedom to anarchy, he merely became *insane*....

In fact, as the hours passed, Stephanie and Colchester had lost themselves as well—but to *him*. He saw himself leading them—subtly manipulating them through the force of his will, and then shaping their souls to the point where he seemed like their *god*.

...It had started out simply: laughing with them, having a good time...buying a few bottles of liquor from the store. He had driven them around Atlanta, ignoring phone calls and red lights and anything else that might challenge his status as a god. Eventually, a policeman had stopped him for speeding; but when the man came to his window to demand his driver's license, Rasmussen had only smiled and handed over his son's teddy bear. The policeman had initially looked at the thing curiously; but before he knew it, he too had been under Rasmussen's spell.

"Go away and enjoy your evening," Rasmussen had told him; and in response, the man had nodded, smiled vapidly, and walked back to his patrol car. ...So, even then, Rasmussen must have been fully aware of how the crystals in the teddy bear's eyes eroded the human will. Maybe he had always known on some subconscious level—which was why he had been able to resist Cassiopeia and the crystal pendant she wore between her breasts. In a world where most people were blind, he had been able to see a faint glimmer of light. That relative power had made him a god—or, perhaps a *devil*.

Reveling in his newfound power, Rasmussen had taken the others to a particularly shady strip club in the black community. At first, the bouncer—a towering black man—had had his doubts about allowing a white man with a baby—and a *teenager*—to enter the club; but once Rasmussen showed him the teddy bear and told him to be cool, all resistance had fallen away. Similarly, after Rasmussen showed the strippers the teddy bear, everyone's face had worn a compliant smile. Everyone had danced; and after a while, they had probably enjoyed themselves without the need for Rasmussen's coaxing.

On the way home, Rasmussen had let young Colchester do the driving. Since the youth had been a little tipsy by then, he had torn up Rasmussen's front lawn as he brought the vehicle to a sliding halt. That was how the kid had injured himself: banging his head when the vehicle came to a stop. However, even then, they had all laughed and been in high spirits. Everything had been fine until Rasmussen saw Cassiopeia and Higginbottom waiting for them. By then, his powers as a god had perhaps surpassed hers, but he had complied with her request to pick up the ransom money—since it had seemed like fun. Young Colchester had wanted to tag along as well, so Rasmussen had taken him in the Porsche. At the mall, they had picked up the money from the caricature of the elder Colchester, and laughed at his outfit on the way back—oblivious of the fact that he had collapsed.

Yet, things had only gotten more chaotic when they returned home. After being in that altered state for a few hours, Rasmussen had been an unstable god. Cassiopeia had wanted them to go deliver the money to the teenagers, but Rasmussen had been bored with her game by then. Indeed, he had taken the others to the back yard, eager to play a new game. While Cassiopeia looked on disapprovingly, he had preached a sermon of freedom and lust. After he made the others strip off their clothes, he had made a bonfire of their garments to celebrate their freedom. Emancipated, they had danced under the moonlight, their naked bodies high-lighted grotesquely by the flames.

With all that commotion, Steinholtz's mother had awakened from sleep and stumbled up to the fence to investigate. Whether it was shock from the scene or the negative effects of being under the mind control for a week, she had had a stroke right there, with her hands gripping the top of the fence and her petrified body held upright—even after death. Rasmussen had noticed her as he danced with the others; but possessed by the godlike euphoria, he had been unable to *care*.

Sleep, when it came, had gripped them totally. Rasmussen had elected to sleep under the stars, his body warmed by the dying embers of the bonfire. The others, finally free of his influence, had wandered off to sleep in the house. Stephanie had found the master bedroom; Colchester had found the Porsche, and Higgin-bottom had become trapped in the closet. Yet, the sleep had reset their minds; and in the morning, they had again been themselves—albeit, in a world that made no sense.

As the recollections began to pour into Jones' mind, he grasped his head, futilely trying to protect it from the onslaught. He saw himself having dinner with the professor and his mom a week ago. His hosts had both been eccentric—but in a way that made them interesting. Plus, Steinholtz's mom had been a prolific drinker; and her stories—about her youth as a chorus girl—had been sordid. Jones had laughed heartily and been at ease as they all enjoyed themselves. However, the mood had changed when Steinholtz's son came over. He lived with his mom, not at Stein-holtz's house—but Steinholtz had made him come to see his grandmother and pretend they were a normal family. The professor had chastised him for being late; Mrs. Steinholtz, fully drunk by then, had called him an orange-haired freak who dressed like a faggot (since he wore those "skinny jeans" that were supposedly fashionable with teenagers). The youth, in turn, had called her a horny old bitch who was probably plotting how to suck Jones' dick.

After that, the melodrama had only escalated, with the son complaining that that was why his mother had left, and the father pointing out that she had not "left"—but had instead been kicked out by *him* when he found her having anal sex with the Pedro, the gardener.

With all that, Jones had lied and said he had to make a phone call, but the others had barely even noticed him leave as they continued bickering. In truth, he would have left entirely if he hadn't been eager to hear about the professor's exciting new project. He had gone outside to get some fresh air. Once he was there, he had called Artemis and joked about the professor's family.

By then, he had been fully in love with her—even though he had only known her for a day. A few hours earlier, he had spotted her walking by the campus bookstore, said hello, and then everything had moved so effortlessly that they had been making love four hours later. From the first moment he met her, he had felt as though he had *always* known her; and so, after joking about Steinholtz's family, they had planned another session for when he returned to Athens.

After those plans were set, it had occurred to him there was no more screaming coming from the house, so he had gone back inside. The professor and his mom had been sitting at the dining room table broodingly, still grumbling about the son—who had probably stormed off to the bathroom or something. Jones had been about to mention the project to the professor—so that he could leave as soon as possible—when the son suddenly returned. As the others looked on, the youth had held something in his hand—a small, handheld device that made the professor turn white when he saw it.

"You've been in my bag!" the professor had squeaked. However, the son had only smiled vindictively; and soon thereafter, there had been a flash of light. Apparently, the son had hacked into his father's computer months ago—and had been reading all his notes. As Jones, Steinholtz and his mom entered the altered state, the teenager had given them elaborate instructions for the revenge he had been planning. Mrs. Steinholtz was to return to Atlanta, become Granny Stanko, and lay the foundation for further revenge he was to take against Colchester.

Even now, Jones was not sure he understood completely; but years ago, when Steinholtz's son was visiting his grandmother during summer vacation, the younger Colchester had slighted him. Both boys had attended the same summer camp, but Colchester had given a party without inviting him; and as Steinhotz's son sat in his bedroom, listening to the loud music coming from the party, he had sworn he would get revenge. That childhood insult, as insignificant as it seemed in the grand scheme of things, had metastasized over the years and become genuine hatred. ...And nothing made you hate your enemy more than seeing him become ridiculously successful doing something you *knew* was idiotic. Bringing down Colchester's rap empire had therefore become his obsession; and with the professor's invention, Steinholtz's son had finally seen a way to settle old scores and take revenge on all his enemies.

In the son's grand scheme, not only would Colchester fall and granny Steinholtz finally start acting like a real grandmother, but by making his father the Roadkill Maniac, he would be killing two birds with one stone. As the Roadkill Maniac, his father would finally take his rightful place as the king of fools; and since the manager of Roadkill Chicken and Bar-b-cue had fired the son a month ago, he figured having a lunatic running around dressed as the mascot would ruin the business.

To take further revenge against his father, the son had instructed Steinholtz to bring over that dominatrix woman he secretly paid to spank his ass. When the son hacked into his father's computer, he had discovered the sordid videos, and had immediately seen how a sexy, manipulative bitch could be used in his grand design.

Yet, before all that, he had instructed the professor to return to his lab that night, in order to get all the paraphernalia—the crystals, envelopes and chemical-treated letters that increased the victims' suggestibility.

As for Jones, he had merely been in the way, so the kid had told him to get lost, forget everything that had happened here tonight, and to never come back—no matter what. Everything with the hillbilly, wild sex with the professor's mom, and waking up in the shower had merely been Jones' own mental projection: his mind filling in the blanks so that he could be a faithful servant of his teenage master.

Higginbottom had been working the night shift at the lab when Steinholtz and his son showed up. As soon as he saw the two of them together, Higginbottom had known something was wrong. From his conversations with Steinholtz over the years, he had known the man *hated* his son. Steinholtz had considered it a cruel joke that one of his spermatozoa could have turned into such a worthless excuse for a human. In truth, Steinholtz blamed his ex-wife's genes for their degenerate offspring. Yet, when Steinholtz showed up that night, the man had held his son around the shoulders fondly, and said the things a proud father was supposed to say—but in a way that a really bad actor would have said them. Steinholtz's sudden need to stay and chat—and grin like a lunatic—had also raised red flags. At the same time, given the professor's status at the research facility, Higginbottom had shrugged at the strangeness of it all and allowed them to go up to the lab.

It had only been when Steinholtz and his son returned half an hour later, hauling all the equipment on two large carts, that alarm bells had really gone off. He had reminded the professor that no one could remove equipment from the lab—especially without the proper paperwork…and definitely not in the middle of the night. Yet, after Higginbottom told them he could not let them leave, the son had only laughed menacingly and produced a handheld device.

After the flash of light, Higginbottom had found himself complying with the youth's instructions. The security video was to be replaced; records were to be destroyed. Witnessing Higginbottom's efficiency, the youth had seen how he could use the man in his plot—or, more accurately, he had seen how he could get more amusement out of ruining someone else's pathetic life.

Once Higginbottom was finished erasing all the evidence, the kid had told him to drive toward Atlanta and await further instructions. Complying, Higginbottom had left his post and driven to the other city. The next morning, he had received a text message on his phone, with a map leading to the woods. His instructions had been to wait there—and that was what he did for the next day. He had eaten nothing but the few snacks in his glove compartment. Luckily, there had been some bottles of water and soda in his car, or he might have died of thirst while he waited compliantly for his master's call.

When the phone call finally came, he had listened attentively before throwing the phone and wallet into the bushes (as he had been ordered). After that, he had returned to the car and allowed himself to "awaken." There actually had been a shack in the valley, but the envelope had always been in his pocket, given to him by the kid when he and Steinholtz were leaving the lab.

By the time he "retrieved" the letter from the shack and returned to the car, Steinholtz's son and his minions had already deposited Cassiopeia on the road and had her waiting there to be "found." Yet, everything that had happened with Big Slug and Goodson had probably only been random chaos within the kid's plot: the unforeseen consequences that came when fools played god....

They all had disillusioned expressions on their faces after their memories returned. The entire thing had taken only seconds, yet they all felt much older now. Worse, even though they had their memories again, none of it really made sense.

Rasmussen suddenly realized his erection was gone. He felt as though a hex had been lifted; but like the others, he had the sense he had been violated on a *spiritual* level. In theory, he was free now, but he sensed it would be a long time before he felt *clean* again.

Steinholtz's son was still lying on the ground, whimpering from his father's attack—but even he seemed more like a pathetic victim of the last week's events than the culprit. Everything just seemed *senseless*, so they stood about restlessly for moments afterwards, trying to find logic where there was none.

Only Steinholtz seemed fully in control of his faculties, and he walked over to his son again. As his rage returned, he contemplated kicking the youth in the ribs or head, but then a sense of deep bewilderment came over him, and looked over to the fence, where his mother was still standing. He stared for a while, before he looked down at his son with heavy eyes. "You killed your *grandmother!*" he said—at first relieved that he had been able to say something besides, "Chicken!" However, there was more sorrow in him now than anger. His mother was dead and as much as he wanted to blame his son, he knew the reason was because he had failed as a father.

"Why'd you *do* all this?" he said at last; but in truth, it was a question that could not possibly have an answer—besides madness. At that moment, one of the police cars at the Colchester estate took off, its blaring sirens serving as a reminder of everything that still needed to be done.

Steinholtz continued to stare at his son, his frame bent from grief and exhaustion. Eventually, when he reached a conclusion in his mind, he reached down and pulled up the teenager. After the beating the kid had taken, he stood on shaky legs, like a pathetic foal standing for the first time. "Damn it, son," Steinholtz said in a low voice; but by then, the kid had begun to weep; and after an awkward moment, they both hugged—so that the kid's cries grew louder and more pathetic. It was unsettling to watch, and the others looked away.

"...We've gotta do better, son," Steinholtz said then, patting the kid on the back. "We've gotta do better...."

When the kid's cries finally died down, Steinholtz sighed and detached from him. "Go wait in your grandmother's house. We'll figure it out later."

The kid nodded, seeming appreciative. As he left, his teenage cronies followed, their frames bent as well—perhaps with dawning shame at what they had done. Being under the control of a madman was always a shameful thing—regardless of whether you were conscious of it or not. Only fools found solace in it, and only genuine psychopaths used their lack of control to exonerate their behavior....

When the three teenagers disappeared around the corner, Steinholtz turned to Rasmussen and the others—who were still standing there in a daze. The professor intended to apologize, but then realized there was nothing he could really say. He took a tentative step toward them before he stopped, thinking something over. After another inner dialogue, Steinholtz nodded his head, glanced back at Jones and his friends (who were still standing behind the fence) and gestured for them to come. Excited to be included in the grand revelation—or whatever Steinholtz was planning—they nodded. Jones helped Artemis over the fence before he and Binkowski hauled themselves over it.

When all of them were standing in Rasmussen's yard, Steinholtz gestured for them to move in closer. Now, he was fiddling with the handheld device—

Rasmussen grew alarmed: "What are you doing?"

Steinholtz looked over at him with tired eyes: "You're all wondering what's happening, but there's only one way to show you."

"What do you mean?" Rasmussen said again, suspicious.

"I'm going to share my thoughts with you."

Jones was wary as well: "I'm not sure I want other people's thoughts in my head anymore."

The others nodded.

Steinholtz sighed; seeing he would have to give them a long explanation, he looked down at the ground, trying to figure out where to start. Once a suitable explanation had settled in his mind, he sighed again and looked up: "Our thoughts are basically a combination of electrical signals and chemicals. You figure out the right balance, and you can control how people think—and *what* they think. You can control what they remember and what they forget. You can tell them what to do and they'll believe it was their own idea."

"...Damn," Rasmussen whispered.

Yet, Steinholtz's expression was matter-of-fact. "It was a government-funded project...but obviously none of this was supposed to happen."

"Obviously," Binkowski said sarcastically.

"...Are there long-term consequences?" Rasmussen asked anxiously.

Steinholtz glanced back at his mother. "Elderly people's brains don't work well with it," he said with a penchant for understatement. "...And people who are..."—he searched for the right word—"under the influence for a long time tend to become unstable. ... It was not meant for *prolonged* exposure—especially for older people. People like my mom and Colchester...their minds can't cope with it." As Steinholtz said these last words, his eyes gravitated to the younger Colchester, and he nodded guiltily. "...Anyway, youthful, healthy people tend to deal with it better—since their minds are more...malleable."

Rasmussen was not sure he had gotten a straight answer: "Are we going to be okay?"

"I'll need to have you all checked out at my lab...but I think so."

There was a long silence after that, while they allowed everything to digest. There was really nothing else to be asked—or, at least they all seemed to sense they had reached the limits of what their minds would be able to *digest*.

Steinholtz seemed to realize their meeting had run its course before the others. He turned to Jones and his friends: "Go back into the house...get something to eat, then we'll figure out the rest later."

After that, Jones and the others left, but Steinholtz stayed behind to talk to Rasmussen's motley crew. "You're staying here now?" he asked Rasmussen, gesturing toward the house.

"Yeah, for about a year and a half."

Steinholtz nodded in acknowledgement. After a deep sigh, he continued, "I'll stop by later…leave contact information for you." Here, he paused and glanced back at his mother. "I'll take care of everything."

When he turned back to Rasmussen, he seemed to notice Higginbottom standing there for the first time. He frowned. "…My son brought you into this too?"

"Yeah," he said shyly.

"…You need a lift back to Athens?"

"Yeah, probably," he said, exhausted.

Steinholtz gestured with his head for Higginbottom to follow him; then, after a final nod to the others, he left, his head bowed.

They all watched the two men turn the corner of the house and disappear; afterwards, they looked at one another anxiously, searching of answers where there were none.

When Rasmussen's eyes fell on young Colchester, he said, "You should probably go to your father now. You want me to take you to the hospital?"

The kid thought about it before he shook his head. "I'll go home first…get some clothes, shower…try to *think*. I'll have one of the guards take me or something…and figure out something to tell the police."

Rasmussen looked at him uneasily, but since Colchester seemed mature for once—or at least *thoughtful*—Rasmussen felt the kid was going to be okay. As Rasmussen nodded his head, Colchester put out his fist for Rasmussen to bump it. After that exchange, the kid began walking away as well, still holding the blanket around his waist like a towel. Rasmussen was about to call him back—and get him some actual clothes (and some shoes)—but by then, the kid had already disappeared around the corner of the house.

It was only Rasmussen and Stephanie standing there now.

"You want to borrow my car or something—to drive home?"

"The Porsche?" she said with a mischievous smile.

He laughed. "Definitely the minivan."

"You trust me with it?" she teased him.

"Well, you have to return anyway, so we can go get ourselves checked out at that guy's lab.

"Yeah," she said, her expression becoming grave at the thought.

"Come into the house with me for a bit," he said, moving toward the house, "and I'll give you my info."

"Okay," she said, following him.

In five minutes, Stephanie was gone. He wrote his number on a piece of paper, walked her over to the minivan, and she drove off. He stood watching the van disappear, then a chill came over him: a sudden sense of loneliness—and perhaps some unresolved feeling of panic at the realization he was still overlooking something obvious.

When he remembered his son, his eyes grew wide and he ran toward the staircase. A sick feeling came over him as he ran; but when he reached the second floor and turned toward the nursery, he saw his son sitting patiently in his crib, staring up at him. When Rasmussen smiled, the baby smiled as well. The little boy's face was now free of all the malevolence Rasmussen had imagined over the last few days. The doll was in the crib as well, but discarded in the corner.

Relieved beyond reason, Rasmussen reached down and picked up his son. He stood there holding and rocking the baby for over a minute, smiling and feeling a deep sense of peace. Eventually, it occurred to him the little boy would probably be hungry by now, so Rasmussen patted him on the back and headed for the kitchen.

As he reached the bottom step, the front door suddenly opened. Rasmussen looked up in time to see his wife step through the entrance, pulling her suitcase behind her. The baby laughed out at the sight of her, and Rasmussen stared at her in amazement, as if he had not seen her in *months*. She was *beautiful*, and he stood there staring at her as if he had to remind himself of that fact. When she noticed the way he was looking at her, she looked over at him quizzically. However, she was home now, after a long trip, and the sight of her little family made her smile. The baby was growing even more excited now, waving his arm; and as his wife laughed at the gesture, Rasmussen marveled at the easy beauty of her smile.

He took a step toward her, but as he remembered everything that had happened over the past week—and everything he had been living with for the last year and a half—his smile faded away.

"...Baby, we need to talk," he began as he continued walking toward her.

Sensing something unsettling in his tone, she paused and looked at him in the same quizzical way. She left her suitcase by the door and was about to go to her family when the powder room door suddenly burst open! They all turned to see a wild-looking woman stumble out holding a briefcase. The woman was panting for air—as if she had been suffocating. Rasmussen's wife screamed and jumped back. At the sound, the woman—Cassiopeia—screamed as well, and stumbled back, so that the briefcase slipped from her hands and fell to the floor. When it did, the half a million dollars came tumbling out, onto the floor. The two women stared down at it, wide-eyed; then, when Rasmussen's wife looked over at

Cassiopeia once more, seeing her suggestive leather outfit—with her breasts practically falling out of the bodice—she glared at Rasmussen with a shocked, accusatory expression.

Yet, after the initial surprise, Rasmussen only chuckled and continued walking over to his wife. "Baby, we *really* need to talk," he said with a smile.

EPILOGUE

With everything that had happened, Higginbottom and Binkowski were the odd men out. Steinholtz and his son had their issues to work out; Jones and Artemis were in love—and therefore had little time for others. That left Higginbottom and Binkowski to fend for themselves. As was usually the case with lonely men, they gravitated to one another, each becoming the other's confessor. Jones and Artemis offered to drive them home, but since nothing was as awkward to single men as being around a couple in love, the two men decided to rent a car and drive back at their leisure.

Besides, after Higginbottom told Binkowski about dismembering Big Slug's corpse, they agreed they needed to make sure there were no loose ends. The fire had probably destroyed most of the physical evidence at Big Slug's house, but Higginbottom realized his finger prints would still be all over the man's truck. Assuming the police had not found it yet, he had to make sure it was clean.

Steinholtz rented them a car from a company that actually dropped off the rental. As Higginbottom drove to where he had parked Big Slug's truck, they went over contingencies. Higginbottom expressed the hope that the government would cover all of this up, and bury all charges, but Binkowski thought it was more likely that the government would deny everything to cover themselves. Either way, they agreed the best course of action was to dump Big

Slug's truck in a ravine somewhere and to wipe it down…and perhaps *burn* it afterwards…assuming the police had not found it yet.

When Higginbottom reached the block where he *thought* he had parked Big Slug's truck, he was confused, because it was nowhere in sight. He panicked, considering the possibility that the police had already impounded it. However, when he turned around to make another sweep, Binkowski noticed a truck frame across the street, resting on some cinderblocks. It had been *stripped*. Big Slug had had one of those "pimped out" vehicles, with expensive rims and a turbo-charged engine. The husk of the vehicle was there, but the insides were gone. The perpetrators had even taken the steering wheel, seats and doors, so that Higginbottom found himself grinning. There was still the chance of a stray finger print being in there, but from the outside, there was nothing that looked like *murder*. It was possible the cops would *search* for Big Slug for a while, but none of this would seem like a priority in a neighborhood like this, where Big Slug was probably hated by all.

Higginbottom breathed deeply, smiling as he pressed the accelerator and moved them forward. When they were heading out of the city, Binkowski looked over at him. "What did you say the name of that book was?"

"Goodson's book?" Higginbottom asked.

"Yeah."

"*The Total Emasculation of the White Man,*" Higginbottom said, looking over at him curiously. "…Why you ask?"

"It's a good title for a novel," Binkowski replied.

"You really think so?" Higginbottom asked, looking over at him oddly. They stared at one another for a while, then they laughed, faced forward and nodded their heads. The men did not say much for the rest of the trip back to Athens, but they sat upright in their seats when they reached the outskirts of town—as if eager to finally begin living their lives.

ABOUT THE AUTHOR

David Valentine Bernard is currently at work finishing his PhD in sociology. Originally from the Caribbean nation of Grenada, he moved to Canada when he was four and Brooklyn, New York when he was nine. This is his seventh novel. For more information, see www.dvbernard.com.

HOW TO KILL YOUR *Boyfriend*

(IN TEN EASY STEPS)

BY D. V. BERNARD
AVAILABLE FROM STREBOR BOOKS

When Stacy thought about it afterwards, she told herself that she had not intended to kill her boyfriend. It certainly had not been something she had planned. However, even she would have admitted that she had been somewhat annoyed with him lately. It had not been anything definite—just the usual ups and downs of a relationship. Once, he had bought the wrong brand of tampons, and she had raged against him mercilessly. If he had really loved her, she had argued, he would have gotten her the right brand. It had all been a sign from God, and she had wept bitterly while he clutched her shoulders and begged for forgiveness. After a few days of brooding and melodrama, she had been able to admit to herself that the entire argument had been stupid, and they had made love. Making love had always been her way of saying she was sorry. In fact, the week before she killed him, they had made love a great deal. It had gotten to the point where she had found herself being aroused as soon as she started yelling at him. And so, maybe the murder, unintentional as it was, had only been an escalation of their sex—a case of arousal gone too far.

D r. Vera Alexander got out of the cab and stood looking at the storefront bookshop. It was in Midtown Manhattan—one of those trendy neighborhoods where everything cost too much and the droves of shoppers took a strange kind of pride from the fact that they were squandering their money. Vera surveyed her reflection in the bookstore's windowpane. She was a slightly plump 31-year-old who always had a tendency to look overdressed. The socially acceptable stereotype at the moment was that gay men had impeccable fashion sense, so she trusted all her clothing, hair and makeup decisions to a flamboyantly gay Haitian called François. The style that year was to have one's hair "long and untamed," so, on François' recommendation, she had adopted a hairdo that was so wild it seemed vicious. All the mousse and red highlights made her hair seem like some kind of diseased porcupine. Yet, it was the style, and she was pleased with her appearance as she stared at her reflection.

When she walked into the bookstore there was a smile on her face, because there were at least two dozen people there, waiting for her to sign copies of her book, *How to Have Great Sex with a So-So Man*. On the cover there was a picture of a beaming woman standing next to a slouching doofus. The bookstore patrons froze and stared at her when she entered; some pointed to her and whispered to their neighbors, as if in awe of her. A couple of them snapped pictures of her, or began to record on their camcorders. Whatever the case, the mass of them moved toward her and put out their hands to be shaken. Soon there was a line to shake hands with her. Of course, all of them were women. Vera shook their hands gladly, smiling at each one and thanking her for coming. The store manager was a bookish-looking woman in her late-twenties: gaunt and severe-looking, with a sarcastic look pasted on her face from years of suppressing her disappointment with life:

"Let Dr. Vera get set-up first!" she chastised the patrons like a kindergarten teacher telling two five-year-olds to stop pulling one another's hair. Some of them groaned in disappointment, but Dr. Vera nodded to them, as if to reassure them that she would shake their hands later. They made room for her to pass, and she walked over to the desk where she was to sign books. A line had already formed; two women tussled with one another in their desire to occupy the same spot on the line. The store manager gave them her stern kindergarten teacher look and they calmed down.

Vera smiled at it all. She got out her fountain pen and sat down at the desk. Soon, she was asking the women their names and writing the same message in their books. She had developed a bad habit of writing and looking up at the person she was signing the book to. As a consequence, the message she wrote was usually illegible. Many people later discovered that she had misspelled their names, or she had written it merely as a line with a squiggly thing in the middle.

She had a good tempo going. In fifteen seconds, she could sign a book, dispense advice on the mysteries of male sexuality and still have time to pose for a picture. Even the sarcastic-looking store manager seemed impressed. The woman did not exactly smile, but she exuded a kind of pleased smugness as she stood to the side, surveying the long line.

"Exactly," Vera said in answer to one woman's declaration of gratitude, "if you can teach a dog to shit outside, why can't teach your man to please you in bed!"

Everyone in the store laughed; some of them applauded. Vera

had used that line about 80 times since she started her book tour a month ago. She had had a dream once, where it had been the only thing she could say…but people loved it when she said it.

She nodded to the woman who had made the declaration of gratitude (as to dismiss her) and the next woman on line stepped up to the table. People were still laughing at Vera's joke. However, the woman who stepped up to the table had a drawn, wretched expression on her face—like in those pictures of war refugees who had watched their children starve to death and their men butchered. The woman seemed about Vera's age, but could have possibly been about ten years older. With her thinness, the woman seemed frail and detached—except for the intensity with which she stared at Vera. It was off-putting, and Vera instinctively looked away. She noticed the woman's blouse: the nape of the neck was slightly frayed and discolored. Vera noticed a peculiar birthmark on the woman's neck. It was heart-shaped with a jagged line through it—a broken heart. The store manager looked at the woman disapprovingly, wondering if she could afford the $21 price of the book.

The woman handed Vera the book to sign, and Vera came back to her senses. She tried to reassure herself by smiling. "To whom am I signing this?" she said.

The woman's voice was low and ominous: "Don't pretend that you don't know me."

Vera's smile disappeared; all the background conversation in the bookstore seemed to cease. "I'm sorry," Vera said, flustered, "…I don't—"

"Don't you dare pretend—you of all people!"

"I'm not—"

"I took the weight for you," the woman went on, suddenly animated. "I carried it while you were doing all this," she said, looking around the bookstore, as if all of it were Vera's and the woman's sacrifice had allowed her to attain it. "But when is it going to be my turn to be free?" the woman lamented. "…The things we did," she said, beginning to sob, "they're killing me—the weight of it all…! I can't take it anymore—it's too much for me."

Vera had sat stunned for most of that; the store patrons had stood staring. Vera remembered that she was a psychologist and stood up, to calm the woman. "Please—"

"I've lost everything," the woman cut her off, talking more to herself now than anything.

"Ma'am, please—"

"Ma'am?" she screamed, outraged by the formality and coldness of the term. "After all we went through—all those things we did…?"

The store manager came over, but Vera warded her off by shaking her head. Vera walked around to the front of the desk and tried to take the woman's hand.

"No!" the woman screamed, as if brushing off a lover's hand. And then, more calmly, "If you don't remember me, it's too late for that. It's too late." Her eyes were full of sorrow and desperation now: "You were all I had left."

"Maybe you should sit down," Vera attempted to reason with her once more. She again tried to take the woman's hand, but the woman pushed her hand away. And then, with a disillusioned expression on her face:

"You really don't know me…?" She stared at Vera's face, as if searching for some clue of recognition; but seeing none, she bowed her head thoughtfully and started talking to herself again: "I guess it's best that you forgot. I took the weight for you, but it's too much."

"Let's talk about it," Vera said, trying to think up every therapist trick she knew. "Maybe you can help me to remember."

The woman started to walk away, as if she had not heard.

"Please," Vera called after her, "—at least tell me your name!"

The woman stopped and stared at her as if considering something. At last she sighed, saying, "I'm the one who helped you to forget." At that, she walked out of the store. When she got to the curb, she looked back at Vera via the display window; then, she turned and took a step into the street. The speeding truck hit her instantly. She was sent flying like a cartoon character. There was something unbelievable about it—like a cheap special effect in a bad movie. The truck tried to stop, but the woman's careening body fell right in its path. There was the sound of tires screeching, and then a thud…and then silence.

For Dr. Vera, four years passed in a blur of success and controversy. As was usually the case, the controversy had fueled her success. The entire episode with the woman at the bookstore had been captured on some of her fans' camcorders. The story got international attention. People called it "The Forget-Me-Not" incident, because of the woman's rant on being forgotten. A couple of networks did exposés on Dr. Vera, trying to figure out the connection between her and the woman: if there really was some deep dark secret that they had shared…but there had been nothing. The woman had spent her entire life in a small town in North Carolina; she had had a history of mental illness and had been living with a family friend until she snuck away to come to New York the day before she died. With all the media attention, the camcorder scenes of Dr. Vera attempting to calm the deranged woman had made her seem compassionate and accessible; and within weeks of the incident, Dr. Vera had been approached to do her own radio call-in show.

Four years later, the Dr. Vera radio call-in show was not exactly a hit, but it was broadcast nationwide, and there was talk of a television version. Since the incident, her agent had been telling her how she was on the verge of greatness. Her last book, *10 Steps to Find Out if Your Man is a Cheating Bastard* had been a number one bestseller...but that was two years ago, and she could not help thinking that her career was languishing.

As for her personal life, despite the fact that she was a relationship counselor, she was single and childless. It had been over a year since she had had sex, and the more she thought about it, the more certain she was that the young stud her agent had set her up with the last time had faked his orgasm just so he could get away from her! In bed, she seemed almost mouse-like—nothing like the voracious sexual beast she wrote about in her books. In college, two of her lovers had fallen asleep while making love to her. Granted, they had both been drunk at the time, but it had all set off a lifelong sense of sexual inadequacy—which was probably why she connected so well with her legion of fans. She knew how they wanted to feel about their sexuality, because she wanted the same feeling—the same fantasy. Her greatest fear was that people would discover she was lousy in bed. To a certain degree, she remained single because she was afraid one of her ex-boyfriends would write one of those tell-all books on her, cataloguing the horrific boredom of her sex. Every lover was a potential blackmailer.

And if all that were not bad enough, she was growing tired of being Dr. Vera. Her last name was actually Alexander, not Vera, but it had become an accepted practice for media doctors to go by their first names—like Dr. Phil and Dr. Ruth—as to give a false sense of intimacy to their fans. Being Dr. Vera required vast amounts of energy—as was usually the case when one lived a lie. Every day, she told lies about lovers who were a figment of her imagination; she dispensed sexual advice on things that she, herself, was terrified to try. And with each passing day, it became clearer to her that she hated doing her call-in show. Five nights a week, it was the same tedious nonsense: women calling up to find out why their husbands or boyfriends did not love them anymore; people trying to manipulate their lovers into doing something (stupid), or who were merely calling to hear a psychological professional justify their scummy behavior. She knew that something would have to change soon or she would crack. Every once in a while she would have a nightmare where she failed totally at this life and again had to return to being a high school guidance counselor. The nightmare would motivate her to work harder for a few weeks, until she again felt herself on the verge of cracking.

"Okay," Dr. Vera said after she had finished answering the last caller's question, "—we have time for one more call." She looked at the computer screen before her to see which caller was to be next, and then she pressed a button: "Matt from Minneapolis, how may I help you today?"

"Thanks for taking my call, Dr. Vera. I'm a longtime listener and first time caller." The man's chipper, excited voice annoyed her for some reason, but she retreated into her usual radio routine:

"Thank you, Matt. How may I help you today?"

"Well, Dr. Vera," Matt began, "I've come to the conclusion that I'm a lesbian."

"Aren't you a man?" she asked, frowning at the computer screen.

"Yes."

Dr. Vera frowned deeper, and looked through the soundproof glass, at the engineer/producer. When she made eye contact with the huge, woolly-mammoth-looking man, he shrugged and bit into a gigantic submarine sandwich. Vera sighed and stared at the computer screen again, as if the answer to everything lay within it. She had trained herself to always give kind, considerate responses—

even to the stupidest questions—but all she could think to say was, "Look, Matt, to be a lesbian, you sort of have to be a woman."

"That's a pretty sexist view!"

"How is that sexist?"

"It's sexist to believe that a man can't be a lesbian, just as it would be sexist to believe that a woman can't be an astronaut, or have her own radio call-in show."

Dr. Vera shook her head: "To be a lesbian, you have to be a woman," she maintained.

"Not at all: a lesbian is simply someone who wants to have sex with a lesbian."

"So, if I had sex with you, I'd be a lesbian?"

"Of course!"

Dr. Vera groaned, despite her usual attempt to maintain a professional/ unflappable radio persona. Maybe it was the fact that it was Friday night and she wanted to go home. She wanted to get away from people and their sexual problems—at least for the weekend—

"Anyway," she said to move things along, "you think you're a lesbian trapped in a man's body?"

"Not at all—I'm secure in my lesbian-ness," he said, making up his own terms.

A side of Dr. Vera wanted to say something sarcastic like, "Good for you, girlfriend!" Instead, she sighed and said, "So what is your problem then?"

"Oh," Matt said, as if he'd forgotten, "...you see, the problem is that my boyfriend doesn't want to be a lesbian."

Dr. Vera hung up the phone and sighed. The theme music began to play in the background, and she glared at the producer as if to say, Aren't you supposed to be screening these calls! However, he was too busy devouring his sandwich to notice her. "Cherished friends," she began her usual sign-off message without enthusiasm, "this brings us to the conclusion of another wonderful show. This is Dr. Vera, reminding you that every day can be a great day if you choose to see it that way. Until next time, my friends...!"

As soon as she was off the air she groaned again, grabbed her huge handbag and walked out of the studio. The summer night was hot and humid. The studio was in midtown Manhattan; when Vera got outside, there were thousands of teenagers milling about on the sidewalk. A rock star named Pastranzo had done an interview at the station about four hours ago, when Vera was coming in to work. Awestruck teenage girls had screamed and passed out at the prospect of meeting their hero; ambulances and huge phalanxes of police officers had had to be called in to quell the hysteria. The worst of it seemed to be over, but even though Pastranzo had left the studio hours ago (through a side entrance) the teenagers refused to believe it. They stood their ground, baking in the summer heat with the crazed obstinacy of goats. Vera, who had had to fight her way through the crowd when coming into work, was now forced to do the same thing upon leaving.

All of a sudden, a squealing 14-year-old ran up to her with arms open wide, perhaps thinking that Vera was Pastranzo. As Vera did not have the patience to explain the difference between herself and a stringy-haired Italian man, she put some sense into the girl's head the most efficient way she knew: with a firm backhand.

When she got to the curb, she hailed a cab and headed to Brooklyn. The cab smelled of vomit, curry and toe jam, so she opened the window and groaned again as she sat there brooding.

The two police officers exited the deli, each carrying a Styrofoam coffee cup in one hand and a paper bag of donuts in the other. Just as they reached their patrol car, the first officer bent his head to take a sip of his coffee and noticed the person standing across the street, in the shadows. The neighborhood always seemed as though it were in the middle of nowhere, even though the Brooklyn and Manhattan Bridges towered overhead. On the bridges, and the major thoroughfares that connected to these bridges, traffic zoomed 24 hours a day—except of course when there was a traffic jam. Either way, on the streets below the bridges, there was always a kind of loneliness. Most of the buildings were industrial warehouses or warehouses that had been converted to luxury condominiums. After dark, the neighborhood was usually deserted. This was why the police officer found the person in the shadows so conspicuous. The first officer got his partner's attention, and then he gestured across the street. His partner stared quizzically in that direction before nodding. They left their coffee and donuts on top of the patrol car and began to walk across the street. Their hands automatically went to their guns. They did not grab them yet, but their fingers were within reach of their weapons. They made no attempt to rush; as they walked, they surveyed the person in the shadows. They took note of where his arms were—if his hands held a weapon. At last, when they were about to step onto the curb, the first officer called to the figure in the shadows:

"Is everything all right?"

Stacy stepped from the shadows, and they saw her. They surveyed her shapely figure—the way her cotton blouse was moist from the humidity and her sweat; they looked at the way her jeans hugged every succulent contour of her legs. She was like an angel standing there before them. Her hair was long and curly from the humidity; she tossed it over her left shoulder and the officers followed the motion as if it were something miraculous. She smiled, and they instinctively smiled. They forgot about their guns and whatever protocol they had learned in the police academy. There was something infectious about her smile, so that the more they looked at it, the more they smiled and felt overcome by an unnamable feeling that made them feel alive and intoxicated.

"Were you guys concerned about me?" Stacy flirted then, breaking the silence. She smiled wider, and the officers, to their amazement, found themselves giggling along, like two teenage morons. They were speechless in that "I wish I could say something cool, but I'm too overcome with awe" sort of way.

Stacy nodded at that moment, as if acknowledging that they were putty in her hands, and then she gestured toward the all-night deli: "Were you guys making a donut run?"

"Yeah, you know how it is," the second officer said, still shy; but looking at her now, and seeing again how beautiful she was, he suddenly remembered the strangeness of her standing in the shadows. "Is everything all right?"

"Sure, I was waiting for a friend."

"Your friend makes you wait here in the dark?" he said, trying to joke. He felt proud of himself; his partner seemed impressed, so they laughed too loudly at his joke.

It was then that a cab drove up and stopped in front of the deli. They all turned to look as Dr. Vera got out.

"There's my friend," Stacy said, smiling again. However, she made no attempt to get Dr. Vera's attention, and the woman walked into the deli. Only after the cab had driven off did Stacy and the officers realize they had all stood staring at the scene. The officers looked at Stacy again, and giggled in the same nervous way as she smiled back at them. "Thanks for looking out for me, officers," she said then.

The officers looked at one another uneasily...